SOFTER THAN STEEL

JESSICA TOPPER

lunabloom books

For my father, Sanford — the original Banana Louie.

And to New York City, with love

RICK

RIDING THE WAVE

Seventeen thousand fans can't be wrong.

Rick Rottenberg clipped his mic into its stand, lifted his face to the spots and hazers shining high above the Palais Omnisports de Paris-Bercy stage, and threw his head back, exalted.

Sweat-soaked ringlets grazed the middle of his slick bare back. It had taken four years to grow his hair back out to acceptable headbanging, rock-and-roll length. Running a hand through the dark, unruly mass of curls, he smiled. Sometimes he forgot it was there, even dreamed his head was still shaved clean. He had kept it shorn like a Buddhist monk for so long, first in solidarity for Simone, then for years after for no reason he could ascertain.

Simone's gone.

Gone.

Even in a sea of thousands, you're alone.

Grimacing, he hoisted his guitar by its neck, high overhead.

The crowd's response was visceral. A rolling current of fists raised, eyes squeezed shut, and a collective hoarse roar emanated from their throats. Rick ripped out his in-ear monitors by their cords, letting the sound hit his eardrums full-force.

Like bracing himself for a hard wave, he took a wide stance in his black leather boots and steeled himself.

I was born to do this.

It was less a thought and more like a full-on sensory experience, as his eyes adjusted to the raised house lights and his ears welcomed the cacophony of applause. Dry ice from the fog machines burned his nose, and the ten-gauge steel of the guitar strings cut into his palm as he used his instrument like a conductor's baton to whip the French crowd into a frenzied cyclone.

And he tasted victory.

It had taken four years. But Riff Rotten was back.

Because seventeen thousand screaming, rabid, shining, elated metal fans can't be wrong.

Right?

He flicked a look side-stage toward the large digital clock sitting on top of the monitor engineer's board. There was still a good eight-minute block for the band to get one last song in before the venue's strict eleven p.m. curfew. But as he turned to his right to suggest it to Digger, he noticed his bandmate exiting the stage. The only encore that interested his lead guitarist was the one waiting for him in the wings.

Kat.

Rick turned away as Adrian grinned like she was the winning lottery ticket and swung her around in a gravity-defying hug.

From his place at center stage, Rick had barely noticed Kat down in the pit tonight, but Adrian obviously had. *He's always been the one to care about the details,* Rick reminded himself. *You're about the big picture.* That's how they'd always functioned.

Or how we malfunctioned, as the case may be.

Corroded Corpse was now back and at the top of their game as the Rotten Graves Project. And Digger Graves was more interested in picking china patterns than tremolo picking his guitar and melting the fans' faces off.

His timing was certainly crap, wasn't it?

The neck of Rick's Gibson slipped through his fatigued and sweaty fingers. In a burst of pent-up energy, he gripped it close to the headstock with both hands and pinwheeled the axe through the air. Sam froze to his left. The bassist had at least had the decency to come downstage for a bow. Now he took a step back and cast a wary glance at Jim, who was leaning over his drum kit.

Guitar met stage floor with a loud crack, like a gunshot. Wood flew and guitar strings popped as Rick pulled it high overhead, sliced it through the air, and smashed it down again and again, to the left, to the right. Jim popped back behind his kit and provided a rising crescendo of cymbals to accompany each upward move and kicked his double bass drum in perfect pace each time Rick's guitar made contact: with the floor, the riser, the amps behind him, and the wedges in front of him. Sam did a little hop as the entire body of the Gibson Memphis guitar separated from the neck and slid toward him.

The kids in the crowd had lost their bloody minds by then.

RICK CLICKED the pause button on his laptop and dragged the bar of the video back so he could watch himself lift the jagged broken neck of his guitar like a conquering hero wielding his sword victoriously—eyes wild, bare chest heaving—while tonight's crowd screamed its approval. Judging from the dozen or so fan-shot videos that had hit YouTube by midnight, his little spectacle had looked pretty damn good from the audience's point of view.

Leaning back in the hotel's desk chair, he twisted his lips into a sardonic smile, shook his glass to loosen up the ice, and took a sip. The single malt's buttery burn was welcome in his whiskey tonight. Subtle notes of orange peel, burnt caramel, and clove teased his tongue and promised to bring the noise in his head down to a dull roar.

The trill of his room phone summoned him. Padding barefoot across the lush carpeting of his Mandarin Oriental suite, he silenced it by placing it to his ear.

Isabelle needed no salutation to get the conversation going. The band's publicist launched into her tirade unprompted.

"So what was with that little hissy fit on stage tonight, huh?"

"*Bonsoir,* Isabelle. *Comment allez-vous?*"

"Don't play cute and French with me, mister."

Rick picked out brash notes of trash talk, Salem Ultra Lights, and Brooklyn in her voice. *Not nearly as smooth as whiskey on the palate,* he thought, wincing as she doused his ear with her version of twenty questions. And label expectations. And SoundScan numbers. And ticket sales. And who's not returning her calls, and who needs to do some serious ass-kissing now that payola bribes were no longer in style.

Rick drained his whiskey glass, but felt completely sober. What had happened to the promise he and Digger made four years ago under the roof of Madison Square Garden? *Of doing things our way,* he asked himself, *this time around?*

He should've known better. This was the music business, after all. Emphasis on *business.* You could have all the talent and drive, but you needed that army behind you. The minute the two of them had buried the hatchet and agreed to play that reunion show, the armies had assembled and performed a coup d'état. The booking agent, the record label, groupies, and hangers-on had all awoken from what appeared to be an enchanted slumber, as if the last twenty years had passed for them in the blink of an eye. Business as usual.

Only their former publicist/self-appointed interim Queen

of Everything had awoken crankier than a disturbed hornets' nest.

If she hadn't been Simone's best friend since childhood, Rick probably would've called the exterminator to fog Isabelle out of his life ages ago.

"Behave yourself, finish the goddamn run, and get your ass back to the States in one piece," Isabelle commanded. "Simone's parents are counting on you for the hospital wing dedication. Then we've got the one-offs in L.A. and Chicago, your Rock and Roll Hall of Fame appearance, and the Northeast leg to get through yet. And two months of lockout booked in the studio here. Oh, and the mayor's office has finally given us the green light for the outdoor video shoot."

"Relax, Isabelle. We've got it under control."

We. The bloody band. Not you.

"Says the guy who just broke a three-thousand-dollar guitar on stage? Yeah. Okay." There was a forced exhale, and Rick bet the bank she was standing on her penthouse balcony, flicking ashes down on the heads of the plebs who dared troll her Upper East Side neighborhood. "And where the hell is Adrian? Would it kill him to return a phone call once in a while?"

"Indisposed."

Rick rubbed his temple, contemplating another glass or the five hours' sleep he could catch before the bus came to pick up the band. He didn't care to contemplate what Adrian and Kat were up to in their fancy hotel suite down the hall at this hour.

"Yeah? What's his drug of choice these days?"

Would you believe me if I said a widowed librarian and her eight-year-old daughter? "Nothing."

"I wasn't born yesterday, Rick."

"And neither was Adrian. In fact, he was born forty-five years ago, this day. It's his birthday. So let's all leave him the fuck alone, shall we?" The sarcasm did a number on his throat, way worse than the whiskey.

"Let me guess." Isabelle gave a dignified snort. "Kat showed up at the show tonight to surprise him?" She barely paused to let Rick respond before throwing out her "Tell me you're not jealous?" card.

Even though he was an ocean away, Rick kept a poker face and his own hand close to his chest.

Whatever the answer was, he sure as hell wouldn't find it in this long-distance phone call, or in the melting ice at the bottom of his whiskey glass.

"Don't ask him to choose," she warned. "You will lose."

"Isabelle. As much as I'd love to listen to you recite more poetic words of wisdom to me, I'm going to—"

"*He* never asked *you* to choose between the band and Simone."

"I'm going to hang up now," Rick finished quietly.

Whether Isabelle responded or not, he'd never know. The roaring in his ears had come back full force. But it wasn't the hordes of screaming masses this time around. It was the roar of the ocean, back home in Hawaii.

He reeled back to 1988, standing with Simone on Kauai's Polihale beach on the westernmost shore. Miles and miles of deserted sand, mostly due to the fierce currents. He had stood on that beach for what seemed like hours, staring at the incredible sand dunes and the cliffs of the Na Pali.

And had experienced his first, full-blown panic attack.

"It's the kind of place that makes one realize how insignificant one really is in the grand scheme of things," he liked to tell people. "Pulled my ego down a few pegs and got my priorities in line straightaway." With the band just a smoking wreck of its former self, he and Simone had relocated to the island with the children shortly after, and family became his number one priority.

Rick was hobbled by the memory, and his legs threatened mutiny as he careened to the bathroom.

"He didn't have to ask me," he said aloud to the mirror, as if he needed to convince the somber dark eyes staring back at him. "I made the choice myself."

His reflection grimly broke the news: *Too late.*

Simone was dead within six years.

He gripped the vanity in front of him as the blackness of the memory washed over him, like it always did. *Keep your head,* he commanded himself now, although he remembered going totally off his nut at the time. The locals had talked about the powerful Polihale heiau, a sacred site believed to be one of the points from which the souls of the dead departed the island into the setting sun. It sounded so beautiful, so peaceful. He had wanted to go and die there, to travel with her. The kids had been the only things holding him back.

The thought of his boys buoyed and anchored him still. All three were now grown up and out in the world on their own. Armed with five college degrees among them, they'd each flown the coop upon graduation without ever looking back.

And what would they have seen had they even bothered?

Rick pulled back his curls from his face with one hand and splashed cool water across his heated cheeks. Face dripping, he let his hair drop into place and contemplated what he saw in the mirror before him. Rangy limbs, their muscles lean from swinging eight pounds of guitar night after night. The strong jut of his jaw, with its dark bristle of five o'clock shadow emerging. Sharp angles where cheekbones met the hollows under his tired eyes. Under his wild mane of charcoal hair, a heavy, determined brow just starting to show the weathered lines of a worrier, aged forty-four this spring.

Father.

Widower.

Rocker.

Empty nester.

His dark brows lifted at that preposterous thought. *How*

could that be? The contradiction in terms describing this current phase of his life brought him back to the present, all threats of his usual, full-blown panic attack abated. He hadn't had one since leaving Hawaii three weeks ago. *So much for that track record.* But the tension eased and a strange sigh of relief blew through his lips.

The storm had passed, for the moment.

Now what?

Sleep. Bus. Show. Repeat. He had no problem jumping through the hoops of the rock and roll traveling circus.

It was the looming prospect of time off the road that terrified him.

RICK
DON'T BREAK THE OATH

One more down, here we go. Another town, another show.

Rick found Adrian backstage in the band's hospitality room in Barcelona, signing black-and-white press pictures in rapid succession. Sharpie marker barely made contact as his hand moved fluidly, his thumb sliding each photo aside before his trademark scrawl had even dried on the page. Jim, who appeared to be building the world's tallest sandwich from the catering deli tray, would stop his task every few seconds to retrieve a photo that escaped to the floor.

"Aren't those the signed promo photos the French label wanted?" Sam asked.

He and Martin, their tour manager, had just returned from a Starbucks run. Some things stayed consistent on the road, and finding the Seattle coffee chain was one of them. It didn't matter the currency or language, one could always order an overpriced Americano and get just that.

"Yeah. Martin can mail them back," Adrian said, scratching an itch on his cheek with the capped end of the Sharpie before getting back to work.

"But weren't you the one who insisted we get them done and out of the way last night?" Sam demanded.

The three others had done their share of signing, cramping their hands before the Paris show, while Adrian had promised to do his straightaway after the gig was over. Anger built within Rick as he watched the photos spread themselves across the entire countertop.

Turned out Adrian had had another itch to scratch last night.

"He was too busy with his pit kitten," Rick said, barely able to keep the contempt out of his voice.

Last night they had been in the midst of a blistering dual bridge toward the end of the second set, playing in perfect guitarmony, neither missing a lick. Suddenly, Adrian started shredding even faster, harder, and more passionately than it seemed possible, leaving Rick completely in the dust. Rick had followed his line of vision and spied his bandmate's prize front and center. Sweat had streamed rivers toward Adrian's grin as he just shook his head slowly in disbelief, the crowd's cacophony reaching an eardrum-splitting crescendo as he wound down to meet the rhythm of Rick and the rest of the band to play the final verse.

"Kat? A pit kitten?" Adrian sputtered a laugh. "Hardly." The glaze of his ice blue eyes denoted his mind was in a far more delightful place.

Yes, Rick could see the appeal of the small-town librarian. The cascade of chestnut hair, the alabaster skin. But it was her eyes, those bright green jewels, that took you beyond the surface. Wit and warmth were sexy tools operated by an expert engineer suited up in a body that wouldn't quit.

What the hell had Kat been thinking? A metal show was a full-contact sport up front. It was a mosh pit down there, Rick thought darkly. Not a coffee klatch. She didn't belong on that side of the barrier.

All evening, security guards had plucked sweaty, battered fans over the railing from the vise grip of center stage. Kat had indicated it was her turn and, with the help of her fellow mates in the trench, she had been lifted up, up, and over. Adrian had signaled to a second guard, who escorted her to the inner sanctum of backstage rather than just expelling her safely back onto the floor. She hadn't even brought her laminate.

Fancy that, someone we know actually buying a ticket for one of our shows. Thanks to Jim's and Sam's social butterfly tendencies, the guest list had begun to grow exponentially every night since the reunion.

"Seeing her down there gave you quite the hard-on, I'm sure."

"Bigger than the one you got from smashing that vintage Gibson," Adrian lobbed right back.

Sam choked on his six-euro cup of coffee, although of the three witnesses in the room, he was the one most familiar with Adrian and Rick's witty brand of bandied insults.

"Right, I'm sure you put yours to good use last night. Giving your groupie her twelve-hundred-dollar orgasm."

Chatter in the room ceased at Rick's comment. All that could be heard was Jim's cold cut hitting bread with a wet slap.

Adrian calmly resumed his task. "How do you figure, mate?" The marker squeaked across another glossy photo as everyone else in the room held their collective breath.

"Let's see: her first-class plane ticket to Paris, the five-star hotel room, the car and driver . . ." Rick ticked them off on his fingers. He knew the expense meant nothing to Adrian. Nor to Kat, compared to witnessing the dawn of recognition on Adrian's face. Surprising her fiancé by showing up for one night in the middle of his band's European tour to celebrate his forty-fifth birthday had probably been, as the MasterCard commercials say, priceless. But Rick couldn't help himself. "Still paying for sex after all these years, Digger?"

Whether it was because of the sneering use of his stage name or the reference to his debauched behavior from decades back, Adrian's patience had clearly thinned to the point of breaking.

Just one more crack—

"I know exactly what you want me to do." In a flash, Adrian was all up in his grill, as his sons would say. Platform boots brought Adrian nose to nose with Rick. "You want me to take a swing, to hit you, so we'll be even." He shook his shaggy blond head of hair, even let a ghost of a smile slip through. "Not gonna happen, mate."

It was Rick who felt the chill through his veins, as the realization sunk in and doused him with icy shame.

"How about you write a song about *my* future wife, have it hit the charts with a bullet, and *I'll* take credit for it? Maybe then we'll be even, huh?" Adrian finished.

From the corner of his eye, Rick saw Sam and Jim exchange a look. He knew what they were thinking. Far be it from Rick to write *any* song, much less a chart-topping song like the one Adrian had penned about Simone so long ago.

Adrian, after all, was all about the details. And Rick, the big picture.

Sanitize my insanity . . . cleanse me, make me whole again, Simone . . .

Darkness loomed, threatening his vision with a fade to black.

Oh ruddy fecking hell.

It was no wonder writer's block had chased him from coast to coast, the muse eluding him both on and off-stage. In an unspoken decree as the King of Doom, Rick had forbidden the band's greatest hit to appear on any set list henceforth. Since reuniting, nobody had dared address the lingering ghost in the room.

Until now.

"I'll have no school yard squabbles on my watch," Martin boomed, "not while I have Isabelle back in the States to reckon with!" His Scottish burr was very apparent. "She'll mop the floor with the lot of us." All six and a half feet and fifteen stone of their tour manager quivered at the utterance of her name. "You'll take the stage in ten, you'll play the poxy gig, and when the tour is done, you two can go your separate ways. Understood?"

Adrian sputtered a laugh. "As if it were that simple! Rick's let Isabelle sell us into indentured servitude. VIP packages, meet and greets, Rock and Roll Fantasy Camp, and propping us up in the Hall of Fame museum like the bloody relics we are, before prodding us like cattle right into the studio. It never ends!"

"Is that what you want, then? For the whole thing to be over with again?" Another wave of anxiety rolled up Rick's frame as he stared his oldest friend down.

Adrian should want for nothing, he thought. *With his instant American family waiting for him back home. But me?*

"Enough," Sam hollered, startling everyone. "It could be worse. It *has* been worse. Remember Cass? Remember Wren?" Everyone bowed their heads at the memory of their fallen crewmate, and scuffed their soles at the mention of Corroded Corpse's wretched ex-manager, who left them broken down in his dust. "It's better now. Because it's ours to make it better, yeah? No one else's."

He plucked the Sharpie out of Adrian's clenched fist and foisted it upon Rick. "Your turn to write the set list, Rotten."

～

THE BAND EXPLODED across the stage in a myriad of lights as Jim's machine-gun drum fills ricocheted through the arena. Sam was up prowling the catwalks, slapping sound out of his bass to the roar of the audience. Opening with "Blood Oath" was always a solid crowd-pleaser, Rick thought as he and Adrian galloped through the intro like a well-oiled machine. Although his excuses and apologies had lodged stubbornly in his throat backstage, he now exorcised them through glass-shatteringly high screams and unwavering, crisp lyrics to the song he and his best friend had penned as school chums.

Adrian's fist rose in solidarity with the masses sprawled below, and one of the movers from the lighting truss overhead highlighted the raised scar on his inner arm. They had been just boys, hopped up on Norse mythology and the idea of *að blanda blóði saman*—"to mix blood together." Rick flicked a glance at the hollow of his own elbow, to the identical mark hatched there.

Blood brothers.

A storm of emotion gathered deep in Rick's chest, and on its bare surface, the thin, simple misericorde dagger tattooed there rose and fell, rose and fell, as he belted out the final chorus to "Blood Oath," of promises kept and tears wept.

A bump to his shoulder told him Adrian had come to share the microphone under the spotlight of center stage. Rick leaned into him, his bare back coming into contact with Adrian's leather-clad one as their fingers scurried across the frets of their guitars, playing rhythm and lead. Beneath the vest he wore, the twin to Rick's dagger graced Adrian's skin, and he breathed life into it as he sang in unison with his blood brother.

We bear some of the same scars, Rick thought, matching Digger's smile with a genuine one of his own as they made peace with a high five of their headstocks and strutted back to their respective spaces on stage.

Sharing war wounds, like the brothers in the song who loved each other dearly, yet hated each other fiercely.

But some we must carry alone.

SIDRA
BEATLES OR ROLLING STONES

Sidra Sullivan dropped herself and her yoga bag down at the table recently bussed clean by her brother, heaving out a potent sigh. *Thank nirvana for the Naked Bagel.* Although their linguist father might argue otherwise, there was a portmanteau for what she felt: *hangry.* It was the impatient and emotional intersection of hungry and angry.

She needed food and serenity—now.

"You know, if you keep showing up here like this, Sid, my boss is going to name a bagel after you." Seamus turned both his ball cap and a chair backward. *Such a guy thing to do,* Sidra thought as her brother pushed the hat down on his thick blond locks with the flat of his large palm before straddling the seat across from her.

At the moment, she was completely disgusted with all guys and their moves.

Although Seamus, to his credit, had at least given her the best table in the house.

"Too late!" Liz breezed out from behind the counter, rocking a tight black T-shirt that proclaimed *Bagels. What's Your Excuse?*

"One Manhattan Goddess bagel, on the house." With a flick of her wrist, she set Sidra's plate spinning down in front of her.

"You know, if you keep giving freebies to your friends, you're going to go broke," Sidra called, but Liz's back, sporting *Go Naked or Go Home* in bold red lettering, had already turned. "Let me pay, for once! I want you to take my money."

"Too bad!" Liz trilled. She had already rocketed herself back behind the counter, slicing a half-dozen to go for the next customer in line before Sidra could even reach into her bag.

"Here," she said to her brother, palming a twenty into his hand. "Go make me a taro bubble tea and put the change in the tip jar."

She had no idea what Liz's rent was like for the Naked Bagel, but she could only imagine it hiked higher with every street sign here on the Upper East Side of Manhattan.

And just like with Evolve, Sidra's yoga studio on the Lower East Side, every little bit counted. Seamus pocketed the soft, worn Andrew Jackson in his apron with a grin. Sidra knew her brother was as honest as the day was long, but he couldn't resist trying to rile her up.

"And don't be a scammer," she added, cocking a dark brow in his direction as he sauntered toward the cash register.

Sidra was pretty fed up with those, too.

Using the length of orange ribbon she never left home without, she tied her glossy black ponytail tight and high and inhaled deeply, relishing the nutty fragrance of the toasted sunflower bagel. It was studded with flax and filled to bursting with albacore tuna and smooth, ripe avocado. Indeed a treat fit for a goddess, and as the shirt Seamus was wearing boasted, *Happiness Is a Warm Bagel.*

"Which one, Sis? Fab Four or Glimmer Twins?"

Seamus held a fistful of bills and coins over the two tip jars on the counter. Like the workers' shirts, the sayings on the jars were clever and changed daily.

"Both," she managed around a mouthful of bagel.

He dropped the bills into the Beatles' jar and the change into the Rolling Stones' jar with a melodic clunk, and then went to work on her tea. Sidra watched as owner and right-hand man swerved around each other in the tight space behind the counter, tossing, reaching, and calling out to each other as they sailed through what was left of the lingering late-lunch crowd. It was like a fluid ballet: Seamus's muscular bronze arms shooting past Liz's pale freckled ones, working in synchronicity.

"Delivery to 55th and Lex," Liz commanded, shoving brown-bagged orders down the counter. "Then the usual two dozen to the doctor's office on York." She relieved him of Sidra's bubble tea and righted his ball cap. "Sixteenth floor."

Sidra had already polished off the first half of her sandwich and was contemplating its equally tempting twin. Teaching always worked up her appetite, especially the free lunch break yoga class she sometimes led at a nearby park. Although her hunger pangs had diminished considerably, her anger and disgust still lingered after this afternoon's episode.

"So, what gives?" Liz plunked herself into the chair Seamus had vacated and slid the pale purple drink across the table.

"Ech. Guys." Sidra swiped a hand in front of her face as if the entire male race were a cloud of gnats annoying her. "Why do they have to be such dogs?"

Liz took a quick scan of tables around them before allowing her mossy green eyes to meet Sidra's brown ones. The lunch crowd had officially dissipated, it seemed she could finally relax.

"Come on, can you blame them? You're standing there with your tight little body, telling them to assume the position. Down dog, up dog . . . Trade that mat for a flogger and you could be dominatrix of all the dogs." She twirled Sidra's abandoned straw wrapper around a finger and added with a devilish wink, "Probably make a helluva lot more money, too."

"Seriously, Sid. Time to grow up and get a *real* job." Seamus grinned, clipping on his space-age-looking bike helmet.

Sidra gave a snort. "Says the guy about to pedal across town with bagels in his basket."

"Bagels that aren't getting any younger, or warmer," Liz added. "Get going, you." She pointed to the front door. "Let us have our girl talk."

"See ya back at the ranch, Sid." Seamus dropped a kiss on the top of her silky head.

"So," Liz said. "Where were we? Oh yeah. Floggers." She snuck a bite of the bagel from Sidra's plate.

"I'm serious. Male yoga teachers probably don't have to put up with this shit."

After five years of teaching every type of yoga across three different boroughs, Sidra thought she had heard every pickup line, from *Hey, I've got a yoga mat built for two*, to *Gee, I bet you could bounce a quarter off that asana!* Frowning, she stabbed her straw at the fat black pearls of tapioca at the bottom of her bubble tea. "Let's just say this guy thought getting in touch with his inner self gave him license to touch me."

"That's not a dog, that's a fucking pig." Finally, Liz was appropriately outraged. "It's not you. And it's not yoga. It's Manhattan. What do we expect, living on an island two miles wide and thirteen miles long?"

"Is that why you're dating a guy who lives twenty-eight hundred miles away?" Sidra teased.

"As if." Liz gave a snort. "Hardly ideal." She sighed, folding the thin wrapper and squeezing it between her thumb and forefinger like a tiny paper accordion. "I'm telling you, this borough's run dry. All the good guys here are spoken for. Or gay. Time to import some new ones."

Sidra chewed on a boba thoughtfully. Liz made it sound easy, like heading down the Jersey Turnpike to IKEA. Sidra didn't want to settle for quick, cheap, and some assembly required. She wanted a drama-free relationship that would stand the test of time, with a solid, decent guy. Was that so wrong?

Yeah, but would you even recognize him if he came along?

The last time Sidra went to IKEA for something practical, like a rug, she ended up coming home with a single bar stool and a string of lights shaped like margarita glasses. Hardly sensible. Hell, she couldn't even choose between the Beatles and the Rolling Stones.

"Could we at least export a few of the bad ones," Sidra joked, "and even out the dating pool?"

Bells above the bagel shop's door clanged, grabbing both women's attentions.

"Anyway, like I'm one to talk." Liz stood and brushed invisible crumbs off her apron-covered miniskirt. "Kevin's true love is his restaurant. He's been talking about moving back east for four years already. I'm beginning to think he only bothers to enter my zip code when his favorite band comes to town. It's starting to give me a complex."

Now it was Sidra's turn to snort. At least Liz's zip code was seeing some occasional action. Ever since Sidra had kicked Charlie out, the only action she got in her zip code was self-addressed, so to speak.

"Be thankful he's just a fan of the band and not in it. Talk about being married to the job," Sidra grumbled. The road had been Charlie's bride for years, and she had had to settle for being mistress muse. "Musicians are the worst."

Liz ducked back behind the counter. "I'm hardly the authority," she began, wielding her huge serrated knife, "but I'd like to think that chivalry isn't quite yet dead." With that, she lopped an everything bagel in half and anointed it with a schmear of cream cheese.

"Oh, sh—" Liz bit her lip, censoring herself in the customers' presence. "Seamus!" She groaned at the sight of the lumpy brown bag still sitting on the counter. "Your flaky brother forgot to take half the order!"

"No worries, I'll take them," Sidra offered.

"Seriously? That would help tremendously. I'm down a guy. I would take them myself, but . . ." She jotted down the address on an order pad and thrust it at Sidra. "I owe you a solid, big-time."

"Well, I owed *you* for my last ten bagels. So we're even." She smiled.

"You sure you have time? It's a bit of a maze in there. Huge medical complex."

"I'm sure. My beginners class downtown isn't till five." Sidra grabbed her yoga bag and the warm order of fresh bagels.

"Still rocking that senior set, huh?"

"You know it." She waved. Actually, Sidra didn't mind teaching the geriatric group that often showed up for her Monday beginners class at Evolve Yoga. They didn't show off, they didn't hit on her, and they were open to new poses. She smiled as she crossed Lexington, remembering how her class had mastered Lizard last week. Age spots and crepe paper–like skin had lent themselves well to the pose.

Lizard pose always reminded Sidra of Charlie's iguana. Banana Louie was the only thing she truly missed about her ex-boyfriend. She used to get nervous when Charlie would let the creature roam free in her apartment. A lash from its powerful tail could easily draw blood or break one of her mother's few remaining sculptures. But with time, she came to like watching Banana Louie. Especially when he'd bask under his UVB bulb and let her feed him green beans.

Turned out Charlie was the one you had to look out for. Chasing tail and biting the hand that fed him. Turning wild when given the allowance to roam free.

Dark thoughts swept in as she crossed 64th Street, clouding

Sidra's mind and tightening her chest. *Set your best intention for the day,* she told herself. *Just let it go.*

Maybe chivalry isn't dead, Sidra reasoned as she breezed through the door of the medical center. *Maybe it's just being kept on life support somewhere. Waiting for the right person to come along and breathe life into it.*

Or to pull the plug and put it out of its misery.

RICK

SHAFTED

Rick surveyed the crowd before him, clearing his throat loudly. Discordant chatter fell to an expectant hush, and all eyes were on him. Camera flashes popped.

I don't belong here.

A prod in the back from Isabelle reminded Rick that this wasn't about him.

He looked down at his hands and almost burst out laughing. It was like one of those horrible dreams you had as a kid, showing up at school and suddenly realizing you're naked. Except he was way overdressed, in a bespoke suit with a horrible Brioni tie strangling him in ways his guitar strap never could.

But that sinking feeling of the dream, of looking down to the utter shock of nakedness? Yeah, that was there. He had no guitar to hide behind. But what he did have in his hands was a pair of gigantic, ceremonial scissors.

"Don't hurt yourself," Isabelle wisecracked from behind him.

"Right." He knew the drill. Welcome everyone, allow the hospital president to say a few words, shake hands for the camera, cut the blasted thing, and call it a day. Both his publicist and the hospital's spokesperson had been over it ad nauseam.

He opened his mouth and words started to flow. But the audience began to murmur again, shaking their heads and raising brows to one another.

"Sorry, sorry." He tapped the dead microphone, then remedied it with a flick of the switch. "It's been a long time since I've had to sound-check my own mic," he joked. "Check, check one-two." That garnered a laugh, mainly from the under forty crowd.

Rick had done the easy stuff earlier. Posing for pictures with various board of director muckety-mucks, signing autographs for them and for some of the doctors, their children, and their children's children. Now came the hard part. He glanced down at the wide, orange satin ribbon stretched out before him as Isabelle gave him another nudge. It was the only thing keeping him from performing a perfect swan dive into the arms of the city officials and dignitaries seated below.

That and social decorum, he supposed.

"Thank you all for coming, and for giving me this honor. Simone would be . . ."

Simone would be what?

Rick glanced around at the shiny new cancer wing of the famed Manhattan hospital. His wife had died far away from here, the city of her birth, and from her parents, who had been unable to make the opening due to unforeseen circumstances. They were the ones who tirelessly raised the money and spoke for the cause, year after bloody year. He was just another checkbook, a token figurehead. Putting money where his mouth—or daresay where his heart—was not. He certainly didn't deserve this honor that had fallen upon him right in the middle of his band's tour, yanking him from the promise of the road and back to the crapshoot of reality.

"Simone would be . . ."

As he searched for the right words, the devil riding shotgun on the shoulder seam of his designer suit provided some choice ones.

Simone would be here if it weren't for you, you pompous, self-centered prick.

His fists clenched, and he heard the crisp bite of stainless steel cutting through the satin. The orange bits fluttered to either side of him, and he stepped back, feeling faint. A collective gasp emanated from below and the president gaped uselessly, unread speech gripped in his hand. Isabelle was at the podium now, not a hair out of place and smiling as the crowd recovered and politely clapped.

"I have to get out of here," Rick hissed at the back of her perfumed neck, "or I'm going to lose it."

"Fine. Go. Take the service elevator," she replied, mouth still frozen in her happy publicist's smile. Isabelle was on the board of the Simone Banquet Memorial Foundation and was certainly equipped to provide the lip service for it. "There's a car waiting downstairs to take you back to the airport."

She relieved him of the Goliath shears and planted what felt like the kiss of Judas on his cheek. Exposing him for what he really was. Why, why, *why* did he let her talk him into this?

Rick bounded behind the pipe and drape toward the old part of the hospital, away from the Simone Banquet Memorial Cancer Center wing that he had just prematurely dedicated.

Why had he even bothered to come? He was useless at these types of things. Beyond useless, actually, and tipping over into the hazardous category. God, he couldn't get out of here fast enough. He should be safely on the other coast with the band in Los Angeles, not here. Anywhere but here. Fingers worked to loosen the tight knot at his throat as he proceeded down the hallway toward the service elevator, which was miraculously opening at that very moment to allow a worker off.

"Hold the lift!" he barked as the doors began to close upon his approach. He saw no one inside move a finger in response. "Dammit!" Curse New York and its bloody New York minute, with everyone rushing and no one taking the time—

A slim, tan leg shot through the gap in the doors, causing them to spring open again.

Rick murmured his thanks as he wormed in, past the tiny sandal dangling from the foot holding the door at bay.

"Crap. My flip-flop!"

The owner of the leg shifted a huge paper sack of heavenly smelling baked goods in her arms, just in time to catch a glimpse of her shoe slipping neatly through the crack as the doors slid shut with a smug *ding*.

"Son of a bitch!"

The expletive hardly matched the wisp of a girl who had uttered it. She had the delicate features of a china doll and barely came up to Rick's chest. Yet he and the other occupants of the elevator cowered as she swore like a trucker.

"Sorry," was all Rick could muster.

"Me too." The girl glared at him with eyes startlingly bright, banded in colors that reminded Rick of the tiger iron stone he used to bring back as gifts for his sons after tour stops in Australia. She mumbled something about good deeds unpunished and left it at that.

As they rode in uncomfortable silence, Rick realized the elevator was going up, not down. He had been so intent on escaping, the thought hadn't even occurred to him that it might not be going the way he wanted.

Nothing was going the way he wanted these days.

He sighed, his eyes drifting down. The girl was balanced like a stork, her bare foot nestled against the inner thigh of her opposite leg. How she was able to stand like that while the elevator took its time to stop at every other floor, Rick had no clue. Not that he could blame her; he wouldn't want his skin coming into contact with any part of Manhattan's terra firma, whether inside or out. Her arms were still clutching the huge bag. Rick caught a whiff of cinnamon swirling with honey and walnuts and realized he had not eaten since landing on American soil.

An older woman in pink scrubs commandeering a cart full of hospital supplies finally spoke up. "Here, *chica*." She rummaged through the items on the bottom shelf of the cart. "You take," she continued in her broken English, smiling and offering up a scrunched handful of something.

Without a word to Rick, the girl handed off her bag to him so she could slide what looked like a pale blue paper shoe over her bare foot.

"*Gracias,*" she said politely and pointedly to the woman. Which seemed to imply *No thanks to you* as far as Rick was concerned. She was a firecracker, this one.

Pink Scrubs got off at the next floor, leaving just the two of them on board. She took back custody of her bagels and kept her eyes on the lighted panel above the door. The only number left lit was sixteen, and they were almost there. Rick leaned past her to press L, feeling like an idiot. *L for Loser.* The girl smirked but didn't comment.

Her hair was straight and glossy, darker than even his, and caught back in a ribbon the same orange hue as the one he had just snipped in half back in the multi-million-dollar wing that bore his wife's name. He had felt so useless earlier. Now he had the sudden urge to do something, say something, to remedy the current situation.

"Can I buy you a coffee?" he blurted. *Lame.* "A new shoe?" That earned him a roll of those tiger iron eyes, flecked with golden jasper and bits as dark as black hematite. "How about a tetanus shot?"

With a dismissive snort, she scuffed down the hall in one paper shoe and didn't look back.

SIDRA
CINDERELLA IN REVERSE

Do a good deed and what do you get? Sidra thought. *The shaft. Literally.*

Truth be told, she had been too busy sneaking a glance at the gorgeous specimen who had entered the tight quarters of the elevator to notice her silly shoe was falling off her foot.

And that accent. Talk about imported!

Guys in power suits usually intimidated her, but something about this guy was different. Make no mistake—he absolutely owned the look. Especially with that cascade of long hair. The unexpected contradiction made him even more intriguing.

His suit had appeared tailor-made for his body, and that tie screamed spendy. Sidra would bet the last bagel in her bag that his shoes were a) Italian and b) worth more than her whole wardrobe combined. Not that her wardrobe contained much more than yoga pants and sports bras, but still. His shoes were really nice. Way too expensive (*and whoa—big!*) to ever lose down an elevator shaft.

She thought back to her "where have all the good guys gone?" conversation with Liz. *Gay?* Maybe. *Taken?* Maybe that, too. He had had a faint but fresh-looking lipstick mark on his cheekbone, she had noticed. Shoot. Oh well.

Sidra delivered the bag of bagels left behind by Seamus with little fanfare. The receptionist even gave her a tip. Enough for the subway ride home, but since she only had one damn shoe, she'd have to spring for a cab. No way was she going to deal with the hassle of the MTA while a paper bootie was cinched to her ankle.

Mr. Import had offered to treat her to a tetanus shot. Cute.

And she totally blew him off for his trouble. *Nice one, Sid. You may as well have given Manhattan's last knight in shining armor the finger.*

She wondered if he was a doctor. Plenty of them seemed to have abandoned the white coats these days. And the way he carried himself gave the impression he was some sort of big cheese, compared to the other lab rats in the maze of a medical center. But why the hell had he been riding the service elevator? Sidra knew why she was on it. Upon checking in at the front desk, she had been relegated to taking the route reserved for deliveries and dirty laundry. Certainly not the preferred mode of transportation for someone so well dressed.

The clap-scuff of her hurried pace echoed through the empty hall. *Back to the scene of the crime,* she thought as the elevator doors slid open.

"Your chariot awaits."

Mr. Import was back, and he had brought a wheelchair.

"You've got to be kidding me." Sidra laughed self-consciously. She hoped the Manhattan Goddess bagel hadn't given her tuna breath.

"It's the least I can do." He pointed to the seat. "In you go."

Sidra humored him. Maybe he could roll her down to the taxi stand, at least.

"Do you make a habit of this?" she asked.

"Of what? Absconding with hospital property?" As his

laugh rumbled above her, she wished she hadn't taken the seat so she could see the smile that went with it. Like his suit, she bet it looked like a million bucks. "Hardly."

"No, of riding the dirty service elevator all day."

They passed by two more floors before he answered. "Only when there's the possibility of rescue and redemption." The handsome stranger's stilted murmur was close to her ear, raising goose bumps and questions she didn't dare ask.

The ride going down was fast and smooth, with no stops in between. He whisked the wheelchair into the busy lobby and finessed his way to the sliding glass doors, humming something in a melodic baritone as he pushed.

"Okay, well. The ride stops here. I'm fine, thanks." She really needed to get downtown so she could grab another pair of shoes from home and hoof it to the studio. "I'm going to be late for work."

"Well, you certainly can't go to work barefoot."

Now it was Sidra's turn to laugh as she accepted his large hand and allowed herself to be helped out of the wheelchair. "Actually, I can."

He raised one heavy, sculpted eyebrow. "Look. You said no to my offer of coffee—"

"And to your offer of immunization," Sidra interjected.

"—so let me at least replace your shoe. I insist." He was already signaling to a—no joke—long, black limousine idling out front. Its driver popped out and stepped lively toward the back door.

"Dude. I'm not getting in a car with a total stranger. Sorry."

Mr. Import's dark brow furrowed as if he didn't quite understand. He *so* wasn't from around here. "You're not getting in a car with a total stranger, you're getting into a car with . . ."

"James, sir." The driver tapped his own name tag with a smile.

"You're getting in a car with James." He turned to the driver and Sidra saw the flash of a bill disappear into the liveryman's breast pocket as they spoke in hushed tones. "James is going to take you to a shoe store, and then he's going to take you to work." Now Sidra caught a glimpse of his smile, which appeared to be tinged with the tiniest bit of regret. "I've actually got a plane to catch."

Sidra watched from the open window of the limo as Mr. Import stepped to the curb and raised his arm. "JFK Airport, please," she heard him say.

So, chivalry isn't dead after all, she thought. *It's hailing a yellow medallion cab to Queens.*

"THERE'S A DUANE READE." Sidra pointed, but James appeared to have strict orders to not stop until he had reached a proper shoe store. They were on Third Avenue, which brimmed with Upper East Side expensive choices. *Step on it, Jeeves. Tick-tock!* She had class in an hour, and her seniors weren't very Zen about being made to wait.

"They're ten-dollar drugstore flip-flops," she insisted impatiently. "And I only lost one. So why not give me five dollars of the hundred he slipped you and we'll call it a day?"

James's eyes met Sidra's in the rearview mirror. "I promised him we'd get you proper shoes, miss."

Of course they had to be proper. Sidra could still hear Mr. Import's oh-so-proper accent ringing in her ears. So smooth. "Pretty elaborate pickup technique, don't you think?"

"Or just a good Samaritan, I suppose."

Sidra contemplated James's reply. For a smooth talker, her Prince Charming hadn't offered up a name, or asked for hers. Perhaps this was just one of those weird pay-it-forward things, like covering the toll of the car behind you, or treating the next customer in line at the drive-thru. Manhattan usually didn't see such random acts of senseless kindness. Or, at least, Sidra didn't.

"Here we are, miss."

Sidra balked at the storefront; she recognized the name brand from flipping through those thick fashion magazines her friend Fiona was partial to.

"Um, the hundred dollars he gave you isn't going to buy an Odor-Eater in this store, James."

Her driver reddened as he ushered her through the front door. "That was just my, um . . . tip. Everything else is on the company account."

Sidra felt her ears burn. As if it weren't embarrassing enough to walk into a high-end boutique wearing a paper hospital bootie! "I'm sorry," she mumbled. "I shouldn't have assumed."

Thankfully, the sales girls didn't bat an eye at Sidra's odd choice of footwear and went to fetch her size. "Just the cheapest you've got. Last season," Sidra called after them. They enlisted James, who brought her a sizable stack of boxes. Even the cardboard looked expensive.

"This is ridiculous," she said to no one in particular. Half the styles she nixed just on the prices alone. The other half she longed to play dress-up with, as they were flirty and fun but totally not practical for walking the uneven and broken sidewalks of her East Village neighborhood. James stood by at the ready, as if he had all the time in the world. But Sidra knew time was a-wasting; she had to get back downtown to teach her beginners class at Evolve.

She slid her feet into the most comfortable and decadent pair of flip-flops she had ever encountered. The suede-covered cork footbed practically sighed as it molded around her foot and supported her arch and heel. The straps were genuine black patent leather, not the plastic stuff, and heavily embellished with rhinestones.

"These are perfect. I'll take them."

James looked on approvingly, and for a millisecond, Sidra entertained a fantasy that instead of a suited chauffeur, her Mr. Import was standing there in all his fineness and finery, helping her choose. A pang of regret reverberated through her. She should have at least asked him his name. Not that it mattered, but . . .

A salesgirl discreetly disposed of the dirty paper shoe while the other clerk rang up the purchase. Sidra cringed at the price, knowing her new flip-flops cost roughly eighteen times more than her old pair.

"What's your return policy?" she asked as James supplied Mr. Import's line of credit. She had half a mind to bring the pretty shoes back tomorrow. Although the other half of her brain must've been connected to her feet, which insisted she was never going to take them off.

"Thirty days. Would you like to keep this?" The salesgirl held up Sidra's lone cheap flip-flop.

"Sure, what the heck." Perhaps she'd tack it to her bedroom wall. It could serve as a reminder that Manhattan hadn't run dry of the good guys just yet.

The limo glided down Second Avenue. Sidra made good use of the surround sound stereo and had James rocking rhymes with the Beastie Boys and singing along to seventies Motown by the time they had reached Houston.

"So this is it, I guess."

"It's been a pleasure, miss."

"Please, call me Sidra."

But it was a little too late for introductions, as the limo pulled away from the dusty, littered curb of Rivington Street and the spell was broken.

Back to reality, I guess.

Sidra glanced up as she gave the doorknob of her family's building a vigorous pull. There was the old sign for Sullivan and Son Bicycles, its red and black letters barely legible amidst the curls of peeling paint and splintered swollen wood. Nailed to its bottom frame was the sign Seamus had painstakingly designed and airbrushed for their cousin Mike: a biomechanical steampunk logo for Revolve Records. While the name was fitting for an establishment that still sold physical forms of music, it was really more of an homage to their family's old trade. Although, Sidra thought grimly, Revolve was quickly on its way to becoming a relic itself. Besides Mikey and a few other purists, no one cared about vinyl. Or even CDs anymore, for that matter. Seamus kidded about just airbrushing over the *R* in the sign once the record store flopped. "Evolve or die," he had joked.

Which was how Sidra came to name Evolve, her month-old business.

She really should have a sign made, too. Word of mouth could only travel so far. Still, it secretly pleased her to know her unlabeled yoga studio brought more income into the property during that short time period than her cousin's record sales had in the last quarter.

"Nice shoes." He whistled from behind the counter. "What, did you mug Paris Hilton?"

"All the better to kick you with, Mikey."

Sidra blew her cousin a kiss as she breezed through the deserted record store and into her back sanctuary. Judging from the number of attendance cards out and lockers in use, it looked like she had ten students waiting for her.

"Good afternoon, everyone." She kicked off her overpriced flip-flops. "Let's begin in Child's pose."

Shedding her tunic in favor of the lightweight black tank top underneath, she grabbed her mat and spread it under the light and shadows cast by the lone Moroccan-style brass lamp hanging high in the back space she had claimed as her own.

All of her seniors folded up and rested their torsos on their thighs like dutiful children. *"Balasana."* Sidra breathed the Sanskrit name as everyone, herself included, surrendered to gravity and the state of non-doing required of this pose. As her forehead met her mat, she was grateful for an excuse to clear her mind of the surreal events of the day.

RICK

SHOT TO HELL

THANK goodness for the Pacific Time Zone. Rick was traveling backward, gaining hours as he lost consciousness against the plush headrest of his first class airline seat.

He drifted in and out of deep and shallow dreams, with images of orange ribbons and scissors. He saw himself back at the new wing of the hospital, wordlessly cutting, then at the hospital in Kauai, watching helplessly as Simone cried while what was left of her beautiful golden hair fell from her pillow to his feet. Then he saw his hands slowly and seductively pulling the tight orange bow that kept the delivery girl's hair in place, imagined the midnight black sweep of her hair covering his eyes as he pulled her to him.

He awoke horny, restless, and ashamed, clutching the armrests of the seat as he catapulted six hundred miles per hour through the air like it was no big deal.

"Anything to drink?" the flight attendant asked.

"Tequila, please. With a lime." Rick sat up straighter.

"I'm sorry, Mr. Rotten. We have a limited beverage menu in-flight." She looked twenty-five if a day, and genuinely sympathetic.

"Well, that's a crying shame, darlin'. I thought I could get anything I wanted in first class."

With the events of New York halfway behind him, Riff Rotten had reached cruising attitude.

"AND HOW WAS YOUR FLIGHT?"

It took Rick a moment to answer Isabelle's long-distance query, as his mouth was full of tequila.

"Uneventful." He dragged his tongue from the flight attendant's navel and up the salt trail of her body, ending at her neck.

"Is there anything you want to tell me?"

Rick teased the lime from between the beautiful girl's lips and sucked on it thoughtfully. "Not that I can think of," he murmured, reaching for the bottle to start the process again.

"Take me off goddamn speakerphone," Isabelle said, clearly annoyed with the girl's squeal as cold alcohol sloshed in her navel once more. "Whatever you're doing, I doubt it requires your hands."

Rick made the lustful loop once more down and back up her body, phone now pressed to his ear.

"Don't you ever sleep?" he asked wearily. If dusk was descending over the Sunset Strip out his hotel window, then it had to be well past midnight in Isabelle's world.

"Not when you're on tour. So . . . no drag queen confessions you'd like to make? Are you developing a shoe fetish in your old age? You owe the Foundation a hundred and eighty-three bucks."

The elevator girl.

Rick spit out the lime and chuckled. *Was that all?* "They were a present. For a friend."

"What, did you go for a quickie before the airport? A booty call?"

He thought of the girl giving him the total piss off as she scuffed out of the elevator in her one shoe and paper slip-on bootie. *"Bootie" call indeed,* Rick joked to himself. He was drawn to her call, all right, like a siren's song. There had been something about her . . .

The flight attendant held out the saltshaker and another shot to him, but he waved it away. She sucked on a lime and pouted. As far as Rick was concerned, their layover was over.

He was tired, he was drunk, and now he couldn't get that girl with the bagels off his mind. He wished he could've stuck around and shopped with her. Maybe she would've given him that lone surviving shoe as a souvenir. Like a jousting knight, he had collected his share of lady favors throughout the years. Rock and roll–style tokens of appreciation: bras, panties . . . but never a flip-flop. Was that considered a fetish?

"What did she buy?"

"How the hell should I know?" Rick heard the scratch of a lighter before she continued. "The receipt said Mephisto Hakira sandals. They hardly sound like Jimmy Choo fuck-me heels." Isabelle's own snobbery definitely extended into stiletto territory, and he knew her preference ran in the four- figure bracket.

Good girl, he thought. He hoped she really liked them.

And would think of him whenever she wore them.

"She seemed the practical type." Down-to-earth—that was a far more apt description. He remembered the way her foot had rooted to the floor while the other balanced effortlessly, her long, tan leg fanned out to the side, almost touching his in the intimate quarters of the lift. Her energy had been subtly powerful, yet seemed to radiate off the walls of the small space.

I want that, he thought. *How does one get that? Can it be bottled?*

The flight attendant had passed out in his hotel bed, having finished off the tequila herself.

"Out of curiosity, can you find out where the driver dropped her?"

Isabelle gave a sigh laced with the usual nicotine and resentment. "Fine. If it will keep you amused. And in a good mood when you get back to New York."

"It just might." Rick smiled. "And could you quit smoking, while you're at it?"

"Not a chance. In other news, you missed Paul."

"Cripes, really?" His eldest had had a final exam to administer and hadn't thought he would be able to make the two o'clock dedication ceremony in time. *My son,* he thought, *the college professor. Good Lord.*

"He showed up moments after you left."

"I'll call him, take him to lunch when I get back to town in a few weeks." He shook the empty bottle before depositing it in the trash. "Has Adrian checked in yet?"

"The rest of the band arrived earlier. He's . . ." Rick patiently waited for Isabelle to fetch her itinerary. "He's in room 609. VIP Meet and Greet at the Forum tomorrow at five o'clock, remember."

"Yes, dear."

"Good. Now get some sleep."

"I will." He planned on crashing in Adrian's room to avoid any turbulence with the flight attendant once her, erm . . . jet lag wore off. "And Isabelle? Thanks. For taking over earlier, at the event."

His publicist was, for once, at a loss for words. Rick knew what was coming. Isabelle shed her tough exterior a few times a year.

Not unlike a snake molting its skin.

"I felt Simone there today. Her presence. Does that sound silly?" she asked softly.

"No. It sounds lucky." Rick tried not to let his envy bleed through. "Good night, luv. Sleep well."

SIDRA
THE DEATH OF THOUGHTS

"Palms up," Sidra intoned as she wound her way through the room, surveying the bodies in supine position on her floor. "Let your thoughts dissolve."

This was *Savasana*, also known as Corpse pose. Sidra felt funny saying the word to the students of this particular yoga class, most of whom had at least forty years over her. "Feel your muscles relax. Everything melts away."

All of her students made good corpses, lying under their colorfully woven Mexican blankets. Sidra shivered as her body temperature dropped under its own relaxation. She tried in vain to keep her thoughts uncluttered, but hiking with Charlie through Mexico came to mind. Arriving in Santa María del Tule just in time for *Día de los Muertos*. Memories of marigolds, white candles, and all those colorful blankets spread out. She and Charlie had danced in the graveyard, then drank the local mescal and made love until dawn.

She had promised herself she wouldn't think about Charlie today. Especially today.

Sidra slowly pulled the orange ribbon that held her tight ponytail, allowing her thick waves of hair to fall like an inky curtain. She wrapped the ribbon around her slim, olive-toned wrist like a reminder and surrendered to her own corpse pose, the words she knew by heart echoing throughout her: *Let it be the death of thoughts, of feelings that do not serve you; the release of everything you don't need.*

Sidra loved *Savasana.* She imagined what it would be like to lie in this pose indefinitely, until her own skin hung loose and crepey, until her hair faded from black to white from loss of melanin and her body ran out of estrogen and her mind turned forgetful.

She wondered if she would grow old alone.

"Let's start to slowly bring awareness back to our bodies," she murmured gently. "Wiggle our toes, our fingers . . . bring our knees up and rock them slowly, to the left and to the right. When you're ready, roll onto your right side and rest there for a moment."

Time to get these seniors rolling, back to their co-ops and walk-ups. Many lived within walking distance of the Rivington Street yoga studio, had probably lived on the Lower East Side of Manhattan their whole lives, back when the Lower East Side stood for something entirely different. The East Village was like a hip shadow slipping down the Bowery and across Houston Street, slowly absorbing the Old World neighborhood. It offended Sidra, and she was only in her early thirties. She wondered how these long-time residents felt about it. Her uncle Sully just laughed from the doorway and shook his head as he watched each Prius and Peg Perego jogging stroller push out the liftgate delivery trucks and their dusty pallets.

"Thank you, dear. That was wonderful." Vivian patted Sidra's forearm. "I always feel so calm after taking your class. Always worth the schlep."

Sidra had to smile. She wondered what the alternative to calm was for the spry seventy-year-old. With her Crayola-red bouffant and full dental bridge, Viv was probably a hell-raiser in her assisted living community. She came all the way from Edgewater, New Jersey, three times a week to attend Sidra's classes at Evolve Yoga, and loved to remind people of it.

Evolve's late evening class was Sidra's favorite class to teach. The entire building was hers. No Uncle Sully in the rear storage room, tinkering with old inventory from his defunct bicycle shop. Her cousin Mikey wasn't hustling up front in the record shop, or nagging his girlfriend, Fiona, to hoist her sizable boobs off the counter and pick up a feather duster once in a while. No clutter, no noise. Just the soft sounds of her yoga mix CDs on the stereo under the ever-glowing exotic brass lamp hanging high overhead.

Sidra strolled up Avenue A in a post-practice haze. It was a short strut from letters to numbers and didn't take long to get to her brownstone on East 5th Street off Second Avenue. Just a block away, the narrow eye of Curry Row blinked invitingly. Her mouth watered at the smell of *rotli* frying in the pan and rice cooking with cardamom. She felt ten years old again, helping her aunties as they made *dal makhani*, the buttery lentil soup her grandparents' restaurant was known for.

While some kids had monkey bars to swing on, Sidra had the front and back doors of every Indian restaurant on 6th Street to zoom through like her own personal culinary playground. There she nicked fresh flatbread *chapatis* hot from the oven and learned how to blend spinach in a cream sauce for *saag*. She'd help her grandma mix chai spices in a baggie to take home and simmer in milk for Seamus and her dad.

Seventh Street was a whole different jungle gym of memories, sounds, and smells. McSorley's Old Ale House was there, had always been there, and probably always would be there. It was just one in a long string of establishments that tolerated Jack Sullivan when he could no longer tolerate himself. She recalled pulling her father off many a bar stool to come home for a hot meal and a change of clothing. The smell of sawdust mixed with the sour sweat of someone who spent his summers drinking indoors. She had been ten then, too, the year her mother died.

She had promised herself she wouldn't think about death today. Especially today.

"Where's yer dot?" was a frequent question from the inebriated clientele on the neighboring bar stools of the Landmark and Molly's Shebeen when she'd arrive, determined to coax her father home. The lighthearted melody of an Irish reel and the piping of a tin whistle would echo cheerily in her head in contrast to the sick thump of her heart later on as she watched her father piss the bed. The first time she saw such a dark stain bloom beneath him, she thought it was blood, that he was dying, too. But somehow, her dad would always spring back, sober and ready for a good Irish roast with the rest of the Sullivan clan come Sunday.

The three streets were a blend of unique memories elemental to her blended Irish-Indian upbringing, a mesh tightly woven. But they were also peppered with thoughts of her first love. She remembered the shock, the burst of summer rain, and the cute boy who walked her all the way home from Great Jones Street just because he happened to have an umbrella when she did not.

That hadn't been chivalry on Charlie's part that day, Sidra realized now. It had been dumb luck and opportunity. Charlie Danahy just always fell into things: cool band gigs, great summer shares, lucrative modeling stints . . . and other women's beds.

She knew exactly which streetlight witnessed their first kiss —the one covered in tiny mirrors and mosaic tiles the color of Charlie's eyes. She could barely stand to walk past it now, afraid to get lost in that sea of mosaic and see her shattered heart reflected in each tiny mirror.

Sidra had lived all her life in Manhattan but had been as

ethnocentric as a small-town girl. She could joke with Liz about importing and exporting for the sake of her love life, but, in all honestly, could never imagine being anywhere else. Yet lately, she felt like she was drowning in the melting pot.

Sidra turned her mind to June and the promise of change. She'd continue teaching her studio classes at night, but her days would be spent outdoors, working at a posh summer camp upstate, away from the dog days of summer in the city. And away from the dogs, like Charlie, who dwelled there. That thought alone became Sidra's new mental mantra for peace.

"Hey, doll."

Speak of the devil. There was the old hound of hell himself, sitting on her stupid, single bar stool and restringing his guitar. He might as well have been sharpening his pitchfork.

"Charlie. *What* are you doing here?" Sidra shrugged the strap of her yoga mat off her weary shoulder and dropped it along with her bag. Her asking for the apartment key back had obviously been a symbolic gesture in his mind. "How many freaking copies of my key did you make?"

Her ex smiled his roguish smile that never failed to cause a pileup on Sidra's heartbeat highway.

His sexy, dark brows arched devilishly. Charlie Danahy was the devil, all right. If the devil had a panty-melting laugh, muttonchops, and a razor-thin goatee eked along his superb jawline.

"Chill, girl." His voice rolled lazily over her. "No law against hanging with my newest bandmate."

Sidra narrowed her eyes. As far as she knew, Evie was his newest bandmate. Unless the lineup had changed since he'd decided to mate with her.

"Hi, Sid." Seamus strolled out of the kitchen, shirtless. Her brother had a slice of bread smeared with peanut butter in one hand, folded over rather than cut. In the other, the quart of milk she had bought just yesterday.

"*Seamus* is in your band now?" Sidra asked incredulously. Seamus chugged milk from the jug innocently, clearly unruffled about being in league with Satan. "Who quit? Or did you kick someone else out?"

Lucifer's lady-killer laugh struck again. "Relax, Sid Vicious. He's not replacing anybody. He's joined the road crew." Sidra watched as her ex gingerly placed his newly strung guitar into its case with the same kind of care he used to lavish on her. How many songs had he played for her—hell, *written* for her on that old thing? Songs those new strings would probably never know, she realized, his fingers never quite falling on them in the same formation. The thought slammed Sidra's emotions into protective lockdown, undoing hours of heart-opening yoga.

"Seamus. On your road crew," she echoed hollowly.

"Yep. The Bold O'Danahys are hitting the road this summer. Someone's gotta hawk the merch, and we're gonna be too busy playing."

Idle hands were the devil's workshop, yet Charlie was ever so busy forming and re-forming rock bands, using his father's popular tavern on St. Mark's as a base. His latest version was an Irish party band he called the Bold O'Danahys, a play on the old traditional folk song "The Bold O'Donahue." Sidra would be the first to begrudgingly admit it: The band was good. But they weren't good enough for her brother to waste his time on.

Seamus may have lacked ambition these days, but he certainly didn't lack musical prowess. Put any type of percussion in front of him and he could play the hell out of it. He had marched with the Boston Crusaders throughout his years at Harvard, effortlessly maintaining top grades while in the elite drum corps. Putting him behind the merch table instead of behind the kit was just another way for Charlie to keep Seamus under his thumb. And to sadistically push Sidra's buttons.

"We're going all the way to the World Music Fest in Vancouver, Sid." Seamus's well-chiseled arm arced overhead, sandwich in hand. Sidra didn't have the heart to call him out on his pathetic personal pronoun usage. She admired his sheer faith and love for the band, but not his illusions of being a real part of it. What was it Uncle Sully would always say? *You can put all your hopes and dreams into the stars, but that doesn't make you a constellation.*

"You'll be selling T-shirts, Seamus. And bumper stickers. What about your jobs here?" *And Dad,* she thought. *And me?* She couldn't imagine getting through the summer without Seamus here.

"I'm sure the Naked Bagel can find someone else to bike their bagels around." Charlie ruffled Seamus's blond locks. "And Mikey will be psyched to cut two less paychecks at Revolve for us. It's only a matter of time before Sully sells that wreck of a building out from under him anyway."

"My uncle would never sell."

Would he?

Charlie shrugged. "Everybody has their price, doll."

His words stung. That wreck of a building had been in her family for three generations. But what did Charlie Danahy know about legacy? He didn't care about long-term or the test of time. And he certainly didn't care about her.

She'd hoped that the growing income from the yoga classes, combined with the cushy pay from her suburban day camp job, would convince her uncle to keep the building in the family, or to at least let her lease-to-own. She hadn't shared her plan with any of her family yet. And she certainly wasn't about to say anything in front of Charlie, who was currently prodding three fingers into her brother's ribs like a trident.

"Come on, Shay. You haven't even told her the best part yet."

"We're opening for Anam-Atman!"

Another thorn spiked in Sidra's side. Another memory tainted by Charlie. He had been the one to discover the energetic Indrish East Village band, but Sidra had connected with them on a cosmic level. "Their name means *soul* in Gaelic. And Hindi," Charlie loved to proclaim.

She didn't need him to tell her what it meant.

Anam-Atman fused bhangra and Celtic music into a fantastic sound track, one that had run through Sidra and Charlie's first summer together. She had finally gotten used to listening to her favorite band without him, and now they were going to be joined at the hip, on the road, with him—and Evie?

"You'll come see us, right?" Seamus asked eagerly. "The first show is at Irving Plaza next month."

"Then on to the Trocadero in Philly, the 9:30 Club in DC, the Middle East in Boston . . ." Charlie began ticking the itinerary off his forked tongue, but Sidra was done listening.

She willed herself to let it go. *Let it be the death of thoughts, of feelings that do not serve you; the release of everything you don't need.* But it was hard to embrace a mantra when Charlie's eyes were on her, grinding her focus down to brittle dust. He leaned back smugly on her cheap IKEA stool, and Sidra wished it would collapse to tinder under him. Then catch fire. *Burn in hell, Devil Man!*

She spied her lone flip-flop, the sole survivor from her adventure in the elevator with Mr. Import a couple weeks ago, in the jumble of sibling footwear by the front door. "Where's our hammer, Shay?" she asked, plucking it from the pile.

"Kitchen drawer, by the microwave."

Both men watched her as she marched past them, retrieved the hammer and a nail from the junk drawer, and made a beeline for her bedroom. While it would give her immense satisfaction to smack Charlie with the shoe—or with the hammer, for that matter—as she passed by, she refrained. She had bigger plans.

Good. Riddance. Two strikes of the hammer punctuated her thought and impaled the thin rubber to the wall above her bed. At least Charlie would be out of her hair—and nowhere near her zip code—this summer.

But Seamus, too? She hated the thought of exporting one of the good guys along with the bad. She hoped the borough would make up for it somehow. Manhattan owed her one.

SIDRA

GODDESS OF NIGHTTIME

SLEEP WASN'T COMING EASILY. Sidra rolled her body to face the ceiling, listening for any evidence that her father was still awake upstairs. She had heard uneven footfalls and the squeaky protest of bedsprings about an hour earlier.

It was the anniversary of a much noisier evening.

Sidra sighed, kicking the sheet down before bringing the bottoms of her feet to touch each other. She kissed her shoulder blades together and let her arms fall away to a forty-five-degree angle. Inhaling deeply and exhaling fully, she felt her knees slowly sink to the bed. This was the pose she recommended to her students when they complained of insomnia. It went by many names: *Supta Baddha Konasana*, which was fun to say, or Reclining Bound Angle pose, which sounded technical. Sidra's favorite choice of words was Nighttime Goddess Stretch. Her mother taught her this, her first pose, when Sidra was just five. Nervous to start kindergarten the next day, she had climbed into her parents' bed, wriggling down like a worm between her mother and her father to inhale both their comforting scents. Her father was Old Spice, plain as that. Her mother was more complicated, a delicate balance of vanilla and cardamom- infused honey.

"Oh, honey," her mother had whispered when Sidra complained she couldn't sleep. "It's time you learned about the Goddess." Although she had just barely opened them, her mother's eyes were shining. "Jack . . . Jack. Out you go. Girls only!"

Sidra had giggled as her father smacked sleepy kisses onto both their cheeks and stumbled to Sidra's bedroom for alternate sleeping quarters. The bed was so big now, with a large warm indent. "This is now our island," her mother had said. Sidra felt her dad's absence and missed him, but was excited to be marooned with just her mother. "Do you feel the moonlight on your face, on your belly?" Sidra did. "Do you hear the gentle waves lapping near your feet, your hands?" She did. Following instructions, she pressed her tiny feet together, splayed her little arms, and let all nervous thoughts drift away in the water. All that was left was a big goddess and a little goddess, relaxing on the sand. "We are the Goddesses of Nighttime."

She opened her eyes. Her dad was definitely sleeping now, as she heard the distant snores through the plaster and drywall. It wasn't an irritating noise to Sidra at all, and wouldn't keep her from sleeping. Her thoughts, on the other hand . . .

A pale green light surrounded the doorjamb. There was either an alien abduction on East 5th Street or Seamus had fired up the Mac in the living room. Come summer and its humid nights, the door would swell enough to block the glow of his nighttime Internet trawling. Then again, come summer, Seamus would be gone.

Sidra pushed her feet into slippers and padded down the hall. "Hey," she said softly.

Her brother greeted her with a distracted grunt. His broad shoulders concealed the screen, but she had no doubt he was checking the online dating sites. He belonged to all the popular ones, but spent most of his time and energy on the Indian-specific ones: Shaadi, Indian Cupid, and the one that made Sidra laugh the most: Simply Marry. As if there were anything simple about deciding who, when, where, and why to marry in the first place.

Poor Seamus. He sounded so promising on paper—or, rather, on screen as bindaasboy76. *Indian- Irish male, 31, vegetarian, Harvard-educated.* But many of the Indian girls—or rather, their more traditional parents—were often shocked to find Seamus Sullivan, the blond-haired, light-skinned, hunky man-boy, at their door. He had stayed at Harvard long enough to pick up the Boston Irish accent, but not long enough to get a diploma or a high-powered career. In person, Seamus was often dismissed as quickly as *pardesi*, a foreigner no doubt out to snare a *desi* girl to cook and clean and cater to him without complaint.

It made Sidra's blood boil to think the majority couldn't see beyond all that to notice the warm, dark eyes he'd inherited from their mother, herself a one-and-a-half-generation Indian-American. His steady, slim, artistic hands, also so like hers. And the dazzling smile she'd passed down to both her children. Sidra's brother was loyal, sweet, crazy-smart, and interesting, with a heart of gold. And according to most of Sidra's girl-friends, totally freakin' hot. Pity none of them were Indian.

"Sorry, did I wake you?" he finally thought to ask, tearing his eyes away from the screen.

"Nah." Plopping into the winged chair beside him, she added, "Hadn't gotten that far yet. So, anyone new out there? What are your intentions?"

Seamus let out a belly laugh. "Oh auntie, please!" It was their usual give-and-take banter, poking fun at and twisting the endless needling Sidra had received from various female relatives and family friends over the years. The questions had dwindled to the occasional hypothetical during her years with

Charlie. Sidra had expected them to resume with a vengeance once they split, but it seemed most of the aunties had since given up hope; Sidra had, after all, hit the magic age considered the unmarriageable marker that year: thirty. And there were a bevy of younger cousins to benefit from such attentions, much to Sidra's relief.

Seamus's finger tapped the wireless mouse as if he were sending out Morse code to the masses with the hope that just one sensational someone was out there to understand him. "I was just taking a look at some profiles out west. You know. It might be nice to chat with someone for a while and have someone new to meet up with when we hit Vancouver."

Sidra nodded, bit at a hangnail that was too short.

"Spit it out, Sid. What's up?" She knew he wasn't talking about her finger maintenance; they were just ten months apart and closer than most siblings ever cared to be.

"Did you remember what today is?"

His eyes flicked to the clock above her head. There were just five minutes left to figure out today before it became yesterday. "May . . . ?"

"It's the day Mom told us she was pregnant."

Both of them immediately glanced where they always did when the topic came up: to the mother dove sculpture sitting on the console table behind the couch.

The dove sculpture was one of the only remaining pieces left of their mother's. And it was both of their favorite. There had been a heartbreaking tug-of-war over who should take it when the siblings had lived in separate quarters. But once Charlie moved out and Seamus moved back in, it became a moot point. Like the Blessed Mother statue that sat on Uncle Sully's lawn (or Mary on the half-shell, as their cousin Mikey called her), the mother dove was a revered household fixture. Something silently considered, but rarely talked about.

"Damn, remember the racket? You grabbed my hand and we ran, hid down here."

Sidra nodded. Mr. Rosenthal, their parents' longtime tenant and friend, had recently vacated the furnished ground-floor apartment. When their dad got to shouting, it became a good place to seek refuge. They had hidden behind the nubby brown-and-gold plaid couch after the first piece of pottery smashed on the hardwood floor above. They had cowered as more burst against the walls and their mother begged him to stop. He wasn't happy at all with her news, but the Irish Catholic in him felt powerless to do anything about it.

"How the hell did you remember it was today?" Seamus demanded, running his hand through his thick locks. It was a nervous habit going on almost three decades. There were times Sidra had to take the shears to his head just to release his fingers; his hair was *that* thick, and tensions were often *that* high.

"I always remember it was Akshaya Tritiya," Sidra murmured. She remembered her mother's excitement upon discovering her happy news coincided with one of the luckiest days on the Hindu calendar, her eyes shining like black-gold star sapphires. *It's a day for a new journey, my love. Both the moon and the sun are at their brightest on Akshaya Tritiya.*

At ten years old, Sidra solemnly absorbed what her mother told her about the auspicious day and made promises to her mother about it. *Promise me when you find the man who makes you happiest in your heart, you will choose Akshaya Tritiya as the day to marry him. You will love him, like I love your father, forever and always.*

Akshaya meant *endless.*

It had been the wrong journey for their mother.

Sidra stared hard at the mother dove. She had been fired in a beautiful white, almost translucent glaze, and in the dim computer light appeared luminescent. Her breast was puffed full and proud, and at her wings, although not completely under them, sat two smaller doves, gazing up lovingly at her. Sidra loved the way her head wasn't bowed in one particular direction or the other, as if she didn't want to play favorites, and loved them equally.

Why hadn't two been enough for her?

"Whoa, wait . . . wait. That means today—it's also your anniversary with Charlie, right? Shit, I'm sorry, Sid. I never would've had him over today if—"

"It's okay. I broke up with him, remember?"

"Yeah, but still. Jeez, I can't even remember Akshaya Tritiya. And I call myself desi?"

Sidra smiled. "It follows the lunar calendar. So it doesn't always fall on the same day." But this year it did. Just like it did the year she met Charlie. *Omens and opportunities,* as their mother would say. Seeing Charlie in the rain that day, of all days. Normally the city-bred chick in her would've blown right past some stranger trying to pick her up under an umbrella. But it was Akshaya Tritiya.

Omens and opportunities.

People clamored to marry on Akshaya Tritiya, to start a new venture. It was a day to buy gold and wear gold. And a day to do charitable acts. Sidra usually spent it with her aunts, volunteering in soup kitchens on the Bowery or raising money for AWB Food Bank, a project in India similar to Meals on Wheels. But the holiday was always a bittersweet one for her.

After meeting Charlie, she had been happy to shift some positive connotation to the day. And she always remembered her promise to her mother. When Charlie proposed a year ago, she reached for a Hindu calendar to plan their happy day. So much for planning . . .

"Dang, I should've been on these sites earlier then!" Seamus bemoaned. "Tons of action on Akshaya Tritiya."

"No doubt." Sidra laughed. "Well, there's always next year.

We'll don some gold bling and take you out on the town. Till then, you always have the west."

His whole demeanor changed. "Oh, Sid. I am itching for the west! A change of scenery will do me some good. I feel bad leaving you and Jack, though."

Both children had begun referring to their father by his first name several years ago. Never to his face, mind you. But in mixed company, saying "Jack threw up on the rug again" or "Jack didn't sleep in his bed last night" sounded more harmless, as if scolding the family dog. "You'll never believe what Jack did yesterday." In unspoken agreement, they just left any mention of a father figure out of it. They loved him, but he wasn't much of one once summer rolled around. He was fine during school semesters, when he took his role as distinguished NYU professor seriously, but come the heat of the summer, he fell apart. He refused to take on summer classes, to go on sabbatical, nothing doing. It was his time to mourn. And remember. It had been like that every year since their mother passed, and they knew to expect it.

"Jack will be fine. Besides, you and Charlie handled him for a month last summer while I was away at my yoga retreat, so it's my turn. My camp day ends at two o'clock, and I'll be back in the city by four. I'll make sure there's food in him each night after yoga. And on weekends, too." She didn't need to waste her free time at the beach anyway. She'd fit in more yoga classes this way, maybe even a kids' yoga workshop. There was money to be had in the prenatal baby yoga craze right now.

"Molly's called. The credit card for his tab expired and he won't give them a new one."

"It's probably sitting upstairs in a pile of mail," Sidra suspected. "I'll go check tomorrow." She yawned, stretched. "You going to bed soon?"

"In a few more minutes. Just wanted to check . . . her." He nodded to the screen. "Wouldn't that be great? The tour bus pulls up in Vancouver, and we all roll out, decked out like rockers. Chicks standing outside yelling for autographs. And there *she* is," he enthused, rubbing his hand in the air between them, as if conjuring up the girl of his dreams. "And she's been waiting for me to arrive. She flirts with me all night from the crowd. And when the show ends, she's boarding the bus to the next town with *me*."

Sidra admired his optimism. She just wished he didn't have to hitch himself to Charlie to make things happen. And she hoped, for his sake, life on the road in a tour bus really had all the romance and excitement he longed for.

RICK

JUMPING SHIP

"BRING OUT YER DEAD . . ."

Rick stretched the full length of his bunk as the voice drew closer.

"Bring out yer dead . . ." Martin had a love for Monty Python, a droll sense of humor, and the command to run a very tight ship. "Gentleman, it's half seven. We are approximately five minutes away from the Guilderland Travel Plaza." Their tour manager's Scottish burr trilled again. "If you're in need of a real loo, 'tis your last one till Boston. *Bring out yer dead!*" His big hands brushed life into the nubby gray bunk curtains as he passed.

Rick rubbed each gritty eye, then the bridge of his nose and yawned. He hated the bunks on the bus, roughly the size of your average coffin. But he didn't mind waking up miles from where he had fallen asleep.

"Riff Rotten! Shift your arse, man!"

Two fingers hooked around the curtain. Rick peeked through the gap and was greeted nose to the button-fly jeans of Digger Graves. Not his ideal wake-up call.

"We're almost there." Adrian's fingers moved to fasten his trousers' top button before pulling Rick's entire curtain asunder, leaving him blinking in the canned light of the Prevost coach. "Look alive, mate." He popped a toothbrush into his mouth and grinned before making his way down the aisle.

At least you have a reason for being so bright-eyed and minty-fresh at this hour, Rick thought dully.

If I were this close to home and to my ladylove, I would go AWOL from tour, too.

Home. Love.

Yeah. There were reasons why Rick kept the show itinerary full.

The last two weeks had passed in a blur. California, Chicago, Cleveland, Pittsburgh, Buffalo, now a two-night stand coming up in Boston . . .

He yanked the curtain half-mast once more, closing his eyes. *Ah, Simone. Sometimes on the road, I find myself looking at the clock and wondering what time it is back home in Hawaii. Not that it matters. You're not there to answer the phone. Or open my letters. Still. If you cannot be my confessional . . .*

Across the aisle, Sam swung massive feet clad in cheap flip-flops out of the top bunk. "Ah, finally a real flusher, thank Christ!" Anyone who harbored illusions that the rock and roll road life was twenty-four-hour glamour had obviously never encountered a musician wandering the streets of some small town early in the morning, waiting for the local McDonald's to open so he could empty his bowels. The tour bus toilet accommodated bladder relief only.

"There're my girls!" Adrian exclaimed as the bus careened up the exit ramp. "I can see the Smurf from here—over there, see? The blue-and-white Mini Cooper."

The door gave a hiss and burped open.

"Morning, Kat!" Sam boomed, as if it were perfectly natural

for them to run into each other here in the middle of the New York State Thruway. No one beat Sam off the bus when he was in need of a bog.

One by one, the awake and the barely awake filtered off and greeted Adrian's instant American family in a hard rock receiving line. Rick lingered, enjoying the obscurity of the tinted bus windows for a few moments longer. He watched his best friend fall into Kat's embrace. Her lips spoke silent words over Adrian's shoulder, ones that only he could hear. Little Abbey wormed her way into the hug, too, as Adrian hiked a thumb backward and Kat turned her eyes up toward the darkened glass.

No doubt telling her about the barmy git on the bus, Rick mused. How the poor sod had discovered his late wife had saved every postcard he'd ever written her, preserved in a hatbox, before he left on tour. And now he can't stop talking about her.

Correction: Now he can't stop talking *to* her.

The hollows of his own dark eyes reflected back, startling Rick into real-time.

"Riff, stop fannying about up there!" Adrian's voice drifted back onto the coach. Small footfalls followed; Abbey loved any excuse to explore the interior of the band's home on wheels, nosing behind the curtains of the bunks and snacking on whatever chips and goodies the crew left lying about.

"Hiya, Bee."

"You're coming with us to the lake."

Rick dropped a pair of sunglasses on. "Says who?"

"Adrian," Abbey stated, her nasally American vowels slightly grating. In the four years Rick had known her and her mother, he had never once heard either refer to his bandmate as Digger. Evidently, stage personas never made it past their front door. "And he said to stop fannying about."

"Is that so?" Rick enjoyed the eight-year-old's mastery of

British lingo, even if she flattened it with her accent. He also admired her quest for anything chocolate-flavored. It reminded him of his twin boys at that age, always nipping Cadbury Buttons from the secret stash Simone had kept in the butler's pantry back home.

"Yes. Is this your bunk?"

"The middle one. On the right." Rick watched as she inspected the row.

"Underwear!" she squealed.

"That's what you get for peeking in Sam's bunk," Rick said with a laugh. "I bet Adrian has a treat for you in his. Third one down, take a look."

Her legs, long and stork-like, stretched as she stood on tiptoe. "Ooh, Cadbury!" She held up a Flake bar as her pilfered bounty.

"The real kind, too." Rick informed her. "Imported." He reached into his bunk, quickly glancing the length of it. Like a man about to jump from a sinking ship, he grabbed what mattered most: his rucksack and his notebook.

"We're busting you out of this rock and roll circus!" Kat shaded her eyes with her hand, smiling at Rick as he emerged with Abbey in tow. She turned to the others. "I hope you guys don't mind; I'm stealing your guitarists for a couple of days." Digger—*No, make that Adrian,* Rick mentally corrected himself —slid his arm around her waist as she added, "Two days off in a row, and so close to the lake house. I couldn't resist."

"Nor could I refuse," Adrian murmured, rubbing his neat goatee of gray and gold against her cheek, eyes closed.

Jim lit a cigarette and mashed his free hand into his jeans pocket. "Cool." The drummer exhaled. "Wish Maryland was a bit closer for me. Soon enough, I guess."

Sam had returned from his lavatory excursion and sputtered in mock outrage. "Riff? At least choose someone worth his salt, Kat!"

"Sam, sometimes the freak show needs a break from the clowns," Rick stated, as slow and dramatic as his descent down the bus stairs.

"Meaning . . . meaning?" Sam echoed like an empty canyon. Everyone else just grinned and looked elsewhere.

"Ah, Kat." Rick leaned to kiss her cheek. "You are the only reason I'd get up at"—he lifted his shades to examine his watch—"stupid o'clock in the morning."

He wasn't sure whether she would consider his compliment a backhanded one. But the way she lobbed a kiss back onto his scruffy cheek told him she didn't—or she didn't care.

"Wait until you see our lake. You may just have one more reason."

"Now this," Adrian remarked as the screen door slammed behind them, "this I missed." He inhaled deeply, and Rick did, too. A mix of odd odors hit him: acrid metallic rust from the old porch screens, earthy clay from the jumble of discarded shoes by the door, and the sharp dewy scent of fresh mowed grass filtering down from a neighboring lawn. Not unpleasant, just different from the last time he had visited the couple. Their summer place by the lake felt light-years away from the Upper West Side apartment they called home, even though the aging chalet bungalow was just under an hour's drive from Manhattan.

"Those are our lake shoes," Kat explained, prodding at a sneaker, caked gray and stiff, with her freshly pedicured toes. "The pile seems to grow larger every summer."

"So this is your old homestead, then?" Rick bent to run his hand down the cat's back as she weaved between his shoes. Even Chelsea, who probably lived a charmed life walking along the huge windows above Central Park most of the year, seemed to welcome the change of scenery. Her tail vibrated with happiness from his attention.

"Born and raised! We try to spend every summer and holiday here now. Just wait until you see your room. The Corroded Corpse time capsule." Kat laughed. "If my brother, Kevin, finds out you're staying here, he'll want to hang an engraved plaque."

"Riff Rotten slept here," Adrian joked.

"Oh, bollocks. Please." Rick scoffed. He had heard all about the attic bedroom, a shrine circa 1984, plastered with posters of Kat's brother's favorite bands.

"Come on in and sit. Coffee? Lemonade?" Kat gestured.

"I'll have a beer, if you've got a proper English one." A myriad of clocks in the living room began their slightly unsynchronized peal, as if to admonish Rick for wanting a beer at eleven o'clock in the morning. "Do I hear the Winchester chimes?"

"Oh, yes. Kat's dad collected clocks in his antique business. Next you'll hear Westminster, and the Whittington. Maddening, isn't it?" Adrian winked at Kat as he uncapped a Newcastle with a vaporous pop and handed it to his friend. "I'll take a glass of your lemonade, my dear."

Kat brought two frosty glasses to the dining room table before settling into a chair with a canary-eating smile. Rick noticed Adrian's pinky immediately curled around hers. Tattooed on his knuckle was a bold, black exclamation point: the punctuation to Kat's very eager response when he proposed to her four years ago. Some people immediately get on the phone to share such happy news, Rick supposed. Others, like Adrian, go to the tattoo parlor so they can fist-pump *YES!*

They both smiled expectantly at him. Suddenly it was clear to Rick just why they had brought him here. Detouring him off the road, away from the rest of the band, forcing rest and relaxation down his throat.

They wanted his blessing.

"So. The wedding." A fluid haul off the beer steeled Rick enough to broach the subject. "You've picked a date, I assume?"

"Look, he's already got his 'side project' face on," Adrian sputtered in disbelief.

"I do not," Rick said indignantly, but he could feel his top lip curling in disgust while his thick dark brow receded in exasperation. It was the same face he pulled any time Adrian decided to take a break from all the sold-their-soul-for-rock-and-roll stuff and play for the under-ten crowd. When they had first reconciled their friendship, Rick had been amused by Digger Graves's new alter ego: the kid-friendly musician Kat had mistakenly hired for a local library program, all because he wrote a stupid-catchy TV theme song about a cartoon cat. But now that their Corroded Corpse legacy had been resurrected as the Rotten Graves Project, Rick no longer regarded Adrian's other pursuits as harmless fancy. Anything that took away from Corpse time was a threat.

"It's my wedding, mate. *Our* wedding." Adrian clutched Kat's hand. "It's not some pesky one-off gig that would be better left unplayed! Oh, but you'd rather walk away from the gigs without big guarantees, right?"

Rick had drained the last of his Newcastle and was picking at the bottle label. "All right," he said, setting it aside and looking at them straight on. "Who am I to deny your happiness? Tell me when and I'll be there."

"As my best man?" Adrian pressed.

"Of course. I always have your back."

"We've got it pretty much planned; small and simple. Ceremony in the park near the Cloisters, reception at New Leaf Café right on the grounds."

"Tell me when," Rick repeated.

"First of November."

Rick was gripping the bottle once again, so tight he feared it would pop to shards in his hand. "Do you not look at the itineraries I send you? Halloween, mate. We've got second hold on Madison Square Garden, and I just had our agent challenge the date. For fuck's sake!"

Kat turned to Adrian. "In English, please."

"Another band is thinking about playing the Garden for Halloween and put in for it first. If we come along and challenge them, they have twenty-four hours to decide if they really want it." Adrian frowned. "Otherwise, it's ours."

Rick was already up and pacing, dialing the band's booking agent on his mobile. "Ach, West Coast. Oliver's not going to answer."

"Look, Rick. Even if it wasn't the wedding date . . . I haven't once trick-or-treated with Abbey, not once in these four years. I just missed her fourth grade play. I don't want to watch her grow up through a video lens."

"Madison Square Garden," Rick repeated, those three words the only bargaining chip he had at the moment.

"Enough," Kat broke in. "You have two days off, then two shows left on this tour."

Adrian's goatee jutted stubbornly as he set his jaw and managed through gritted teeth, "I'll show you your room."

They both clomped up the steep attic stairs in silence. The scene was set most ironically for their comically tragic little play, Rick observed: Two men in their midlife, arguing under a scrapbook ceiling lined with tattered pictures of their much-younger selves.

"I'm on your side, Dig. Just trying to stay one step ahead. You remember the last time the music industry machine left us behind."

"I don't care. I *will* take a sledgehammer to that machine."

Rick listened to the heavy tread of his bandmate's motorcycle boots on the stairs, followed by Kat's murmur, "You okay?"

"Yeah."

"And Rick?"

"Rick needs to get laid," came Adrian's gruff reply, and the angry roar of the shower could be heard moments later.

RICK
I NEVER PROMISED YOU THE GARDEN

"Hey, let me show you the lake."

Rick rose slowly to Kat's request. He and Adrian were out by the grill, having another beer as Adrian painstakingly built a pyre out of twigs and stick matches inside a huge pyramid of charcoal briquettes and Abbey serenaded them with the little pink ukulele Rick had sent from Hawaii for her birthday last year.

"Want to join us?" mother asked daughter.

"Nope." Abbey handed Adrian her instrument. "Your turn."

Rick looked to his best friend for backup. Surely Adrian wasn't going to allow him to be subjected to some sort of heart-to-heart alone with Kat?

"Sorry, mate. It doesn't matter how metal you are. If an eight-year-old hands you a pink ukulele, you sure as hell better play it." Adrian smiled and began to strum as Abbey made hula motions with her hands to wave Rick and her mother out of the yard.

Bugger.

Kat led the way toward the road. Neighbors were just ending their day's commute, coming home from work in town or from the city. A car rolled past, giving a beep before crunching into the gravel driveway a few doors down. As Kat lifted a hand in greeting, Rick wondered what most people would think about their odd little commute this morning. Nine to five had no meaning in the music world.

"So," he grunted, "you've enough food for an army." Small talk. "Who's coming?"

"Oh, Marissa and her family."

"The chesty one?"

Kat laughed. "She'll love that! And you, for noticing. Yep, that's her."

"How about the ginger? Your brother's girl?"

"Liz?" She shook her head. "First time she's missed spending the holiday up here in years. She's taking inventory in her bagel shop over the long weekend. So it'll just be us. Oh, and my neighbor, Karen, with her family. They won't eat much, though. They've recently gone macrobiotic."

"Sounds painful."

"It's not too crazy. Mostly raw veggies, grains, and—"

"I was kidding, Kat. I know what it is. We tried it with Simone, after her diagnosis."

Rick hoped his grim and halting tone would stick a pin in any widow-to-widower heart-to-heart Kat was considering. Yes, they had both lost spouses. When Kat rang him up out of the blue four years ago, they had instantly bonded over their heartbreak. And over Adrian, of course. But the parallels ended there.

"This." Kat allowed Rick to punctuate her pause with a gasp upon sight of the lake. "This is my Polihale, where I come to ponder things."

In that first phone conversation, Rick had mentioned the vast beach near his house back in Hawaii, and how it had been a savior to him. Obviously Kat had not forgotten.

"Superb, Kat . . . really." Rick stood at the shore, hips jutted slightly forward in his cargo shorts. The far horizon hovering over the watery expanse had his undivided attention. Who would've thought there would be such a vista hidden at the end of a sleepy suburban block?

"I can't believe we've never gotten you up here before now."

Rick shrugged. "Ah, you know. Touring, recording. Now, if you were to build a midsize venue back here . . ." His laugh dwindled. "Listen, Kat. I'm sorry for ranting earlier. I really like you, and cripes, Adrian is the happiest I've ever seen him. It's just . . . well. Marriage can be a shock on the rock and roll system. And vice versa."

Kat cringed at his stress on the word *vice*. Adrian had obviously confessed Digger's every sin to her, long before any talk of marriage had taken place. *It was a cheap shot,* Rick silently admitted. He was fairly confident, even though the Digger persona was present and accounted for these days, that Adrian was the person in control.

"Are you both sure you're ready for it?" he continued. "I've seen Adrian on marriage." Adrian didn't speak of his ex-wife Robyn very often, but Rick knew the knife of that relationship still twisted in him every so often, especially when their daughter, Natalie, was involved. An old TV commercial popped into Rick's head, of an egg hitting a sizzling frying pan. *This is your brain . . . and this is your brain on drugs.* Would "Adrian on marriage" appear any different to Kat than he did now, after four years of cohabitating?

"I'm not Robyn," she said slowly.

"Thank the bloody Lord for that."

I'm not Simone, either, her eyes seemed to say, or perhaps it was his own imagination inflicting such cruel and unusual punishment. After all, he found new ways to torture himself daily, thinking about the way he had abused his own marriage. He'd give anything to take the wasted hours back: the affairs, the lies, the excuses. How he wished he could make it up to his loyal wife tenfold. But how could a sinner repent when his confessor had slipped from his grasp, languishing under her lover's touch before he could fully redeem himself?

Rick hurled a rock into the watery gray expanse. "All this talk of making it legal after four years of engagement, did this stem from Miles's passing?" he wanted to know.

Miles, the band's longtime sound engineer, had passed away a few months before, leaving behind a wife, a girlfriend, four children, and a big heartbreaking mess. Married to one, living long-term with the other, children in both houses needing the benefits and life insurance that neither woman was willing to swallow their pride and share.

Kat scooped up a handful of sand and let it sift through her fingers. "His death certainly made us reconsider our current arrangement, yes."

"So why not make it a quick, small thing and be done with it?"

"Believe me, I suggested that. He's the one who wants his mother and Natalie, and my family and *all* the friends, mutual and exclusive, together for one big shindig." She squinted out to where the late-day sun was bouncing blindingly off the water before turning back to Rick. "Adrian may say it's me who wants the fairy-tale wedding, but it's really him."

"He always did like tales." Rick smirked. "But they usually had bloodletting and gore and medieval weaponry of some kind."

"I don't care if he shows up for the wedding in full chain mail, carrying a cat-o'-nine-tails. As long as he comes home with me at the end of the night as my husband."

Kat's comment caused the tension in Rick to break like the tiny whitecaps rushing to the shoreline. An unbridled laugh escaped. "You really do love the hell out of him, don't you?"

She responded, just as Adrian had happily reported she had after he proposed to her using just a Sharpie marker, an antique emerald ring and two stone lions as his witnesses. "YES!"

~

25 MAY

It's evening, my love. I'm in bed in a stranger's room, staring up at a photo collage of twenty-five-year-old me. It feels very odd—not so much that I'm in a strange bed; I've gotten used to that again. No, it's the fact that I have no recollection of even being present when these pictures were taken, let alone printed in magazines for the world to see. I'm wearing that shirt you gave me, the loud tropical one I never liked, but you loved. As if you foresaw us destined for Hanalei one day.

The purple naupaka on the mauka side of the house was blooming like mad when I left for our European tour. I hacked away the lot last year, but it all came back with a vengeance. Its half flower shape saddens me, and they still smell like you. Impossible to think a flower could mimic a person's scent, but I swear on my life, these do.

There's a picture of you and me with Miles up here on the wall as well. Remember our sound engineer? We lost Miles this spring— prostate cancer took him quick. Did you know he was Jewish? I didn't. We never talked about that kind of thing on the road. The family needed a minyan, so yours truly got a starring role. I recited the Mourner's Kaddish, like I do for you each year. Yitgadal v'yitkadash . . .

Fuck cancer in its motherfucking arse.

I've almost filled a notebook, writing to you since the tour started. Ever since I found those postcards, I've felt compelled. I cannot believe you saved every single one.

I should've written you more, Simone. Out of the blue, just because. Love notes for when just walls, not even continents, sepa-rated us.

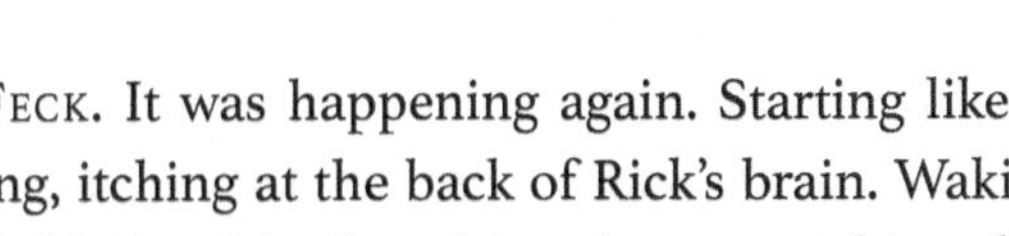

FECK. It was happening again. Starting like a seedling. Nudging, itching at the back of Rick's brain. Waking him with a jolt. Cold dread iced up his spine, nourishing the fear in his head until it became a reedy whip of a sapling. It smacked him with horrible thoughts of *this may be it, this may be the big one, are you ready for this, you're going to die, you're dying alone, it's here.* When he tried to shake away the thoughts, his mind began to buzz like an amplifier. Rendered helpless, unable to think logically with all the static and feedback.

Then the sweating began, flashes of toxic heat irradiating his entire six-foot frame. The bowels in an uproar. He vaulted from the attic bed to the bathroom and back again. *Lie down. Calm down. It's nothing. The doctor checked you out before the tour started. You're fine.* His heart blasting beats as quick as Lars Ulrich on the double bass drum pedals.

Why me? Why now?

Stress. Don't they call it the silent killer?

Rick cursed himself. He should never have stepped off that bus in the first place. He should be in Boston with the others, not stuck with the consolation prize of Adrian and Kat's company as they talked nonstop for two days about their wedding plans.

He tried to keep his breathing measured and deep. *Focus, man.* His eyes hit the ceiling, reeling in their sockets for a focal point.

And there's your wasted life, flashing before your ruddy eyes.

Thoughts Rick relied upon to bring joy and comfort under normal circumstances—his children, his home, the ocean— cruelly magnified the panic. And now, faced with the time line of his career sloping down from above, he felt a double betrayal. *You quixotic tosser, still tilting at windmills, chasing cheap thrills, the meaningless attention, and at what cost? Your wife, your sons? What are you doing here? What were you thinking?*

Each and every photo mocked him, accused him.

You never should have boarded that bus. You should be home.

"Home" was as empty as the porcelain bowl Rick hung his head over, dry heaving, burping, gasping. The twins were newly graduated; coming home wasn't on their agenda this year. Their older brother, Paul, hadn't been back for an age, and rarely called.

The band. It's what matters now. You run the show. It's your gig. Madison Square Garden.

The other band they had challenged was unapologetically huge. The masses loved them. But Corroded Corpse had always owned Madison Square Garden on Halloween in their heyday. And it had been the date and place of their first reunion show as the Rotten Graves Project. It was territory worth pissing in.

If they got the date, and Adrian refused to play it . . .

You left him behind before.

You left him in jail. And the band played on briefly before spiraling down in flames. Some bandleader you are.

Thankfully, the pulse pounding behind his eardrums drowned out the voice in Rick's head. He felt dizzy.

Their agent would be calling tomorrow with the outcome.

Rick wondered if he'd last that long.

Far below him, he heard the bells begin to toll from Kat's father's clocks striking two, over and over, as unsynchronized as his thoughts. He needed air.

Stealth and silent, he descended the steep steps, mindful that Abbey was sleeping in the room at the foot of them. Just the action of moving, doing, seeking out sanctuary, improved his condition. He slunk past the menagerie of ticking clocks.

Perhaps a good Bo-Peep on the lanai will do the trick, he thought. After more than twenty years of living on Kauai, Rick's British tongue had become Hawaiianized. It wasn't unusual to mix Cockney rhyming slang with something exotically Austronesian. His lingo certainly elevated the status of his hosts' musty screened-in porch, which contained a few potted plants and a lopsided futon.

"Hey."

To his surprise, Kat had already beaten him there.

"Bugger, you scared me!" As if his heart needed any more reason to knock like the clock hammers against their chime rods. "What are you doing up?"

Kat laughed softly, but Rick could see the balled-up tissues in her fist, the reddened eyes. "Stupid insomnia. It always hits me before he leaves again." She swiped at her eyes. "Like my brain has decided to not miss a minute of his furlough."

She shimmied over to make room for him, but he couldn't sit. Adrenaline was flooding through him, and suddenly even the lanai felt claustrophobic. He began to pace.

"Maybe we shouldn't have come . . . for the off-days," he managed. "Spare you and Abbey . . ." He gulped. "The roller coaster."

Kat frowned. "You're the one who looks like you've been through one too many loop-dee-loops. You okay?"

"I think . . ." *I'm dying it's a heart attack aneurysm stroke I need to get to the hospital something's happening I can't stop it I don't know how to stop it and it feels like—*

He stopped and pressed his cheek against the old porch screen. *You've dealt with this before. Now breathe.* "I'll be okay," he managed.

"I think you're having a panic attack."

Rick closed his eyes and turned the other cheek to the screen.

"Anxiety isn't a sign of weakness, Rick." Kat paused a moment, then quietly added, "I've been told it's a sign of being strong for too long."

He didn't feel strong. He felt wiped out. It was as if all the miles logged had suddenly caught up to him, and he couldn't fathom taking another step.

"Maybe you should take—"

Rick cut her off at the pass. "No drugs, Kat. No way." He had made it through raising three teenagers on his own without "mother's little helpers"; he certainly wasn't going to start taking anything now as an empty-nester. He was only forty-four years old; wasn't this supposed to be the prime of his life?

"I was going to suggest taking a *class*. Meditation, Tai Chi, yoga, something. Find an outlet."

Rick smirked. "It used to be as simple as finding a wall socket and plugging an amplifier in."

"Promise me you'll look into it?"

"Yes, I promise." He rolled his eyes. "In all my spare time, I will look into it."

"Speaking of time, you'll know about that date in twenty-four hours, right?"

"Less, actually." Hence the sweating and the trembling panic.

"I'll give you your Garden date," she began, and Rick braced himself for the conditions.

"If?"

"If the other band holding the Garden drops out and you get first hold, we will pick another date for the wedding," she stated simply. "The world won't end."

Rick nodded in agreement, grateful for the ability to breathe naturally and think clearly. *The world won't end. Fancy that!*

"But—"

Ah, but here's the rub, Rick thought. Behind every rock band, there were usually a half dozen women who thought they could run the show better than the myriad of agents, managers, and publicists hired for the very job.

"But whatever date we end up with, you need to support

him. And I need him home. No touring before the wedding," she advised.

"No problem there. We'll be in the studio all summer."

"And no touring right after the wedding, either."

"Kat, we are releasing a new album. A street date's all but set. We'll need to tour it. I can't promise you that."

"Then I can't promise you the Garden date." She hugged herself tight. "I've waited a long time. I can't let the road take him."

He saw loss dulling the luster of her emerald eyes. It occurred to him that she, too, was versed in cruel and unusual punishment. For how could she not help but wonder whether each kiss good-bye to Adrian before a tour might be their last? Kat's first husband had boarded a train for a quick business trip that ended up ripping a hole through her and Abbey's hearts and well-being.

"Deal," Rick heard himself saying. "But I have one condition. You cannot tell Adrian about my panic attacks." Kat raised her brows at his use of the plural. "I know you two probably share everything, but I beg of you. Please keep this to yourself, all right?"

She gave him a small, tired smile and reached to squeeze his hand. "Deal."

"I think I'm going to sleep on the lanai tonight, if that's all right with you."

Kat yawned and unfolded herself from the futon. "It's all yours." She paused at the doorway, turning back to look up at him. "I sleep out here sometimes, too," she admitted. "If you really quiet your mind and listen, you can hear the lake. It's no ocean, but . . ."

"It'll do."

SIDRA
FIGHTING WORDS

SIDRA CAREFULLY CLOSED the quotation marks with two more strokes of the paintbrush and leaned back on the stepladder to observe her work. Not bad:

"In life you only need to journey twelve inches. That is the distance from your head to your heart."

She had given the yoga room a sunny wash of pale yellow paint last month, with flowing pale green accents and trim. Now she was adding various quotes she had gathered over time to the walls for inspiration.

If only twelve inches were necessary, why did she feel like the only loser who hadn't left the city over Memorial Day weekend? Her classes were empty; the record shop was a ghost town. She should've checked in with friends, made plans. She climbed down the ladder and lugged it over to the far wall. Even a barbecue out on a postage stamp of a lawn in Queens would've been something. Sighing, she climbed back up.

Seamus was gearing up for his journey through twelve states. He would leave next month and not return until late August. It had taken Sidra a week to let that sink in, but she accepted it now. If anyone needed to travel out of his head and heart for a while and do some living, it was Seamus.

She was excited to paint her next quote, one by the famous Yogacharya B.K.S. Iyengar:

"Yoga is a light, which once lit, will never dim. The better your practice, the brighter the flame."

She knew it would be a perfect complement for the wall where she demonstrated her poses, under the old exotic hanging lamp. *That lamp must have a good history,* she thought, wondering just what its origins were. She needed to ask her uncle if he knew.

"Looks good."

Sidra twisted on her ladder to face her cousin. "Thanks, Mikey. Figured I'd do it while no one was around to smell the fumes."

Her logic received a curt nod. "You know Shay and Char are bailing on me?"

"Yeah." She often found herself resorting to monosyllabic Manhattanese tough-girl tone around her older cousin.

"You'll put in some hours for me up front, right?"

Sidra painstakingly stroked the curl of a thick cursive capital *Y* onto the wall freehand. Dexterity inherited from her mother's side of the family had been perfected through her formative years in Montessori school. Thousands of Downward Facing Dog poses kept her armpits strong as she leaned and stretched her entire arm's length to finish the word.

She hated working in the record shop, where hipsters and homeless guys were always trying to pick her up. Revolve Records was a haven for the weirdo and wayward population of the Lower East Side, who would linger for hours, hogging the listening stations and never spending a dime.

"One night a week, Mikey. And a few weekend hours, but that's it."

"All right." He grinned. Mikey Sullivan was a huge trash-talking teddy bear of a guy. He didn't even need a ladder to land his kiss on her cheek. "Thanks. You all set here?"

"All good," Sidra replied happily, and resumed her lettering. She loved her space and appreciated all the help her family had lent in making it come to fruition. Mikey and his dad had sanded down and refinished every floorboard, Seamus had expertly installed recessed dimmer lights and wide fans on the ceiling, and Fiona had sewn vibrant pillows in earthy fabrics for the small lounge area. Enduring a few hours behind the cash register in return wouldn't be a hardship.

Mikey's large frame filled the doorway once again. "Hey, did you see the For Sale sign up next door?"

Sidra lost her grip on the paintbrush, earning a pale green stripe down her leg as it clattered to the floor. "No! Shit. The dry cleaner's?"

"Yeah. Fuckin' A, right?" Mikey said grimly. He swooped his arm down to retrieve the thin brush, like a grizzly bear swiping a fish from the river current. "And with the corner property still vacant, our asses are officially on the line."

Every couple of months, Mikey Senior—or Sully, as he was called by everyone who knew him— threatened to dip his toe into the sellers' market that was skyrocketing around his family's building. But Sidra had always assumed that, like his son, Uncle Sully was just a big trash-talker. Investors routinely came sniffing around these streets to snap up the last of the genuine New York up-and-coming, next-hot locales, trying to make him an offer he couldn't refuse, but he had yet to really bite. However, if his building was sitting pretty with two ugly wallflowers on either side, it was bound to be the most popular girl at the dance.

Mikey emphatically pointed the brush at her. "We gotta drum the shit up outta these businesses, okay?"

Sidra plucked it from his hand. "Hell yeah." She didn't know how or to whom she was going to drum the shit up out of yoga, but going down without a fight wasn't in the Sullivan vocabulary.

"Come up front for a second, I wanna show you something."

Ever the gentlemen when he wanted to be, her cousin swept his hand and let Sidra take the lead up the long corridor to the front of the record store. Over the PA, Dropkick Murphys were blasting out their own brand of pirate punk, and Fiona was sitting on the counter, swinging her legs to the beat as she flipped through one of her fat fashion magazines.

"When can I borrow your new shoes, Sid?" she hollered over the music.

"When you grow a size-five foot," Sidra quipped, earning herself a playful kick in the butt by one of Fiona's Doc Martens, easily a size eight. She hadn't even worn the fancy footwear herself today, opting for ratty tennis sneakers in case she splattered paint.

"Mikey, will you buy me sandals like Sidra's?" Fiona batted her eyelashes his way.

"If you want a sugar daddy, go date someone over at Doughnut Plant," Mikey teased his girlfriend. "Now get your ass off the counter and rotate some of the end displays, would-ja?" Holding the door, he motioned impatiently. "Letting all the AC out, Sid. Come on."

Out on the sidewalk, Mikey adjusted the brim of his flat black cap and squinted upward. "Well, what do you think?"

Under the old Sullivan and Son Bicycles sign now hung a sign for Evolve, in equal billing with the one for the record store.

"Oh, Mike. I love everything about it!" And she did, from the yellow swirling motif to the orange flaming sun. "Thank you!"

Mikey allowed himself to be hugged. "Thank Seamus. He painted. I just hung it."

Sidra had figured as much. Whether it was a paintbrush or a drumstick, Seamus itched to create with whatever was in his hands. "It brightens up the neighborhood," Sidra observed.

"Yeah. So let's not give my dad any good reason to tear it down, okay?"

As Sidra stepped back toward the curb to get a better look at her new sign, a flash of the sun's glare off a moving windshield caught her eye from down the block. Her pulse rate quickened at the sight of a sleek black limo sliding down Rivington's narrow passage. Mr. Import had crossed her mind more than once since he had hailed that cab to JFK.

"Someone must be lost," Mikey muttered under his breath, watching the tinted windows as the car slowed to a crawl past them. Sidra felt heat rise to her cheeks, no doubt matching the red of the luxury car's taillights as it braked to a smooth stop. She chastised herself for even fantasizing that it could be the handsome stranger who had come to her rescue with a wheelchair.

Yeah, like he's gonna pop out of that car with a dozen roses and a glass flip-flop for you?

"Forget what I said," Fiona breathed. Now she was the one letting all the air-conditioning out, her curvaceous body propping the shop door open. "Mikey, I want you to buy me shoes like *those*."

A spike heel, capped with silver, speared a candy bar wrapper in the gutter as its owner swung her other leg out of the limo and stood to full height. She surveyed the block from behind large sunglasses, her lips pursing slightly as she brought manicured hands to her hips.

"Loubies." Fiona's worshipping tone brought Sidra out of her trance, but lit a flame under Mikey's temper.

"Christ almighty, Fi! I'm not paying to cool the entire East Side. Close the friggin' door!"

"Yeah, well, wipe the drool from your chin, Mike," Fiona

snapped. "She's clearly outta your league . . . and I doubt she's here to trade in her used records."

The woman cast a furtive glance in their direction before sliding back into the car. Long nails flicked the candy wrapper from her heel to the curb as if it were a cockroach before the door slammed and the limo sped off.

"Nah, she's probably one of those bendy, trendy yoga bitches." Mike pulled his cap from his head, wiped his sweaty brow, and grinned at his cousin. "Looking for *you*, Sid. There goes the freakin' neighborhood."

WHEN ONE WENT poking around in Uncle Sully's backspace, there was no telling what one might find. "Uncle Sul?"

Sidra's foot came down on something soft and pliable. It protested with a baritone squawk, causing her to jump about a foot. She picked up the old bike horn and laughed to herself. Although the bicycle shop had been closed for years, her uncle's inventory mysteriously seemed to keep growing.

She stepped deftly over snakelike coils of bicycle tubing, but stopped short when she heard a strange, staccato hiss coming from her left. She backtracked around a pile of shipping cartons and spotted her uncle kneeling on the cement floor. Sunlight streamed through the open roll-up door behind him, yet it was the cascade of soldering sparks that caused her to squint.

A masked figure stepped into her path, causing her to yelp.

"Boo." Seamus laughed, flipping up his welding mask. His gloved hands plucked the bicycle horn from her grasp. "Hey, I've been looking for one of these. Thanks!"

Sidra watched her brother circle around their uncle. Sully passed him the blowtorch, and they both bent their heads with the concentration of surgeons conducting a delicate operation.

Sidra stayed at a safe distance until the iron's flame was extinguished and both men stepped away, lifting their masks triumphantly.

"Oh Shay, it's beautiful!" Sidra gasped. "I can't believe you finally finished it."

Seamus had a knack for Frankensteining spare parts together into something functional. This time, he had taken one of the frames left to languish in the back of the bike shop and turned it into an aesthetically pleasing, aerodynamic riding machine.

Sidra ran her hand over the ruby leather seat. Gold ornamentation against the black frame gave it an elegance that far surpassed any other steampunk-inspired bike she had ever seen. And she had seen many, as Seamus insisted on thrusting magazine photos and blueprints under her nose regularly. This one had a coachman's lamp mounted on the front, and ample gears, clocks, springs, and wooden rims to complete the look.

"I used old army ammo boxes for storage in back," Seamus explained, rubbing his nose with the back of his hand. "Steampimped my ride." He grinned.

"Your grandfather—God rest his soul—would be proud, Seamus." Uncle Sully pointed upward at another Sullivan and Son sign, this one hanging over his workbench, and then touched his heart with as much reverence as making the sign of the cross. "Bikes," he announced, gathering up his tools. "Bikes are in the Sullivan blood."

Or, in Mikey's case, in the Sullivan blood alcohol content, Sidra thought wryly. Several years ago, her uncle and cousin attempted to get in on the rickshaw craze. Sully blew a wad of dough on a fleet of pedicabs, and then had to spend a bundle to bail out Mikey for drunk driving (drunk pedaling?) when he crashed into a cab coming off the Brooklyn Bridge. Luckily, no one was hurt and he had no fare in the rickshaw at the time, but it was a dark period in the evolution of the Sullivan bicycle business.

"I bet you could sell it for a mint," Sidra mused, running a finger along the sleek handlebars.

"The hell with that! I'm riding this old girl. Come with me." Seamus threw a leg over the frame and pounded the seat behind him. Sidra gave him a withering, skeptical look, then turned to her uncle.

"Hey, Uncle Sul?"

"Yes, angel?"

She was about to recite a litany of reasons why selling the building would not be in the family's best interests, but when he looked down at her with those watery blue eyes so much like her father's, she lost her nerve. "What's the story with that light?"

"The one in your space?"

"Yeah. Does it ever turn off?"

Sully polished the tip of the soldering iron thoughtfully. "Your grandfather"—he gave a heavenward jab, this time with the torch—"God love him. He always said not to mess with it. That's all I know."

It was a nonanswer at best. Which was rare, since Sullivans rarely minced their words.

Seamus gave the mounted horn an impatient squeak. "Gitawnup!"

Sidra threw her own leg over the bike with a laugh, and her uncle gave her a boost to land her on the seat.

"Hang on," Seamus warned, shoving off with one foot and catching a pedal beneath his other. Sidra squealed as they bumped out the roll-up door and into the bright light, shooting through the alleyway. "Lean with me," he instructed. "I won't let us fall."

Brother promised, and sister trusted. And off went the two siblings through lower Manhattan on a bicycle built for one.

RICK

SON KNOWS BEST

"Don't be daft, mate. We move to the lake house for the summer as soon as school's over next week. The apartment is yours for the asking. All the comforts of home."

Rick hadn't remotely considered asking. Holing himself up for the past two weeks in generic well- appointed anonymity had eased the anxiety triggers. "Eh. I don't know, Dig. There's something to be said for hotel living."

He had to practically grind his mobile into his ear canal for Adrian's response to register over the din of Bedford Avenue. *Cripes, Brooklyn is just as loud as Manhattan.* Rick had assumed the outer boroughs might be a bit more laid-back.

"Spending your summer in a hotel sounds downright depressing. And like a waste of bloody cash."

"Yet clean towels and a well-made bed every day," Rick countered.

"Right, well, you wouldn't have my housekeeper every day for *that*." Adrian laughed. "But Ana does come once a week to keep up with things. And think, you'll be close to the park, to the studio."

Truth be told, the appeal of the Benjamin was wearing thin.

Rick had chosen the luxury boutique hotel as his home base during the band's recording session before remembering how much he loathed Midtown East. The location was convenient for meeting his in-laws out at an occasional dinner, but little else. Simone's parents tirelessly tolerated him, but he wondered how many more East Side dinners he could handle out with the Banquets before taking a fork to his eyes. They felt the need to return, item by bloody item, everything he'd ever given Simone that had stayed behind in her childhood shrine.

Bad enough he had found the letters she had saved back home. Now he had possession of dusty stuffed animals, bad poetry he'd written her, and a crate full of warped record albums.

He'd beg off embarrassingly early after each meal, not exaggerating when he used the early morning schlep to the recording studio as an excuse. West 54th might as well have been the West Bank and Gaza Strip, for all the trouble it took him to get there.

Rick cracked his neck from side to side, catching in his peripheral the loping stride of his eldest son. Paul was twenty minutes late for the brunch date of his own making.

"Gone are the days of just kipping on the studio floor, I reckon?"

"Not advisable at our advanced age." Adrian tutted.

"Thanks, mate. I'll consider your offer."

Adrian's spacious flat on Central Park West certainly trumped that attic bedroom at the lake house; its ceiling, held together by the cello tape of broken dreams and wasted years, appeared to sink lower to Rick with each visit.

"Oh, and Kat insists you continue to join us upstate on the weekends."

Bugger and blast.

American hospitality. *Bah.* Simone would've offered the same thing for any of his bandmates, left to their own devices in a rented town. But for some reason, this got under his skin. The last thing Rick wanted was Kat examining and fussing over him. He hoped she was at least keeping her promise not to reveal his panic spells to Adrian.

"Right, mate. Isabelle's clicking in. Cheers!"

"I found your little match girl," Isabelle opened with. "A hop, skip, and a jump from skid row. Rivington. Under the Bowery."

"You sure?" A stir of excitement, followed by a pang of something else he couldn't quite define, shifted inside him.

"Of course I'm sure. Do you want me to draw you a fucking map?" She hung up before Rick had a chance to thank her or tell her to piss off.

"Ready for the best breakfast in Brooklyn, Dad? They serve it until five o'clock in the evening!"

Rick clapped a hand on Paul's shoulder. "So you're still four hours early then, not a half hour late?"

"Sorry, got held up printing our boarding passes." Rick's blank look prompted his son to add, "Ilana and I leave for Greece tomorrow, remember?" Paul gripped his father's forearm and pulled him into the closest thing resembling a hug between them in the last six months. "Good to see you, Dad."

They entered the narrow, glass-fronted space of Egg and squeezed their way to one of the few unoccupied tables. Paul signaled for a pot of the restaurant's signature French press, giving Rick a chance to survey his son. The dark Rottenberg hair tamed to a hip, shaggy swoop, the Banquet blue eyes slightly magnified behind chunky-framed lenses. The beard was new. "What's this?" Rick gestured. "You're looking a bit Orthodox."

Paul laughed, slowly preparing their coffee. Rick envied the patience it took, along with his son's youthful elegant nonchalance in performing the task. "Williamsburg certainly has its fair share of Hasidim, but the hipsters are slowly outnumbering them."

Rick wondered whether he could channel his own inner Grizzly Adams, don the serial killer glasses, and pull off the look. Nah, too old for it. And he certainly wasn't ready for the Professor Calculus look just yet. He noticed the ladies were giving Digger dewy-eyed looks whenever he succumbed to his reading glasses on the road, more and more so these days. Rick still preferred to stumble around like Captain Haddock, blind on too much Loch Lomond, like in those old Belgian *Tintin* comics he used to read to his sons during those rare nights he wasn't on tour.

"So, Greece?"

Paul nodded. "We're backpacking around the islands for a month before I'm due in Thessaloniki. My second summer at ISSON."

Now Rick remembered. "The nanosciences and nanotechnologies summer program. Right, blimey. A doctor in front of me," he marveled as his son grinned from behind a mouthful of candied bacon. "And doctors behind me." His own parents boasted PhDs in art history. "How did all that brilliance skip a generation?"

"Come on. You're the mastermind behind a legendary band, and you managed to raise three normal children despite all the rock and roll craziness. No easy feat."

Simone was owed most of the credit, Rick felt. The children were raised out of the spotlight and under her maiden name of Banquet. *My legacy,* she would jokingly boast, *my greatest hits.*

"Thessaloniki." Rick cleared his throat. "Beautiful, beautiful city. We played the Theatro Dassous in '86, if I recall. Digger drank enough ouzo on that run to put hair on *both* our chests."

Paul smiled, his eyes shining behind those thick glasses. He and his younger brothers had loved the stories of their road warrior father almost as much as they had loved *Tintin*. Rick couldn't recall if he had ever shared that tour tale before.

"How is Adrian these days?"

"Fine. Better than fine." Rick busied himself separating the Grafton cheddar oozing from between his omelet using the tines of his fork. "Marrying soon."

"Wow, that's so great!" Paul scraped the front legs of his chair up off the floor in a "Hi-ho, Silver" move, as if to physically display how taken aback he was by the news. Rick wasn't fooled.

"And not at all a surprise to you."

"Well." Paul gave a sheepish grin. "Ilana babysits Abbey now and then. She and Kat *do* talk." He folded his arms, still tipping confidently back in his seat. "I figured I'd let you bring it up. You okay?"

"Of course I am okay! He's my best mate. And Kat is wonderful. I've her to thank for reconciling us in the first place. It's just . . . timing, that's all. Dig's at the top of his game right now." Rick bit into one of the sticky buns Paul had insisted upon ordering. He felt his jaw lock in protest and worked to wrench it back into place. "Musically," he said with a wince.

"And emotionally, wouldn't you say? It's all woven together."

Rick concentrated on chewing. He fixated on Paul's fingers, staring as they tapped against their owner's elbows now. *He has my hands,* Rick marveled. Long capable fingers, a dusting of dark hair at the knuckles, flat square tips. "Doctor's hands," Rick's mother often remarked, as if she could channel a self-fulfilling prophecy with an oft-repeated compliment.

He turned his own hands over to study them now. Where Paul's were probably kept smooth in academia, Rick's were permanently calloused, grooved from years of hard play and heavy-gauge steel. They weren't doctor's hands; they weren't helping hands. Sure, they had helped themselves to a fair number of women over the years. But they had no power to heal. To Rick they felt heavy, useless now. Scraping the bottom of the barrel. Nowhere near the top of his game anymore.

"I just thought . . . maybe they'd wait a while longer. Hold off till we really got the band back on track and sorted. I guess it would be too much to ask . . ." He drifted off, shifting his jaw back and forth. *Crikey,* he thought. *I'm like the bloody Wizard of Oz tin man in need of oil.*

"Ask him to give up what he loves, to choose between the two?" Paul supplied the words Rick didn't dare speak. "What purpose would that serve? Mom never made you choose."

Rick did little to hide his pained expression. Having the rusty jaw of a tin man didn't hurt as much as knowing the cavity where his heart used to beat was empty by his own making.

"Dad. Fourteen years is a long time. More than half my lifetime."

"Don't."

"It's okay to hold on to your memories . . . but don't let them hold you back."

Rick gritted his teeth, swallowed hard. "Again, how did you get so bloody brilliant?"

"You and Mom raised us well," Paul replied, gently righting his chair to solid ground. "You did a good job."

Rick opened his mouth to speak, but only elicited a pop as his jaw cracked out of alignment again.

"Jeez, is that your *mouth*? You'd better have that looked at. Sounds like TMJ."

"I just came off the road and we're in the studio for the next two months. It can wait a little longer."

"You look ropy. Carrying all your tension here." Paul rubbed the back of his own neck. "When was the last time you had a massage?"

Rick gave a laugh. Women from every *arrondissement* in

Paris were clamoring to touch him just a short while ago. Did that count?

"Seriously. Have you ever thought of taking yoga?"

"Okay. Now I think *you've* been talking to Kat. She's into all that poxy new age mumbo jumbo, too."

"So try it. Here." Paul pushed his faculty ID across the table. "Ilana swears by these classes at NYU. She says people line up around the block during the semester, but I'm sure you'd have no problem getting in during the summer. But you have to be faculty, staff, or alumni. I won't need this back till September."

Rick practically choked on the last swallow of coffee from his mug. "You want me to impersonate you?"

Paul gave his father a piteous withering look. "No, I want you to fit in with all the nanobots self- replicating down at the Commons as they perform their DoS attack in pursuit of total mass exercise ecophagy."

"Eco-what?"

"Ecophagy," his son repeated. "As in consumption of the entire ecosphere."

"Nanonerd humor. Nice."

"Just swipe the card at the door for entry. You probably won't even have to interact with another human."

"It's not one of those fire-and-brimstone classes, is it?"

"Hot yoga, you mean?" Paul laughed. "The only thing hot will be the scenery. That might do you some good, as well."

Rick ran his index finger with its permanent E string groove around the laminated edge of Paul's ID card. "I'll have a go," he said finally.

"Give it hell, Riff!"

Now it was Rick's turn to throw a look of mock disdain, just as he threw bills down on the table for the check. "Riff Rotten gives as good as he gets." *I'm in hell now,* he thought. *So what more do I have to lose?*

"Hey, where's Rivington Street?" he thought to ask.

"Lower East Side. But up-and-coming. If you see a bail bonds place next to a pho restaurant, you are probably in the right place." Paul gave a laugh.

Father and son exchanged a real hug back on the street. "By the way, your grandparents gave me some of your mom's old LPs last time I saw them. Any interest?"

Paul threw up an apologetic hand. "I don't even own a CD player anymore, Dad. Let alone a turntable. MP3s are where it's at."

"Think your brothers would like them?"

"*Dad.* They probably don't even know what LP stands for."

Rick watched as his son strode off, Greece putting an extra spring in his step.

"Yo, yo, on your left!"

Rick managed to sidestep last-minute to avoid being taken out by a blond guy on a bicycle that looked like something straight out of a Terry Gilliam movie. It appeared to be a high-performance mountain bike retrofitted with antique parts, capable of flattening random passersby and the occasional stray dog. A box attached to the back towered with paper sacks.

"Thanks, man!" The blond boy gave a wave and a honk from an old brass bicycle horn as he sailed effortlessly into the intersection and disappeared into the sea of taxis.

Rick just shook his head, feeling ancient. Retrofitted into the modern-day metropolis. There had been a time when New York felt like it belonged to him. Was it in the seventies, when he first met Simone here? Or had it been in the eighties, when he decimated it with rock and roll? Talk about ecophagy. Either way, too many decades had piled on since then. He walked slowly, trying to find his bearings and the correct subway line to get him back to Manhattan. Pre-production work in the studio was almost complete. Time to start chipping away at the rock.

SIDRA
PROPOSITIONS

"Just the girl I was looking for!"

Sidra didn't look up from the register tape in one hand or the pile of cash in the other. Charlie's hair could be on fire, for all she cared. She and Mikey shared a cash register, and each week she reconciled her books.

"Favor to ask you, Sid."

"Shush. Counting." *Seven-eighty? Or was it . . . Shit.* She crushed the tape in her hand. "What. Do. You. Want." Each word suffered between her clenched teeth. *Two more weeks,* she told herself. *Two more weeks until he's out of the borough, out of my sight.*

Charlie stood directly in her line of vision, hips cocked. His hair was not on fire, but spiked as prickly as Sidra's mood had turned at the sound of his voice.

"It's not me. It's Banana Louie. He misses you."

Sidra shoved the money into a paper bag. There was no way she was going to be able to count straight with her ex-boyfriend leaning over the counter and giving her the sad eyes.

"I'm not watching him while you're on the road, if that's what you're getting at."

Charlie pulled his six-feet-two frame over the counter instead of walking around it like a normal person. The chain leashed to his wallet rattled like a ghost's shackles as he went. "Come on, Sid. It would only be on the weekends." He followed her into the back room. "Reggie just landed a sweet deal on a Fire Island summer share."

"Reggie's taking care of him during the week?" There was one person on the planet who detested Charlie's new girlfriend even more than Sidra, and that was Reggie. Sidra was surprised to hear their mutual friend was involving himself. "At his apartment?"

"Are you kidding? His girlfriend would kill him if he tried to bring Louie in there. No, at my place." *His place.*

Charlie's place was Evie's place. Sidra could barely walk into Alphabet City; just the thought of the two of them cohabitating within a four-block radius made her throat form a sickly lump and her palms sweat profusely. "I can't," she said weakly.

"You can't. Or you won't?" Charlie plucked the bag from her hand and nimbly worked the safe tucked between Mikey's desk and the wall. Sidra helplessly watched his fingers, so capable of quickly manipulating the dial while hers just fumbled under pressure.

There were days when she thought Charlie was just a senseless oaf, incapable of realizing the torment he put her through. And then there were the days when she realized Charlie knew precisely what he was doing. The safe sprang open at his bidding.

Sidra bent to collect her yoga bag. "Tell me Evie *really* wants me in her apartment."

"She'd rather have *you* in there than a smelly dead iguana." Charlie grinned, tossing the money in and securing the steel door with a clunk. Sidra wished she could lock up her heart and her feelings as easily.

"I'll think about it. For Louie. Don't ask me again in the meantime."

"Excellent!" Charlie reached to give her shoulder a squeeze, but she turned quickly with a shrug, causing her yoga bag to knock his hand away. "Oh, and before I forget . . ."

He bounded back to the counter and began rummaging through his messenger bag. "For the show next week," he said, handing her a satin stick-on pass. It was just a house pass, generic to the venue. Someone had added the date of the show in Sharpie. "It'll get you in the door without being hassled."

Sidra nodded, slipping it into her bag. "Gotta go. Class."

RICK
BLANK PAGES

"You boys ready to make a piece of music history?"

Rick cast a quick glance up at Thor. Their producer was rubbing his hands a bit too maniacally to be taken seriously.

The album was a piece, all right. Of what, Rick wasn't quite sure. But his gut told him it wasn't quite right. Any old dinosaur could leave a fossil behind; they needed to leave a legacy. The rest of the band was having lunch and listening to the playback, but Rick had lost his appetite four tracks ago.

"As soon as Sam devours that U-boat, I'd say we're good to go," he murmured, dropping his gaze back to his notebook.

Rick wasn't used to blank pages.

The band had spent the past week live tracking in the studio. They had the basics of ten songs nailed down. But Rick wasn't convinced they were the right ten for the project. Yet he could tell Thor's brain was working five paces ahead, his sights already set on overdubbing.

Rick wasn't in the mood for another battle of wills. He was still smarting from yesterday, after Thor suggested he try the growling approach to his vocals popular with the newer screamo and grindcore bands. "Where are those brass balls of yours?" the producer had razzed. "You used to be such a beast back in the day."

Rick knew he was having trouble nailing some of the high notes, but he had no desire to sing in what he called "Cookie Monster tones." "I'm a vocalist," Rick had informed him. "Not a bloody Muppet."

Thorton Young III was no young upstart in the business. In fact, he had spent years in the trenches with Corroded Corpse, back in the eighties when they were spinning their souls into platters of gold. But Rick knew the tides had turned in the business. It wasn't just about album sales; not when bands like Radiohead were practically giving away albums in a pay-what-you-want environment and unsigned acts were getting five million hits on their YouTube videos.

It was about relevance.

The band could no longer just keep singing about Vikings and rats and pillaging, the fodder that had made them famous in the eighties. Mythology and history were not as progressive or cool as the new dystopian view. Kids these days wanted to hear about surviving the zombie apocalypse and landfills in the sky, doomsday stuff. It should be a no-brainer, since the Rotten Graves Project was descended from doom metal royalty.

"Heavy is the head that wears the metal crown, eh, Rotten?" Thor's voice niggled.

Rick tapped his pen against the empty page, staring absently at his bandmates. The King of Doom had been cursed with silence, a writer's block that was growing roots and thick, thorny vines that snaked up the walls of the fortress he had built. Luckily, the jesters holding court were full of ideas.

Speaking of mighty Norsemen . . . Sam was wrestling with a submarine sandwich, his Viking beard catching bits of lettuce as they dropped. Although not the most serious musician, he had at least managed to keep the rust off his bass strings during the band's hiatus by doing session work with just about half of Los Angeles.

To his right sat Jim, looking just as redneck American as Sam appeared red- cheeked British. The lad didn't seem to own a shirt with sleeves. Rick stared at the colorful creatures inked around the drummer's bulging biceps. It was as if the three-eyed Fujins, Asian devil dragons, and Kabuki demons had been summoned to spur Jim on like a man possessed when he stepped behind the kit.

He was the only member not original to the lineup, having been plucked from the helm of his own successful group, Dead Can Dream. He set the pace for his idols, refusing to let the moss grow under their aging feet. Jim's own feet were in constant tapping mode, and his hands were rarely without sticks.

Currently, he was keeping time on an empty pizza box balanced atop Thor's swivel chair.

And then there was Adrian. His skid-row sensibilities made him every metalhead's man. Even with his Madison Avenue wardrobe. He had the knack of making music effortlessly, fluidly, yet with a passion that was enviable. And he had figured out how to hang his cap at the end of the day, switching from one world to the other. Which was *very* enviable. With his reading glasses perched on his nose and his Fluevog motor-cycle boots propped up, Rick's lead guitarist was immersed in the Sunday *New York Times* crossword puzzle, oblivious to the din around him.

Adrian defied logic, God bless him. The former loose cannon of the band had achieved a Zen-like balance. Mean-while, Rick had achieved bloody little since the regrouping. Maybe it really was time to try a yoga class. He felt—

"Well, spit it out, man."

"Come again?"

"I figured you must have it, since you've been staring at me for an age." Adrian pulled off his glasses. "The opposite of 'pro-lific.' Eight letters, ends with *t*."

Rick cleared his throat. "Impotent."

Adrian raised a brow and placed pen to paper once more. He clucked amusedly before smacking the paper down triumphantly. "First time for everything!"

"What, is that the first time you've ever finished a puzzle?" Sam mocked, pulling a slimy tomato

from between the bread and flicking it onto Jim's pizza box. All drumming stopped abruptly.

"*The* puzzle. As in the Sunday puzzle. In *pen*."

Jim whistled his awe before popping out for a cigarette break. Sam simply hoisted himself out of his chair and announced, "Finished the U-boat. Now time to drop a missile."

"Keep that bit of intelligence to yourself next time, Summerisle!" Adrian groaned.

"Hey Riff, I wanna show you something."

Rick dropped notebook and pen and approached the control board. Thor had what looked like blueprints up on his laptop screen.

"I'm tired of renting a chair under my ass. Or rather, having you or a record label rent it for me. I'm thinking of opening my own recording studio. Was wondering if you'd want in?" Thor stroked the keyboard, and the screen filled with thumbnail images of commercial properties.

"You mean investing?"

"Yeah. I've found some spaces that have real potential. This location here would be a steal." He nudged the screen with his knuckle. "Old dry cleaning business, Lower East Side."

Rick studied it doubtfully. "Looks like it should be condemned."

"Scaffolding," Thor scoffed. "That'll be gone in a New York minute. Probably just some facade work."

"I'll think about it," Rick replied, sensing Adrian at his

shoulder. "Might be cool to have a stake in some Manhattan realty."

"Your own floor to kip on, at least," Adrian joked.

"What do you think, Dig?" Rick wanted to know.

"No way. I think Kat would kill me." He just shrugged as the other two made whip-cracking noises. "I've got a wedding to think about, guys. And school tuition."

In other words, a life, Rick thought darkly. "You know what?" he blurted. "Hell, I'm in." *Who cares what Adrian thinks? Thor asked me, not him.* Rick took a bit of perverse pleasure in that.

"Really? Sweet!" Thor slapped the Mac closed. "I'll set up a meeting with the other guys on board. Mostly suits. But they're cool. They'll be psyched to have an artist on board."

"Set it up," Rick agreed. He glanced at the clock. "I've got an appointment; mind if I roll?"

"What about the overdubs?"

"First thing tomorrow," Rick promised. *Right now,* he thought, *there's a first time for everything.*

SIDRA
SEEKING SANCTUARY

Sometimes it was better to get out of your own way, thought Sidra, and your own studio. In fact, there was a reason she held no classes on Thursdays. There were times when she liked to practice yoga alone, and other times when she needed someone else's prompts and cues in her head. She headed toward NYU. Her friend Gretchen ran a serious class that people clamored for. She wanted to be worked hard, forced to concentrate on poses so that all else left her mind.

Of course Charlie assumed she would take care of the iguana. Wasn't she always there to take care of everything? To take the brunt of everything? She remembered all the times she'd come home after a grueling day of exams, just longing to crawl into her pajamas, eat a can of soup, and fall asleep, only to find starving musicians had emptied her entire kitchen. Couldn't they have ordered a pizza? Then there was the time Charlie let some dreadlocked ska band crash at her place. "It's only for one night," Charlie had said. Yeah. And the band *only* gave the two of them, and her pullout sofa, a horrible case of crabs. It took her weeks to get rid of *those* unwanted guests.

She had long suffered as the girlfriend of a musician.

Supporting his dream. Being used. Being made a fool of. As if the creative life gave him license to fool around. She should have kept walking that day she saw him in the rain. She was still paying for it now, unable to say no to him. No more, flat out.

Charlie and his freaking passes.

She remembered the first real gig the Bold O'Danahys landed in New York, at a hip club now long gone. Charlie had made laminates for the band members and their girlfriends, and Sidra remembered the thrill of winding through the crowd importantly, that all-access pass hanging from her neck. Silly, but it finally felt like all the time she had invested in Charlie's dream had paid off. She loved gliding past the bouncers, behind the velvet rope, backstage. Many eyes were on her as she passed by, checking out the wardrobe she had cultivated over the course of the weeks leading up to the show. She was impeccably, stylishly "with the band." Her man was the main man on stage, she thought proudly. And she was his sexy muse. How lucky was she?

"How fuckable is he?"

"Who, the lead singer? Totally."

Two girls swayed their hips to the music by the balcony rail, blocking Sidra's view and talking about Charlie.

"Even with that banjo he's playing," the first girl drawled loudly, buzzed on her drink. "He can pluck me any time!"

"Electric banjo!" Girl number two laughed and curled her tongue to capture the lone ice cube remaining in her cup. "Too bad he's taken."

"Seriously?"

Damn straight, Sidra felt like saying. But the music was too loud and she was feeling too good to care. Charlie *was* hot, banjo slung low on his hips and looking as cocky and confident as any rock star. Girls could look at the menu all they wanted.

"Jenny's working coat check tonight. She said he snuck in there with the fiddle player during set break!"

"Eww, I hope they weren't grinding all naked on *my* coat!"

"Jenny said he was totally fingering her up that short skirt."

Sidra was in a tunnel, the music now far away. She was alone on a balcony full of people. Laughter and talking and singing and drinking and dancing were no longer within her realm of possibility. She stood frozen, staring at the stage. Seeing, as if for the first time, the chemistry on stage between Evie and Charlie.

"We needed a new fiddle player." Charlie loved to defend his lineup choice to anyone who asked. "So might as well get a smoking hot one! Maybe more people will come see us." To Sidra he'd assure, "She's just like one of the guys."

Evie was a great draw. She wore crazy high heels, adding to her already Amazonian stature, and played the fiddle like she played the entire audience. She'd bounce one knee, her slim thigh quivering beneath her impossibly short skirts and tight dresses, and smirk a pretty little smirk as she pointed her bow in the direction of every guy and girl in the front row. Her nose would wrinkle and then she'd shake her hips to the beat. Now she was arching her eyebrows, dyed fiery red to match her mane of hair, in Charlie's direction as they both fingered their respective string instruments in perfect unison to wrap up their last song in their set. *Fingered.* Sidra felt nauseated.

Charlie had called a band meeting backstage after the show, their most successful gig yet. Drunken fans hollered for one more song as security began to do a sweep, moving people out into the frigid Manhattan night. A couple of A&R guys lingered, hot to talk to the band about representation. Sidra pushed her way into the tight back room. The air in there was claustrophobic, thick with smoke and sweat and tired laughter. "Hey, we're in the middle of— Oh, it's okay, it's only Sidra. Hey, doll."

Charlie reached for her with a hand already clasping a bottle of beer.

"Yep, only me," Sidra said loudly. She spied Evie sitting on a couch next to their drummer, Justin. A beer was poised at her mouth, a smile playing on her beautiful lips over something Justin was saying. "I'm just like one of the guys." Sidra grabbed the beer from Charlie's hand and took a swig. "In fact, let me smell your fingers, Charlie."

Charlie opened his mouth, and the room grew quiet. "What the fuck, Sid?"

"Yeah, that's what I thought. Go to hell." She catapulted the remaining beer across his chest and then dropped the bottle to the floor, where it smashed at his feet. With her heart in smithereens, she fled.

"Watch your step, miss."

A voice brought her back to the here and now. The mile walk had barely registered with her, she had been so caught up in the memories.

"Thanks." In her fancy new shoes, Sidra dodged shards of glass littering the sidewalk in front of the Gallatin building where a bottle must've broken, and nodded at the passerby who had issued the warning. She could smell the aroma of wine staining the pavement as she bowed her head and ducked into NYU.

RICK
NEW GUY ON THE BLOCK

Ah, spandex the way God intended it. Or better yet, mused Rick, *the devil.* In every direction, girls dotted the landscape like gumdrops in their shiny, colorful exercise garb. Paul had been right about the scenery, Rick thought. He didn't remember university looking this appealing. Then again, he hadn't lasted long in higher education, trading the books for baby nappies and band commitments.

He waited patiently in line to scan Paul's faculty ID card and gain entrance into the inner sanctum of supposed yoga nirvana. The modern expanse of glass and chrome within the whitewashed lobby was in severe contrast to the view outside on Washington Place. A sudden summer storm had shaded the sky as gray as the pavement, and rain looked imminent.

"Hi, here for the six thirty?"

A nubile blonde encased in a sexy black tracksuit addressed him from behind the front desk. In her hand, she wielded a scanner gun that would either allow him to proceed or would Taser him senseless on the spot.

"Indeed. Hi." Rick gave his best winning smile. He felt

underdressed in his football kit, consisting of a pair of West Ham shorts and collared player's shirt.

"What do you teach?" she asked, her eyes on the plastic faculty card as she scanned it.

"Currently," Rick murmured dryly, "I'm trying to teach an old dog some new tricks."

The blonde cocked her head. "How's that working out for you?"

"Considering I'm the old dog . . . it's pretty crap."

She laughed as she buzzed him through. "Enjoy the class."

He could stride onto legendary stages before throngs of screaming thousands without a second thought, but the utter silence of the small, windowless yoga room gave Rick pause. It was unsettling. He observed two dozen or so participants, mostly women, sitting rod-straight on mats, some with their buttocks resting on colorful bricks. Not an open eye among them. The instructor, a wisp of a woman with an umbrella of kinky ginger curls cascading from the crown of her head, motioned him toward the general vicinity of where the mats and blocks were stockpiled. Her body reminded Rick of rubber bands, shapely but taut, not an ounce of fat to be seen.

"Have you practiced yoga before?" she whispered as he passed her.

He surprised himself by giving her a noncommittal shake of the wrist, as if to say, *Oh, a little here, a little there.* He had toured Southeast Asia extensively, had visited Buddhist temples in Japan, and had certainly *observed* yoga. Then there was that bird from Australia who had roped him into some Tantric sexual escapades for a brief spell. But "practice" was something that implied eventual perfection to Rick. And he didn't want to admit he wasn't perfect at something.

He settled onto a block in his best cross-legged pose, allowing his eyes to close. The only sound reaching his ears was the second hand sweeping in five-second, hushed intervals on the wall clock high overhead. *This could pass for relaxing,* he thought. Then he chastised himself for thinking; *if yoga is about clearing the mind, have I already failed the test?* Soft air and the scent of sandalwood breezed by; the instructor had moved to turn on the stereo. *Commencing airy-fairy jingle jangle.* New age flute and sitar filled the room.

He stood and followed the others as gracefully as possible into his very first Swan Dive, and the instructor began to work them through some sun salutations. Moving without the customary eight pounds of guitar hanging from his neck felt foreign, like one of his limbs was missing.

From there, they moved into a position true to its namesake, Awkward Chair. He felt like a royal twonk, trying to balance in his wee invisible chair. Thankfully, the instructor cued them into what she called 'the first Down Dog of the day.' Rick was perfectly content to hang out here for a while. It felt legit.

"Wag your tail, lift your sit-bones high. Shoulders down."

Rick felt like an obedient doggy indeed, only to be rewarded by the torturous Plank. *Good God!* His abs launched a shaky protest, but he held strong until he was told to transform into an ark-load of other animals: Cobra, Locust, Cat, Cow, Dog, Pigeon. Internally, he cursed Kat and Paul. Infernally. How on earth had they convinced him this would be good? This was hell.

He shook out his limbs, willing himself not to glance at the clock. *Soon it will be over and I never have to come again.*

"Standing Half Lotus," the rubber band lady commanded, and the entire room bent their right legs like hypnotized storks. Rick followed suit, cheating with his hands in order to prop his foot firmly upon his opposite thigh. He achieved balance, slowly stretching out his arms.

Yes, master of the bloody universe.

He had no problem following the instructor's cue of focusing his gaze on one spot on the floor, as the view was exquisite. The girl positioned on the mat in front of him had an ass that could stop traffic. Her tiny black yoga shorts hugged its ripe curves and ended spectacularly, showcasing her smooth tan thighs. Her top, a pale pink spandex contraption that criss-crossed along her shoulder blades, did not betray an ounce of excess body fat along her torso, and he marveled as he noticed the way she tucked her tailbone at the instructor's cue. The thought of that slight pivot in her hips almost caused Rick to groan aloud. He wanted to run his fingers down her spine; it was perfectly aligned, like the fretboard of his favorite guitar.

Focus, ruddy focus. You pathetic geezer. She's probably half your age.

"Very good. Let's bring our right hands to the center of our chests in *Anjali Mudra*. Yes, that's half prayer position. Now bring your left hand to meet your right, pressing your palms together. Don't drop your right foot!"

Rick was lost. He held his current position, silently praying to God above or the devil below to keep him upright. He did not want to fall on his arse in front of—or behind, for that matter—this lovely creature. She was like Devon cream tea, he thought stupidly. A memory surfaced of his aunt Bootsy pouring out a lovely cup of tea using her best china. The sweet stickiness of fresh apricot jam and dollops of clotted cream came to mind as he considered this yoga girl's flesh. *I'd like to split her scones and cream them.*

"Bring your awareness to the center of your body," the instructor was saying. *No bloody problem there.* "Think of the vertical line that runs directly through the center of your head, neck, and torso. If this is your limit and your comfort zone, stay here." Rick wanted to laugh, but he was too uncomfortable to do so. "If you're more advanced, slowly move into *Ardha Baddha Padmottanasana*."

He watched in amazement as half of the class, Miss Cream Tea included, proceeded to reach for the sky with their right hands. With a deep breath and fluid movement, the girl lowered her hand behind her back until she was grasping her left elbow. "Create that bind and connection," the instructor breathed, winding through the class to observe their progress. Rick concentrated on keeping the sole of his foot facing the sky, locking his gaze on the girl ahead. She, of course, was oblivious to him.

From there, she glided her fingertips down her left forearm. Rick felt a shiver, watching what seemed like such an intimate gesture. With the assistance of her left hand, she wrapped the fingers of her right hand around her toes where they were still perfectly balanced on her left hip. Her right shoulder pulled back, giving him a stellar view of the swell of her breast. He swallowed hard. *Calm, clear mind. God, she is beautiful.*

Her left arm went up, straight as an arrow to the sky. Just when he didn't think her body and his imagination could take any more, she exhaled audibly, hinged from the hip, and bent forward, slowly, mindfully, until her left fingertips were touching the floor. She kept folding her body, torso lowering farther and farther, until she was staring right at him from upside down with eyes startlingly light, flecked with golden jasper and bits as dark as black hematite.

It was the one-shoed bagel girl from the lift.

Rick gave her his most charming smile, then toppled unceremoniously like a felled spruce.

SIDRA
IMPORTED GOODS

SIDRA HAD TUCKED her issue with Charlie under the yoga mat for the session, but the new guy behind her had made it difficult to concentrate. And once she bent over, ass in the air, and realized who he was? *Impossible.*

What the hell was Mr. Import doing here?

He had no business even attempting the Half Bound Lotus Forward Bend, and Gretchen should have modified the pose for him. Anyone could tell he was as green as new bamboo. If this were her class . . . Ah, but that was the beauty of it. She just had to follow instruction. It was nice to be led down the path without having to be the ever-vigilant guide, with someone else pointing out the beauty and the dangers nature presented along the way. Sidra knew the pitfalls surrounding *Ardha Baddha Padmottanasana* were ego and greed, pushing too far too fast. Yoga students, often so eager to master the pose, blew out their knees before even getting a proper chance.

Gretchen was a good instructor, but she was definitely from the school of competition and comparison. Yoga was a tough market in Manhattan, just like everything else. All the crazy fads, from aerial yoga to naked yoga to dog yoga, had many scrambling to find the next hot thing, and it was every yogi and yogini for themselves out there. Gretchen had built her popular adjunct yoga classes at NYU into something along the lines of a Cirque du Soleil training camp, a precise and exotic blend of cutthroat yoga. It definitely wasn't newbie territory. Sidra gave the guy mad props for even trying.

How the hell did he end up here?

"Nice shoes."

Sidra pushed her feet into the sandals he had gifted her. "Thanks. Nice mat technique."

He was adorable when he blushed.

"It gets easier." Gretchen had purred up alongside him like a cat in heat and placed a hand on his chiseled biceps.

Typical. Sidra had witnessed firsthand Gretchen's propensity to treat yoga class as if it were speed dating, especially when eligible men were at stake. Whether this guy was eligible or not still wasn't readily apparent. He wore no ring, but that meant nothing in yoga. Or in other social situations. Sidra thought of the Celtic knot ring she had given Charlie, but didn't want to think about where it had been during the night of Evie and the coat check wall.

"And there are easier classes, too," Sidra felt the need to add.

"Sidra, your Monday night class would be perfect for him! Season him up . . . then toss him back to me," Gretchen joked.

Season and toss him? He's not a meatball, Gretchen. Sidra cringed at the way her colleague was drooling over him like he was.

"Here." She fished a card for Evolve from the pocket of her mat bag. "It's a great way to start the week. Five p.m. And the first class is always on me."

Oh jeez. Like *that* didn't sound like a come-on. But Mr. Import just smiled, fingering the card and flipping it over.

"Don't let the address fool you," Gretchen supplied. "Sidra's the real deal."

"Thanks, then. Cheers."

Sidra watched as Gretchen practically peed her Lululemons and melted to the floor at the sound of his voice. And then they both got to watch him from the back view as he left.

Gretchen squeezed Sidra's arm with both hands now in a vise grip. "Holy hotness, I'm a sucker for those curls. And that accent! Where did he come from?"

His presence was definitely the most intriguing thing to hit —literally—the dojo floor in a long time.

Gretchen didn't wait for her to answer. "Let's ask Beth!"

Sidra trailed behind Gretchen in her quest to the front desk, where the pretty grad student was scanning IDs. "Oh yeah, he was funny," Beth recalled. "His ID was faculty. PhD, I think."

Ah. Mr. Doctor *Import,* Sidra thought triumphantly. She'd been half right.

"Think he'll be back?" Beth asked.

"I don't think he'll last a week in yoga," Gretchen said with a laugh. "If he's a creeper, he picked the wrong class. He's going to try Sidra's Kool-Aid next."

"Perhaps he was at yoga for *yoga,* not to pick up women. When your practice goes well, it removes gender and lets you see people for who they really are." It was a high and mighty stance to take, but Sidra thought it was especially fitting here. Seeing as Gretchen had practically thrown herself at her supposed "creeper." She yanked her umbrella from the mesh pocket of her yoga bag. "See you next week."

"Look at you, Miss Prepared! I think I'll stay in here till it lets up." Gretchen shivered. "The forecast didn't even say rain today."

"I always have one." Sidra gave a half smile and wave. She had gotten caught out in the rain once. Never again.

RICK

KARMA CALLING

LED ZEPPELIN's "Fool in the Rain" came to Rick's mind as he sloshed through Washington Square Park. Breathless, smiling, curls plastered to the side of his face—who cared? He knew it was only a business card in his pocket, but it felt like a connection.

That yoga class had been bloody awful. Perhaps it was karmic justice for making fun of the airy- fairy music and salivating over the eye candy earlier. He had felt like a piece of meat. An uncoordinated piece of meat, more specifically. That rubber band of a woman had been no different than a chick front row at a show, eyeing his crotch and flubbing all the lyrics. Thank goodness for the other one. Miss Cream Tea. What had the instructor called her? *The real deal.*

Sidra.

The rain had soaked his Hammers shirt from claret to black. It clung to his skin and he remembered the warmth of Sidra's smile as she handed over her card. She taught yoga, too? He laughed out loud, realizing he just got the punch line to her joke about not needing shoes for work.

The thought made him want to stop in his tracks and . . . sing.

"Thor." He sheltered his mobile from the downpour with his hand. "It's Riff. You still at the studio?"

"No. But I can be there in ten minutes. Why, what's up?"

"I'm ready to nail that verse from yesterday."

"Seriously?"

"Yeah. You up for it?"

"I'll see you in ten."

Grinning, Rick ended the call and began to jog up Fifth Avenue. He was bound to find an available cab at some point, but for now he didn't mind running in the rain.

SIDRA
ROLL CALL

SIDRA POPPED out of bed early on Monday morning. *First day of camp!* she thought happily, as eager and excited as no doubt hundreds of waking children throughout Westchester County. It was a perfect summer day, too. Not too warm, yet the sun was already soaking the streets with bright light as she bounded down the steps of her brownstone with her yoga mat, bag, and a fresh new book to read on the train.

When the conductor announced Lauder Lake, Sidra lurched her way to the front of the car to exit. The slumped form of a man sleeping in a backward-facing seat caught her eye, making her think of her father. His head was pressed against the window and his hand clutched a small brown paper bag. Sidra wondered if the guy had already slept through his stop, or if his intentions were just to ride until he slept the drink off.

I forgot to check on Jack this morning.

She shook off the thought. Seamus was still home; she shouldn't feel the least bit guilty of shirking duty.

"Sidra! Yoo-hoo! Hello!"

She shaded her eyes, seeking out the voice. Her friend

Karen was standing in the train station lot by her Prius, waving wildly with one hand and clasping the swathed head of a baby, cradled against her breast in a colorful cotton sling, with her other. There were several clusters of mothers with kids around her, all waiting for the camp bus to arrive.

"Oh my God, it's been forever!" Sidra carefully hugged her yoga retreat pal over the baby's sleeping head. "Look at Mina, she's so big! And where's my little man?"

"Jasper's too cool for Mom; he's hanging with his friends over there." Karen laughed, gesturing toward the six-year-old who was kicking up dust and gravel with two other boys. "Oh, and these are my friends, Katrina and Marissa. Ladies, this is Sidra. She's the one I told you about; she'll be teaching yoga to the kids."

Sidra nodded and smiled at the two other mothers. They were juggling coffee cups and camp backpacks as their two daughters dawdled behind them.

"Sorry, we could've brought you a coffee, too, if we knew how you liked yours." The one with thick wavy curls handed Karen a cup.

"No worries, I had a venti on the train," Sidra supplied.

"Oh, to have a venti again!" the other woman groaned. She was dark-haired and voluptuous, with large sunglasses. "Two kids later, my bladder is barely strong enough to hold a small cup of coffee through the ride here. Where's that freakin' bus?"

"Miz-ess, Miz-ess!"

Sidra heard the familiar salutation her younger yoga students loved to greet her with before feeling solid little arms bear-hugging her waist. "Do you remember me, Miz-ess?"

Sidra regularly visited several of the public and private schools in the five boroughs. She hated the formal "Ms. Sullivan," yet found the kids didn't listen as well when she went by "Sidra." So "Miss S." became the happy medium by which she taught the youngsters basic poses throughout the school year.

"Of course, you were my best Tree pose this spring, Abbey!" Sidra gave the girl's ponytail a tiny tug. She had nice waves in her hair, just like her mom. "What are you doing here?"

"I'm going to camp!" Abbey stated as she demonstrated her Tree for her little friend next to her. "My mom does even better Tree poses than me, because of her name: Katrina! Actually, she has *two* poses named after her—Cat pose *and* Tree pose!"

"My childhood friends call me Tree for short," her mom explained. "But I go by Kat more these days. So you taught at Abbey's school in the city?"

"Yeah, there was a special grant last year for alternative exercise. I went in to teach the kids, as well as the phys ed teachers," Sidra explained. "I didn't think I'd see any of my city kids up here."

"We summer in Lauder Lake." Kat turned to Marissa, who snorted. "God, that didn't sound pretentious, did it?"

"Kat grew up on the street where I live," Karen said. "You should come up some weekend, Sidra. We could all do sunrise yoga on the beach."

"You can all kiss my big fat lilywhite ass," Marissa stated. "I'll sleep in, then cook you skinny yoga bitches bacon and eggs."

"Mariss!" Karen scolded. She pushed her palms over Mina's ears, but the baby slept snuggly on. Kat just rolled her eyes with a smile.

Sidra decided she liked Karen's friends. "So what are you ladies going to do with your five hours of freedom?" she inquired.

"Mina and I have a StrollerFit class," Karen said, bouncing the baby gently. "Then a much-needed nap . . . for both of us, isn't that right, Mina-girl?"

"And we're sneaking into Manhattan on a mission. Wedding reconnaissance," Marissa said. "Kat's going to book a wedding venue and date without telling her fiancé."

"Not exactly," Kat said. "I'm *changing* the date, because his best man is being—"

"A total asshole?" Marissa supplied.

"He's being high maintenance," Kat said diplomatically. "They're in a band," she explained. "And our original date conflicted with the weekend of a big show. So I agreed to change it. No biggie. I just haven't told Adrian yet. I don't want the two of them fighting."

"Sounds like the best man needs to get over himself," Sidra said sympathetically.

"Either that or get laid, as my fiancé so eloquently put it," Kat said with a laugh. "But I can't even imagine this guy on a date. His version of a pickup line would probably be 'nice humbucker.'"

Sidra was the only one who genuinely laughed at Kat's joke. "My ex is a musician. I get it."

Kat smiled warmly at her.

"The bus! The bus!" Abbey and the other kids began to hop and crow excitedly as the big yellow school bus began its descent down the long drive into the station lot.

"Um, text from Red." Marissa poked Kat. "She's not meeting us. 'Too busy at work.' I call bull. Something is up with that girl; she's been dodging us."

"You know how she gets. She throws herself into one thing to avoid another. I say we ambush her."

Sidra turned and helped the kids with their backpacks, not wanting to eavesdrop. She missed having her own close-knit pack of girlfriends. Most of her college crew had scattered to the four winds after graduation, and those who had stayed in Manhattan were busy popping out kids. Since new moms and single gals were about as likely to run in the same social circles —or to keep the same hours—as nuns and vampires, they just didn't see one another that much. Liz was cool, but always so busy with work. Spending time with Fiona usually meant spending time with Mikey, and when you threw Seamus into the mix, it was more along the lines of a Roddy Doyle comedy than a Ya-Ya Sisterhood. And befriending any of her students, even the nicest ones, blurred the teacher-student line a bit too much for her comfort.

Kat kissed her daughter's forehead. "You be good. Listen to Miss S. and the other counselors, okay?" Abbey nodded.

"Nice meeting you all; enjoy the peace and quiet," Sidra called, and got in the line to board the bus with the kids. She didn't mind hanging out with children, as long as she got to hand them back at the end of the day.

Motherhood was definitely not a path she planned to walk down. She watched out the bus window as Karen carefully transferred Mina from sling to car seat and drove away with her coffee cup balancing, forgotten, on the roof of her Prius. It was neither a sacrifice nor a priority Sidra was remotely interested in.

RICK

AS GOOD A DAY AS ANY

"THINK we can finish sometime in this century, Summerisle?"

Sam flipped a fat middle finger in Rick's direction from behind the slanted glass wall of the studio.

Overdubs had begun that morning. It was going to be a long week.

"We're experiencing some timbral inconsistencies," Thor murmured, barely glancing up from the console.

Rick muted himself from Sam. "Tell him to quit the five-string, then."

"He needs that B string," Adrian argued. "You're the one who wrote the bloody bridge."

"I didn't think it was going to come off sounding so hollow," Rick said.

"It's my favorite fucking part of the song," Jim piped in. "Don't kill it."

"I'll use the compressor to get it into shape. A multiband." Thor ran his index finger across his neck, signaling to Sam they were done for the time being. Sam practically threw off his headphones in disgust.

There was a reason the rest of the band was on the other

side of the glass. Their bassist had been working on the same track for the better part of the day and looked fairly murderous. And since Rick was the creator of the song, he was certain he'd be Sam's first victim.

Musically and vocally, "Demons Above" was a monster. Rick had done live takes on every other song, but this particular track had been hell on his voice. Sam's day had been a walk in the park compared to Rick's. At one point, he had to put himself in an isolation booth and talk his way down from the ledge, skittering on the edge of a panic attack. He could feel he was distancing himself from the others, and the last thing a band needed in the studio was dissention among the ranks.

During his final stab before calling it quits earlier, he had pushed his fingertips together out in front of him as he went for the difficult notes. It was a traditional technique for opening the rib cage, and for some reason, Miss Cream Tea occurred to him. The card she had given him was good for one free class, and it listed her yoga schedule on the back. Perhaps he'd take her up on her suggestion today.

"For fuck's sake, that one bloomin' note!"

"No worries, Sam. Thor will salvage it," Adrian assured him, ever the peacekeeper.

"Attack and release!" Thor boomed. "I'll get the ratios right, even if I have to stay here all night."

"You just about live here anyway, am I right?" Riff chided. "Digger and I were just joking last week about our days of kipping on the studio floor. You know"—he tapped a finger to his lips in thought—"maybe you should look into a bigger property for the studio, one that could actually house musicians during the recording process."

Thor's brow shot up in contemplation. "I like that. Good thinking, Riff."

"Always thinking like a CFO," Adrian joked. "Why else would we keep him around?"

Rick gave his best mate an elbow jostle. "It would certainly be a draw for artists who don't live here in town."

"Well I, for one, like to rely on the hospitality of the local ladies." Sam grinned. "Any port in a storm, I say!"

"And which port is your cock docking in tonight?" Jim asked.

"It's Monday, so let's see." Sam licked his fat thumb and began to tick off on his fingers. "Today, it's Monica. Then Tuesday, on to Tabitha. Haven't found a Wendy yet for Wednesday, but I'm managing. Thursday is always Trixie. On Friday, there's Franny. Then the twins get me over the weekend. Serena." He shivered happily. "And Sabine."

"Good God, man!" Adrian laughed. "Do you make them wear Day of the Week panties?"

"How else would I keep track?"

"All right, all right. Speaking of tracks . . . we done here? It's almost half four." Rick glanced at the clock above Jim's head.

"What's your hurry?" Sam demanded.

"I've got a five o'clock class."

"Control Freaks Anonymous? I'm glad you've finally admitted you have a problem."

"Go ahead, Summerisle. Take the piss. It's a gym class, if you must know."

"Mixed martial arts?" Jim piped in. "Jazzercise?" Everyone had a laugh.

"So witty, you lot. I'm going to a yoga class. And before you open your gobs to anyone about it"— he wagged a finger in warning—"think of all the skeletons I could drag out of *your* closets. You"—he pointed at Sam—"codpiece and lipstick. I've got photographic proof. Digger . . . I won't even go there," he said, and shook his head. Adrian held up his hands, surrendering quickly. "Jim, just because you're the new guy doesn't mean you escape unscathed. I'm recalling a certain night . . . oh yes, last summer. The Brass Rail will never be the same." Jim reddened at Rick's mention of the famous strip club in Toronto. "And even you, Thor." Rick turned on their producer, who was practically doubled up in laughter over the console. "Three words: Vietnamese basket trick. Oh, and five-hundred-dollar daily cocaine habit."

"That's more than three words," Thor pointed out, sobering a bit. "And I've been clean—*and* I've been practicing Tai Chi— for over seven years now. Nothing wrong with yoga."

"Yeah, mate. Kat has me doing a bit," Adrian admitted. "I like it."

"My wife loves hot yoga," Jim supplied. "We have some great sex," he added randomly.

Sam perked up at the notion. "Think there's room in your class for one more?"

"No, bugger off!"

RICK GLANCED down at the address on the card once he located Rivington Street. He wasn't very familiar with Manhattan beyond the numbered grid. "Don't let the address fool you," were the words of the NYU instructor. *Whatever that means,* he thought. Isabelle had called the area skid row, but she rarely ventured off Park Avenue. His thumb rubbed over the name of the studio, Evolve, printed on the slightly dog-eared card as if it were trying to coax a genie out of a lamp. *Come on now,* he thought. *Show yourself.*

Like the East End of London, the Lower East Side of Manhattan still had a whisper of old world Judaism to it. He passed Streit's, the old matzo maker, with its Kosher food items lining the shelves. Paul had been right; the area was clearly in a state of hyper gentrification. Trendy bars and shops were muscling their way in between the dirty brick buildings with their ancient fire escapes, and a newish glass boutique hotel hulked over the tenement landscape. It may have stuck out like a sore thumb, but the structure clearly just thumbed its nose at everyone walking by, daring them to question its foresight. Yes, this area was an up-and-comer. While touring, he and the band were always happy to discover there were places like this, apart from the Ritz-Carltons and Four Seasons of the world.

He found the building that matched the number on the card, sandwiched between two empty storefronts. But it was a record shop, not anything resembling a yoga studio. Could she have gone out of business in the half a week span since he had seen her? It would be a pity.

His eyes were drawn to the flickering neon Open sign in the record store's window. Tiny lights raced around each letter, highlighting them one by one, then blinking the entire word madly, on off, on off. He imagined his brain doing quite the same thing as it sent out its messages during one of his anxiety attacks. *S-T-O-P, stop- stop-stop. H-E-L-P, help-help-help.*

He felt something cold and yielding under his palm and realized he had his hand on the shop's doorknob. *Well, if I can't find peace through yoga, I may as well take a gander.* Music shops ranked high in his comfort zone, at the opposite side of the spectrum from yoga. He sighed. Was it in relief, or disappointment? He wasn't quite sure.

The smell of vinyl and cardboard hit him instantly. It brought home a rush of memories, some dating back as far as the seventies. He remembered himself and Digger as kids at Ditcham Park School. His Aunt Bootsy piling them in her Karmann Ghia and dragging them to various shops, from Oxford Street to Camden Town, in hunt of new music. Introducing the boys to Deep Purple's *In Rock*, the album that would become their favorite and most influential. He had forgotten this particular smell, and the thrill of walking into a treasure trove just waiting to be excavated. Having fifteen quid in his pocket as a lad and endless hours to peruse.

Rows and rows of used vinyl beckoned Rick. But he was surprised to also see the number of new releases on vinyl, displayed on the wall above the register. It hadn't occurred to him to offer a simultaneous vinyl release. Label executives and their distributors were always going on about metadata and the digital formats these days. He wondered how many record manufacturers still existed out there, in the world of the compact disc and MP3.

He skipped over the Metal section and went straight for the *D*s in Rock. Looking for that old album, ironically titled *In Rock*. In a simpler time, it was the heaviest thing Rick had ever experienced. He could picture the cover in his mind, the band members' heads in stone as a rock and roll Mount Rushmore, set against a brilliant blue sky. Even their long hair, a style so coveted by the two schoolboys, chiseled into the rock. The store had some oldies, like *Made in Japan* and *Machine Head*. Rick chuckled to think his fifteen quid would barely cover one these days.

"Hi, need some help?"

A very curvy shopgirl stood before him, her elbow propped on the *B*s.

"Just browsing. I once had this, pressed on purple vinyl." He held up *Machine Head*. "French import."

"Sweet!" The jet-black fringe above her brow ruffled with her exhale. "Mikey's always looking to buy, as well as sell. He's the owner."

"Cripes, I wish I still had it. Lost along the way, I'm sure." *Probably before you were born,* he almost added, but didn't. "Hey, erm . . . do you know about . . ."

"Sidra's classes?" She gestured toward his hand, and he looked down. Cripes, he'd been clutching the card she had given him the whole time, and now it was sweaty and rumpled in addition to slightly dog-eared. "Her students usually use the other door. But I'll take you through the shop; come on."

Rick followed the girl, his face curiously hot at the notion of being someone's "student."

Sidra's student.

The shopgirl led him away from the familiar and into a serene yellow corridor through the back of the shop. Rick glanced over his shoulder. Had he not been so fixated on the record store at the time, he may have noticed this long corridor when walking through the front door. It was a straight shot, whereas he had had to make an abrupt right turn through another entryway to get to the music store.

"Better hurry, I think she's starting. Changing room is over there. It's a one-staller, so always knock. Use any of these"—she gestured to a row of pale green lockers—"for valuables and shoes. Grab a mat and you're all set."

"Right. Thank you." Rick felt compelled to keep his voice low, although there was still a door separating the yoga studio from the outer lounge. Once left on his own, he surveyed the cozy space. It was decorated in an East Indian style, with dark pipe and drape. Spicy Votivo candles burned on a low table between two couches. It was a place, as his sons would say, to "chillax." He had experienced dressing rooms backstage that had tried hard to achieve this same vibe, yet fell flat.

He studied the class schedule tacked to the wall. With the exception of Thursdays, each day of the week offered a variety of classes to choose from. Rick smirked as Sam's Day of the Week panty girls came to mind. *Different day, different flavor.* He contemplated sitting out the class in the lounge, waiting until he could just speak with Sidra privately. Maybe he didn't need a bevy of classes, but instead a breathing technique to quell the anxiety. Something he could practice at home. He didn't have hours to devote to lying on some floor with a bunch of strangers.

Hell, it's a one-hour session, you big baby. He kicked his shoes into an available locker, shucked his wallet and keys from his pocket, and breathed deep. The lockers had a small keypad for temporary customized passwords. He pecked out 3683, which spelled *DOVE*. The Hebrew name of his youngest son, Jonah, was his easy-to-remember, go-to alphanumeric password.

Nothing to be scared of, he chastised himself. Noiselessly, he turned the doorknob and crept in.

The first thing that hit him was the cavernous space. The building's facade had been deceiving; one would never imagine such a space existed beyond it. The ceiling was curved, probably rising forty to fifty feet above them. Tall torchiere lamps in the corners cast just enough light on the nine participants on their mats.

Sidra was settled on a mat not far from them, but up a few steps, under a slightly brighter hanging lamp. The focal point of the room, Rick observed, as he settled into an open space on the floor. She cast a glance at him, smiled briefly in recognition, but kept going.

"Continue with the deep cleansing breaths, cross-legged, straightest back possible." Rick fell right in line with the other students, although he noticed he had to be the youngest in the room by at least twenty years. "Let the belly go this time," Sidra instructed. "Inflate it like a balloon, then your rib cage. Feel it lift, too."

Rick was a little too proud to let his abs completely go, not in front of this delicious specimen before him. He was sad to see she had covered those tan thighs today in long black yoga pants. Through her thin yellow T-shirt, though, he could see the rise and fall of her flat stomach as she breathed. *Was that a ring in her navel?*

"Now out through your mouth," she was saying. "First from your upper chest, then feel your rib cage fall, then draw the belly in." *Who breathes like this in real life?* Rick asked himself. His head felt a little light, as if he had climbed to thinner atmosphere. "Most people are too busy rushing around to breathe properly," Sidra answered his question. "This helps us focus on the moment; it calms the mind."

Rick liked that idea. He closed his eyes and tried it again, following only the sound of her voice. One of the old folks let out a ragged hacking cough. Rick allowed one eye to open, his brow arching as he peeked toward the culprit, a woman in her eighties, from the looks of her. To the other side of him, a balding geezer released air from both ends. *What have I entered into?* Rick thought helplessly. *Heaven's waiting room?* His next thought filled him with embarrassed horror: Did Sidra consider him an old geezer as well? Is that why she recommended this particular class?

"Let's stretch out those legs, get some warmth going." Sidra bounced her legs out on the mat in front of her, and her overage pupils all followed suit. "For Boat pose, you're going to start out sitting, with your legs out in front of you. I'll turn so you can see me." She turned sideways, but Rick, who was positioned off to the side, got more of a back view than a side view. "You want to use your tailbone and your sit-bones like a tripod, balancing on the area between them, like so." She tilted her pelvis slightly, and just as she rolled back, Rick caught a flash of red peeking between the black strip of her waistband and the dash of yellow as her shirt rode up.

Fuck me, she's wearing a red thong!

Sidra was explaining the benefits of Boat pose as she hovered and they all shakily followed along, but mentally, Rick was capsized and lost at sea. The tiny red triangle at the base of her spine was not unlike one of those warning flags staked in the sand back home. *High Hazard. Strong Currents. Danger.* He was being sucked in.

Everyone else was staring straight ahead. Did they not notice the exquisite ass of their instructor, trussed up in red satin and lace? Maybe he was the only one with eyesight good enough to see. Did she wear a thong to every class? Was it a testing tool designed to determine who could shut out distractions? If so, he was failing.

The next fifty minutes were a dreamlike state. He handled the class better than the NYU fiasco, but he certainly didn't have the Zen-like look that many of the participants had as they shuffled out the door. Rolling his borrowed mat slowly, he watched her bid people farewell, her hand resting lightly on a shoulder or a forearm here and there. Gentle laughter. That smile was disarming.

"So . . ." She approached him. "What did you think?"

"I thought it was . . . fine. But do *you* think I belong in a senior citizens' class?"

"I think you belong in a beginners class," she snapped back.

"Do you always wear a thong to beginners class?"

Rick watched as his retort sent her eyes wide open, and her hand flew to her tailbone. He realized she hadn't a clue and hadn't done it deliberately.

Idiot, he fumed. *You bloody fool.* "That was extremely rude of me," he sputtered stupidly. "Thank you for the class. I'll be back."

SIDRA

DOWN DOG

FIGURES, the moment a man under the age of fifty enters my class, sex demands entrance, too. Sidra angrily pushed the broom through the space, now devoid of mats and bodies. Boy, had she sure pegged him wrong. She thought of his last words, uttered in that clipped British accent: "I'll be back." Like she was supposed to drop to her knees—or strip to her thong—and thank him?

She had hurriedly dressed for camp that day, grabbing any old thing from her drawers, and hadn't had time to even stop home before class. *I work my ass off,* she thought, *and some uppity know-it-all professor has the nerve to comment on its attire?* Irritation swirled around her, not unlike the dust her broom was kicking up. Eyes and throat stinging, she paused. *Enough,* she thought. *Moving on.*

Wednesday night was Irving Plaza. She'd get to dance to her favorite band, Anam-Atman, have a couple of drinks, and relax with friends. She had that new handkerchief tank top she was dying to wear, and those Robin's Jeans Fiona had convinced her to spend way too much money on. Of course she wasn't looking forward to Charlie's opening set, but she was perfectly content to hang out in the lobby and keep Seamus company while he peddled the merch.

Sidra straightened the mats and blankets in their baskets and readied the bricks and straps for the next day. After blowing out the candles in her tiny lounge, she collected the day's punch cards.

While many gyms and studios around the city were selling classes in packs of five and ten, Sidra's was the only place that utilized a novel and nostalgic way of tracking clients: using a punch clock that still hung on the wall from the old Sullivan and Son Bicycles days. She loved the retro chrome of the machine and its resolute thump as it clocked each and every person in. Not only was she able to keep track of the time and date for each student, she also had the ability to leave them quotes and notes of progress and encouragement on their cards. And when a student punched a total of ten times, she would leave them a gentle reminder about purchasing another punch card at the front register.

Twenty cards today, she tallied. But twenty-one students, if she counted the freebie she gave Mr. Import. No more Get Out of Jail Free cards for him. If he wanted to learn and work, he'd have to make a commitment like everyone else.

Sidra breathed deep and plopped herself down on one of the couches. The newly extinguished candles gave up their last aromatic gasps. She loved the candles' name as much as she loved the scent: Forgotten Sage. The smell was like nothing else in Sidra's life: cedar and twigs, sage and sweet grasses from a faraway plain. It was foreign, yet peaceful. Smiling, she leaned forward and began to make notes on the cards.

Cindy: Your side angle pose is looking great! Just remember not to collapse forward.

Marilyn: Don't lose patience! "Yoga doesn't take time, it gives time." (Ganga White)

Jonathon: You should be able to do Warrior II between two panes of glass. Check your stance! Great high lunge today.

Vivian: Don't forget to breathe, breathe, BREATHE!

Lia: It's not about a $100 mat. As the great Rodney Yee would say: "The most important pieces of equipment you need for doing yoga are your body and your mind."

Morty: If your hamstrings are still bothering you tomorrow, use a block to bring the earth up a little closer to you. Don't be a hero!

Gina: You made it to your thirty-ninth class—holla! Hit up the front counter for a new punch card. :)

There was a rhythm to her method as she plucked each card from the pile, turned it over, and placed the pen tip down. But with each movement, her thoughts unconsciously and automatically drifted back to her conversation with that guy. The PhD professor. She wondered if he went by "Doctor." And whether he wore a lab coat to class.

Do you always wear a thong to beginners class? Her cheeks burned as his words echoed in her head. She recalled his smug, surveying smile, as if he were watching her swinging from a pole. Oh, if only she had a card for him. She'd share a few choice words in return.

Charlie's devil-may-care whinny galloped down the corridor, adding to Sidra's annoyance. Whether it was by coincidence or not, Mikey had an uncanny habit of scheduling her ex for closing on the nights Sidra worked late. She hastily finished up the rest of the cards and filed them back alphabetically into an accordion folder near the door. If Charlie was working up front tonight, Evie was probably keeping him company. *All the more reason to take the back—and the easy—way out,* Sidra reasoned, and slipped out the rear exit door.

RICK
CHANGE FROM WITHIN

"Are you kidding me?" Rick swore under his breath as Sam approached. The rest of the band had been marooned on a barge in the East River since ten o'clock, sweating under the June sun and photographer's lights. And now Sam was strolling in come high noon, wearing Bermuda shorts, a loud tropical shirt, those ruddy flip-flops, and a shit-eating grin on his face? Unacceptable.

Rick felt his stomach lurch, his body sway sickly in unison with the waves lapping impatiently at the side of the moored, flat boat.

"Let me handle it." Adrian's hand was on Rick's shoulder briefly before he hopped to dry land and approached their bass player. Rick could feel sweat in rivulets behind his knees, and he was only in dark jeans. He could only imagine how Adrian was fairing in those leather trousers of his. A crowd had gathered on one of the South Street Seaport landings, watching as the band was made to mimic and mime for hours to the incessant whirl of the camera's shutter.

Whose idea had this photo and video shoot been?

Isabelle's, of course. The scenery was admittedly a cool back-drop, with not one, not two, but three Manhattan bridges in steely gray against the brilliant blue sky. Rick glanced up at the faces peering down at them in generic curiosity and felt the all-too- familiar hot buzz of panic prickle down his nerve endings.

He quickly dropped his eyes to the water. Amazing how much one body of water could differ from another. Back home in Hawaii the shores were clear and sparkling. Here, the East River dirtily churned with a myriad of sins, and Rick shuddered to think what was floating on the surface: used condoms, syringes . . . and then there were his own ominous thoughts and secrets lurking below, hovering as silent and heavy as cement shoes at the bottom. He recalled how different his first view of this river had been from high atop the Upper East Side pent-house where Simone had lived as a girl.

Adrian's steel-toed boots made heavy contact on the deck, followed by Sam's weighty, slapping footfalls. While Rick had been hobnobbing through New York society as a teen with his parents on holiday, his two bandmates had been toiling day labor on the Portsmouth docks back in England. As they made their way toward him on confident sea legs, he felt his own quiver. The barge workers sprang into action at Isabelle's command.

"You're letting this thing loose?" Rick called out anxiously.

"We need some movement, some air flowing behind the band." The video crew scuttled around Isabelle as she barked directions, but Rick's ears only took in what he imagined was the call of the swallowing sea. How ridiculous to be out on a rusting barge with their amps and their instruments, posturing. A conceited cruise to nowhere, the band members basking in their own egos. If the boat went down, who would even care in the end?

"The three of us look like 'the band,'" Rick stated, thumbing back at Adrian and Jim. "Sam looks like he stepped off the set of *Weekend at Bernie's.* Unacceptable, mate. Thanks for wasting our whole day and the media budget."

Sam stuttered apologies and excuses that Rick didn't want to hear.

"We'll stick him behind that oil drum so no one sees his flip-flops, and we'll shoot in black and white. No one will notice." Isabelle scoffed. "You are way too wired, Riff."

Adrian unbuttoned his black Western-style short sleeve and tossed it to Sam. There was little chance Sam would be able to rebutton the shirt over his own girth, but at least it looked better than the loud tropical print.

"Let's get this show on the road," Adrian stated, slinging his guitar strap over his naked, tattooed shoulder. Jim turned his baseball cap backward in determination and pulled a pair of ever-present sticks from the back pocket of his jeans.

Rick felt a dull ache blossom in his rib cage, followed by a sharp one in his arm. He loosened his grip on the neck of his guitar, trying to shake away the impending sense of doom as the dock receded from his sight line. *Deep breaths,* he thought, trying to conjure up the exercise Sidra had had them do in class yesterday. But with each inhalation, he felt a searing pain between his shoulder blades.

A gull flapped its wings above, then seemed to float frozen in midair. Rick's head joined it, suspended. *Symptoms? Of what? It's nothing. My heart. Attack. No.* Another prickly wave of adrenaline rushed up his legs and through his core, radiating out his fingertips and buzzing up his spinal cord. *Yes. Listen to your body.* His heart began to pound wildly, as if competing with the ache that was beginning to spread a leaden weight across his chest. *Dying!*

He would die on this godforsaken barge, collapse in front of his brothers and all the strangers on board. And then what? *Nothing.* He wasn't ready.

He lost his footing, arms flailing behind him in a futile search for stability. Strong fingers grabbed his forearm, and he looked straight into the concerned eyes of his best friend.

"It's . . . the heat. And the water," Rick gasped.

"Turn this thing around, we're done for the day," Adrian hollered, much to Rick's relief.

"I'M FINE," Rick insisted. "Feeling much better." In the air-conditioned confines of the cab, with a water bottle in hand, he was speaking the truth. *Silly. It was nothing.* "Let's go back and salvage the shoot."

Adrian shook his head. "Nothing doing. Let's get you checked out first. I've got a guy."

"That sounds ominous."

"Not a dealer. A doctor."

"Pill-pusher just the same."

Adrian pushed his sweaty locks off his forehead. "He's my family doctor. And he's fitting you in. Deal with it."

Rick thought to mention the recent clean bill of health from his own doctor, but realized it might unleash a flurry of fifty questions from his best mate that he wasn't quite ready to answer. So he dealt. Besides, a second opinion couldn't hurt.

The Upper West Side waiting room was utilitarian. Hard-backed chairs for long waits. A plant of undetermined species looked a little too green to be true, given the windowless room. Rick was tempted to dump his water into the soil hiding under its leaves, but refrained. Adrian checked them in with the receptionist and took a seat next to his friend.

"You don't have to wait for me."

"I will. And then you'll come back to Lauder Lake with me for the night."

"What, for bloody observation?" It was Tuesday. He had

hoped to make Sidra's six o'clock class. And to hopefully make up for his horrid thong comment. "No."

"Why are you arguing with me? Here, read a magazine."

Rick glanced at the men's health magazine Adrian was offering and shook his head.

"Have you already read it?"

"No, but look at the date. December of last year."

"So?"

"So it's old news. Expired. Possibly misinformation at this point."

"You're impossible."

Adrian's mobile rang, giving them both an excuse to stop talking. Rick listened to the one-sided conversation. "Yes, luv. No problem . . . Uh-huh. Probably sixish. Can do . . ." Adrian procured a pen from the front desk and began to hatch letters in the crook of his forearm, one of the few places the tattoo needle hadn't touched. "Yes, I've written it down so I won't forget. Love you." He slid the phone back into the front pocket of his leather pants.

"What's that, then?"

Adrian held out his arm with a grin so his friend could read it.

"Kitty litter, lemonade?"

"Shopping list. Kat's without the car today; I drove it in."

He had scrawled the words in a slanting, jagged font, almost like they were an extension of his tattooed time line.

"Sounds like the makings of a new song lyric. *Kitty litter LEMONADE!*" Rick sang in a growling grindcore, followed by a King Diamond–inspired falsetto. Adrian joined in, laughing, as they made a mocking parody of their own genre.

"*Kit-ty. Kit-ty Litterrrrrr. LE-MON-ADE!*"

Luckily, the waiting room was empty. A nurse came to fetch Rick, and he could still hear Adrian singing under his breath of the perils of kitty litter as the door closed behind them.

The nurse was comfortingly schoolmarmish and took his vitals quickly. The symptoms he recited were pecked into the keyboard in the corner of the room, its monitor blacked from Rick using a privacy screen. "The doctor will be with you in a minute."

Left alone, he surveyed the room. Glass containers held cotton and tongue depressors. More outdated magazines hung from a rack on the wall. Rick shivered, even though he was still fully dressed in head-to-toe black. He contemplated the sealed sharps container hanging from the wall next to him and thought of Adrian out in the lobby. What did his friend, an ex-junkie, think about when he saw the discarded needles jumbled inside? Was there ever a yearning, a nostalgia, for that life of escape? To break back into that biohazard, that haphazard habit?

Adrian was the strongest man he knew.

The nurse hadn't lied; the doctor was indeed with him in a minute, filling the room with his large presence and the scent of antibacterial soap as he quickly pumped Rick's hand. "Richard Rottenberg! Another member of the tribe?"

"I guess you could say that." Rick studied the man's name tag—*Phillip Rosenberg, MD*—as well as the heavy gold Star of David pendant that hung from his neck. New York Jews were fiercely proud of their tribe, it seemed. More Jewish here than in many other parts of the world.

"I've got one for you," Dr. Rosenberg said, reaching for the blood pressure cuff. "Jewish guy and a Chinese guy walk into a bar..."

The doctor paused to listen to Rick's pulse as it pounded beneath the strangling cuff before continuing. Less than a minute and one politically incorrect punchline later, Rick burst out laughing. What a difference an hour made.

"Blood pressure is perfect, now let's give a listen." Dr. Rosenberg dropped the Mel Brooks act and set his stethoscope with a no-nonsense thump onto Rick's chest. "Don't hold your breath, it's okay to breathe normally." He moved behind Rick. "So . . . you married, Richard? Now a deep breath, please."

Rick drew in as much air as he could muster. "Widowed," he expelled with a hefty sigh. The doctor slid the stethoscope to more areas of Rick's back, as if contemplating moves on a chessboard. Rick continued to inhale deeply, exhale fully, and answer his questions. *Where's home?* Hawaii. *Kids?* Three boys. *Ages?* Twenty-five and the twins are twenty-one. Rick wished they would stop with the small talk. How on earth was this man supposed to detect possible abnormalities or arrhythmia if he wouldn't shut up?

"And you're here in New York for work?" Dr. Rosenberg tilted Rick's head gently and set his stethoscope on the side of his patient's neck. Rick didn't want to speak, and he couldn't even nod. Luckily, the doctor answered his own question. "I've been Adrian's doctor going on ten years now. I see other musicians, too. Carpal tunnel, pinched nerves, bulging discs, tendonitis. Not to mention the hearing loss. It's a hard life, rock and roll." He draped the stethoscope around his neck, apparently finished with it. "You guys make it look easy. It's not. I give you all a lot of credit."

"Thanks," Rick said, feeling humbled and undeserving. Here was a man who studied to save lives, acknowledging the lowly profession of rock musician.

"Your heart sounds fine. Strong. Healthy. I'm going to do an EKG just to make sure, but I suspect it will be normal."

Relief flooded Rick. The same nurse brought in a cart, and together, she and Dr. Rosenberg began sticking patches on Rick's arms, legs, and chest.

"Sorry, not exactly dressed for this," he mumbled. Although he had removed his leather motorcycle boots, his jeans were second-skin. The nurse shimmied them up his calves just the same.

"Shirt off, if you would."

Rick peeled the black T-shirt off. He saw the nurse's eyes flicker over his body art before she strategically placed the sticky discs.

"Now lie back and relax, but stay as still as possible," the doctor said as his nurse began to wire Rick to the machine, clipping the leads to each patch. "Will this hurt?"

"Asks the guy with the body piercings and tattoos?" the doctor said with a laugh. "Worst part will be pulling those electrodes off at the end." He winked.

The EKG machine hummed, and Rick attempted to relax.

"Perfect, perfect." The doctor consulted the computer screen, clucking happily. "All done." Just as systematically, the nurse unhooked each wire and pulled off the patches.

"That's it?" It seemed too easy. "Don't I need a stress test, too?" Rick pulled his damp T back over his head.

"Certainly not today; can't have you running on a treadmill in boots. I can write you a script for one, but honestly, I don't think it's necessary at this point." The doctor patted Rick's knees. "Your heart appears healthy. You gave us no history of heart disease in your family. Stress and anxiety can wreak havoc on your mind and your body, I'm not downplaying that. I can give you something to take the edge off—"

"No. No drugs, thank you." He pulled on his motorcycle boots resolutely.

"Are you exercising, off-stage?"

"Yoga." Rick said the word with such conviction that he actually startled himself. He expected the doctor to raise a brow or roll an eye. Instead, he gave a curt nod.

"That's a great start. Take some time for yourself. Here's one: A yogi walks into a bar, orders a drink, and slaps a twenty down. The bartender brings him a drink and pockets the twenty. 'Hey,' says the yogi. 'Don't I get any change?' And the bartender replies . . ." Dr. Rosenberg paused for effect, eyes twinkling. "'Change must come from within . . .'"

SIDRA
DONE DEAL

Contrary to his threat, Mr. Import did not come back for Sidra's Tuesday classes. He wasn't the first to come in with all guns blazing, only to fire blanks by the second round. Sidra worked her regulars through sun salutations, trying to pinpoint the nagging sensation at the base of her brain. Was it disappointment? Relief? She knew yoga wasn't everyone's cup of tea. Still. She enjoyed the challenge and the opportunity to work with students new to the practice. But it was, in the end, a practice that depended entirely on the individual. And if he wasn't willing or ready, that was no reflection on her.

She barely remembered the asanas that brought the last class to their final relaxation. "Thank you for allowing me to lead you in your practice," she said, a bit guiltily. "Namaste."

As her students echoed back reciprocal valedictions and began to file out, she heard one "Namaste" that stood out from the others. Mr. Import leaned in the doorway, watching her. Fully clothed and with shoes on his feet. With not a trace of respect or humility, his utterance of the word completely voided its meaning.

"A little late for class, don't you think?"

"Or just insanely early for your next one." His smile was disarming.

Or just insane, period, Sidra thought. She bent and began winding the yoga straps used in class into tight coils.

"I had all good intentions. Long day at work. Bloody unending."

"Yeah, well. Tomorrow's another day." She brushed past him into the now empty lounge. "Did you get a punch card yet?" She called over her shoulder.

"Come again?"

"Ten class punch card. They're sold up front in the record store." When she was met with silence, she grabbed a card to demonstrate. "See? Card. Ten classes, a hundred bucks." She inserted it roughly. "You won't find a better deal in Manhattan," she assured him, allowing the clunk of the machine to punctuate her sentence.

"What, you running a bloody factory?" He cast such a look of distain that Sidra wanted to smack him with the card, but refrained. "I can't be bothered with that."

"I am the farthest from a factory that you will find in the city, and believe me, there are plenty of them. If you are looking for the girls in the hundred-dollar yoga pants, you've come to the wrong place. If you can't be bothered with my system, or even getting here on time, then I suggest you practice somewhere else."

"Is yoga always this hostile?" he snarled.

"No, but you have a knack for insulting it!"

She expected a snappy retort or a lame excuse. But instead, all she heard was the flat smack as his credit card hit the low table between the two couches.

"Name a price. Charge me however you want, and let me come to any class I want. All of them. And some private sessions."

Fury broiled in her core. Hours of good yoga therapy were

undone within just a few short moments in the presence of this prick and his Platinum card. It was like Jack starting a tab at the bar and acting like he owned the place. "I run fifteen classes a week. That's sixty in a month. No offense, but you aren't in any shape to handle sixty classes a month."

"I'm in no shape, full-stop. I need to force myself . . ." He paused. "To slow down and relax. Before I have a bleedin' heart attack. If I know I have a place . . ." His voice drifted as he gazed around. "A place like this, with someone who won't blow smoke up my arse and will just teach me how, I will pay and do whatever it takes."

Sidra stared hard at him. She already had her father to deal with. And Seamus. And soon, the freakin' iguana. Did she really need one more body to take care of? "I'm not a therapist," she mumbled.

"And I'm not a head case. I'm just really, really stressed. And even after taking just one of your classes, I can tell . . . this grounds me. It helps. So what do you say?"

Take his money. That's what Mikey would say.

"Six hundred a month. Unlimited group classes."

"And one-on-one?"

"Double it. And I'll give you three private hours a week."

"Starting now?"

"Starting Thursday. But I can't do days."

"And Sunday nights? Reentry is tough."

"Come for class at seven and we'll work together for an hour after that. And Tuesday nights at around this time."

He didn't smile, nor did he thank her. But he nodded in such a way that told her he was serious about this, and grateful.

"Let's go see Mikey up front." She nodded toward his credit card. "He'll set you up." *And if he's in a good mood, he'll probably bust your balls,* she almost added, but didn't.

"Brilliant."

Sidra didn't feel brilliant. She felt desperate. Her cousin's decree had been to drum up business in order to save both of their enterprises. She didn't realize it would mean selling her soul and giving up what was left of her pathetic social life.

"T-SHIRTS! GETCHER ICE-COLD T-SHIRTS HERE!" Seamus would've made a great hawker selling peanuts and beer at Yankee Stadium. He was on fire behind the merch booth in the lobby of Irving Plaza, flattering and flirting with the ladies and making deals with the men. Sidra sat on the edge of the table, making change and people-watching. She had breezed through the venue earlier to say hi to a few friends before the Bold O'Danahys went on, and the room had already begun to reach sweatbox conditions. She could only imagine what it would be like once Anam-Atman took the stage.

"You don't have to stay if you don't want to," Seamus called to her, flipping a medium ladies' tank top up and presenting it with a flourish to a girl who was clearly in denial that her boobs needed a double XL.

"I don't mind." Sidra could hear the muted set from where she was. The band was currently plowing through half of the Irish traditional ballad back catalog, singing a rousing version of "Johnny Jump Up." She didn't need to see Charlie and Evie making music together.

It wasn't that their songs were romantic; the closest the Bold O'Danahys came to a love song was "I Only Tell You I Love You When I'm Drunk," and the only odes were dedicated to the many kinds of whiskey Charlie loved to sing about. No, it had more to do with Evie having a piece of Charlie that Sidra never truly had: the piece that lived on the stage. And now Evie had it all.

Oh never, oh never oh never again. If I live to be a hundred or a hundred and ten . . .

Sidra raked a hand through her thick mane of hair, shaking it out along with all thoughts of the two lovers on stage.

"Girl, you are looking F-I-N-E fine! Whatchu hidin' out here for?"

"Hey, Reggie!" Sidra hopped off the table, tottering on her wedge sandals. She and Charlie shared custody of the six-feet-three teddy bear of a best friend. Reggie's embrace practically swallowed her, but her hug in return nearly knocked him over.

"You should be on the dance floor in those dead-sexy shoes, not hanging with your brother. He's cramping your style."

"Please. I'm the one scaring all the girls away from him."

Seamus laughed. "Take her, man. I keep telling her."

Reggie didn't need to be told twice, nor did he listen to Sidra's weak protests. He was a Wall Street trader by day and a boogying funk machine by night. He never needed an excuse to move. "Let's go get jiggy wit' it!"

Sidra squealed as Reggie practically carried her out into the hot, dark room. "At least get me a drink first!" She let him muscle through the bar crowd three people deep while she hung back, watching Charlie work the crowd. She had to admit, he still had it. Charlie was like a different person when he took the stage. He became everyone's best friend, everyone's protector, everyone's lover. Perhaps that had been part of the problem.

Something icy nudged at her breastbone. "Thanks, Reg." She accepted the clear plastic cup and gulped until she felt the sweet-tart burn. Red Bull and vodka. It was the drink that said Reggie meant business; he planned to dance all night.

They wormed their way toward the front, where the crowd had broken into small clusters. This was normal for a Bold O'Danahys show. There was the usual female pack that swayed with their drinks, staring up at Charlie and hanging on to his every word. Shain, the bass player, had his loyal posse who pogoed and managed to spill beer on everyone, and Justin's huge family was usually off to one side, craning their necks to proudly beam at their drumming wonder. A generic smattering of those Sidra called "Plastic Paddies" formed tiny groups, dancing up a storm with their Guinnesses in hand and singing every word at the top of their lungs. Similar to those who became instantly Irish every St. Patrick's Day, they used a Bold O'Danahys show for a Wearing o' the Green and a Getting o' the Drunk.

And then there were Evie's followers. They formed an eclectic mix: art students, models, hippie chicks in twirly skirts. Frat boys and pierced punks. Guys in suits and lumberjack lesbians. God only knows where she had collected them along the way. She was like the Pied Piper with that fiddle and bow, Sidra thought darkly. Tonight she wore a big fake rose in her hair, its ruby red clashing with her fading russet-dyed updo. A strip of leopard-print fabric was her dress choice for the evening, barely covering her cooch. *Classy.*

The Plastic Paddies glanced suspiciously at Sidra and Reggie as they claimed a prime spot for dancing. "We're making the white folks nervous," she yelled in his general direction.

"Who? *Us?* No!" Reggie had been soft-shoeing to the sound of Charlie's music way before any of these fans had discovered him. Back before Reggie wore a size fourteen shoe, and back when the only instrument Charlie could play was harmonica. The two boys had been friends for twenty-five years. Similarly, Sidra had danced her way through her first *Feis* in Irish ghillies way before any of these posers had even heard of Michael Flatley. While the unlikely pair may not have looked the part, people stepped aside when Sidra and Reggie started to step dance.

Charlie reached down to fist-bump Reggie with a grin before resuming his mad strumming on "The Hero of Happy Hour," a song Sidra was pretty sure Charlie had penned after spending a booze-soaked weekend with her father last summer while she was away on a yoga retreat. Jack's benders made for good song fodder.

Sidra drained her drink and did a good job of ignoring Evie as she aimed her bow at Reggie and winked theatrically. There was no love lost between the pair, but performance was everything. Reg made a 'talk to the hand" gesture in the fiddle player's general direction and grabbed Sidra around the waist. She swung her dark curtain of hair and laughed as they began to move. Fiona deserved a medal, Sidra realized. The expensive black jeans Fi had convinced her to buy, with their signature silver-stitched wings perched above her ass, were dynamite.

Sidra kept her back to the stage as she danced, giving both her ex and his fiddler a stellar view. She loved the silky feel of her handkerchief top gracing her skin as she lifted her arms and all her gold bangles shifted. She and Reggie had the floor on fire when some bimbo from Evie's corner started yelling, "'Ring the Bells,' Charlie! 'Ring the Bells'!"

She was either drunk or she was a troublemaker. Most fans of the band knew Charlie had written "Ring the Bells" for a girlfriend. And not the new one sharing the stage with him. No, he had written it for the one dancing in the crowd. And it had been dropped from the set list right around the time that Charlie dropped Sidra.

"You broke up with him, remember?" Reggie's warm breath was on her earlobe, as if reading her thoughts. The yelling crowd had reached deafening proportions, but it was as if his whisper was the only sound in the room. "He's an idiot, Sid. I love him, but he never deserved you."

Up on stage, Charlie's chin jutted and his eyes betrayed nothing. Evie was playing the modest mouse, with a *Shucks, that little ol' song?* look upon her face. Sidra wouldn't have been surprised to learn Evie had put the girl up to it, instructing her to yell out for the song if Sidra came within thirty feet of Charlie.

"Play it, Charlie! I really don't give a shit," Sidra called between cupped hands.

"This one's called 'Third Stool to the Left,'" Charlie mumbled instead, and Justin counted off the beats. It was a newer song, Dropkick Murphys–style, played at breakneck speed. Sidra felt diminutive as people began to pogo and slam-dance around her.

"Let's get out of here," she hollered to Reggie. "I don't want to be showered with beer."

Reggie parted the crowd like Moses at the Red Sea, providing Sidra safe passage back to the bar where it was at least ten degrees cooler. Fresh vodka–Red Bulls were procured before pushing back out into the lobby to see how Seamus was doing.

"Is that Ravi?"

The lead singer of Anam-Atman was in the merch booth with Seamus, his dark head bent toward Seamus's blond top in serious discussion. Sidra broke into a smile.

Ravi was asking Seamus to play. She could tell by the look on her brother's face.

Anam-Atman's manager was leaning on the table as well. He had waited tables in Sidra's grandparents' restaurant for years before his foray into music management. Now he dressed a bit like a gangsta rapper, or as Seamus liked to call it, an ABCD: "American-Born Confused Desi." Manish had done pretty well for himself, but Sidra would always think fondly of him as the boy who fetched the bread.

"What's up?" Sidra sidled up to Manish and bumped his hip.

"Our drummer got delayed out of town," he answered gruffly. "I remembered Seamus played dhol." Manish's begrudging tone also conveyed he remembered Seamus courting his twin sister, Manisha, incessantly during the summer of 1999.

"What about the merch?" Seamus thought to ask.

"I got you covered, bro." Reggie slid behind the table and clapped Seamus on the shoulder. Charlie was going to have a freak attack when he realized his merch boy was up on stage with the headliner, Sidra thought with glee.

"Our merch guy can help, too," Ravi said. He flashed a dazzling Bollywood smile Sidra's way. "We need you, man."

Sidra saw Seamus flex his left hand, as if already feeling the curved wood of the *dagga* stick in it. "Lead the way."

Sidra waited for the three of them to head backstage before cheering and jumping up and down with excitement. "I'm going to get a good spot up front, okay?"

"Dance your ass off, and dance for me, too!" Reggie called.

It was set change. The house lights had come up, making it easy for Sidra to locate Mikey and Fiona and some of their friends. "No shit?" Mikey exclaimed when Sidra told them of the lineup addition.

While the Plastic Paddies had receded back to the bar and Evie's groupies trouped backstage, the bhangra contingent moved up. It was like Old Home Days for Sidra, seeing school friends and cousins on her mother's side that had turned up for the show, along with neighbors and vaguely recognizable musicians from around the East Village. Anam-Atman was that kind of band, respected by both fans and the industry alike. To be asked to sit in with them was an honor, and Sidra trembled with anticipation, sending out good vibes for Seamus.

The lights went down and the crowd began to chant.

Anam-Atman was a feast for the eyes and the ears. Indian dancers in colorful saris and Bollywood dancers with bare midriffs floated across the stage as Ravi began to sing a cappella over the roar of the audience. Their fiddle player started up, making Evie look like a country bumpkin, and the women really began to dance in a Celtic-bhangra blend of flashing feet and fluid hand motion. Sidra loved the global lineup Ravi had assembled, which included an Asian guy who just smoked on electric sitar and guitar, Sarah, who was straight from County Cork and sang backup, a Jewish fiddle player, and now, as the strobe lights began to flash, Seamus.

Her brother strutted out, beaming from ear to ear. Seamus was still wearing his street clothes: a pair of tattered, faded jeans, Birks, and a Bold O'Danahys T-shirt. And he was whacking the bass side of the dhol with the *dagga*, keeping the beat, while his right hand provided a funky higher-pitched rhythm so fast, making the *chanti* stick a blur. Sidra and Fiona screamed like it was Beatlemania and began to dance. Mikey was doing a crazy dubstep pogo around them as the music heated up.

Sidra closed her eyes, smiling and letting the music course through her. This was her world, her sound track. The fiddle made her feet fly, and the sitar made her heart sing. Ravi was all over the stage, rapping to the crowd, doing call-and-response. His shoulder-length dreadlocks were tucked neatly behind a black bandana, and girls in the audience were already flexing their hands like pincers, ready to catch it when he whipped it off and threw it like he always did when he got heated up.

Sidra twisted her hands, imitating the *mudras* the dancers on stage were gesturing with, when she felt a strong arm around her waist. Shain, the Bold O'Danahys' bass player, began to spin her this way and that, then entwined his fingers with hers, pulling both their arms up in a bridge at shoulder height.

"What, are we going to *céilí* dance in the middle of Irving Plaza?" she hollered.

"Sure, why the hell not?" Shain yelled back, and began to do the traditional jig-step of the Irish folk dance. Mikey and Fiona joined in, laughing, and the two pairs went around and around to the crazy Celtic-Punjabi funk happening on stage.

"Seamus sounds great! I'm so happy for him," Shain confided. "Too bad they don't need a bassist; I'd be all over that."

"Don't let Charlie hear you say that," Sidra warned as they side-stepped together.

"Don't think Charlie doesn't already know," Shain scoffed, and moved to grab Fiona as Mikey came to call for Sidra and they began another round.

Out of the corner of her eye, Sidra noticed Charlie, watching from side-stage. His arms were crossed and his eyes were fixed on Seamus. She trailed her own eyes to where her brother was now perched behind the tabla, a pair of low, lopsided drums similar to a bongo. He used his fingers and the heel of his palm self-assuredly to tap out a complex solo, but you could see the music run through his whole being in the way he moved his shoulders and his head. He was totally in the zone. Sidra flicked her eyes back to side-stage. Charlie was now staring at her.

Fiona was reaching for Sidra now, and they crossed wrists and linked hands, laughing tipsily as they danced and hopped through the rest of the song. Mikey had disappeared and reappeared with fresh drinks, and they stayed front and center for the rest of the blistering set.

"Gimme ten," Seamus called down from the stage after the band played their last encore. "I just have to settle out the merch."

"And you're having a celebratory beer with us, right, *bhaiya*?" Ravi slung an arm around the man he had just called brother. Sidra watched Seamus's eyes, just as dark as Ravi's, widen in response.

"Hell yeah!"

"I need air," Sidra complained, fanning her face with her hands. "Meet me out front when you're done."

The night air wasn't much cooler, but it beat the stale,

sweaty venue. Sidra lingered under the marquee but inched her way off to the side as the smokers puffed into the warm sky.

"Sid, come on!" Fiona called, yanking the door of a cab open.

"Go ahead, I'm waiting for Shay." Sidra gave a tired flip of her wrist. Damn, it was late, and she had had one too many VRBs. She tried not to think about having to face a long day at camp come morning. Lifting her heavy, damp locks off the back of her neck and leaning back against the building, she willed her brother to hurry the hell up.

RICK
ON THE CORNER, OUT OF CONTEXT

RICK HAD FINISHED his sushi twenty minutes ago, and had had it with the conversation ten minutes before that. Thor had insisted they meet the other studio investors at Yama, a tiny basement sushi bar near Gramercy Park. Rick played nice for a while, answering questions patiently, posing for photos when asked.

Being the only musician involved in a music-related project funded by money-making money guys was a bit unsettling. Thor was ass-kissing and talking a little too much about the Rotten Graves Project's current studio trials and tribulations, as if its bandleader weren't sitting two feet away from him.

Rick checked his phone, feigning interest in an imaginary text message before begging off. Handshakes and slaps on the back ensued before he was able to escape up the stairs and out into the humid evening. *Finally,* he thought, and thanked God he didn't have to do bloody boring business like that for his livelihood.

Building a studio from the ground up was exciting, and he was eager to help make a place that musicians would find sanc-tuary, different from the ordinary lockout room. His dollars were going toward customization, dictating what the facility needed on a first-hand basis. Thinking about owning a tiny piece of Manhattan kept his mind off the small chunk of Kauai that bore his name, now sitting empty.

He knew Union Square was somewhere close by, with a train line that would take him back to Adrian's apartment. Taxis were cued up around the corner, but an event must've just let out. People were pouring out building exit doors and into yellow cabs. Realizing he was headed in the wrong direction, he spun on the heel of his shoe to backtrack toward Yama again.

"Oh, hey. Hi!"

His yoga teacher was propped up against the side of the corner building, one knee bent in front of her. The gold bracelets circling her arms mingled with the midnight tangle of her hair as she held it up off her neck to keep herself cool.

"Fancy running into you," he murmured, feeling warmth spread from the pit of his stomach. It was not the customary prick of panic that often originated there, but a much more pleasant, comfortable feeling. "Outside of yoga," he added.

Sidra snorted. "I'm not a cloistered nun, you know." She pushed off with her foot against the brick to approach him. He'd only ever seen her in workout wear, he realized. Tonight, she balanced in impossibly high sandals, and, with tight black jeans, she looked leggy and divine.

"Were you at the show?" She stumbled and reached out to use him to steady herself. Quick reflexes forced his hands under her elbows before he even realized it was happening.

"No, just . . . out to dinner."

He thought she'd pull away, but instead she surprised him by melting a little closer.

Hmm, was Miss Cream Tea a little tipsy? The engaging warmth of her was a nice distraction from the humid Manhattan air.

In the yoga studio, he was used to seeing her arms and shoulders bare. But tonight, something about the way her silky top dipped at her cleavage and its ribbon straps cut across her bronze skin left him speechless. "You look . . . fun." Maybe it was all the sake at dinner, but he couldn't find the words. "Like you're having a lot of fun," he quickly recovered.

"Oh my God, the best!" she gushed, whipping her head back toward the door of the club. She turned to him again, tilting her head. "You." She dropped her palms against his chest in emphasis. "You look *important*, Mr. Import." She eyed his crisp, white dress shirt and loose trousers of black linen. "But I like you in your gym clothes the best."

"Thanks." It was hard to keep the amusement out of his voice. "Likewise."

A side door burst open down the block, and a boisterous blond fellow sailed out yelling her name.

He looked vaguely familiar. Like a fisherman in New York's sea of faces, Rick cast out a line for a memory, but reeled in a blank.

"I've got to go! You're coming to the studio tomorrow, right?" she hollered back to Rick as the bloke draped both his arms around her neck.

"I'll be there," he called, and caught one last smile from her, dazzling him from halfway down the dark block, before she grabbed her companion around the waist and they merrily stumbled away, bumping hips.

SIDRA

HANGING TOUGH

"Lemonade . . ." *Clap clap clap.*

"Crunchy ice . . ." *Clap clap clap.*

"Sip it once . . ." *Clap clap clap.*

"Sip it twice . . ."

Sidra rubbed her temple and sunk a little lower in her camp bus seat. She wished she had had the brains last night to drink lemonade instead of Reggie's lethal speedball concoction. Nothing was worse than doing yoga while hungover . . . except doing yoga with a bunch of children in the hot sun while hungover. The camp day had felt endless.

"Turn around, touch the ground . . . kick your boyfriend out of town!"

Sidra smiled, listening to the chant dissolve into giggles. Charlie was taking his band on the road that night, down to Philly and then on to DC. They'd come back through New York for a week before heading up to Boston and beyond. This thought made the day seem brighter, despite the faint throbbing in her head from dehydration and all the clapping.

"Miz-ess, why aren't you singing along?"

Sidra glanced up at the cute head full of curls that was

hanging over the top of the high bus seat. "I don't know the clapping part on this one, Abbey."

"I can teach you, come on!"

The girl's enthusiasm was irresistible. Sidra swung her feet into the aisle and joined the other counselor and several campers as they ran through the rhyme again. "Lemonade, crunchy ice. Sip it once, sip it twice . . ." Abbey sat across the aisle from Sidra, clapping her small hands down onto Sidra's upturned palms.

Sidra sang along. "Kick your boyfriend out of town —FREEZE!"

She made a crazy frozen statue face, arms up, and all of the girls followed suit, laughing hysterically.

"Again, again!" they begged her until she relented. "You're a good singer, Miz-ess."

"Thank you, Abbey. You too!"

"Do *you* have a boyfriend?" Abbey wanted to know. "Nope." *Kicked that boyfriend out of town . . .*

"My uncle sings good, too. Well, he's not my real uncle, but I call him that. Maybe you can meet him some day. He comes from Hawaii."

"Maybe." The bus was swinging down the gravel drive for its final stop at the Lauder Lake train station. "Hawaii is pretty far away."

"He can sing the Queen's Bone Man Rap," Abbey hollered over her shoulder as she hopped down the bus steps. "Mamma Mia, Figaro! All the parts!"

Just what I need, Sidra thought. *A surfing opera singer boyfriend.*

"Hey, Sidra!" Karen called as her son, Jasper, piled a week's collection of arts and crafts creations—sand-art bottle, tie-dye T-shirt, mysterious spray-painted tinfoil structure—on her like she was his own personal Sherpa. "Mitch is home with Mina today. Want to grab a coffee?"

"I'd love to, but I've got a private session with a client," Sidra called back as she searched her bag for her Metro-North monthly pass. "Maybe next week sometime?"

Private client, she thought, settling into the next padded seat in her daily commute. *One-on-one session with the prof.* The throb in her head was gone, replaced by a pancake flip in her belly.

She hoped she hadn't come off like an idiot in front of him last night, all hyper from Red Bull and fuzzy from the vodka. Not a good impression for a supposed yogini to make. Good thing Seamus had rescued her from that street corner, or she might still be standing there with her hands on his chest. *Ugh . .*

Sidra rolled her eyes at her reflection in the train window. She got a little touchy-feely when she drank, that was all. So what? Mr. Import still had a lot more redeeming to do than she did.

~

"What in green hell are you doing, Seamus?"

"What does it look like?" Seamus punched into his oversize army duffel bag and came up with a fistful of sock rolls. "I'm unpacking."

Sidra glanced in dismay at the disarray that had leaked from his bedroom into the living room. T- shirts that had been packed neatly for the first quick leg of the tour were now taking up residence on the couch. CDs were stacked precariously on the desk, and at least five different pairs of shoes were scattered like breadcrumbs on a trail. She had almost tripped twice on her way through the apartment to find her brother.

"You're exploding." She swiped the pile of jeans from his hands before he was able to deposit them on the floor. "Slow down. No, actually . . . stop. Stop!"

Seamus gripped the zipper of his now-deflated duffel and slipped down to sit on the floor. "I can't go, Sid."

"Don't be silly. It's your time to tour, butthead. Hanging with Anam-Atman every night," she reminded him. More than just hanging. Seamus would be playing every night with them; it turned out their drummer had been more than just delayed out of town. More like arrested and in jail down South for a bag of Viagra and an underage girl in his car.

"I can't leave. Liz is pregnant."

"What?"

"Not by me," Seamus added hastily.

A car alarm whooped outside. Sidra merely stared, waiting for him to go on.

"Kevin's the father, I assume. You know, the guy who lives out west, but he's kind of out of the picture now. She doesn't talk about it. Not with me, not with anyone, really. But her group of friends came in and confronted her, and she's . . . she's going to keep it. I guess it's his, but . . . I gotta be there for her, Sid. I can't leave her in the lurch."

"Shay, she's a grown woman with her own business, her own life. Her choices. It's not your duty—

"I can't just abandon her, Sid!"

Sidra heard his tears as a tremor in his voice; she felt his anger as a memory blew a hole through her heart. She fell to her knees and saw her brother as a boy before her, forlornly clutching his army duffel bag.

While other kids his age were making out their lists for Santa, Seamus was busy circling various sleepaway camps advertised in the back of the *New York Times Magazine*. Year after year he approached their parents with the fervent wish of being allowed to attend, and year after year he was met with opposition. He was too young. The camps were too expensive. Their locales were just so far away. Finally after much bargaining and begging, Seamus got his wish.

Sidra remembered the drive to the Catskills, where Seamus's ultra-nerdy science camp was located. Their parents sang along with almost every song on the car radio. "Just think," their mother had said, leaning over the seat. "This is one of our last road trips as a foursome." The seat belt had stretched comically over her large belly.

"I think we're going to need a bigger car," their father had deadpanned. And they all had laughed, since it was Uncle Sully's Volkswagen Jetta they had borrowed for the ride.

Who had picked Seamus up?

Someone had brought him home in time for the funeral.

"I'm not going," he whispered.

"Yes, you are." Sidra took his hands. "She'll be fine." She didn't want to utter the words, but he needed to hear them. "Women have babies all the time just fine." Her own voice sounded foreign to her, preaching some gospel she knew she didn't believe in.

"You're right. I'm being dumb."

"That's the last thing I would ever call you, you nutball." Sidra kissed his crazy blond locks to punctuate each sisterly sentence. "Now, go decimate Philadelphia." *And Charlie's ego.* "Then conquer the District of Columbia." *And your fears.* "You'll be back up here before you know it."

"But then the real tour starts. Cross-country. And I won't be back till August. A lot can happen in two months."

"But nothing can happen if you sit here, watching the dust bunnies under your bed grow."

RICK

MERMAIDS OF ST. MARKS

Although Rick himself had asked for it, the thought of a private yoga session sent him into heart palpitations come Thursday. His mouth got dry and his palms sweaty as he considered the lengthy questionnaire Sidra had wanted him to fill out before commencing, needing an in-depth medical history, symptoms, etc. He could barely talk about them, let alone commit them to paper.

This isn't going to help, he thought. *I was delusional to even think it would in the first place.* Then he remembered the way she had smiled at him last night on the street. She struck him as genuine, even when they were butting heads the other day. And last night, that smile channeled happiness. Tipsy or no, she had been happy to run into him.

He wanted to show Sidra he was serious about their deal. At lunch, he sent Thor's assistant out to buy him a yoga mat. "What color, Riff?" Mason had asked nervously.

"The most manly, metal color you can find," was Rick's response.

Mason returned with a mat slightly thicker than the ones at the studio, in a slate gray. "The salesperson assured me it was the top pick for men," Mason relayed. "It's longer than average mats, and thicker."

"It's not a penis, or a representation of my penis, Mason!" Rick exclaimed. "It's a ruddy rubber exercise mat. It'll do." Luckily, the rest of the band was in the live room at the time.

He wasn't able to escape their eyes before leaving for the day, however. Adrian had given him the squinty once-over. "Something different about you, mate."

"Bah, go ahead. Pull the other one."

"Just don't start wearing Jesus sandals next. I won't be able to bear it."

RICK DELAYED AND DAWDLED, rambling down Second Avenue, then across St. Marks. His first visit to the East Village had been in the 1970s, and each decade brought more change and less familiarity. His feet slowed as he admired a pair of stone statues flanking the doorway of one building. They'd certainly stood the test of time.

Noting architecture was an old habit, born from having renowned art historians for parents. Ornate caryatids, mermaid-like and legless, looked down upon him. Each figure held the same feminine and timeless pose: One hand hovered near its small stone breast, while the other arm was flung over-head. The hint of humor in their smiles reminded him of Sidra's. With thoughts of her, he let his feet beat out a path toward Houston.

But as he rounded the corner onto Rivington, he began to have doubts once more. Visions of the blond bloke wrapping both arms around Sidra's shoulders from behind and the sound of their drunken happy laughter stopped Rick in his tracks. *Why do you care? What are you trying to prove?* He cursed himself. *Are you trying to achieve inner peace, or just trying to get in her pants? Have you learned nothing?*

The now familiar, but certainly not welcome, tingling began to radiate into his brain stem. *Shit, shit, shit.* It clouded his thoughts and fed his fears, moving up to the tips of his ears and down to the base of his spine, paralyzing him with indecision. Stay or go? Fight or flight? He needed to salvage a good memory, a comfortable thought.

The vinyl.

He moved past the sign blinking *O-P-E-N, open-open-open,* breathed deep, and reached for the doorknob just as it was being yanked from the inside.

"Yo, Fi! I'm cutting out early, gotta head down to Philly." The culprit responsible for practically ripping Rick's rotator cuff didn't acknowledge him, nor did he apologize.

"Mikey say you could?" The girl who Rick had talked to earlier in the week cracked her gum and smiled big.

"Mikey said I stopped getting paid yesterday, so yuh-huh. I guess so."

Rick nodded toward the guy's hard-shell case. "What's your weapon of choice?"

"What?" He grimaced, as if Rick's words were a fly to the face.

"Your axe."

"I haven't heard *that* term since mideighties MTV!" the guy crowed. His laugh was as cringeworthy to Rick as screeching feedback from a stack of Marshall amps. "It's a Takamine."

"Electric-acoustic?"

"Yep." The guy jutted his hips forward in a cocky stance.

Rick gripped his strap, but then remembered there was a flimsy rubber mat on the other end rather than the solid body guitar he was used to slinging. "Nice, mate."

"One of Sidra's followers, I guess?" The guy gestured at the mat. "I could never quite get behind her *that way.*" He gave another cackle, obviously impressed with his attempt at a witty double entendre. "But the view is great, regardless. Have fun, man." And with that, he breezed out the door.

"Ladies and gents," the salesgirl boomed into the store intercom, satire mixed with static, "the ego has left the building."

Rick laughed.

"Don't mind Charlie," she said, off-mic. "He's got a bad case of LSD. You know, Lead Singer Disease. It runs rampant in the East Village."

"Well, I hope it's not catching," Rick said slowly. Could he possibly be a carrier?

"If you experience swelling of your ego, difficulty working well with others, or similar megalomaniacal symptoms, you'd better run for the hills."

Or grab a yoga mat, thought Rick. He gave the girl called Fi a two-fingered salute before ducking down the corridor toward the studio.

The door to the cavernous space was open. Drums were beating a rhythm way too lively to be yoga music. He peeked in, and there was Sidra. She was holding what looked like a pretty complicated pose, on the floor with one leg tucked close to her body and the other bent up so that her foot fit into the crease of her elbow. Her gaze was upward as she gracefully held herself still. One arm was arcing over her head, hand clasping the opposite one behind her head. Like a majestic caryatid come to life. Rick must've been holding his breath, because the sigh that finally escaped was potent enough to announce his presence.

SIDRA

SLOW START

"You're on time." Sidra looked up expectantly. "Did you bring your intake form?"

"One out of two isn't bad." His brow half crinkled, but his voice didn't sound apologetic.

Unbelievable, Sidra thought. *So much for redemption.* "I can't help you if I don't know what's going on. Get it to me tomorrow. Okay?"

"All right. Can I, erm, ask you a favor?"

Already with the favors? "What?"

"Can I store my mat here? I'm afraid it's a bit . . . distracting to my coworkers."

"What are they, Neanderthals?"

"In some ways, yes."

"All men?"

"Oh yes."

"Mat envy. I'm serious," she insisted when he just sputtered a laugh. "Roll that bad boy out."

He wrestled with the straps of his obviously new, deliberately expensive-looking mat until he had it under submission.

Sidra gave it an exaggerated once-over and an approving

smile. "Up there"—she pointed toward the front of the building —"it's all guys. And none of them have the balls to admit they could benefit from a little time on the mat. You're here. And you are attempting it. You're open to it. That's good."

Her words coaxed a broad smile out of him. "But wait. I've noticed a girl behind the register."

"Oh, Fiona. She's like one of the guys. Don't get any ideas about her. She's taken. Very taken."

"Wouldn't dream of it," he said hastily. "Lovely, but . . . not my type."

The words hung in the air of the studio, buzzing with a voltage that vied with the serene vibe of Sidra's workspace. She wondered what his type was. Being a professor, he probably preferred young blonde coeds, or quickies in the faculty lounge. Or he was having a torrid affair with the whiskey bottle, like her father.

"And yours?"

"My . . ." Sidra shook her head. Her thoughts were both racy and fuzzy, and this time she didn't have vodka–Red Bulls to blame. "My what?"

"Your type."

"That has no bearing on your practice."

"Just trying to get to know my teacher." His smile was little-boy mischievous, while his eyes conveyed weariness well beyond his years. "Unless you've filled out an intake form yourself?"

He was either attempting to flirt with her or mock her. Either way, he was doing a piss-poor job of it. On her clock, and on his dime. Sidra crossed her arms and waited.

"Let me take a guess. Blond? Strapping? Prone to public displays of affection on street corners?" Sidra snorted. "With what looks like a killer tan? You've just described my *brother*. Seamus." No one ever assumed they were kin at first glance. "I would've introduced you two last night. But I was drunk. And obviously forgot my manners." She waited for the customary reaction of surprise and confusion, but neither came.

"Your manners were impeccable, if I recall." Recognition lit his eyes. "As were your brother's, actually." He squinted and nodded as a memory dawned. "He thanked me after almost flattening me with his bicycle in Williamsburg last week."

Sidra laughed. "Yeah, that's my brother, all right. Seamus is hell on wheels in all five boroughs. Watch out."

He swallowed hard. Was that a sign of . . . nervousness? Relief? The talisman on the leather choker he wore shifted. Had he been wearing that the night before? If so, her fingertips had just been inches from it when she had teetered drunkenly against him.

Her heart sped up to match the double-heeled drumbeat of the song at the thought of his hands catching her.

"All right, shall we start?" She moved to change the music in the player to something mellower.

"Wait, don't. What is that?"

"They're called Delhi 2 Dublin." Sidra was delighted he'd noticed. She was very proud of her unique Indrish heritage, and happy there was a genre of music out in the world that reflected it perfectly.

He approached the stereo, squatting down near the speaker. "I've never heard anything like it. It's like . . . like a . . ."

"Like a jig and a bhangra rolled into one?" Sidra laughed. "Oh, if only you walked by Irving Plaza an hour earlier last night. You could have heard my favorite band, Anam-Atman. When they play, it's like a dance party."

"It certainly doesn't sound like yoga music." He took the liberty to adjust a few of the tiny knobs Sidra never knew what to do with. Instantly, the song sounded more vibrant to her, more alive. And the wistful smile on his face made it feel like she was hearing the music's magic for the first time. "Your midrange was a little off. That's the heart of the music."

Something tugged inside her. It made her want to move closer, where his fingers were still hovering near the knobs. "Any music can be used for yoga, I think. As long as you like it and it moves you."

"Even heavy metal?" he joked.

"Sure, I guess! It doesn't all have to be birds and waterfalls." She smiled. "I just figure, for the masses, mellower is better." A laugh escaped. "Can you see Gerta headbanging?"

"Which one is Gerta?"

"She was right up front, with the gray bob. Tiny. Guess how old she is?"

"I don't know . . . eighty?"

"Ninety-three," Sidra revealed, watching the wonderment cross his face. "Yoga. Pretty amazing stuff."

"I'll say."

"On that note . . ." Sidra kneeled at the end of his extra-long mat and pointed to the other end. He joined her, sitting on his knees, facing her. "I think you need a mantra."

"Bloody hell. Really?"

"Really. It doesn't have to be anything fancy. People think they need to memorize Sanskrit or pick something spiritual. But all words are energy-based. It can be one simple, meaningful word to help you focus."

He was silent a moment, lost in thought. "One word . . . wow. Sometimes it's harder to extract one word than to blurt a whole sentence of them."

"Exactly."

"I feel like a right twonk." He closed his eyes, and Sidra saw for the first time what perfect dark eyelashes he had. It wasn't something she usually noticed on a guy.

"Come on, I'll do it with you." Heat infused her cheeks at her suggestive choice of words, causing her to hastily add, "Chanting helps remind us we are all together in this process."

"Okay. I'm going to go with . . . dove."

Her heart reacted like it did when Seamus used to practice his marching bass drum in the house. "Dove?" *How?* "Did you say dove?" *How could he know?*

"Yeah. Silly?"

"No." Her word barely made it out past a whisper. She swallowed. "Okay. Let's use dove."

She chanted it softly, stretching the word out. Hesitantly, he echoed her, before falling in unison as she repeated it. She smiled as his voice soon became the stronger of the two. "Feel the vibration?" Eyes still closed, he nodded. "The repetition can be stimulating, yet it can also be calming. And distracting."

Sidra watched the way his top teeth made gentle contact with his lower lip as he pressed out the final consonant of the word. *Distracting, indeed.*

"A mantra forces your mind to think about it, and only it. Leaving less mental energy to think about the things that stress you out."

"It's calming," he agreed. But his hands, curled to tight fists in his lap, weren't very convincing.

She had a feeling he had a lot more going on than what her simple intake form was going to reveal. He needed his head on the mat. Big-time.

"You know Child's pose, right? A great pose for stretching the quadratus lumborum muscles in your back. Prayer stretch is similar. Since you're already on your knees . . ." She demonstrated the pose, talking her way through it. "Rest your butt on your heels, spread your knees wide, if you can, with big toes touching. Forehead to the mat. Arms out in front of you, as far as they can go." She slowly rose to watch him assume the position. "How's the breathing down there?"

"Different."

She gently pressed his shoulders. "Armpits down; drive them toward the mat. I know it feels weird, but it will become more natural as time goes by. Spread those fingers. Wider." He had beautiful hands, she noticed. With long, elegant fingers. *Skilled* was the word that came to mind. Sidra felt a blush creep up under her hair and was thankful her student was facedown, ass-up on the mat.

He's your student. Do not contemplate his ass. Even if he noticed yours.

As if on cue, a jarring ringtone emanated from his back pocket.

"Are you kidding me?" she sputtered as he disrupted his perfect prayer stretch to reach for it. "Gimme that." With her hand firmly on his back to keep him in place, she plucked the phone from his pocket. "You're on my time right now."

"What is this, tough love yoga? At least have the courtesy to tell me who it is."

She noticed he dropped his *h* sounds when he was worked up. "I'll tell you ''oo it 'tis,'" she imitated, glancing at the caller ID. "It's someone named Thor."

Every one of his vertebrae stiffened under her touch. "Then it's very important. Give me my mobile, please."

"I don't care if Zeus or every other Greek god is on the line; no phones in my studio."

"Fine," he barked resignedly, and she felt his back lower in defeat. "Norse."

"What?"

"Thor is a Norse god, not Greek. He's the god of thunder."

"Well, whatever." She silenced the ringer and set the phone aside. "You'd think he's got more important things to worry about, then, than not being able to get a hold of you."

"You'd think so," came a mutter from the mat. It almost made Sidra laugh.

"Okay, let's shake it out. Downward Facing Dog."

She talked him through Dog and into Plank, down through Chaturanga and up to Cobra, then back to Child's pose, reminding him to breathe all the while. It was enjoyable, actually. To work one-on-one with someone and to watch their demeanor change. Mr. Import had been wound tighter than an old bicycle chain from her uncle's shop when they had begun, and she had him stretched on the floor and moving fluidly by hour's end.

"That pose you were doing earlier, when I came in," he commented as he slowly rolled his mat. "That was . . ."

"Mermaid."

He smiled and gave a slight nod, as if she had confirmed something. *If he tries to compare me to Aphrodite or some other goddess of the sea,* she silently vowed, *I'll slug him.*

"Stunning."

Sidra traded him his phone for his mat. "See you Sunday."

RICK

FIRE UP THE CORE

WARRIOR STANCE, Fierce pose, hissing breath, Fists of Fire—it turned out yoga and heavy metal shared a lot of similar imagery. Powerful, primal. Rick moved mindfully, fluidly through the group session. He enjoyed the preciseness, the balance, and the control. Especially when he felt he lacked those qualities off the mat.

Sleep had been troubled and elusive lately. Progress in the recording studio was stalling. The last time he asked Isabelle if the label had scheduled a street date for the album, she'd quipped, "Yeah, right after you shit but before you get off the pot." Her way of trying to light a fire under him, but it wasn't helping. Yoga was quickly becoming the only place he felt like he had license to truly be himself.

"If you're struggling at your edge," Sidra instructed, "don't fight your breath. Soften."

It was a word she used a lot, but he had yet to fully grasp her meaning.

"Soft" had never gone well with heavy metal. "Soft" was the ballad that destroyed his friendship with Adrian and strained his marriage.

No, you wanker. You did that all on your fucking own, with your hard heart and stubborn exterior.

She moved them into a deep forward bend, then instructed the class to clasp their elbows and let their heads hang heavy. "Nod your head yes," she gently intoned. "Now shake your head no." A wave of emotion followed Rick's movements, surprising him. He felt as if he was giving himself the green light and saying "fuck off" to the rest of the world at large. *Fancy that,* he thought. *When was the last time I allowed that to happen?* Tears pricked at his eyes. He was so tired.

Sidra wove her way in between each student, checking their stances, suggesting adjustments and modifications where needed. "If you are holding on to any anger, resentment, fear, or anxiety, yoga offers the opportunity to let it go." Rick had a hard time keeping his eyes off her.

Half-Forward Fold to Plank, Plank to Down Dog . . . He was getting the hang of this. Moving through Chaturanga Dandasana like a pushup and transforming into Cobra. "This is great for strengthening the muscles across your back. The latissimus dorsi."

God, he loved when she spoke Latin. At her bidding, he folded, along with the other participants, into Child's pose.

"Let's focus on some different kinds of breaths."

Sidra had already taught them Ujjayi breathing, with a constricted throat. Otherwise known as "ocean breath," she had told him during one of their private sessions. He liked the thought of the ocean in his breath, and he had even used it with success the night before, when the panic threatened to sift down from the darkened ceiling like a burial shroud and smother him in bed.

His twisted mind had tortured him with the same horrible dream again. In it, he was dressed to the nines; it was his wedding day. He was happy. Simone was waiting for him at the end of the flower- strewn aisle. Dress, veil, everything perfect.

He couldn't wait to get down the aisle to be with her. But his feet moved so slowly; it seemed he'd never get there. He kept stopping, seven times. Then he'd notice there weren't rose petals at his feet. Just a trail of dirt, leading up to . . .

To have and to hold, to love and to cherish . . . till death . . .

That was always the part that wrenched him to waking, back to reality.

"Lion's breath," Sidra was saying now. Her voice sounded sacred, assured. "This is a great one. It may look silly with your tongue hanging out, but no one can see you. It gets rid of tension in the face, and it feels great."

She instructed them to widen their mouths and loll out their tongues. With his head to the mat, Rick could hear his own breath roaring in his ears as he took his first lion's breath. Then another, and another.

He saw himself leaping through the surf of the rolling blue Pacific, scooping up Jonah and sailing him, like the dove of his Hebrew name, high overhead. "Me next, Daddy! Now me!" Rick had deposited his youngest son, dripping, laughing, and fearless, into Simone's arms, and had reached for Ari next. Unlike his twin, Ari was pensive, cautious. The quiet middle child. He, too, had wanted to fly, but once aloft, he was scared. "You won't drop me, will you?"

"Never," Rick had promised, swirling with Ari in his arms as the sea churned below them. "I'll never let you go, my little lion."

He missed his family so much.

"Stay with the breath," Sidra was saying. And she was saying it directly to him, for he had stopped; he was holding it deep within his lungs. "Stay in the present moment," she added as she brought them to a kneeling position and her gaze met his.

～

Y*OUR OLD DOG is learning some new tricks, Simone. My body is learning a whole new language through yoga. Yes, laugh all you want. Roll in your grave, my love.*

My favorite new vocabulary word, I have to say, is scapulae. It's fancy talk for shoulder blades. If Digger and I were to part ways once more, I think I would form a new metal band called Scapulae.

My instructor is very good. She works us hard, harder than I ever imagined I would allow. There are times I'm so grateful for prayer stretch, I feel like weeping. She tells us to let gravity do the work. What a revelation! All this time, it never occurred to me. I've always clawed my way to the top in an attempt to fight gravity. No, to defy gravity. Now, I revel in Child's pose. The feeling of my forehead on the mat humbles me. It's very grounding.

Did you know there's an edge you reach in yoga? She tells us the body's edge is the place just before pain, but not pain itself. And that our body knows to automatically steel itself, to protect us? Apparently, in time, we learn to listen and trust and move ourselves past it. Both mind and body.

I'm quite addicted to breathing now that I know how to do it correctly. How we cheat ourselves of, yet take for granted, the air that's there. It's as heady to me as whipping a crowd of ten thousand into frenzied applause, a quality high no drug can compare to. Sidra —that's my instructor's name—gives us these breaths as a gift. Then she takes them away, telling us to fit our breaths in the spaces left open by the twists, between the knots. Bloody hard, but I spend so much time on my body and my breathing, I forget about the outside world and I truly relax.

She's saving my life. Please don't hate her for it.

⁓

"C*AN I ASK YOU A QUESTION*?"

"Shoot," Rick groaned. They were in Pigeon pose, side by side. It was a grueling hip stretch. When Sidra had first taught it to him, he had likened it to a self-guided tour of a torture rack. *Someone shoot me now,* he had thought. *Put me out of my misery.*

His left leg was out straight behind him, pubic bone pressed to the floor, while his right leg was bent, practically parallel to the top of the mat, beneath his torso. *Who would willingly put their body through this?* But now, as he settled into the pose, minding the bits and bobs, he marveled at how his body had allowed him to take it deeper over time. It was just their third private session.

"Why dove?"

"Come again?"

"Your focus word. Dove."

"Dove," he grunted, propping himself up on his elbows and swaying his top half gently, "is for my son Jonah. It's his Hebrew name."

He gave a small sigh and slowly dropped to his forearms. Just past the edge of comfort. Sidra was a step ahead of him. She had walked her hands out in front of her and practically brought her torso to the floor over the bent knee.

"I love this pose." She inhaled deeply. *"Kapotasana."* With her left ear down on the mat, she regarded him with those bright, intense eyes. *"Kapota* actually means both 'pigeon' and 'dove.' "

There were so many things he wanted to ask her. Like whether that wanker with the guitar and the cheap cracks, Charlie, meant anything to her. And how did she end up here, behind a record store? Who was this girl, beneath all her Latin and her Sanskrit and ancient knowledge?

"Why do you ask?" he questioned instead, lowering his head in increments until he was able to meet her face-to-face.

"Because it's my mantra, too," she replied quietly.

SIDRA

REVERSE WARRIOR

SHE COULD SEE curiosity in his eyes as he tried to unearth more of her secrets with his stare. *Why did I just tell him that?* she chastised herself. *My mantra has no bearing on his practice.* She could've kicked herself for opening up. She would've, had she not been in Pigeon stretch.

It was the type of pose the body just knew when it had had enough and couldn't stand it a minute longer. She pushed up and out of it, back into Downward Dog. He followed suit.

A son. *He's a dad. Downward Facing Dad.*

Sidra shook out her leg in Dog Split and hopped to the top of her mat. Now, with each pose she led him into, she could feel his eyes. It was unnerving.

"Warrior One. Why are you looking at me like that?" "Like what?"

"Like I'm your *drishti.*"

His brow wrinkled quizzically.

"Your gazing point," she supplied. "Warrior Two."

He adjusted his stance and glided his arms into position, but his eyes remained on hers.

"Maybe you are," he murmured, that ghost of a smirk ever-present.

Sidra felt her face heat. This guy needed to back the hell off. "Reverse Warrior," she commanded.

"One line of energy, from fingertip to fingertip." The pose caused him to drop his back arm to his thigh and reach for the sky with the other, forcing his gaze upward. She circled him, checking his alignment, making him hold the position a bit longer than necessary. There was a fine line between enjoying a counterpose and discomfort. But she needed a moment for composure and to recover herself. She struck her own Warrior, straight as an arrow, next to him, wondering who would quiver first.

"Well, find a different one," she finally managed. "I'm not always going to be there for you."

RICK

SHEDDING LIGHT

RICK WATCHED as Sidra patiently and thoughtfully gave modifications to her current pose. She seemed to have memorized every student's ailment or quirk, like the most sought-after waitress in a restaurant could remember how each of her customers took their coffee.

Not that there were many students on a day like today, Rick observed. He had forgotten the sauna- like conditions Manhattan could push to. The climate-controlled recording studio hadn't been a bad place to wait out the heat of the day, but the air had still been oppressive as he made his way down to the not-so-climatically-disciplined yoga studio that evening.

Sidra had the ceiling fans, as well as floor fans, going strong, and the air-conditioning of the old building was churning out a bit of relief. But Rick had noted the concern crossing her face each time the lights would dim and the motors would hum instead of purr.

Her Friday evening Hatha class was gentler and seemed to attract mostly seniors. *And the occasional rogue rocker,* Rick humored himself.

"Do you mind if I . . . Your Dog isn't quite . . ." She was next to him, smelling like mandarin oranges and buttercream frosting.

"Not at all," he murmured, wishing he could see her from the downward facing position he was currently holding. Delicate fingers found his waistline, and with a strength he didn't realize she had, she pulled him higher to God. It wasn't a natural position to be in at all, he marveled, with his arse in the air and the rest of him bent like a triangle, but it felt surprisingly good. And her hands now gently holding his rib cage felt even better.

"Believe it or not, it's a recovery pose," she said breathily, as if she were the one in the compromising position, defying gravity. Rick cocked his head and watched, through shakily supporting arms, as she moved on.

He thought she was beautiful, even down to the star-shaped sweat mark staining her shirt at the small of her back.

The lights flickered once more, and everything in the room seemed to give a dull hum. "Brownout," the lady called Vivian announced. She popped out of her Downward Dog position and calmly began rolling her mat. "I need to get back to Jersey while I still can."

A few others murmured in agreement. "This area is prone to brownouts," Sidra relayed. "If you choose to leave, I understand. But we've already punched cards and are halfway through the class."

"That's all right, dear. Carry on." Vivian gave a wave, a few of her posse following close at her heels.

The lights of the yoga studio continued to burn at the normal dim rate, but Rick noticed the motors of the cooling systems were struggling. He didn't even want to consider how suboptimal voltage could affect the recording equipment. *You're not in the studio,* he reminded himself. *Not in your studio, anyway. Relax.*

The word no sooner came to his head than the room

plunged into darkness. Bleats of surprise could be heard from the few students left. "Careful, everyone. Slowly come out of Dog, recover in Child's pose," Sidra calmly dictated. "It's probably a rolling blackout. This area is prone to them as well."

"Rolling!" An older man huffed. "We're always the first to lose power and the last to regain. Mendez could give a fig about her constituents on the Lower East Side!"

"Less politics, more yoga, Morty." Sidra was trying to keep control of the situation. In the shadow of the few emergency lights, Riff could see her moving through the room with purpose. She propped open the exit door, which allowed natural light to stream in, but provided no relief to the mounting heat.

Like moths to a flame, Rick observed. The majority of the class fled, all eager to get home before Friday's rush hour to check on their own power situations. Only he and Benny remained. Rick only knew the bloke's name because he consistently referred to himself in the third person, mostly to complain about something.

"We can still work," Sidra said slowly. "Let's just take it easy. We can pretend we're in a Bikram class." Rick had no doubt the room temperature was pushing into the nineties, so it was more of a reality than a joke.

"Sid, you okay back here?" A hulking shadow appeared in the entryway. "Freakin' Con Ed. I'm gonna close up. No registers, no AC. I'm dying up there."

"We're good, Mikey. Just finishing a class. You can lock up the front."

The guy, Mikey, turned and gave both Benny and Rick a stare-down before turning on his heel and leaving. Rick was familiar with the type. Lord knows he had had plenty of brawny Irish men working crew for him over the years. *A hardchaw,* he decided. That was the term. He suspected this guy was full of bark and not much bite. He wondered how long the bloke had known Sidra, and felt strangely envious of the way he looked out for her.

"Shall we, gentlemen?"

"Benny's fine with that!" The old man scrubbed his gray mustache with the back of his hand. "I like to get what I paid for," he confided in Rick with a wink, his eyes magnified to almost cartoon character proportions behind thick glasses.

Rick wanted to laugh, or at least catch Sidra's eye and share a private smirk behind the old guy's back. But she was struggling with a long wooden pole, trying to raise the shades on the windows that were easily thirty feet above her.

"Can I help shed some light on the situation?" he asked, hopping up to help her.

"Thanks. Not sure if any of them open as well. You know, to release some of the hot air." She raised her brow, and he figured she was referring to Benny.

Most were leaded glass, stained in hues of beautiful blues and greens that literally took Rick's breath away. They reminded him of the darkest shards of sea glass found washed up from the ocean floor. A shame these windows were covered most of the time, he thought. It wasn't until he backed up to wrestle with the last shade that he realized there were Stars of David in intricate patterns on each one. "This was a synagogue!" he marveled.

"Of course, any meshuggener knows that!" Benny clucked his tongue against the roof of his mouth. "So many old tenement synagogues in this neighborhood. 'Cuz we were here long before your people, missy. Am I right?" He turned to Rick for backup. "My parents belonged to Temple Beth-El. This one had a fire. The congregation rebuilt on Amsterdam Avenue."

"So that explains the *ner tamid*." The look upon Sidra's face told Rick she had no clue what he was referring to. "Your lamp up there. It never goes out, does it?"

Her gaze followed his pointer finger, and she allowed a

slight, baffled smile. "I've never been able to find a switch for it. I figured it was on the same circuit as the emergency exit signs and stuff."

"Gas!" Benny exclaimed impatiently. "It runs on gas. If you could switch it off, it wouldn't be eternal, now, would it? Can we get on with things? Benny's not getting any younger!"

"All right, Benny. Shall we move into Crow?" When the older man balked, Sidra continued, "Let me demonstrate." Within a half minute, Sidra was defying gravity in a move neither man would ever achieve in their lifetime. "From here, it's fairly easy to move into a headstand."

"Whoa, whoa, whoa. Should we try something so advanced, and under these conditions?" Benny gestured around them.

Sidra slowly lowered and righted herself. "You know, I think you're right. In fact, I don't think I should really charge you for a class under these conditions, Benny. Here." She sauntered over to a small table in the corner of the room. "Here's a new punch card. It's my new five-class card. On the house. Or should I say, on the sweathouse?"

"Well, that's nothing to sniff at." Happy his perseverance paid off in spades, Benny rolled up his mat. "You get the power fixed, and I'll be back. None of that Blimblam hot yoga nonsense for Benny."

"Now, what about you?" Sidra turned to Rick.

"What about me?"

"There's twenty more minutes of class. Want to call it quits?"

Rick couldn't read her. "Stone the crows! Time flies when you're sweating half to death," he murmured. That got a smile out of her. "I mean, seriously. No Crow. But I would like to try something less death-defying, more calming. I had a really shitty day at work. But if you're ready to knock off . . ."

"No, no, we can work through our vinyasa," she mumbled. "But you sure you want to stick around? It's going to get really hot in here." She paused a moment, then peeled off her damp top, revealing just a sports bra underneath.

"Really." *You've obviously never played the Cotton Bowl in Dallas during 104-degree heat in leather pants,* he thought. "I'm sure."

As he had suspected, a small silver ring graced her navel. It had a tiny orange jewel dangling from it. *Now* there's *a perfect focal point,* he thought. "May I?" He pinched his own T-shirt, fanning it on and off his damp skin.

"Knock yourself out."

Rick slowly pulled his shirt over his head, suddenly feeling a bit exposed. *God, I hope she doesn't ask about the misericorde,* he prayed. The dagger inked into his chest and similarly into Digger's paid homage to their shared adolescent obsession with medieval weaponry and Nordic legends. His pat response when anyone—from women to other musicians to journalists—inquired about the origin of his tattoo was always a flippant "Never you mind," but he had a feeling he would confess everything to this one.

SIDRA

BODY IN SPACE

HOLY HELL, thought Sidra. *It's a hundred degrees and I've lost my shirt and most of my willpower.* She almost wished she hadn't driven Benny away, now that she found herself alone with the hot prof.

She no longer thought of him as Mr. Import. As much as his attitude had irked her during those first few sessions, she now looked forward to his presence in class. There was something electric about him. Her fantasies had multiplied exponentially over the last week. She'd sneak glances after sending him into a challenging pose, just to observe how his muscle groups handled the strain.

As much as she enjoyed his bare limbs on display, she wondered how he looked out of the gym and in front of a classroom. Did he stand behind a podium and dryly lecture, or was he animated, pacing, provoking his students to think? She liked to believe the latter. She tried to picture him in a faculty meeting in well- fitting jeans and a blazer, still with that ever-present leather choker at his throat. It made her slightly dizzy to think of peeling the blazer off, unbuttoning the crisp oxford he'd be wearing beneath . . .

Now he was shirtless, and she was actually dizzy. *It's got to be the heat,* she thought, turning and retreating toward her mat under the lamp. Eternally burning. *Yep.* She and the lamp had something in common.

"That quote above the bimah is perfect—about yoga being a flame that never dims."

"Above the what?"

"Bee-mah," he enunciated. "The platform where you usually demonstrate. That's called the bimah. I guess like a pulpit in a church?"

She turned to face him. He stood on his mat, curls framing his face. Her face heated at the sight of the heavy-gauge silver rings piercing his nipples. One lone tattoo graced his bare torso; it was a sword of some kind. "You surprise me."

"How so?"

Gee, where do I begin? "I didn't peg you for a religious type."

"I'm not. In fact, *I'm* surprised I haven't burst into flames standing on such hallowed ground." He gave a short laugh. "But seriously. I've felt a connection to this place all along that I couldn't explain. It's mostly the yoga, I think, yet there's something more."

He had the most intense and intelligent eyes. While most people conveyed emotions through their mouths, literally or figuratively through words and facial expressions, this guy spoke through his eyes. Sidra was almost afraid to look into them, and she definitely didn't want to continue this line of conversation any further.

She bent and pulled a burgundy-colored scarf from the basket by her mat. She often used scarves of various colors in her kids yoga classes, especially to teach them about belly breathing. They loved when she would lay scarves over their faces and have them try to blow them upward and off.

"Do you know what proprioception is?" she asked, winding the scarf through her fingers. "No? It's the awareness of your body in space." She moved closer, close enough to ascertain that there was writing surrounding the blade of the dagger on his chest. It wasn't in English, or any language she was familiar with. "Like when I cue you for Table"—she waited while he assumed the Table position —"you know exactly where your knees and hands should be."

Sidra circled him. She smiled as he made the tiniest adjustments to correct himself. He had come a long way since day one. "Let's see that Down Dog again." He arched up, and this time she didn't have to adjust him. "You've got amazing muscle." She gulped involuntarily. "Muscle memory."

"Job perk." He grinned smugly up at her. "Or job hazard."

"Plank," she replied, refusing to return his smile. He rolled his eyes, but obeyed. "And don't forget to breathe."

"Impossible," he managed.

"To forget? Or to breathe? Dog once more." She moved in front of him. "Can you move from there to High Lunge?"

She observed him as he swept a foot through and came up, thighs shaking, arms glistening. In lunge, they were about the same height. "Use that back foot to really ground you. Up, up, up. Nice. But can you stay balanced if you close your eyes?" His dark lashes fanned his cheeks as he allowed his eyes to close. "Keeping you honest," she explained, and reached to tie the scarf around his head.

"Shouldn't I be paying you extra for this?"

"You already are."

He gave a laugh, but Sidra detected some nervous energy.

"Does this make you anxious?"

"No, I'm . . . it's fine."

She was so close to him now, tucking the loose ends of the scarf to secure it. Clichéd fantasies flitted past her, but she refused to give chase and let her imagination run wild.

Move away, she chastised herself. *Stop inhaling him!* He

smelled good, though, despite the stale heat of the room. Like lime and clove.

She touched his shoulders lightly, under the pretense of steadying him. *God, am I pathetic or what?*

She never wanted anyone to touch her when she was doing yoga, and never liked the idea of couples yoga. But around him, she found herself breaking her own rules and wanting to be closer.

"I tried this at a yoga retreat once. Remember, body in space."

"Body in space," he repeated.

"Awkward Chair."

He groaned, but did it anyway.

"Fists of Fire." She took him through several sequences, and even blindfolded, he never wavered. "Tree pose," she said quietly. He shakily attempted to kickstand his right heel to his left ankle, bringing his hands out. Once he steadied himself, he slowly raised his leg higher against his calf and raised his arms high.

"Never against your knee," she scolded. "And those shoulders should be nowhere near your ears." She ran her palms over his bare shoulders to cue them lower. She wanted to explore further, imagining the solid resistance of his biceps as she squeezed them. "Come on, I shouldn't have to correct you."

Her harsh tone of annoyance surprised her, but not as much as the realization that she was annoyed with herself. *I shouldn't want to touch him.*

"Don't keep your breath to yourself," she commanded, taking a step back from her sightless charge. "You've got it. Bind the pose."

She felt his warm exhale as his hands met high above his head. She sighed, longing to melt into him, but as she leaned closer, he almost toppled into her.

"Sod it," he mustered under his next inhale, and she felt a

rush of air as his arms swept to pull her toward him, his lips landing on hers in a decadent crush.

"I always know where your body is in space," he murmured, capturing her top lip in both of his. "I can't get you off my mind, Sidra."

It may have been the first time she heard him say her name, but the flow of it off his tongue sounded ancient, sacred.

Sidra moved to pull the blindfold off him, just as he reached to push her sports bra up. She raised her arms for him. It wasn't the sexiest thing she had ever had to slip out of, but she felt like a goddess under his gaze and his touch. Her hair tickled the small of her back as she arched luxuriously and allowed him to rain gentle, open-mouthed nips down her neck.

God, was she insane? She barely knew him.

Her nipples pebbled up under the nimble caress of his tongue. When was the last time anyone had touched her like this? She ran her fingers down his strong jaw line, savoring the rough scruff before tilting his chin and bringing her lips down to meet his once more. She felt him tremble as her tongue landed on his in a bold, exploring kiss.

Down they went, onto the mat as one, arms tangled languidly around necks. The kisses were less pressing now, more lingering as they teased and tasted each other's skin. She had a crazy urge to memorize his tattoo with her mouth, starting at the tip of it right above his navel. She licked her way up the blade of the knife, only leaving it to flick each steel ring and their captive beads. She had never encountered piercings on a man before, not this intimately. He groaned and bucked up against her.

The thin cotton of her yoga pants and the mesh of his athletic shorts barely provided a barrier, but nonetheless they were a line Sidra allowed fingers to dance upon but not cross. She was on top and she was in charge.

Zero 7 flowed softly from the stereo in the corner. It was one of her favorites: a flowing, soaring melody with lyrics she always thought would be perfect to make love to. But not here, in her workspace with this almost perfect stranger. What were they doing, dry-humping like two horny teenagers on a yoga mat?

She needed to collect herself, gather her head, but his body felt so amazing under hers, those dark eyes pools of serious depth that had drawn her in. She swept down for one last gentle kiss upon his waiting lips, her hair spilling across his bare shoulders. Their sighs and movements had an almost vinyasa-like flow to them, in calm unison, but she knew—no, she feared—how quickly they could lose control if given the chance. It felt way too good to keep it contained for much longer.

"*Savasana*," she breathed, peeling her body away from his and rolling onto her back beside him. "We forgot to end with *Savasana*."

"I didn't realize we were finished," he countered, his breathing rough. She smiled to herself as his fingers found hers and they lay, staring up at the scattering of shadows cast on the ceiling by the eternal light.

"What's that called again?"

"*Ner tamid.*"

She repeated the words, wishing her pulse would settle down.

"Why do we always need *Savasana* anyway?" He closed his eyes and drew a ragged breath. "Hardly seems necessary; wasted time that could be spent on more yoga."

"The body needs this time," she explained, turning so her lips grazed his earlobe. "To understand the new information it's received . . . through practicing yoga."

Sidra closed her eyes, too, needing to contemplate her words and how they applied to this unexpected and not unpleasant turn of events. She liked the feel of his strong fingers, confidently clasped over hers.

"Corpse pose." He laughed. "Gets me every time you call it that in class."

"Why?"

Propping himself up on an elbow, he traced lazy circles around her navel. "I've spent half my life in a different kind of Corpse pose. Traded my soul for a guitar at age seventeen, and the devil made me famous by twenty. Ever since, I've had to fight gravity to stay at the top, to be the big star. I never knew the view was so good from down here."

It took a moment for his words to register with Sidra, but she had already gone into protection mode, sliding out of his grasp. "I—I don't understand. I thought . . . you're a professor, right?"

"What? Good God, no! Why would . . . Oh, because of Paul's ID? I took that first class at NYU on recommendation from my son. He's the professor, not me. Cripes, this is a bit roundabout, but . . ." He sat up, extending his hand toward the one she had pulled away. "I'm Rick."

Sidra snatched her damp T-shirt from the floor, turning away. "Well, *Rick.* I think you'd better leave now."

He sputtered a laugh. "Are you—"

"Seriously. Please go. Now."

A BAND, of all things! Another musician. *It figures,* Sidra fumed. The city streets flared with a hot temper to match hers.

She propelled herself around clusters of people clogging the sidewalk, all slowed to a sluggish pace by the heat. *Another huge ego in tight pants. Not interested.* The endless red light at Houston and Essex had forced her to a stop, but her brain was still reeling full speed ahead. She hammered the pedestrian walk button with an impatient thumb. Seamus had recently told her of a study revealing those buttons as nothing but a placebo, designed to give New Yorkers an illusion of control while the crossing signal just continued its operation as programmed.

"Well, that figures, too," she said aloud, not caring if anyone took her for crazy, ranting on the corner.

Rick—so that was his name—Rick had pushed her buttons something fierce. She had no doubt he was probably used to rolling around half-naked with girls all the time before bothering to learn their names. Well, that wasn't the way she operated.

A professor. God, she was stupid.

It may as well have been her wearing the blindfold tonight.

Out with the briefcase and hipster tweed fantasies. No suede elbow patches or lecterns. Once again, a musician had her heart pounding an uncontrollable beat. A tattooed, pierced, brooding, totally sexy musician.

She recalled his breath on her cheek, the song he had made out of her name.

He had known her name.

I can't get you off my mind, Sidra.

The light was now in her favor, but she stood rooted to the spot, cheeks burning.

RICK

TANGLED UP IN BLUE

THE RAMONES STUTTERED about the number of hours in a day at top volume from the car stereo of the Mini. *'Kin hell,* Rick thought. Twenty-four hours prior, he had had his hands and his mouth full of Sidra. As soft and as intoxicating as the wild tiger lilies whizzing by his window, dizzying him.

How ever was he going to get through the weekend without seeing her, without talking to her? Perhaps the Ramones were on to something. He wanted to be sedated, too. *Put me in a coma til Monday night,* he thought.

Sidra had all but kicked him to the curb last night. Rick wasn't sure if "go now" meant "come back later" or "fuck off don't bother." He thought of a million things he could have done differently, starting with the fact that he could have cleared up the issue of his bloody name from the get-go.

He had lived in a town of less than five hundred people for the last twenty years. Hanalei was just small enough for everyone to know their neighbor and just quirky enough not to care about Riff Rotten or the handful of other famous freaks who sought refuge from their nonsensical notoriety there. And since coming to New York, he had been living in a sort of similar limbo.

Take any given day on the subway. Strangers felt compelled to strike up conversation like they knew him, or chose to inhabit comfortable silence; the looks on many of their faces revealed they knew *of* him. New Yorkers conveyed an aloof reverence, for the most part. When was the last time he had had to introduce himself, cold, to another person? Let alone a beautiful woman in a state of half undress?

Oh, he had fucked up big-time.

"What's got your tongue?" Kat asked, glancing in the rearview. "You're awfully quiet, Riff."

"Didn't he tell you? He's gone all yogi on us," Adrian teased.

Rick had half a mind to give the front seat a kick, wishing it were a direct blow to Adrian's arse instead.

"Are Sheena and Judy friends?" Abbey broke in. "Uncle Riff, do you know Sheena and Judy?"

"I'm sorry, luv. Who?"

"Sheena is a punk rocker. And Judy is a punk. In these songs," she pointed out. "So I wanna know if they know each other."

God bless the Ramones. "I'm sure Johnny and Joey really knew girls like Sheena and Judy," Rick explained.

"And Jackie, too," Adrian reminded them.

"I think that's great," Kat said, her eyes meeting Rick's in the mirror.

"Do you mind if I nip down to the beach?"

"No, go right ahead." Kat was reaching in the cupboard for pasta. "*Mi casa es su casa,* and the beach, too. Dinner in about half an hour."

"Thanks, Kat."

The arc of soft sand was a mere fingernail clipping compared to the vast Polihale beach back home. Still, Rick felt transported the minute he let his toes sink down. Actually, the shape of the lake, with its seclusion of trees, reminded him very much of Hanalei Bay, a smaller beach closer to his house.

He walked to the lip of the water. He glanced left, then right. Alone with his body and his thoughts, he nestled one elbow in the crook of the other and wound his arms into Eagle pose, with his palms meeting in prayer.

Splaying the toes of his left foot in the firm wet sand, he carefully lifted and balanced his right leg before crossing it over his left. He hinged at the hip, bowing to the watery blue horizon. He had never felt so entangled yet so calm in all his life.

And he had Sidra to thank for that.

SIDRA

SNOGGING AND CELIBACY

"Who's going to paint my toes while you're gone?" Sidra pouted, inspecting her brother's perfect pedicure work.

"Jeez, Sid. Go to a professional. Pretty toes are part of your job; I would think it could be a tax write-off." Seamus blew gently to dry the polish. His hands were the steadiest in the household, and he had always claimed the practice, and the vapors, were therapeutic.

Fiona looked out from behind her gossip magazine. "Do me next, do me!" She leaned back on the couch and perched her own bare feet up on the coffee table in anticipation.

Seamus gave her an eyebrow raise and directed a snort toward Sidra. Fiona hadn't exactly played hard to get when they were teens, before Mikey had made an honest woman of her.

"Fuck you, Shay." Fiona rolled her magazine and whacked him for being a dirty dog.

"Hello, *ladies*." Mikey lugged himself through the front door of the brownstone apartment and collapsed, work boots and all, across Fiona's lap on the couch. "Christ, what a day. Dad had me moving ten tons of shit in the back room this after-noon. I don't understand. For a retired guy, why does he still have so much work to do?" Fiona leaned down and laid a kiss on his sweaty cheek in consolation. "Just what I want to see at the end of the day: My cousin down on his knees, servicing everyone. Jesus."

Seamus grinned and went to work threading tissues through Mikey's girlfriend's toes to prep them for polishing. "Sully could've asked me to help. I don't leave for tour again until Tuesday."

"Probably didn't want to risk damaging those talented hands of yours." The rivalry shared between the elder Sullivan brothers, Jack and Sully, had been unquestionably inherited by each of their firstborn male children. Jack had been the scholar; Sully the laborer. Now Seamus, with his Harvard credentials and fragile interior, played straight man to Mikey's crude tough-guy act. "You were needed in the nail salon."

"Sidra, what color is that?" Fiona inquired. "I want it, too."

"It's called Snog." Sidra inspected her hot pink toes. "Don't you love it?"

"*Snog?* Isn't that when you, like, backwash into someone else's drink?" Mikey wanted to know. "Why the hell would someone name their product after that?"

"You're thinking *snarf*, Mike." Seamus rolled the fat square bottle of polish between his hands like a pro. "*Snog* is slang for kissing. Fancy a snog with me?" His dead-accurate British accent earned him a chaste kiss from Fiona and a scowl from Mikey.

Sidra blushed, thinking of her behavior at the studio the day before. Rick's clipped accent in her ear, his lips on hers. She needed to set some better boundaries and make it a new policy: *No snogging with your yoga students.* Maybe she needed to paint that motto on the damn wall.

"Look at Sid! She's got some dirty thoughts going on," Mikey crowed.

"Do not," Sidra countered, slowly and nonchalantly pulling

out the tissue separating her toes and balling it up in her fist. "Quite the opposite. I'm thinking of trying *brahmacharya* for the summer, actually."

"What's that? Like a singles cruise or something?" Fiona arched her back as Seamus went to work on her big toe.

Sidra chuckled. "Not quite. It's like conscious celibacy, to help you harness the energy of your senses. It's one of the *yamas*, like a yoga rule."

"No sex allowed?" Fiona looked alarmed. "What about . . . you know?" She flittered her hand back and forth so rapidly that there was no misunderstanding what she was getting at.

"I guess a concession could be made for that."

"So if Sidra's manning her own boat, it is kinda like a singles cruise after all, Fi." Mikey held his belly and laughed.

Seamus pretended to plug his ears. "*La la la* not listening, happy birthday, not listening to you talking about my sister self-pleasuring."

"Quit, Mikey, you're shaking the couch," Fiona complained, as Mikey had become quite hysterical. "No offense, Sid, but aren't you kinda already doing bra-ma-ya-ya or whatever you call it, now?"

"*Brahmacharya*." It was true; she hadn't been intimate with anyone since Charlie. "It's more than just that. It's . . . I don't know. Gaining a greater understanding of myself, maybe? Sexual impulse is a big drain on your energy. I just want . . . more contentment in my life."

She sat back, grew quiet. Was that what she wanted? She wasn't even sure. What she had felt briefly with Rick was delicious and terrifying. It was so outside of the rules she had structured for herself and all the reasoning she had gathered in order to protect her heart from further damage.

"The hell with the celibate talk. If I were into yoga, I'd be like Sting. All tantric and shit."

"Lovely image, Mike." Seamus propped Fiona's left ankle

over his right shoulder, allowing the fresh polish on that foot to dry unmarred, while he held her right heel fast between his knees to begin work on the rest of her toes.

Between Mikey's narration, Fiona's compromised position, and Seamus's focused gaze, Sidra felt like she was in the middle of the most bizarre porno movie ever. She hopped up and hobbled to the door.

"Hey, Sis, where are you going?"

"Carry on with your Snog. I'm gonna go check on Jack."

RICK
OPERATION HOLY G.R.A.I.L.

"Refrain from getting piss-drunk tonight, please," Adrian requested before handing Rick a bottle of Newcastle. "We've got company coming."

"Wasn't planning on it. Who else is coming to dinner?" Rick glanced around. Over the past few weekends, he had come to know all present company sitting around the backyard patio. They weren't guests; they were Adrian and Kat's extended Lake family.

The chesty one, Marissa, and her husband, Rob. Karen and Mitch, the macrobiotic duo. Leanna, who was a bit of a piss-up and whose other half never seemed to materialize during the regular gatherings. And then there were the numerous children of varying ages, all belonging somehow to at least one or more of them.

"Wait, don't tell me. Another blind date?"

Last week, it had been drinks in town with a divorcée around his age, no offspring. Kat had thought they would hit it off. "She's Jewish and she's a singer" had apparently been the basis of criteria. "Yes, and so is Barbra Streisand," Rick had bristled defensively. "Doesn't mean I want to date her."

Adrian smirked. "The women have apparently initiated Operation Holy G.R.A.I.L. in full force."

"Good God, they've got a code name for it?"

Marissa sidled up to grab a beer from the cooler near the back door. "Get Riff Amazingly, Intensely Laid. That's our mission."

"You should choose to accept it," Leanna supplied.

"Totally Abbey's idea." Marissa twisted the beer top off in the hollow of her thumb, her nails curling like raven's claws. "Well, not the verbiage." All heads turned to the children, who were innocently turning cartwheels on the lawn.

"All she wants is to be a flower girl, and for you to have a date for the wedding, Uncle Riff." Adrian grinned. "She's got her eye on one of her camp counselors for you."

Rick pictured a nature girl, bare feet and a guitar, leading a group through a rousing rendition of "Kumbaya." Flowers in her straight blond hair. Freckles on her nose. Twenty years ago, she may have been his flavor of the day. But not now.

"I've got some single gals in the city office, Riff. I'd be happy to introduce you to some," Mitch offered a bit too eagerly and lasciviously. Karen's husband reminded Rick of the hangers-on backstage, just waiting to be thrown the groupie leftovers.

"Doubt he needs your help," Rob deadpanned. "These dudes were probably drowning in tail back in the eighties. Am I right?"

Neither Adrian nor Rick refuted the statement, causing Mitch's eyes to grow saucer-wide.

"What's it really like, being a rock star?" he asked.

Rick gave him a dark look. "Close your eyes and imagine all the women you've ever slept with."

Mitch obeyed. "See them all?" Rick asked. Mitch nodded. "Yeah? I wouldn't touch any of them."

"Riff!" Adrian scolded, but he was snickering as well.

"Ignore him, mate. He's taking the piss." Mitch smiled slowly, a bit unsure whether he was in on the joke or the butt of it.

"Well." Rick tipped his head in the direction of Karen, who was nestled under a tree in the far corner of the lawn and quietly nursing her youngest. "Except for your lovely wife . . . *if* she were single."

Mitch's smile took on a frozen, pasted-upon look. The women quickly intervened. Plates were shoved into Rick's hands, and Mitch was put in charge of rounding up the kids for dinner.

"Behave," Marissa warned Rick. "Robbie, keep an eye on them while we grab the rest of the food from inside."

"Here's Kat with Gloria now." Adrian raised the barbecue tongs in greeting as Kat rounded the side of the house with a platinum blond bombshell. "A friend from her Columbia library school days."

"G-l-o-r-i-a," Rob breathed. "Hot damn, why can't the school librarians where I teach look like that?"

Rick kept his eyes down, setting the plates on the table with calculated nonchalance. It turned out yoga wasn't the torture chamber he'd thought it would be. No, it was surviving these suburban weekends with his self-dignity and discipline intact. These setups were a form of emotional waterboarding.

"Rick, I'd like you to meet Gloria. She's the head of research for the New York City Landmarks Preservation Commission. Gloria . . . this is Rick."

Kat's friend was beautiful, and no doubt had a brain to go with the beauty. Like Rob's had, Rick's brain summoned up the old classic Van Morrison song proclaiming her name . . . before allowing it to mutate into the far dirtier Jim Morrison version involving her legs and his neck.

But it was Sidra he wanted to do those things to. He remembered her hair upon his skin and her kiss upon his tattoo with trembling clarity. It took all of Rick's resolve to politely smile and say hello, when all he wanted to do was hightail it down to the Lower East Side and drop to his knees under Sidra's gaze, beneath the glow of the *ner tamid*.

SIDRA

STANDING IN MOUNTAIN

Sidra gazed upon a room full of closed eyes. She had her students sitting as straight as possible, focus in, and rolling their shoulders up, back, and down. "Now roll them in the other direction," she instructed softly. The last spot of the middle row, the place she had come to think of as *his*, was vacant.

Rick.

His name had been on her tongue all weekend. At odd times, she almost caught herself saying it aloud. While brushing her hair, while teaching the kids how to do Gorilla pose in class. While making change for the record store customers. While rinsing empties and ridding her dad's apartment of them. While closing up last night, after he didn't show up for class or his session. And this evening, as she unrolled her yoga mat under the *ner tamid*.

The door clicked closed. She hadn't realized someone had even opened it. Rick strode briskly to his spot, as if heir to the throne.

A mixture of resentment and shame flooded Sidra. *Don't even give him the satisfaction,* she thought. *Don't even look his way.*

Teach your students. He's just another ten dollar bill. Cha-ching. Eighteen students, three classes tonight. $540 more than she had yesterday.

But she couldn't think of her students like that. She enjoyed teaching them. Even crotchety old Benny. If anyone had an ache or a pain, she wanted yoga to have eased it by session's end.

"Continue focusing on your breathing, keeping your eyes closed." *Coward.* It was easier for her to face Rick if he couldn't look back at her. But she knew she couldn't keep the eyes of her entire class shut for the duration. "Take a minute to place your hands on any part of your body that needs work today. Any spot you want to pay particular attention to."

"I don't have that many hands," Vivian piped up, and titters of laughter could be heard from all around.

Sidra watched as her students placed hands on shoulders, on spines, on knees, and on hips. At last, she allowed herself to steal a glance at Rick. *Oh God.* He had a hand up, those long, strong fingers gently resting above his heavy brow. His other hand, closed in a half fist, was pushed firmly against his chest. His eyes, like everyone else's, were closed. Not squeezed shut, but the look on his face expressed a fervent wish for peace in his head and his heart.

Sidra knew the feeling well.

"All right. Table." She gulped. She no longer wanted to gaze upon any of their faces. Or see their hands as indicators of where their weaknesses lay. She was going to work them hard and get through this hour as best she could.

"Best class yet!"

Sidra smiled, thanked those who came up to express themselves as they shuffled out the door.

Three new students, women in their early forties with colorful Gaiam mats and sleek ponytails, vowed to return and to bring their friends. Sidra had been able to tell from their movements in class they were fairly practiced, yet now, with their cheeks flushed and eyes sparkling, she knew they were converts to her method.

They peppered their praise with questions about a particular song she played, a pose known by another name, and whether she sold gift certificates. She immersed herself in the conversation, enjoying the fleeting barrier it provided. She could feel Rick's presence still taking up energy within the room.

"Ten-class punch cards are available up front with Fiona." She scooped up a stray foam yoga brick from the floor and gave a wave to the last of them. "See you."

"You've got quite the fan club," she heard him say. "You deserve it."

Ignoring him, Sidra tossed the brick into the basket. In her mind's eye, she saw herself throw it at his head instead. *You deserve it.*

She had been about to roll up her mat, but thought better of it. Calmly, she closed her eyes and stood in Mountain, her back to him. Maybe he would get the hint and leave.

"Are we going to talk about last week?"

Rick's words produced an effervescence that radiated through her core, and heat rushed to all the places he had lingered upon Friday night. She took a deep breath. *Stillness. Stillness leads to clarity.*

"Because it wasn't just some whim, some cheap thrill. And I wouldn't have done it if I didn't think you wanted to just as much."

Stillness, strength, power. Sidra took the pose as active as she could, aiming for the immovable stability of mountains that the pose was named for.

She heard a gusty sigh rake from his throat; he was in front of her now. If she opened her eyes, if she saw the tangle of curls that always fell over one temple, the squint and furrow of that dark, defined brow as it focused his intense gaze upon her, she knew she would crumble and dissolve on the spot. She sensed how close he was; close enough for her to effortlessly raise a hand and trace the contour of his cheekbone down to his stubborn jaw line and over to those full, fierce lips and down the scratchy-soft stripe of scruff on his chin.

"How can you just stand there, doing nothing? Saying nothing?"

Sidra's eyes flew open, her face instantly matching the look of defiance he wore on his. "I am doing *everything* right now. *Tadasana* is not just standing," she pointed out. "My toes are spreading the mat apart. My thighs are inner-spiraled. My shoulders are set upon my back, and my muscles are hugging my arms. My fingers are wide, my abs are engaged. My chest is collected." She watched as he took every detail as an order. "Skin to muscle to bone. It's a very active pose."

And it took all of her concentration; she was doing everything to keep herself from thinking about kissing him.

His stance now mirrored hers, and she felt the energy radiating out from him. "The crown of your head is reaching to the sky while your feet are pressing firmly in the earth. You may think you're still, but you are moving," she said softly. "Do you feel it?"

He was as rigid as any mountain, until he tilted his chin to catch her gaze. "Is there a fancy yoga name for what I'm feeling?"

It was as if his mere glance released her from one spell, yet trapped her in another. She stepped into his orbit.

"It's called dynamic tension," she breathed, her lips resting on the hollow of his throat, right above that ever-present rope of leather. A sigh escaped from him as he leaned into her touch, but his feet remained rooted, arms outstretched from his sides with his palms up and fingers wide, as if offering himself wholly up to her.

She gave him a shove, surprising him as much as herself.

"Bloody hell, what was that for?" he swore, stumbling back a foot.

"If you were truly in *Tadasana*, you wouldn't move when I pushed you. Like a mountain." She could feel her pulse hammering in her neck, her face heating up.

"What's your problem with me, Sidra?"

"I don't date musicians."

He folded his arms across his chest and cocked a brow. "And I don't date yoga instructors. So why don't you stop teaching yoga?"

"That's like," she sputtered, "that's like asking me not to breathe!"

Rick bit back a smile. "Exactly." He ducked down and caught her bottom lip between both of his.

"The mountain's not going anywhere this time," he chided, grabbing her wrists to keep her from shoving him again. "In fact, the mountain will wait for you. It's got all the time in the world."

Another kiss was stolen, but under mutual acquiescence; it wasn't clear who initiated it this time around, and Sidra no longer cared. It felt so good. Too good. The rhythmic thump of the time clock could be heard from behind the door, signaling the arrival of her students punching in for the next class. She pulled back just as he decided to be the one to push away this time.

"See? Dynamic tension at work," she managed.

"Well, then. We'll just have to get away from work, now won't we?"

RICK
ROCKS AND HARD PLACES

No wonder I haven't been out here in ages. The traffic out to Brooklyn had moved at the speed of sloths, cramping Rick's long legs within the confines of Kat's borrowed Mini Cooper, and now it had taken him a dizzying walk through a labyrinth of graves to try to find the Banquet family plot.

This isn't about your convenience, he reminded himself as random raindrops began to darken the path and decorate the tops of the tombstones. *This isn't about your comfort at all. It's the least you can do.*

The early summer shower turned to a soaker just as he spotted the pink granite marker in a sea of white and gray. He stopped in his tracks, eyes falling out of focus for a moment. The only thing that kept him tethered to the here and now was the cool drench, plastering his shirt to his skin. He felt the material strain and shrink with each breath he took. *Focus. Breathe. Walk.*

It took him seven small steps to reach Simone's grave. He remembered the seven pauses the processional had made, from hearse to burial site. Simone's parents had insisted on a traditional service, and who was he to object? Seven times they halted at the rabbi's signal, the pallbearers shifting their weight, friends and family shuffling to a stop, his young sons bumping into his knees and stepping on his heels in confusion. "Why, Dad?" Paul had asked him. "Why are we stopping?"

"To show our reluctance," Rick had explained. "Our unwillingness to end the service." When all the while, he'd wanted to break away and run, far from this place he had no connection to. Simone didn't belong here. She wasn't in that box that rocked and paused, rocked and paused, seven times.

Heading toward a hole of fresh-dug earth.

Now the rain pooled and dammed at the soil close to the stone, beating the grass down. Fourteen years had manicured the spot to blend into the landscape, generations of deceased resting eternally under perfect and level terrain. Not like that day, when the precarious gap in the earth accepted the wooden casket. Rick remembered tossing the first shovelful of dirt, balancing it on the back of the spade before heaving it in. Another tradition. Another reluctance. Each mourner one by one, even the twins, took their turn. There was no noise in the world quite so forlorn as their shovelfuls of dirt and rocks hitting that casket. It sounded so hollow.

Simone wasn't in there.

After the service had finished and the crowd straggled away, Rick had grabbed a waiting shovel once more. Side by side with the gravediggers, he heaved in pile after pile, returning the earth from whence it came. He worked until the calluses on his hands bled, his sons sniffling stoically by his side. He worked until he could no longer see wood. And he worked until he no longer heard that haunting, hollow sound.

Fourteen years, but I still can't shake the hollow feeling inside.

As quickly as the rain came, it ceased. Rick glanced up. A short shuttle bus had pulled through the cemetery gates, and a group of senior citizens was slowly dispelling in various directions from its doors. Like homing pigeons, they navigated their way to the resting places of loved ones. Some with canes, even one with a walker. Many were spry and sure-footed, but he noticed they slowed their pace as they approached their destinations.

Rick reached a finger out and traced the engraving of his wife's full name.

I always thought it would be me. What kind of God out there would take you first?

He watched as the old folks from the shuttle bus began to pull small stones from their pockets and purses and place them on top of their loved ones' graves. More eternal than flowers, lasting as long as love and memory.

Bugger. Rick patted his jeans pockets and came up with a money clip and two guitar picks. What exactly did that say about him? That fame and fortune were always at the forefront of his mind, and honoring family, an afterthought? He searched the pristine, soggy grounds in vain for a stone.

Spying a flat rock nearby, he reached to pry it up. It turned out to be deeper than he had realized. He leaned his weight in, mud sucking up the sides of his motorcycle boot. His legs twisted and down he went, arse first, in the wet grass, his shoulder smacking against the unyielding curves of Simone's headstone.

Talk about being caught between a rock and a hard place. The thought coaxed an exhausted laugh out of him.

"Oh my dear. Are you all right?"

An elegant older woman leaned over him. She looked familiar, in that timeless beauty sort of way. She wore a hair scarf to protect her russet hair from the elements, like a movie starlet riding in a convertible would.

Rick pushed himself up and out of his predicament, careful not to spatter her with mud. The rock he had been trying to free was like a tectonic plate, still moored to the earth and much larger than he had assumed.

"Here, dear. I have extras."

Jeweled rings and smooth nail polish graced her knobby, wrinkled fingers, and her touch was tissue-soft. As she placed two small stones in his hand, he finally placed her. Vivian. She was one of the women in Sidra's beginners class. Whether she recognized him outside of class was debatable. With his long hair loose and clinging wet to his face, he hardly looked Zen.

"Thank you." Rick carefully set them on the top of the smooth granite, one from the boys and one from him. He tried to think of a prayer or a good thought or wish. Words swirled in his head, but nothing intelligible formed.

"Simone . . . *Zichrona livracha*." She must've interpreted the crumple of his brow as puzzled. "That's what it says right there," she added. "'Of Blessed Memory.'"

Other than the pink color, which was chosen by the boys for their mother, Simone's parents had made all the decisions about the headstone. Had Rick not been so numb at the time, he may have opted for a different saying.

She patted his hand. "May her memory always be a blessing to you."

Rick nodded and mouthed his thanks. But in the hollow space inside him dwelled the unspoken truth: *If her memory is supposed to be a blessing, why do I feel cursed?*

SIDRA
BIG REVEAL

"Trivia time," Sidra called across the store to Fiona. It was a common way for Revolve Records employees to pass the time when the store was devoid of customers and no one felt like restocking shelves or rotating displays. It was hard to restock when product wasn't moving.

"I'm in!" Fiona was like a human jukebox, and always up for a challenge. Sidra surmised that resilient trait applied to all aspects of her life, since she had been Mikey's girlfriend for eight years now. She earned extra brownie points for working with him, too. "Dead or Alive? Or do you want to play Cover or Original?"

"How about naming all the artists you know named Rick?"

After yesterday's encounter, Sidra had been unable to think of much else. She still felt his pounding pulse point on her lips, where she had rested them against his neck. She was crazy for even entertaining the idea of getting involved with a student, let alone another musician, and yet . . .

"With or without a *K*? Or both?" Fiona asked, clearly in it to win it. She had yet to notice the madness behind Sidra's methods.

"Gee, I don't know. Both, I guess. As many as you can in five minutes." Mikey had just left on a late lunch run down to Lucky's Famous for burgers, and Charlie was in the back room sorting merch for the road.

Fiona began rattling off names like nobody's business. "Rik Emmett, Ric Ocasek, Rick Savage, Rick Allen . . . um, Rick Derringer. Ricky Martin! Rikki Rocket—does that count?"

"Sure."

"So what game am I paying you girls to play today?"

Damn, Mikey was back. He plopped a sack down on the counter and pulled a fistful of French fries out.

"Guess the name of the hot guy in Sidra's yoga class," Fiona said nonchalantly.

"Fi!" Sidra sputtered.

"Well, isn't that what we're doing? Oh, oh, I got one!" Fiona hopped up and scurried down the main Pop-Rock aisle. "How about . . ." She pulled an album from the bin and danced it back and forth between her airbrushed nails. "Rick Springfield?"

"No way." Sidra gave an embarrassed laugh. "Anyway, five minutes are up. Game over." She grabbed a stack of albums from the rack next to the listening station and moved to shelve them. It had been a silly undertaking, anyway. Who's to say this guy was even a household name? Any yahoo with a guitar these days called himself a musician. Then again . . .

The devil made me famous by twenty, he'd said. Her fingers gripped the pile of records to her chest, and she wondered if any of his music could possibly be here in the store. The thought made her heart pound.

"Here ya go." Mikey held his half-eaten burger in one hand and a cardboard sleeve in the other. "Rick James."

"Mikey," Fiona scolded. "You've seen the guy. He's not black."

"Or dead," Sidra added, laughing.

"So who's the guy Sid's getting all superfreaky with?" Charlie had emerged from the back room, apparently having eavesdropped on the entire conversation.

"Mikey, his credit card!" Sidra exclaimed, completely ignoring Charlie. "You charged him for an unlimited month. Do you remember the name on the card?"

"I remember a Platinum freakin' Am Ex." Mikey pulled a manila envelope from the drawer beneath the register. "Go nuts."

Sidra pulled the sheaf of curling credit card slips from the envelope. It didn't take her long to locate Rick's; his was the only twelve-hundred-dollar transaction in the bunch. She expected a signature that was doctor-on-prescription-pad-worthy in terms of its illegibility, but he had signed in a neat, left- slanted scrawl:

Richard Rottenberg

She committed the name to memory before sliding the receipts back where they belonged. Apparently her cousin, who had been looking over her shoulder, had, too. He was on the Internet in a flash. "Oh my God. No fucking way." He began to hee-haw loudly.

"What? Come on. I hope you choke on your burger."

Mikey stopped laughing long enough to make his way over to the Metal section. Apart from some early Megaforce pressings of Metallica's first album and several used Iron Maiden imports, not much moved from those bins.

"Here's . . . Rrrricky!" her cousin said in his best Jack Nicholson, poking his face out between two horrid-looking album covers.

Fiona marched up and grabbed one. "Corroded Corpse . . . lovely."

I've spent half my life in a different kind of Corpse pose. Sidra heard his words in her head as clearly as he had uttered them the night of the blackout.

"Corroded Corpse? There's no way Riff Rotten is hiding out in Sid's yoga class." Charlie laughed. "Although it does say here"—his finger traced along the monitor screen—"there's a new album in the works this year, and it's being recorded in New York."

Sidra accepted the albums Mikey and Fiona handed her. She paid no mind to the gruesome graphics, rife with flames and blood splatter. She inspected the photos on the back cover and inside sleeves. She couldn't reconcile any of the ass-clowns posturing in the pictures with the soft-spoken and eloquent student who knelt on his mat and awaited her instruction. Who shared her same mantra and who kissed her with such passion and reverence that it made her want to weep.

"Hell, Sid, you'd better wear a full-body condom—no telling how many skanks that guy has slept with," Mikey warned.

"I'm not having sex with *anyone!*" Sidra announced, right as the door jangled and Evie walked in with Seamus in tow. An amused but sympathetic smile played on the fiddle player's lips, but she said nothing of Sidra's outburst.

"Vaniel Day Lewis is packed and ready to roll." Although he had hoped for a tour bus, Seamus had willingly adopted the fifteen-passenger Ford Econoline the band had procured through Reggie's uncle last week. Good thing, since Charlie had appointed him primary driver.

"Don't forget the two Gildan boxes in the back, okay?" Charlie gestured but didn't take his eyes off the computer screen. Seamus gave his sister's shoulder a squeeze as he made his way toward the back room.

"Holy balls," Mikey exclaimed. "Look at the size of his"—Sidra took the bait, glancing backward just as he finished—"Wiki entry."

"Har har."

"Made you look!"

"What are you, five?"

"I know you are, but what am I?"

Sidra stuck her tongue out at Mikey. He retaliated just as he had since they were in grade school, by thrusting his hand toward her chin in an attempt to make her bite her tongue. She ducked away and went to help Seamus with the front door, since no one else was making a move to do it.

"So."

"Sew buttons on your underwear."

Sidra smiled at Seamus's retort. The Sullivans all seemed to be stuck in retro mode today. "So, what are your intentions?"

Seamus rolled his eyes at his sister. "I assume you don't mean auntie intentions."

"Nope. Gimme some good old-fashioned yoga intentions."

Like many yogis who set their intentions before their practice, the Sullivan children had been encouraged at a young age to be mindful and present and to choose words to lead them through their days. In this case, Sidra was referring to Seamus's summer on the road.

"Creativity. Positivity. Openness."

She hugged him tight, her fingers falling on his damp-from-the-shower curls. "Those sound great, Big Brother," she whispered. "Proud of you."

"Love you, Sid."

"Love you, too, you nutball. Text, call . . . I'll be here."

There were classes to teach and iguanas to feed, after all.

Sidra glanced over Seamus's shoulder and spotted Mikey in the window, rubbing the LP cover over his chest in mock ecstasy as if he were in some porno. She bit her lip to keep from smiling. Staying in the city this summer might not be so bad, after all.

RICK

DISCORD AND RHYME

"So this is the velvet rope club of Lauder Lake, then?" Rick took in the neon décor with a roll of his eyes. "Sergeant Pepperoni's Karaoke Night."

Adrian cracked a smile. "What did you expect? Neal Kay's Bandwagon?"

Rick snorted at the mention of the infamous club, just a back room in the North London pub where Corroded Corpse rode the New Wave of British Heavy Metal like conquering heroes back in the eighties. It was postage stamp–size in relation to the arenas that followed over the next decade, but unarguably one of the most prized pieces within their collective memories.

Never forget your roots, as their former manager, Wren, had always reminded them.

Even as he had been kicking them to the gutter.

Adrian led Abbey by the hand through the vestibule clogged with impatient families: adults who looked as if they had already had one too many slices of pizza pie in their lifetime, prodding at their whinging children.

Rick found himself automatically falling into the old habit

of scouting mode, as he did in most unfamiliar social settings. He looked for the hottest female in the place and imagined having sex with her. It brought a strange comfort to him, even though he had no intention of going home with someone that night. Sidra was all he wanted.

A knockout brunette stood near the hostess station with a group of girlfriends. Rick recognized the group's behavior: lots of teeth flashing, hair flipping, bursts of laughter at seemingly nothing. *Here comes the turn,* he thought. And sure enough, she flicked her eyes nonchalantly over her shoulder. Eyes that were, as it turned out, strictly for Adrian only. They zeroed in on his left hand, the one that happened to still be grasping Abbey's. Her smile got hopeful, huge.

Rick knew the type. A woman got to a certain age and stage in her life where the sight of a man tending to a child was sexier and more appealing than a guy in a hot rod with no strings attached. Abbey was a chick magnet, he realized. And Adrian was either ambivalent or oblivious. The woman kept smiling at Abbey, clucking her tongue at the banter between apparent father figure and angelic child.

Banter, ha. More like relentless bargaining by Abbey on why she needed a second dinner of pizza. She'd make a fine attorney some day, Rick thought, with her single-minded quest for pepperoni and justice. He stood back and watched as the eight-year-old ruthlessly pursued her goal of wearing Digger Graves down.

Adrian and Rick had been in charge of dinner for Abbey while Kat spent a girls' night out with friends. The guitarists had grilled steaks earlier; spent the day marinating them, in fact. And when Adrian suggested they take Abbey for an ice cream in town, Rick had been game. It hadn't exactly been Rick's idea of a rockin' Saturday evening, but he was along for the ride. Now, as they threaded through half the population of Lauder Lake, Rick wondered if Adrian's next suggestion of "popping in on the girls" was just a clever ruse for another disastrous blind date situation.

"Come on then, let's at least find your mum. Shall we?" Adrian pushed Abbey by the shoulders past the clogged bar and into a side room.

It took a moment for Rick's eyes to adjust from fluorescent pizzeria atmosphere to the darkened space, peppered by strobe effect lighting and a long-suffering disco ball slowly revolving overhead. The karaoke PA system assaulted their ears with an "in the style" version of Green Day. Rick, cursed with perfect pitch, winced and longed to adjust the treble and bass knobs.

"Hi, guys!" Empty beer pitchers rattled as Kat pushed back from the table to greet them. "Fancy meeting you." The kiss she granted Adrian was short but sensuous, and probably far steamier than Sergeant Pepperoni's was used to.

"We were down the road for ice cream, drawn in by your siren song," Adrian said, grinning. Kat gave him a playful shove.

"Lizzie's up next, check her out."

Abbey bear-hugged her mother around the waist, eyeing the metal tray of half-eaten pizza on the table behind them. Rick raised a hand in greeting to all present and blew a sigh of relief. Besides the ginger channeling her inner Billie Joe Armstrong up on the stage, it appeared to be only the chesty one called Marissa and Leanna, the sarcastic one, out with Kat tonight.

"Double Jack, please," he called out to the passing waitress. It wouldn't hurt to have reinforcements, just in case Kat and her friends decided to bring in some of their own during this Holy G.R.A.I.L. quest.

"Woooo, go, Red! Ain't she great?" Kat wolf-whistled.

"Methinks your ladylove is blotto," Rick observed.

Adrian grimaced. "Let's see . . . First she had to change our wedding date because *someone* had a conflict. Next she had to change the locale because it turns out Natalie won't step foot on

Manhattan soil after 9/11. And she's been doing all the legwork because I'm locked in the studio all week, every week. So I think she deserves a drink or three."

"Could be worse. Isabelle could be her wedding planner."

"Bite your tongue. And by the way . . . the new date is August 17. At the lake. So pen that into your busy social calendar, okay?"

"Noted."

Rick turned his attention toward the stage. Liz wasn't half-bad, actually, although "Boulevard of Broken Dreams" wasn't exactly a song known for its challenging range. She had the moves down. There was something stoic tonight about the otherwise freewheeling party girl; Rick knew she was the only unmarried one in the bunch, and most recently had been in a long-distance relationship with her high school sweetheart, Kat's brother, Kevin.

She was also the only girlfriend they had to import back from Manhattan to hang out on a night like tonight. He had met her on several occasions; she was Kat's concert buddy when the Rotten Graves Project played live, raging just as hard as Kat from side-stage. And he and Rick had popped into her Manhattan eatery more than once on a break from the studio and ravenous.

Liz swayed to the beat, marched in place. Beneath the fiery red fringe of her bangs, she let her eyes rest on no one. Repeatedly, she let the hand not gripping the microphone rest near her abdomen while singing about walking alone. *Was she—*

"She's pregnant," Adrian murmured at close range. "Kat's furious with her brother."

Rick recovered quickly. "Has he pulled a runner?"

"Not exactly sure what's going on. The ladies confronted her at the Naked Bagel a while back; she had been MIA and they suspected something was up."

"Speaking of the ladies . . ." Rick glanced around, causing

Adrian to laugh. "They're not plotting to shanghai me here with another blind date, are they?"

"Not to worry, mate. I think they're only interested in getting their drink, and their tunes, on." He perused the karaoke schedule. "Pity. Looks like the playlist is totally full. No time for us to steal the spotlight, I reckon."

"Very funny. Look, I've been meaning to ask . . . Could you tell them to call off their search?" He tipped the waitress heavily and relieved her drink tray of the double Jack. "I beg of you. In the name of all that is holy."

"Oh?"

He caught the mischievous gleam in Adrian's baby blues, sky-high with the limitless possibilities of taking the piss out of him if given the chance.

"What happened to being a free agent?" Adrian wanted to know.

"I've narrowed down my options. To one." If he downed his drink, he wouldn't have to elaborate.

"I'm not goin' on stage by myself!" Marissa's voice was even brassier when doused with drink. "Le's in the can! Oh, man . . . we're up. Who's with me?"

Kat was quick to find new recruits. "Hey guys. All the slots are filled tonight. If you want to have a turn, you're going to have to take Marissa and Leanna's song."

Rick allowed Adrian to humor his slightly inebriated fiancée. It was going to take a helluva lot more than a few shots of Jack to get—

Abbey handed Rick the wireless karaoke mic and gave him her best puppy dog eyes. No doubt her mum's clan had put her up to it.

"Shall we have a go? We've certainly done a lot worse," Adrian prompted. Grinning, Kat plucked Rick's drink from his other hand.

"Oh, bloody hell. At least tell me what they've got cued for us."

The men strode to the low stage, then hopped on. Rick tried to remember the last time they played to a crowd of roughly thirty. Give or take. Mostly women. Mostly drunk. And one child who cupped her hands to her mouth and shouted a request, mangling the pronunciation of "Bohemian Rhapsody."

"So . . . about this *option* you've narrowed your sights on," Adrian began, grabbing the back-up mic.

"She's a nice girl. Do I have your blessing?" Rick tossed back his curls and allowed the meager spotlights to warm his face. *A stage is a stage is a stage. All the world's a stage.* Being on one was more than just comfortable; it was as natural as taking a slash.

The caption machine flashed Duran Duran's "Hungry Like the Wolf" title in big purple letters.

"Seriously? Can't we get a last-minute change request?" Adrian sputtered. The guy in charge of the PA just shook his head and pointed to the sign typed in seventy-two-point font next to the machine. ALL SONG CHOICES FINAL—NO EXCEPTIONS!

"You got us into this, Simon Poxy Le Bon. You're singing lead."

"Fine. You can do all the doot-do-do-doos." Adrian laughed and signaled for the track to start. He began to snap his fingers to fall in with the eighties synthpop beat. "By the way . . . lightning always strikes the lucky ones twice. You and your nice girl totally have my blessing."

SIDRA

SUN SALUTE

RICK'S WAS the only body still lying in Corpse pose.

"Are you all right, dear?"

"Yes, Vivian. Just taking full advantage of *Savasana*."

Sidra, straightening props with her back to the departing class, smiled as she listened to their interchange. Rick had slowly opened to the idea of being a student in her beginners class, and he had far exceeded her expectations, as well as the abilities of most of his neighbors on the mats. He was now habitually prompt, he was courteous, and his was the face she looked forward to seeing most when she walked into the room.

And his kisses sent her out of this world.

Nothing wrong with a little bit of snogging. Off the clock and off the mat. Right?

Yeah, keep telling yourself that, Sullivan.

She turned, glimpsing the old woman pat his shoulder with a gnarled but gentle hand before rising. Rick handed Sidra a card as he was leaving. "My turn. Can you meet me here tomorrow? At around five fifteen?"

She scanned the address scrawled on it before searching his

face. "Central Park West?" Curiosity trumped suspicion . . . but she waited for him to elaborate.

"Doorman building, security cameras . . . perfectly safe to arrive at that hour."

"I've got a class starting at five."

"I meant in the morning, luv. There's something I want to show you. I swear it's on the up-and-up. Nothing untoward is going to happen."

She tilted her head and studied him. He'd looked like hell and had complained of a rough night's sleep when he'd arrived, but as usual, her class appeared to breathe life and energy back into him. "You doing okay?"

"Other than not sleeping, I'm tip-top. Oh, and bring your yoga mat." He gave her a tired smile as he exited, choosing the narrow hall to the front door rather than the passage through the record shop. She noticed him meandering in there sometimes, before and after class. Lost in some sort of musical memory lane, no doubt.

"Amazing class, as usual," Vivian said as she passed her. "That poor man," she added under her breath with a *tsk* and a shake of her rosy hair.

"What do you mean?"

"I think I know a broken heart when I see one."

"I DON'T NORMALLY MAKE house calls," Sidra joked nervously. She had been in sensory overload since stepping out of the cab in front of the landmark building. As she waited for the doorman to phone up her arrival, she had wondered if Rick entertained women at this bizarre hour often. Now, as she paused in the threshold, she began to question not so much her safety, but her reputation.

Last night, she'd looked up the word he'd used—*untoward*

—in the dictionary. *Inappropriate,* the definition began. *Or inconvenient. Unexpected. Improper. Contrary to your interests or welfare,* it had warned further.

Rick stood before her. She had witnessed him in minimal dress at the studio, obviously, since yoga required comfortable clothing and bare feet. But the change of scenery changed everything. Wearing just a plain white T, a pair of black board shorts, and a warm, sleepy smile, he appeared much more sexy and self-assured.

"Come on in; perfect timing."

"I guess I'm not the only one who gets up at the ass-crack of dawn. Wow." She slowly dropped her bag as she took in the main living space and its floor-to-ceiling windows. Rick had just a few candles burning on the coffee table, but combined with the ambient light slowly increasing through the uncovered windows, it was perfect.

"I didn't get up this early . . . I just never went to bed." He picked up her yoga mat and gently took her hand. "Over here."

"Why aren't you sleeping? Are you still having the panic attacks?" She wondered just where his bed was, and imagined what the rest of the apartment must look like based on the palatial living room. He rolled out her mat right in front of the center window.

"I had a whopper of one the other night. It started as a dream. Well, nightmare, I suppose. So I came downstairs, did a few tree poses, and paced until dawn." He stood in Mountain on the Persian rug and beckoned for her to join him.

The hollows under his dark eyes were more pronounced than usual, giving him a tortured artist look that plucked at her very heartstrings. She thought about Vivian's comment yesterday and wondered what it was she did not know. But his eyes themselves were bright as he turned his head to the east. "This is what I wanted to show you," he stated in a breath barely above a whisper.

Sidra followed his gaze. A shimmering red-gold sun was just making its debut above the tiny LEGO brick–like buildings across the park. Its rays began to burst through each and every treetop. "All my life I've lived on the East Side of the island," she gasped. "But I've never, *never* seen the sun rise like this."

"And I've been living in the West for far too long," Rick murmured. "Only watching the sun set."

She stared, enraptured as the light continued to stream at a pace not unlike one of those time-lapse videos. She didn't want to move and miss a moment of it, but at the same time, she wanted to honor the view as well. "How perfect for Sun Salutations."

"*Carpe punctum.* Seize the moment." He smiled.

She smiled back, knotting her loose cotton top at her waist and pulling her hair back with the orange ribbon she kept around her wrist. "*Surya Namaskara,*" she pronounced, standing in Mountain, hands in prayer position.

It felt glorious to close her eyes and bask in the glow now illuminating the entire room. She began to silently flow through all twelve poses. It wasn't until she lifted into Downward Facing Dog that she realized Rick had moved behind her and was settled on the couch, watching her.

"How can you just sit there, doing nothing?" she mocked him with a version of his own words from last week. "And I'm up here doing all the work."

"I'm memorizing your every move," he said quietly. "For when I'm not graced by the pleasure of your company."

She smoothly swept her right foot through and came up into a lunge, inhaling deeply. With Rick's eyes on her, she stepped her left foot forward to meet the front and folded her body into a deep forward bend. "How's the view?" she asked after her exhale.

"Spectacular," came his strangled reply.

Smiling, she lengthened her spine, reaching up and out

with her arms, her pelvis tilted forward. "Gentle backbend. This is a great chest opener," she pointed out to him. "Might be good for prepping to sing."

"I'm taking notes." He laughed, his eyes zeroing in on hers. *Is it possible he's even cuter from upside down?* The thought made her dizzy. She released back into Mountain, her back to him. *If I had a view like this,* she thought, *I'd be up doing yoga every morning at sunrise. Then again, if I had a tall, dark, and sexy guy lounging on my couch every day . . .* She breathed deep, summoning up her courage before turning toward him.

"Still memorizing?" she asked, slowly skimming off her top to reveal a purple lace demi bra.

Moment seized.

"One might call it that," he said slowly, leaning slightly forward.

Locking her eyes on his, she released her hair and shook it out to its full length. With one snap and push, she was stepping out of her cut-off shorts and moving toward him. She mentally congratulated herself on having the foresight to pair the matching lace panties that morning. Rick obviously approved, biting his bottom lip and drinking in her every curve.

"You once asked me if yoga was always so hostile," she teased, straddling his lap.

"Never again," he swore, tangling his fingers through her tresses and pulling her gently closer. The kiss she dropped on his lips was complicated, a mixture of pent-up longing and sheer desire, yet still tentative, unsure of its message.

Rick responded fully, his lips mirroring hers in every subtle movement. The sun baked against her back while his warm hands explored the hollow of her collarbones, causing her to feel absolutely worshipped. She sighed as his fingers slipped down to her cleavage, then danced around her navel before traveling farther south.

"Hey, before we get too . . . you know?" She ran her hands

down his strong shoulders, fingers climbing up his muscle-hugging short sleeves. "Do you have anything?"

"I've had a vasectomy, luv," he whispered, lightly biting her earlobe.

Oh God. His tongue in her ear, combined with that knowledge, revved her drive up to double speed. *Still,* she reasoned, *there's so much I don't know.*

"And I'm on the pill. But there are other things to worry about, and I don't—"

"You don't want any worries," he finished for her.

"And I don't want to talk about it all right now. And kill the mood."

"Hang on." He planted a kiss on her shoulder as she reluctantly shifted to free him. She smiled, watching him race up the spiral staircase in the corner, and she could hear his feet pounding a path from room to room. Hugging a velvety throw pillow to her bare stomach, she waited. She wondered what made him tick and just what turned him on. Her head craved to learn more, and her heart flitted madly.

Rick bounded down the stairs moments later, and she interpreted his smile as a successful quest. "Good thing . . . Otherwise I was ready to go door to door," he joked, kneeling at her feet.

"Rick!" She bopped him on the head with the pillow, laughing.

"Easy now!" He plucked it from her hands and tossed it aside. "Come 'ere, Goddess." Sidra gasped at the first flick of his tongue against her inner thigh. "You can stop me at any time, you know." She simply nodded, not wanting to add words to the moment. He licked his way up one leg, pausing only for an open-mouthed kiss right against the silk of her panties. She felt her whole being quiver with delight she had never known before. Up he went, tonguing her stomach, popping the front clasp of her lacy demi with his thumb, covering her torso with his kisses.

She drew a ragged breath and leaned back as his lips gave attention to each side of her neck, then lingered at the hollow of her throat. He was rock-hard and right between her legs now, and moaned as she imprinted her back to the couch and pushed up her hips to meet him.

That tiny movement had changed the dynamic. A low growl emanated from Rick's throat as he hitched his hands under her ass and peeled her panties off. She clawed at his back, rendering him shirtless. The dagger inked on his chest quivered as he heaved a breath and shucked his shorts.

"Top," she said huskily, and he willingly flipped her. She had him on the couch and under her touch now, running fingertips down the silky hair of his legs. She teased him, barely letting her fingers linger as she ran her hand up past his knee and over to his navel. His entire frame stiffened, then surrendered to her. Head bent, she began to slowly lick each nipple, erect between their rings of steel. His fingers sought out their own prize, and she cried out as he hooked his thumb between the slickness of her folds, as if he had already memorized exactly what her body needed.

He kissed her as she came, his open mouth capturing every moan as she bucked against his palm. She couldn't remember experiencing such prolonged waves of pleasure, and realized she was on the peak of another orgasm as Rick sheathed himself.

"You need to fuck me — now." His voice had a rough catch, opening her eyes to a different part of him. There was something primal yet sacred in the way he closed the gap between them, locking his elbows around her arms. She felt his hot mouth on her throat, his hands tangling through her hair.

"Oh my God, yes!" She began to ride him hard, rhythmically. He met her, matched her, then pulled her down deep. "Oh, Rick!"

"Don't stop, luv."

"I want to come with you." She barely got the words out before he heaved toward her and they reached the peak of pleasure together, their gazes locked. He touched her face, her hair, so tenderly that Sidra wanted to stay at the top of whatever magic they had created in the cosmos. But gently, beautifully, they were descending together, sighing, kissing, smiling.

"The sun," he whispered, his eyes glistening. "You've got flames in your hair, my golden goddess. So stunning . . ."

She shifted, breaking contact for a moment, but then sidling up to cuddle close. They watched in silence, tangled together, as the sky matured from pinky-yellow to summer blue, and their breaths and pulse rates resumed their normal rhythms.

"I've got a train to catch," she said regretfully.

"No, you don't." Rick laughed. He hoisted himself up and padded down the hall. Sidra heard water running.

"I'm not joking. Day job." She reached for her discarded garments.

"I'll pay you twice as much as whatever day job you have." He strode back in bare-assed, as unabashed as she was incensed.

"And *that* didn't make me feel like a prostitute *at all*," she quipped, mistaking his shorts for her top. She hurled them in anger, and he deftly caught them against his naked form. *Good hand-eye coordination, of course,* she fumed. *Fucking musician.*

"Ah, come on, Sidra. I didn't mean it like that."

"No? You can screw me on your couch or grab a quick feel on the yoga mat, but God forbid you bring me into your bed."

"I would love nothing better than to have you in my bed, luv. But it's very far from here, and you would surely miss your train."

The humor in his voice, scantily clad by his calm tone, infuriated her. *You rich, conceited prick,* she seethed. *You're fucking amused?* "It all comes down to money in the end, doesn't it? I'm just like some bar tab to you." Dressed now, she jerked her mat from the floor, barely even bothering to roll it.

"What? No, luv. You've got me all wrong."

"Must be nice to be *all right*, then. Here on Central Park West. I'm working my ass off, just trying to have a prayer of keeping my studio open. It *does* come down to money for me."

"Whoa, can we back this conversation up and start over?"

Sidra wished she could back up all the way to the front door, when she said she usually didn't make house calls.

"I'm minding the flat for a friend. This place isn't mine . . . It isn't me. And you." He pulled the mat from her hands, squeezing it into a tight, neat roll. "You are not just a charge on my credit card. Your classes . . . I'm going to go as far as to say I think they've saved my life. So tell me how I can help you," he finished quietly.

Emotion swelled to a lump in her throat. Was it her pride lodged there? she wondered. Or her doubt? Could she trust another musician with her hopes and dreams? Charlie hadn't just broken her heart. He had put it in a blender and pulverized it.

"You tell your students to open their hearts," he chided, barely above a whisper. "Time to practice what you preach, teacher."

"You can't *manipulate* a heart to open," she insisted. The words sounded lame, even to her ears.

Rick's fingertips tilted her chin, and his stare became her personal *drishti.* Her eyes threatened tears as she locked her focus, losing herself in his gaze.

"But you can allow it to open, under the right circumstances."

Deep within the embers of his pupils, she saw a spark as he

spoke those words. It reminded her of the yoga lamp, like a light that never dimmed, no matter what it had been through. And surrounding the light, Sidra saw a tiny part of herself reflecting back.

Sullivans didn't go down without a fight. But they also rarely called for backup. She didn't even know where to begin. *Try me,* the light seemed to say.

"My uncle"—she swallowed hard—"wants to sell the building. It's been in my family for three generations, but he doesn't think yoga, or music, are worthwhile pursuits. Make that *lucrative* pursuits."

"What about your dreams? What about destiny?" Rick wanted to know.

"Two things Mike Sullivan does not believe in, I'm afraid." She allowed herself to be gathered, to be held. His touch had a way of making her feel like a precious thing, even though his earlier words had hit a sore spot.

"Let's show him lucrative." Rick kissed her forehead. "I know some people. We'll bring in more business. Make it happen."

"Thanks," she whispered.

"And just so we are clear, I'm a new believer in destiny."

"Yeah?"

"Yeah. It hit me the first time you looked my way in class."

"Hit you like a ton of bricks, huh?"

"Yeah. Why else do you think I fell on my arse?"

RICK

HONOR THY COMMANDMENTS

RICK'S MOBILE rattled across the glass coffee table, jarring him awake. He had collapsed on the couch after Sidra's departure, naked but for his shorts, and had slept like the dead. His thumb brushed against something silky as he sat up. *What on earth . . . ?* Threaded through his fingers was the bit of orange ribbon Sidra had tied her hair up with. He must have found it in the cushions and grasped it in his fist during slumber.

Ten thirty-five. Thor was calling.

Thor could wait.

Sidra. Just like the ribbon, she had woven through his dreams.

Leaning back against the couch, Rick let a ragged breath go. Furling and unfurling the ribbon, he thought about the morning's events. Her look of delight upon seeing the rising sun, the confidence in which she had glided through her salutations, her silhouette as she presented herself to him . . . all gifts. And then he had opened her up; that had been the best gift of them all. The way her body had delicately shaken above his and then had melted over him. Dynamic tension surrendered.

Why, then, did he open his great gaping gob and insult her?

Couldn't have just let her gracefully go, now could you? Abandonment issues? You feckless weakling.

He had never touched rosary beads, but he could understand the fervent handling, the tactile desire. Sidra's ribbon was comforting as he worked it between his callused hands with mantra-like devotion.

He remembered watching his grandfather wrapping tefillin every morning, mysterious little boxes with connecting leather straps for Jewish prayer. As a young boy, he had been fascinated, yet afraid, an outsider looking in. Like any ritual, Rick supposed. Yet when the time came for him to learn the mitzvah, he still felt like an outsider. Different. Or perhaps "indifferent" was a better description. Embarrassed to don such crude-looking items, to bow and sway in prayer. Resentful.

Rick looked down. Without even realizing it, he had wound the ribbon three times around his middle finger—once above his knuckle, twice below—and around his left palm and thumb, bound and tucked neatly. He flipped his hand over, marveling at the fact that he still remembered how.

He stood and stretched, remembering Sidra's backbend. Adrian had three guitars on stands by the window. *Pick a Les, any Les.* He grabbed a late seventies Gibson Goldtop and threw the strap over his bare chest. Standing at the tall window with the noon sun baking down, he began working out a heavy, bluesy riff. It scorched like his body had under Sidra's touch, blazed like the fiery sun through her hair, and then it wound down into melancholy minor notes as he saw the hurt in her eyes. Rick was tired of hurting others; he was tired of hurting himself.

He obeyed different commandments than his forefathers. Rock and roll was his religion and his law. Yet, in theory, it was similar; he was connecting his mind and his heart with his hands. His fingers formed bar chords, and he could feel the ribbon as he lingered on certain notes. The satin, matte on one side and shiny on the other, was surprisingly strong. *Like her.*

Gazing through the glass, he thought about all the trains that wound above and below the city, and wondered which one had taken her. And where she had had to go, and why.

He supposed he should get over to the studio, try to salvage a few hours of work. But first, he had a few phone calls to make.

SIDRA
SUPPLY AND DEMAND

THE CAMP DAY FLEW BY, and the rowdy bus ride felt like a dream. Sidra barely remembered her Metro- North ride.

Rick. Destiny.

Could she get on board with that? Even if she got over the fact that he was a musician, he was her student. Verboten conduct, as far as much of the yoga community was concerned. And Sidra had always been a poster child for keeping her boundaries very clear.

So much for celibacy. And *brahmacharya* for the summer.

As she unrolled her mat in the solitude of her studio, patterns of light fell from the *ner tamid*, reminding her of the morning's practice. Of basking in the sunrise, and in Rick's gaze. *Focus,* she chided herself. Since beginning the private sessions with him, she hadn't had a chance to attend an NYU class or spent time on her own mat work. She planned to use every minute of the free hour before her first class wisely.

Her thoughts, however, couldn't be contained, no matter how deep and deliberate she went in her poses. Rick was ingrained in her vinyasas; she felt his presence shadowing her as she flowed. Each time she turned her gaze up to the sky, he occurred to her.

She planked for a good four minutes or so, her ego playing drill sergeant to her id. *Drop and give me twenty, sailor. You're spineless and weak.*

He had made her tremble, and the thought almost flattened her. Determined, she rolled swiftly into Side Plank. *Vasisthasana* required all her focus. She performed a mental checklist, making sure she was in perfect alignment as she stacked her legs, flexed her feet. Wrist balanced directly under shoulder. Sagely, calmly, she mastered the pose.

What had brought him here? Loneliness?

Taking a deep breath, she transferred her weight to her right hand, rooting herself to the earth. His tiredness worried her. *Had he finally been able to sleep?* She closed her eyes and raised her hips. She saw Rick's face, so serene below her as they had reached their release. They had both, for a moment, been rendered speechless, the sun beating down on them as they had come tumbling down.

She flipped herself up, left foot planting down, and offered her heart up to the sky. *Wild Thing.* She dropped her head back in the full expression of the pose, her left arm extended from her heart. *Freedom. Power.* She felt the *ner tamid* shining down its eternal light on her.

You've got flames in your hair, my golden goddess.

Rick's words stayed with her as she brought herself slowly back to center, then over to her left-side plank and performed Wild Thing pose once more. She felt so free and weightless, freed from chains that had long tethered her.

Sidra moved into Reclining Hero pose, on her back. All thoughts had been released, her mind was clear. Voices emanated from down the long hall, but she paid no attention. Her body hugged the earth, through the floorboards down past the concrete and into the Manhattan bedrock, but her spirit felt higher than the rafters. As much as she loved to teach in it, she loved having a place like Evolve all to herself.

"And the true gem of the building is right this way." Her uncle was bullshitting his way down the corridor. Sidra extended her arms out above her head to intensify the stretch, but otherwise didn't move.

"She's a jewel, all right." The chuckle on the tail end of the statement was deep and throaty. Sidra opened her eyes to see Sully standing over her, along with another man. The stranger's face, lined but handsomely rugged, leaned down. He was dressed business casual, but Sidra could smell "buyer" from a mile away.

"Oh, that's just my niece, Sidra. She runs a little exercise thing out of here. As you can see, it's a room that can lend itself to all kinds of purposes."

"Perfect for our purpose," he said admiringly.

Sidra popped out of Reclining Hero, which was not the easiest nor the safest thing to do. She felt a hitch in her lower back, but there was no time to counterpose. "Uncle Sully, I have a class coming in fifteen minutes." She hoped her class constituted more than just Morty, Benny, and Vivian tonight.

"Your uncle was just giving me a little tour of the property, and you were our last stop. Hi." He stretched out his hand. "Thorton Young."

Sidra briefly pressed her hand into his. "Sidra Sullivan. Welcome to Evolve Yoga." His shoes looked too clean for New York, and his sleek ponytail of blond hair had years of sun streaks running through it. If she had to venture a guess, she'd say California. Maybe she'd have a chance in hell of staying open, even under new ownership. "What exactly *is* your purpose?" She crossed her arms.

He barked another raspy laugh. "It's more a vision than a

purpose, darlin'. And not just mine to share. I was hoping my investment partner could make it down to see the place as well, but I couldn't reach him. He's in entertainment, keeps odd hours. Today was an exploratory visit, more than anything. Just wanted to get a feel for how things were situated, that's all." His icy blue eyes trailed over her prAna tank top and hovered somewhere around her hips in their tightly clad yoga capris. "So much more than meets the eye from the exterior."

The first punch card of the day registered just outside the door. "My students are arriving," Sidra said flatly.

"I'll walk you out." Sully held up an arm. "Three fire exits, as you can see, and more storage back here." He kept up a running monologue, but Sidra could see Thorton Young's attention was up in the rafters.

He wanted her space.

SIDRA WATCHED, amazed, as her studio began to fill with faces she had never seen before. The first group of women who appeared were expensively highlighted and manicured and made themselves right at home on the yoga mats. Next came a rougher looking bunch, biker chick types. They were slightly less at ease, but nonetheless smiled and grabbed bricks, mats, and blankets. Then a trio of guys in Carhartt strode in and instantly fell in line between the biker girls and Sidra's regulars.

"Hi, wow, some new faces. Have any of you taken yoga before?" A smattering of hands went up. She heard the steady *kerthunk* of class cards being punched. More men were coming through the door, hipster types thumbing at their iPhones as they made one last contact with the outside world before succumbing to gravity and the silence of the yoga studio.

In walked Rick, causing Sidra's tummy to do a Wild Thing flip-flop. He was flanked by a tiny punk chick with hair the color of a blueberry sno-cone and a guy who looked as if he had traded in his leather Hells Angels jacket for the day in favor of a tracksuit. Tattoos blossomed from his tree trunk of a neck, and his knuckles were dusted with skulls of silver. His gray beard was split into two braids, and he had a bandana with flames tied pirate-style to his shaved head.

"I hope you don't mind; I brought a few friends," Rick said with a grin.

"I see," Sidra said slowly, handing over his mat to him. "I think I'm just about out of mats."

"Load in, guys," Rick called. A half dozen more wandered in, lumberjack-large, and unrolled mats of their own.

"I'm Pixy," said the punk girl. "And that's Deuce. We run catering and hospitality over at the Garden." She waved to the tough-looking chicks.

"The Local 1," Rick explained, raising a hand in greeting. "And the Local 4. IATSE." Her blank look prompted him to add, "International Alliance of Theatrical Stage Employees."

"Stagehands," the Carhartts interpreted, waving back.

"And electricians. And these are the publicists from the label." Rick nodded toward the hipsters, who were beginning to show signs of smartphone withdrawal. "And personal assistants."

"Hi, Riff," the pretty girls chorused.

"And a few of my favorite roadies, whose bands happen to be in town this week." He pointed down the line of the lumberjacks. "Blondie, Social D, Avenged Sevenfold, and Springsteen." Each guy raised a hand in turn. Rick turned to Sidra with a grin. "I told you I knew people."

"Well, let's get started then. How about we begin today in Child's pose? Big toes touching, knees apart. Forehead to the mat." Rick gave her one last smile and a wink before lowering his head, and she felt her knees literally wobble. His hands, which had ignited her this morning with their very touch, were now flat on the mat, fingers spread as wide as he could take them. "If the earth isn't close enough, you can bring your forehead to a block if you'd like." She wound through the fresh crowd, distributing blocks as needed. "Great form, everybody. I want you to think about how your breathing changes while you're down here."

Sidra moved fluidly over to the bimah and touched a button on her stereo. Opium Jukebox covered Bhangra versions of everything from the Sex Pistols to the Rolling Stones. She wondered what all these grizzled working guys and rock chicks would think of her music choice. Assuming the position on her own mat under the *ner tamid*, she quietly talked them through filling their belly first, then chest, then neck with their breath. The entire room did a collective inhale.

"Room for one more?"

Sidra lifted her head at the sound of the heavy British accent. The first thing she saw were mammoth bare feet, followed by solid calves. One was decorated with a large Celtic cross tattoo, the other a fire-spitting dragon. Sidra came to a kneeling position and noticed Rick had, too.

"Put him next to me." Rick shifted his mat to make room. "I don't trust this one as far as I can throw him."

The blond guy grinned from beneath an ample beard and lumbered over next to Rick. Sidra brought him her last available mat. "Thanks, gorgeous."

"Be respectful, Summerisle." Rick turned to Sidra. "My bandmate," he explained. "Sam."

"Otherwise known as Samson Steel, at your service. Had to come see what all the fuss was about." The Viking-size guy gave a lick of his bottom lip as he stole a glance at the personal assistants' spandex-clad bottoms resting on their heels. "All the fuss, indeed," he murmured lasciviously.

Sidra put her finger to her lips in warning and pointed

down to the mat. Sam obeyed like a big furry dog that was eager to play, but bound to please.

"Please set your intentions for the day before coming out of Child's pose and into the first Down Dog of the day. No lofty goals, no . . . Just a silent little reminder to yourself of what you want to release or bring, right here and now, into your life."

RICK

TRANSCEND

Peace, productivity. Peace, productivity.

Rick felt pretty productive already. His quick sweep through the ol' rock and roll Rolodex had scared up enough bodies to fill Sidra's entire yoga studio. He'd made a deal with everyone: The first punch card was on his dime, and if they made it through all ten classes on the card, he'd comp them and a guest for his next show at the Garden. He was banking on the fact that most of the locals would be converts by their tenth class. He smiled into the mat and used his abs to raise himself up into the first Down Dog of the day.

Sidra talked the newbies through the pose, and Rick remembered how his Dog had looked more like a crippled hyena when he had first begun. Now he could feel when he hit the pose correctly, and it was an addictive stretch for the spine and the shins. Sam fidgeted next to him and cursed under his breath as they collectively moved into Plank. Sidra lowered them down slowly and then up to Cobra. Rick lengthened his neck and looked around, marveling at everyone's form; they were giving it their all. Even Deuce, who had a lot more "all" to give than the others.

"And back to Child's pose, everyone. Come up on your fingers. Really spread them wide, like prongs. Deuce, like this —see? Cupcake hands." The jumbo-size chef understood the food-inspired cue, and she moved on.

Soon she had them up and moving through Warriors. Rick moved from One to Two, keeping his eyes on her. Thank goodness she had changed into yoga gear; seeing her in those cut-off shorts from earlier in the day would've driven him mad. Her thick, shiny hair was drawn back once again with an orange ribbon. As the class all leaned back to capture Peaceful Warrior, Rick discreetly slid his hand into the pocket of his shorts. Yep, the ribbon she had left behind at the apartment was still there. She must have an endless supply of them. His fingers stroked the smooth silk once more before coming back to Warrior Two, his energy buzzing through him in a straight line from fingertip to fingertip.

A sense of peace, well-being, and power overwhelmed him as he revolved into Extended Side Angle. Maybe it was being surrounded by so many people from the different paths of his world. Maybe it was Black Sabbath's "N.I.B." being played in a smoked-out, South Asian downtempo and breakbeat rhythm. Maybe it was Sidra. He loved her for choosing music that his people could relate to, yet for introducing it to them in a style that meshed perfectly with what she was teaching them.

He loved her.

"Let's nestle down to a small seed and grow our tree from there."

Freud would have a field day with him; Rick had read enough psychotherapy books to know the term *transference*. Sidra and her yoga teachings had helped him immensely. But this was way beyond her throwing him the life preserver, and he knew he would defend his feelings until the ship went down and he sucked his very last breath of air.

This was transcendence.

He blossomed from a compact seed, a slow, steady balance up to a strong, high tree, and for the first time ever, he was able to lift his eyes to the sky and find stillness in the infinite possibility.

SIDRA
ONENESS

"How many girls have you been with?"

Rick's warm fingers paused a moment, then gently continued massaging out the knot in her lower back. "Enough."

"Come on. Ballpark?"

"No, not enough to fill a ballpark," he murmured, stifling a laugh against her bare shoulder.

Sidra turned, meeting his eyes just inches from hers. "I'm serious."

They were sitting lotus-style on pillows in front of that fabulous Central Park view once again, their Mediterranean feast spread across the coffee table now abandoned as they watched the sky reverse its colors from the morning. From unseen speakers, Jeff Buckley filled the spacious room with his cherubic voice and crystal clear guitar.

Sidra had sworn to herself she wouldn't pry, but Sam's comment after their yoga session had been echoing off the canyon that housed her better judgment ever since.

It used to take far less clothing, copious amounts of T&A, and a grow house of quality cannabis strain to get Riff Rotten this euphoric.

"You first."

Fair enough. "I've slept with five men before you. And I ended up breaking things off with each of them."

"Why?"

She took a deep breath and a sip from his wineglass. "Four of them I just knew I didn't love, would never love. Great guys, loyal guys. Not their faults."

"And the fifth one?"

"I fell in love with the fifth one. And he broke my heart."

Rick continued to rub small circles on her sore back, and Sidra leaned back, allowing him to claim the spot as his. No more Reclining Hero Pose for her. She wished she had the patience to wait for him to speak. "So," she prompted, wincing. "Your turn."

He reached for his wineglass. "Honestly? I don't know."

"So many you lost track?"

"I never wanted to keep track. How can I impress upon you—"

"This is never going to work." Sidra moved to stand, but Rick pulled her gently back. He kissed her cheekbones sweetly, touched a ripe Greek olive to her lips. The briny taste burst on her tongue, as salty as the tears that were threatening to spill any moment as he touched his lips to her neck.

"I can tell you . . . I married the first girl I slept with. And I loved her very much." He relayed this truth so softly against her skin. "Despite the craziness my life required, I am a forever kind of guy."

Enough, she chastised herself. *Stop, do not ask him.* "Where is she now?" She hated herself for not being able to keep herself in check around him.

Rick sat up, drained his wine, and stared into the empty glass. "Brooklyn."

Sidra felt a queer mix of jealousy and dread rise. *So close . . .*

"Salem Fields Cemetery."

Now she really hated herself. "Oh Rick." She reached for

him, and he let himself be gathered. "I'm so sorry." She was. Sorry for his loss, sorry for asking, sorry for making him talk about it.

"Thank you," he said simply, and kissed her temple.

At some point during their conversation, dusk had crept in. Darkness had settled into the treetops, causing Sidra to contemplate the secrets that possibly lurked beneath them. She hadn't ever asked Rick about the root of his panic attacks; come to think of it, he had never turned in that silly intake form she had given him for their private yoga sessions. She could only assume his loss gnawed just as hard at the raw and vulnerable corners of his consciousness as her own loss did.

She had once told him, like she instructed all of her students, to "stay in the present moment," yet her mother was never far from her thoughts as she journeyed from one pose to another, to another. She strove to master her practice with evenness and precision, yet coming to peace and stillness about her mother's death always seemed just beyond her reach. Who was she to teach, to try and bring others on a journey to awareness and healing? She could think of at least a dozen heart-opening poses when it came to yoga, but when it came to her own heart . . . ?

"I'd better go." She moved to stand. "Day job. And all that."

Rick's mouth opened, then he bit his lip thoughtfully, his eyes dancing questions that shot heat right down to her pelvic floor. It would be so easy to fall back on the couch with him and resume their play from the morning. But she would eventually have to leave, and he would inevitably want to know why.

He had obviously absolved himself of his earlier transgression, but that didn't mean she was ready to confess all her secrets to him. Where would she start? *I have to teach yoga to spoiled rich kids upstate all day for an obscene amount of money? I have to make sure my father doesn't choke on his own vomit in his sleep? I have to iguana-sit on the weekends for my ex, in the apart-*

ment where he screws the girl he left me for? I have to figure out how to stop my uncle from pimping out the one place in Manhattan where I feel the world makes sense?

"Sidra." Rick's voice pulled her from her reverie. He stood before her now. Gathering both her hands in his, he lifted them together to his chest and dropped his lips to rest on them. "Namaste," he whispered.

"Namaste, Rick," she replied softly.

RICK

IN DEEP

"So Romeo," Thor's voice came through Rick's monitor crisp and clear. "I've been doing a lot of legwork while you've been out a-courtin'."

Rick jerked his head up so fast that the headphones nearly came off. After spending the entire day in the isolation room, laying down vocals, he had gotten used to hearing only the sound of his own voice. In fact, he would go as far as to say it had induced somewhat of a meditative state. He readjusted the headphones as Thor continued his intimate invasion.

"It's the perfect space. I've made an offer on it."

"Mazel tov," Rick baritoned fluidly into the mic. "Where is it?"

Thor twirled in his chair behind the mixing board, looking pleased with himself. "Lower East Side. The street's a little sketchy, but this property, mmm-hmmm." He pushed his fingers to his lips and blew a kiss toward the glass wall separating them. "Cathedral ceilings, hardwood floors . . . the acoustics will border on orgasmic."

Lower East Side . . . closer to Sidra. "Orgasmic?"

Thor goofed around with the input channel, sending reverb

into Rick's monitors so the word ping-ponged between his closed cans in a never-ending echo.

"Oh yeah. Remember the place I showed you, with all the scaffolding? She cleaned up nice. Owner is hot to unload. Got a couple family businesses in there, but nothing that can't relocate. I'm telling you, this building is the gem of—"

Rick had ripped the headphones off but could still read Thor's lips as he stormed out of the isolation room and into the control room. "Rivington Street? You're joking, right?"

Thor seemed taken aback. "I've scoured the city, Riff. Studios are a dime a dozen in Midtown, Chelsea, Brooklyn. The price is right; it's a dream spot," he rambled as Rick took a closer look at the external shots, blueprints, and paperwork Thor had scattered across the console. "Just hit the market with two adjacent storefronts on either side. It's destiny."

Dreams, Destiny. Now it was Sidra's voice reverberating in his head. *Two things Mike Sullivan does not believe in.* "You need to pull your offer."

"What the fuck are you talking about?"

"I know that building. I know the people." He swallowed hard, biting back the panic that threatened to rise and strangle him. He closed his eyes and saw Mikey's Open sign flashing; he felt his hand make solid contact with the doorknob leading into Revolve Records and Evolve. Sidra's space.

He remembered her hands on his rib cage, adjusting his pose on the night of the brownout, and his hands finding her body later, unassisted by his blindfolded eyes. He saw the yoga studio full of new bodies, heard that old lady Vivian in his head, calling him a mensch, a good person, telling him he did a mitzvah by bringing so many people to class. "It will hurt a lot of good people."

"Please." Thor scoffed. "If it's not our money this week, it will be some real estate mogul's next week. That area is ripe for the taking. What's your problem, man?"

Rick had problems, plural. But since meeting Sidra and stepping into her yoga studio, he had hope as well. "Either pull your offer, or I am pulling out my money. I'm serious, Thor."

"Dude. I've already spent the hundred grand in seed money you paid in. Surveyors, architects . . . it's a sure thing."

"I don't care about the seed money." A hundred grand was a small price to pay to begin to wash the blood from his hands.

"You're crazy." Thor's eyes blazed as he yanked the papers off the console and gathered them to his chest. "You don't know a sure thing when you see it, and you've fucked up every good thing that's ever come into your life!"

Rick wanted to yank the blueprints from Thor's grasp and rip them to pieces; he wanted to smash the console with the smug producer's ugly face. Instead, he squeezed his hands into Fists of Fire and inhaled a cleansing breath. "Do it. Or I'm out."

He wasn't going to fuck up a good thing this time.

RICK HEADED DOWNTOWN, not really hearing or seeing what was around him. *Fucking Thor.* The last thing the band needed was bad blood in the studio, messing with their creative process. But Rick wanted to tear the guy limb from limb.

One phone call to the label. That's all it would take. Thor would be out on his ass. But that still wouldn't solve the problem. In fact, it could potentially make it worse. Having to scrap their project, or shelve it until they could find a new producer, might drive the final nail into the coffin. And it would only leave more free time in Thor's hands to ruthlessly pursue his real estate venture, regardless of Rick's involvement.

He was damned either way.

He strode across street after street until he hit the wide expanse of Houston. Then Delancey. The Lower East Side patiently took him in. He was hours too early for yoga; Sidra wouldn't even be there. But he didn't care. Where once he was uncomfortable off the numbered grid, now he relished it. While waiting for a light to change, he stood and breathed deep, tilting his head ever so slightly to the sky.

A complicated maze of string and wire stretched overhead, encompassing the telephone and light poles and snaking their way downtown.

"That's an *eruv*."

Rick glanced down at the voice that addressed him. He realized that while he had been staring up, the light had changed and the entire crowd next to him had moved on. Except for the young man who had spoken. He had long brown curls, like Rick's. But while the rocker had many, this boy only had two. One on each side of his head. *Payot*, Rick realized. Besides the long sidelocks, only the kippah perched low on the back of his skull and the fringe of the prayer shawl peeking out at his waist gave away his faith. Otherwise, he appeared to be an average teenager, earbuds and all.

The lad pointed up to the enclosure. "It's both conceptual and physical, you see, in our community. It allows us to accomplish certain activities that Jewish law would otherwise restrict on the Sabbath. We can carry our house keys, deliver food to the elderly, and push our babies in carriages within the *eruv*."

Rick noted how the young man had stressed the pronunciation, *ay-roov*, and carefully explained its purpose to him, the outsider. Yet his use of *our*, *us*, and *we* were not lost on Rick.

He remembered his grandfather, who would not so much as flick on a lightbulb from sundown Friday until sundown Saturday. What had been important, had been *law*, to the old man had made little sense to the impatient young man that Rick had been. Friday nights were gig nights, after all. Dosh in the pocket.

Now Rick saw there were ways to respect, and adapt to, your

environment. There were ways to get around things without destroying them completely.

"Well, that's a beautiful quality," Rick murmured to the boy, and to himself. Together, they stepped off the curb, and Rick reached for his mobile.

"Ay up, mate?"

"Favor to ask, Dig. Gloria . . . that friend of Kat's. Could you get her number for me?"

Rick could almost hear Adrian pondering in silence on the other end of the call.

"Really? I thought the holy grail had been found."

"Yeah, well. I'm on a different crusade now."

SIDRA

SOFTEN THE STEEL

"Hold the pose, not the drama. Lose the drama."

Sidra delighted in the myriad of protests and grumbling. For the second straight week, her classes were wonderfully, happily filled to capacity. Like a chain reaction, the PAs from the label and the secretaries Rick had enticed to come brought their significant others to class. The publicists showed up with dates they wanted to impress. And the roadies, surprisingly enough, had fans and followers of their own, just as loyal and eager as groupies. Pixy brought her mother, who was an older, just as adorable version. Blue hair and all. And Deuce brought himself, faithfully, every other day. He was already standing taller, his skin was brighter, and he was able to go deeper into his spinal twists in record time.

She wound through the students, observing their progress. "No matter how awful or awkward it feels, you need to find stillness in this pose."

No question: They were giving it their best effort. Concentrating, focused, serious. "I know you hate me when I say it," Sidra said with a grin, "but smile. It's yoga for your face, people." That got a few laughs.

While it wasn't possible for Rick to attend every single class with his charges, Sidra couldn't help but think of him each time she stepped under the *ner tamid*, ready to teach. And with each final relaxation pose, he drifted to mind.

She was smiling a lot more during class these days, too.

At the session's end, she had them cross their arms and pull down on their shoulders. "That's a hug from me," she said happily, then instructed them to open their arms and cross them again, opposite arm on top this time. "And that's a hug from you. Thank you for sharing your practice with me."

The collective "Namaste" that emanated from her students was music to her ears. High fives and fist bumps abounded.

"Girl, the energy in your studio could power half the borough!"

Sidra grinned; that was high praise coming from a powerhouse yogini like Gretchen. Like Sidra, she often craved a change of scenery from her own practice once in a while. Evolve's gentle Hatha Flow class provided the perfect counterbalance. "I want to bottle it up and bring it over to NYU," Gretchen continued. "Where did all these people come from?"

The time machine gave its double clunk: Rick was punching in for his session. He teased her about sticking to formalities at this point, but she wanted to track his progress like she did everyone else's.

"Sorry, Gretch . . . no time to chat. Private client coming in."

"Anyone I know?" Her tone was casual as she deftly rolled up her mat, but Sidra was well aware that the yoga grapevine was just as juicy and tangled as any other profession. No water cooler was needed to spread gossip; it hopped from mat to mat.

"I think he took your class once," Sidra allowed, keeping her voice just as controlled.

"Omigod, the hottie with the accent?"

"Shhh. Yes, he's my client, and he's right behind that door."

"How long have you been keeping him all to yourself?"

Gretchen mock-pouted and rearranged her prAna top just so. As in "just so" her boobs would spill out. Sidra took her gaze up to the rafters. "So is he single? Just kidding, Teach. I'm sure you don't go there in conversations with your students. Except for me, but I don't count." She giggled.

Sidra was allergic to giggling. It took all her energy to not thwack Gretchen with a yoga strap on her scrawny ass.

"Sorry I'm late; I had to change. Am I interrupting?"

Gretchen discreetly eyed Rick up and down and smiled like she wouldn't change a thing about him. "Good to see you again," she gushed. "I hear you're good. I mean, you're getting really good at yoga."

"A reflection of a good teacher," he said, moving past her to roll out his mat. With barely a glance at Sidra, he did a Swan Dive and a Deep Forward Fold. He was done talking.

Gretchen shot Sidra a glance, then shrugged.

"Here, I'll walk you out."

In the small waiting area, she noticed Rick had left his guitar case propped in the corner. It was too big to fit in any of the lockers. Sometimes he brought "work home from the office," and Sidra loved when he'd play for her after their sessions, the sound ethereal as it floated up to the high beams of the old building.

A buzzing sound stopped both women in their tracks. Rick had left his cell phone out, too, on the low table under the time clock. Sidra caught a quick glance of the incoming text before the screen went black. The display showed two missed calls, plus a text from someone named Gloria.

My pleasure...

Before Sidra could even comprehend the first, another text sparked up the display. Same number, same name. Gloria. Like a deer in headlights, Sidra couldn't look away.

Great to see you again. I'll be in touch.

"Well," Gretchen said with a smirk. "I guess that answers

my question. Looks like he's got ladies blowing up his phone. See ya, babe."

When Sidra turned back to the phone, it had faded to black. She felt her vision tunnel to a pinhole as well. Thoughts of Charlie pried their way in. How he had suddenly developed a habit of carrying his phone everywhere in their tiny apartment, even into the bathroom when he took a shower. Strangely possessive of it, sneaking glances and smiling when he thought she wasn't looking.

Let go of thoughts that do not serve you.

Gloria could be anyone. Her "pleasure" could mean anything. Sidra was done thinking about it. For now.

Rick was still in his inversion and stayed there, even after Sidra had closed the door firmly behind her and they were alone. "Hey," she started softly. With his head hanging, the curls cascaded down and almost touched the floor, and she couldn't see his face. "Hard day at the office?"

It was a lame joke at best, but she didn't expect it to fall so flat.

"Yes."

"Do you—"

He straightened, flipping his hair back with help from his hand. "I really don't want to talk about it."

"I was going to ask, do you want music tonight? Or not?" She turned on her heel and moved to the stereo. What the hell? Gretchen's obnoxious behavior had snipped her fuse short, and now Rick's tone took a match to it.

"No. Thank you. I'm surrounded by noise all day."

Oh, this is going to be fun. "Fine. Turn your awareness inward . . ." *And see how you're acting like a total prick to me.* Her face burned at the thought. It shocked her, really. Yoga was neutral territory. No room here for lovers' quarrels. Especially one that came out of nowhere. She shook her own head, trying to unload the personal junk. *Take an inventory, clear your mental in-box . . .*

Who the hell was Gloria?

Pushing her hands firmly in prayer position in front of her chest, she began again. "Let's set our intentions."

Oh, he did not *just roll his eyes at me!*

She dropped her hands.

"Sorry," he mumbled. "I'm feeling a bit off."

"Well, yoga does not have an On/Off button. Focus, okay? How about some intentions, like gratitude, forgiveness, guidance—"

To her surprise, he seized her by the elbows, crushing her against him as he kissed her. It was all fire, no heat. As if he had something to prove. She broke away, furious.

"If all you *intend* to do is get in my pants by the end of the night, why don't you leave now!" She had half a mind to yank the mat out from under him and send him on his way.

"Christ, Sidra. I had a rough day. Okay? Am I not allowed to be in a shitty mood? Holding it in is what started the panic attacks in the first place." The talisman at his throat shifted on its tight cord. "I haven't had one since you came to the apartment that morning."

All at once, Sidra felt a myriad of emotions, from longing to dread to tenderness to shame.

"Then maybe we're done here."

Gretchen was right. She shouldn't have "gone there"—she shouldn't have gotten close to him, learned of his problems, opened her own . . . or looked at his damn phone.

"What the fuck does that mean? We're done with yoga? Or *we're* done?"

She stomped over to the corner and began to straighten the foam bricks, angrily shoving them into place.

"Are you breaking up with me, like you did those other blokes, because you don't think you could ever love me?"

Sidra bit her lip and kept stacking. *No. I think you're going to be like the other one. You're going to break my heart.*

He grabbed the bricks out of her hands and let them drop. "Don't shut me out!"

"Isn't that what you're doing?" She kicked the fallen blocks at his feet. "Building the walls of your lonely castle right back up? I don't know what you want, Rick!"

"You. I want *you*. And *this*." He gestured, hands up in supplication. "I want us. *Here*." His voice was a throaty hush, and his eyes deepened into even darker pools than usual. "Forgive me."

It was a whisper so low, it could have been a vibration, as nebulous as a chant of *Om* in the empty room.

For what?

"Who's Gloria?" The words were out, and she couldn't pull them back. "You left your phone out." She swallowed hard. "A text came through and it . . . it was hard to *not* see it."

Rick bent and swept up a brick with a heavy sigh. "She's doing some research for me." Sidra took the brick he offered, but he didn't let it go right away. "Sid . . . You don't have to worry about Gloria."

"I'm sorry." Again, the brick tumbled to the floor as she fell into his arms. "It's just, jeez, Gretchen was all judgy about you being my client, and then she pissed me off by flirting with you herself, and then the text came, and—" For the first time that evening, Rick chuckled. His breath warmed her neck and infused her with relief. "—and Charlie . . . my ex. He cheated on me with his bandmate Evie. Giving a whole new meaning to the term 'fiddle player,'" she muttered.

Rick clasped her hands and brought them to his chest. "I'm not Charlie. You're not Gretchen. And Gloria is not a threat." He tucked his chin and ducked his head to the side so he could seek out her eyes. "Okay?"

"So you want this to be . . . Are we . . . exclusive?"

"Nothing would make me happier. And contrary to my foul

mood tonight, I haven't been this happy in a long time. I'm finally able to live in my skin again. Because of you, Goddess. Because you've given me a chance."

His voice melted her heart, and she softened against him, like dissolving into a pose. He sighed and pulled her closer. It was as if they had both reached their edge, and then took things deeper. Settling into what was. Not worrying about the "what if" and "if only."

They managed to soften the steel they'd both girded themselves with, systemically, for so long, and stepped into the process of letting themselves be vulnerable. It was okay to be vulnerable sometimes. It was strangely liberating, and powerful.

"I do think we need to make a slight change to this dynamic, though," Sidra admitted.

Rick pulled back to regard her.

"I can't take your money for unlimited classes anymore . . . or the private sessions. It's just a little too . . ." Okay, she wasn't going to go there. "I don't need your money, Rick. Not anymore. We can still practice together. Same times and everything. But honestly, with Pixy, Deuce, and all the others, you've brought more business and loyalty to the studio than I could've ever hoped to do on my own. Thank you for taking that gamble, for me."

He laced his fingers through hers and pulled her close once again. "The wisest investment I've ever made," he murmured against her hair.

RICK

DISCOVERY AND DENIAL

SHE WAS VELVET PERSONIFIED. From the inky drape of her hair as it pooled over his bare shoulder to the softness of her earlobe as he caught it lightly between his teeth and right down to her inner walls, guiding his every move, gripping him and making him feel like a fucking Adonis. Good God, she was the lushest thing he had ever experienced. Rick wanted to shout to the rafters, but he kept his praise private, his breathing measured. Sidra was nestled in his lap, her exquisite spine pressed in perfect alignment against the misericorde tattooed down his chest. They were on the step leading down from the former bimah, pillows bolstered behind them.

Every evening they somehow ended up like this, together, after the final yoga class. They knew they must have been violating some sacred order in doing so, desecrating the *Savasana* as they reached for each other, stripping clothes and licking skin. They didn't care. His desire would build, slow and strong, during class as he concentrated on nothing but his breathing and his body to the sound of her voice. Like waves out in the distant sea, his passion churned until he had her alone, the doors locked behind them. Then she would join him, as warm and as yielding as the sand, and they'd meld together as he crashed against her, becoming one.

Other times, she was the ocean demanding his attention, teasing and lapping at him as he lay in exhilarated exhaustion. Then pulling away from him like the tide and letting him pursue.

Her shoulders now trembled as she bucked and buried him to the hilt. "Rick," she gasped, his name like chocolate melting on her tongue as she panted. His thumbs circled along her lower back and she arched forward, relinquishing all power to him. He eclipsed her firm breasts with his large hands and held her as he began to meet her pleas with measured thrusts.

She reached her first pinnacle, quaking under his hands as he began to catch up to her. She felt so amazing to him, she felt—

No. Not now. This can't be happening.

"Sidra, oh luv . . ." His hands were still cradling her breasts, his lips frozen between her shoulder blades.

"Baby . . . what?" They were so new, yet he knew she could sense the subtle shift in his demeanor.

"Luv, I . . . I've found a lump."

SIDRA
SURREAL REALITY

SIDRA FELT the tremor in her hand as Rick guided it to her left breast. He gently lifted, then pressed a spot underneath. Her fingers pushed his out of the way, needing to palpitate the place herself. Her breasts were small, and something she barely gave a thought to each morning as she squeezed into a sports bra or ensconced them in a tank top.

There. Yes, he was right. Her fingers rolled over a marble-size hardness.

"How long do you think it's been there?"

"How the hell should I know?" She was up and moving away from him, yanking the lace of her panties into place. No one else had touched her since Charlie, and she hadn't ever thought to self-examine. The thing would've probably grown to the size of a golf ball if Rick hadn't come along.

She frowned at her breasts in the mirror along the side wall, running her hand over the spot again. Beyond her shoulder, Rick's reflection was pulling up boxers, gaze on her.

Perhaps . . . ? No, there it was again. A knotty nodule. Rick's mirror image grew larger, but her eyes were quickly filling and blurring him out.

"For fuck's sake, Sidra! With all the wellness and self-aware-ness you tout? You could've checked yourself—"

"When? Yesterday? Last week? Tomorrow? Who cares? It's there!" It was *her* body, and *he* had the nerve to get angry? "Just leave, okay? Go. I don't need you, your sucky bedside manner, or your lectures!"

His face contorted before quickly steeling itself. "If you need someone, I'll be there, Sidra."

Sidra trembled, white-hot, as she stared him down. *How could you be there?* her mind screamed. *You're already a million miles away.*

"Sid? You still here?" Mikey's voice sounded dangerously close.

"Shit. You'd better—"

Rick dropped a kiss on her lips. His jeans and shirt littered the path to the rear exit, but he was back in them and out the door before her cousin rattled the doorknob.

"Just a sec," she called, shimmying back into her yoga pants and reaching for a hoodie she kept on a peg by the door. She couldn't bear to bind herself back into a sports bra tonight. She zipped the sweatshirt up over her bare chest and opened the door.

"What the hell?" Mike stood, massive hands on hips. "You shouldn't lock yourself in here."

"I was changing," she mumbled. "What's up?"

"My dad wants a meeting."

RICK

TOUGH LOVE

RICK MADE it as far as the Bowery before he lost it, retching in the gutter like some homeless bum on a bender. Bile replaced the sweet taste of Sidra in his mouth as he choked on the bitter thought of his discovery.

Don't jump to conclusions. It's probably nothing.

Yeah. Right.

Simone's "nothing" was stage four by the time it was discovered.

A car horn blared, sending his heart into slingshot mode as he reeled off the curb, trying to get his bearings. He propelled his feet forward, not caring if he headed north or south. Anywhere, away from the hell that was going on in his mind. Streets intersected at odd angles, and Rick expected to meet his Maker at the crossroads, any minute now.

A young street musician paced the corner with his guitar, strumming away on the battered acoustic despite his meager audience. Rick allowed his feet to slow and willed his pulse rate to match the chord progressions. The kid was good. He reminded Rick of Adrian, loaded with talent and not a pot to piss in, as evident from the open guitar case at his feet. Three dollars, give or take, was scattered in coins across the thread-bare velvet lining.

But he also reminded Rick of himself. The dark, rebel hair. The strong jut of his jaw as he sang about life passing him by, eyes burning with a cause.

Rick scrounged in his pocket and threw a bill into the case. Ten dollars didn't seem quite enough. In went a fifty. That didn't feel sufficient. Two crisp hundreds. The busker's eyes widened, but his fingers never broke contact with the strings. *Remember being that pure, that driven? That devil-may- care?*

"Your cell phone's ringing."

It took Rick a moment to distinguish lyrics from layman's terms. Fantasy from reality. He focused on the device clutched in his hand. Isabelle.

"Not a good time."

"When is it ever, Riff? I swear to Christ. While you've been living out your *Slumdog Millionaire* fantasies in yogaland, I've had to play nice with the label heads. They aren't happy with the rough cuts Thor sent."

Rick closed his eyes. He couldn't do this. Not tonight. "That's why they're called 'rough,' Iz. They're nowhere near done."

"How did they put it? Oh, yeah. 'This album might be too *complicated* to market through traditional label means.' Translation: The Daddy Warbuckses up top have no qualms about orphaning your ass and abandoning this project, Rick."

"Can you stall them?"

"No amount of record executive dick sucking is going to make the album sound better! It's all on you."

Busker boy was playing to beat the band, but there was no escaping the publicist's verbal assault. Had it been this bad with Wren? It had been different, Rick reasoned. He'd employed a wholly original brand of tough love.

"For fuck's sake, Iz! A little lip service doesn't require you to *suck* anything. Can you get behind me, for once?"

"A is for effort, honey . . . not for amateur hour." Her murmur led Rick to believe she was lighting one cigarette off another, chain smoking while tightening the noose around his neck. "You've been shooting blanks since you got into the goddamn studio! And butting heads with Thor, when he's only trying to help. It's not going to be perfect, so get over yourself. God, you're impossible. I don't know how Simone lived with you."

She didn't.

Perhaps that was Isabelle's point.

Rick bit his lip. He contemplated the guitar case once more, with its purple threads of velvet. Frayed, like his nerves, as she laundry-listed the consequences of delivering a dud. He was tempted to drop his phone in, to dump the whole lot—the record contracts, the merch licensing, the tours—but at this point, he wouldn't wish it on anyone.

"You've made yourself clear."

"Well, *you'd* better make it your priority."

The young man doffed his hat as if bidding Rick adieu, or paying his respects. *Hell,* Rick thought, slowly lowering the phone, *maybe he was offering his condolences.* Dead man walking.

"Any advice for someone like me, just starting out?" the bloke asked, scraping up the cash and coin and pocketing it before his next song. They were, after all, still on the sketchy side of Lower East Manhattan.

"Here's my *real* tip: If someone like me offers you a million dollars to trade places with him . . . don't."

SIDRA
EXPECTATIONS

"HE SAID *WHAT*?"

Liz punched the register keys angrily and thrust change at the hapless customer who dared interrupt Sidra's story. The Naked Bagel, it turned out, wasn't just down a man with Seamus gone. Sidra's brother had done the work of three people.

"It wasn't so much *what* he said. It was how he said it," Sidra mumbled, straightening the tip jars on the counter. Today they were labeled Dumbledore and Gandalf. Sidra would've gladly paid off either fictional wizard to rid her of any feelings for Rick. "He *barked* at me."

Like a dog.

"He sounds like a dick, from what little you've told me. You're better off without him."

"You're right. I don't need a boyfriend. I'd be better off with one of those tumor-sniffing dogs."

"Oh, Sid." Liz's brow wrinkled sympathetically. "It's probably not . . ." She couldn't seem to voice it. "Probably not anything serious. A cyst, perhaps? You'll get it checked out. It'll be okay."

"Yeah," she whispered.

"Any family history . . . ?" Liz trailed off.

Sidra shook her head no, but what she really meant was she didn't know. Her mother died young.

Who knows what may have developed over time? An aunt had it—but wait, no, that was an aunt by marriage. Her mind swam laps around her family gene pool.

A gentle hand eclipsed her wrist. "I'll go with you."

"No, it's fine." Sidra backed away. She didn't like the thought of Liz and her baby bump anywhere near her potentially poisonous self. Or the toxic radiation from machinery the doctors would use to confirm or refute her fears. "I'll get Fiona to go with me."

Fiona, with her massive, nonlumpy rack.

Liz gave a stink eye to the Con Ed worker who was next in line, and he quickly switched his order from "for here" to "to go."

"I'm gonna jet. My problems are bad for business." If she lingered any longer, she'd no doubt wax neurotic on the fact that her uncle had jumped on the first offer made on the building. Was he that desperate to unload? She'd be teaching yoga out of a cardboard box on the Bowery by next week, at this rate.

Liz huffed a sigh of protest. "No. It's not you. It's the damn hormones. Some women get a pregnancy glow. I'm phosphorescent with rage." She expertly wrapped Con Ed guy's Hell Hole—aptly named for the heat level of the jalapeño bagel stuffed with turkey and pepper jack cheese—and thrust it at him. Forcing a smile, she managed, "Thank you, come again soon."

When he was out of earshot, she muttered, "Come again and go. That's all men ever do. They're dicks, every single one of them. Dicks with arms, Sidra."

Sidra couldn't help it. Despite the last hellish twelve hours, she laughed. The mental image of Liz's words, along with the utter conviction in which she said them, was too funny.

Liz just shrugged and grabbed a huge apple from the fruit bowl next to her. Chomping down with gusto, she mumbled between mouthfuls, "Eve was an idiot to give Adam a taste of anything."

"When's the last time you saw Kevin?"

"Isn't it obvious?" Liz gestured toward the general vicinity of her abdomen and snorted. "It's been at least a trimester or so."

"Oh, jeez." Like preparing to clear her mind for yoga practice, Sidra tucked her worries under her mental mat to concentrate on her friend. "You have every right to be upset with him. Does he expect you to deal with this all on your own?"

"He's not . . . *expecting* anything." Liz tossed the apple core into the trash.

Sidra gasped. "Liz! You haven't told him?"

"My baby. My problem." Her friend pushed her lip out, aiming for strong, but Sidra wasn't fooled by the way her voice broke.

"That's it." Sidra marched to the door. Flipping the lock and the sign from OPEN to CLOSED, she ignored Liz's protests. "You need a break. And you're too stubborn to see it." She forced Liz off her feet by sliding a stool behind her knees. "What, were you going to hide out from him for nine months, and then what?"

Liz pulled an unsliced bagel from the basket behind her and nibbled at it like a manic little mouse. "I'll tell him as it gets closer."

"Closer? Liz, you're half-baked! That bun is cooked more than your bagels."

"Let's become lesbians," Liz begged. "We'll swear off guys and raise the baby ourselves."

Sidra quirked a brow.

"Okay, okay. At least be my date, then? His sister is getting married next month and I'm going to need a buffer."

"Next *month*? To hell with a buffer!" Sidra joked. "You'll need an epidural and a midwife by then."

"Nuh-uh. Not till after I get my money out of wearing that bridesmaid's dress."

Sidra's eyes bugged. Liz was delusional. "When's your due date, anyway?" Having demolished the bagel, Liz reached for a bear claw next. "Maybe eat a calendar, so the baby will know exactly when to be born." Sidra plucked the pastry out of her friend's hand and took a flaky bite. Liz's eyes immediately brimmed, like emerald pools at the base of a waterfall. "Jeez, I take it back! Sorry, sorry." Sidra pushed the treat back.

"It's not you," Liz blubbered. "Or this." She waved the bear claw forlornly. "It's me. I . . . I've never told anyone this. Not even my oldest, closest girlfriends. But when Kev and I dated in high school, I . . ."

Sidra waited patiently as Liz took a deep sniff, composed herself, and continued. "*We* got pregnant. It was just as much on him as it was on me. He was great about it. I mean, as great as any scared-out-of-his-wits sixteen-year-old could be. We . . . you know. Made it all go away."

"Oh, honey." Sidra embraced her friend.

"And maybe afterward, I regretted it a little. Even though I knew it was for the best, at the time. But now?" Liz reciprocated, tightening her arms around Sidra. "The longer I wait to tell Kev . . ." She dwindled, but Sidra caught the drift. "I may lose him because I didn't include him in the choice, but . . . I want to keep it."

Her abdomen, straining at the hem of her Naked Bagel T-shirt, felt like a strong bundle of energy against Sidra's own. It was both humbling and terrifying to think about the cycle of cells rapidly dividing. Ever since Rick discovered the lump, Sidra couldn't stop imagining the worst within her own body.

But now, pressed up against the amazing life force growing inside her friend, she allowed her mind to conjure up strength and positivity. Life and its unknowns were scary, but amazing at the same time.

You are stronger than you know, Sidra advised herself, and her friend, silently. She felt a strong jab to her belly, as if Liz's baby had decided to say, *Hey! Me too!*

"Whoa, did you feel that?" Liz backed up, hands clapping against the little mound.

Sidra smiled. "I think your little yogi just did a perfect Standing Split."

RICK
BOMBED

RICK CAME SO CLOSE. He could practically feel the doorknob, solid and warm beneath his fingers. But his feet continued to make tracks. He passed the blinking Open sign as his brain flashed messages like *C-A-N' T can't-can't-can't.*

Can't.

Cancer.

I can't do it again.

He found himself on Essex Street, walking fast and close to the storefronts with no destination in mind. A bloke in a black leather waistcoat burst through a doorway, with more belly and beard than Santa Claus. Rick halted in his tracks to keep from being barreled over, but the man had paused, too, propping the door open for Rick with a chubby elbow.

"Going in?"

Rick considered the lettering above the door. "Yes, cheers."

I can't do it again because I'm a selfish bastard, he thought, making his way toward the mostly empty stools lining the bar of the Whiskey Ward.

Rick contemplated the rows of bottles lining the exposed

brick of the wall. In his mind, he saw rows and rows of yoga mats. And Sidra, sitting in lotus, all alone.

"Jameson, please." He stared dully at the wood of the bar, even after the drink was placed in front of him.

"It's all well and good to drink the Irish whiskey," came a voice thick with malt, and Rick smelled the eighty-proof breath that followed it. "Marco," the man called, holding up two fingers as he dropped unsteadily onto the stool next to Rick. He looked to be in his midsixties, with close-cropped silver hair and a face ruddy and puffy from drink. The bartender barely glanced up, but began to pull a pint of Guinness from the tap, apparently the customer's drink of choice.

"Jesus Christ, am I the only one seeing double here?" the guy wanted to know. "I meant two, Marco. *Dos, zwei, deux,* two!" Another Guinness was poured. "Now bring us the Baileys."

Us? Rick hated instant alcohol-infused camaraderie. He threw back his drink, letting the whiskey burn dull the longing and regret he felt for altering his course that evening. Instantly, his empty glass was replaced with a foaming, blended shot of Irish cream and whiskey.

"Erm, many thanks but—" Rick stopped when his stool mate slid one of the pints of dark ruby velvet toward him.

"As I was saying, it's all well and good to drink the Irish whiskey, but it's really no fun to drink it alone." And with that, the guy plunked his own shot directly into the thick head of his Guinness. He grabbed the overflowing glass and lobbed it in the direction of his mouth. Foam dappled the collar of his checkered shirt and ran down his fingers, but he didn't pause until the pint glass was emptied.

"What in bloody hell was that?" Rick asked.

Marco threw down a bar rag and sopped up the aftermath. "Some places call it an Irish Car Bomb. We just call it the Jack #5 Combo."

The drink's namesake gave Rick a broad grin. His watery

blue eyes didn't seem to be smiling, though. "Well, son. Are you with me or against me?"

Rick contemplated the two vessels before him. He thought of Sidra's creamy tan skin under his touch, the dark velvet of her hair whispering across his lips. The cold, unyielding glass was in his hands now, and he chugged the blended concoction before it could curdle.

No cheers or pats on the back. His drinking partner just lurched off to the toilet, leaving Rick with thoughts that soured in the back of his throat.

Feckless bastard. You should be with her. You told her you would be there for her.

Your lies will poison her.

You're the poison.

The fire in his belly hadn't dulled a thing. In fact, it flicked hot sparks, riling his nerves and smoldering up to his brain. *One more drink,* he thought. Although he must've thought it out loud, because Marco came down to his end of the bar, staring at him expectantly. "One more Jameson. With ginger, this time." He needed something nonflammable. "And whatever he's drinking next."

Marco nodded. "Lime?"

"Sure, mate."

A large figure had taken over the stool to Rick's right and was nursing a bottle of beer that looked toylike under his great mitts. He appeared Native American, with a mane of hair to rival the length of Rick's back in his heyday, worn in a long straight ponytail.

Marco delivered Rick's drink and another Jack #5 Combo. Jack reappeared on Rick's left.

"Ah, more spirits to lift my spirits!"

"Cheers, mate." Rick clinked glasses and hoped that he was now relieved of his social obligations. The knock of pool cues and a bit of trumpet bursting from the jukebox replaced conversation. The Rolling Stones were singing "Bitch." Simone had always loved Jagger. Rick remembered buying her *Sticky Fingers* on vinyl during one of his visits to New York as a teen, and the cover had had a real working zipper to the trouser pants. It was probably in that big crate of vinyl her parents had pawned off on him.

He wondered if Revolve Records ever saw copies come through their door. The image of his hand almost on the doorknob forced an audible sigh. Sidra would be livid. Or hurt. Probably both. *Bloody hell.*

"Women!" Jack proclaimed to no one in particular. "Women are always gonna leave." The giant to Rick's right flicked an annoyed glance. "Whether they go out with another man" —*burp*—"or they go out in a pine box. They leave."

"Shut up, old man." The big guy stood.

Rick threw down some bills. It was not a line of discussion he wished to get into.

He didn't see the fist coming, but heard the pop. Like a cue breaking and scattering the pool balls on the table. Then he felt the punch and went down, sunk like the eight ball.

SIDRA

IT TAKES A VILLAGE

Sidra paced the floor of her father's living room. It was after nine, yet he still wasn't home. The hour could be considered early for those who went out to drink socially, but since Jack made a summer career out of it, he was usually tucked in bed by now to get an early start on the stool the next morning. She had had a quick dinner at Molly's with him, and he had been in good spirits, claiming he'd be heading home after the next round.

"We put him in a cab a couple hours ago, gave the cabbie the address. He ain't home yet?"

Sidra hung up with Molly's and paced some more. It felt better to do it up here in his quarters than down in hers. She didn't want to bring the worry and the loneliness down to hers, with no Seamus and no Charlie down there.

Did I just say Charlie?

Setting aside his many obvious faults, Charlie had a knack for dealing with her dad. Or maybe, since he himself had grown up in the tavern setting, he had a knack for dealing with drunks. Her dad had loved Charlie like a second son. And Charlie had always treated Jack with respect. When the doorbell rang at three a.m. because Jack was locked out or the cops had given him a ride home, Charlie would handle it. Better than Seamus could ever handle it. Shay had the brute strength to get Jack up into bed, but his inner emotional strength was still that of a scared little boy, hiding behind the couch from his dad's demons. It collapsed upon itself quickly.

Sidra paced back to the phone. She called all the usual hangouts she could think of. Finally, she got a lead.

"Oh yeah, he was here. Left maybe a half hour ago? I offered to grab him a cab, but he wanted to walk. Don't worry, Sid. He had another patron looking out for him."

"Thanks, Marco." She slowly hung up, shaking her head. *Great. Freaking drunks.* Walking all the way from the Whiskey Ward? And with company? It takes a village of idiots to stumble home, apparently.

She sat out on the stoop of the brownstone to wait and watch for any sign. Sure enough, two hobbling specks materialized from the direction of Cooper Union. They had obviously taken the scenic route. Sidra stared, elbows on knees, palms on cheeks, waiting for her eyes and her memory to mold one of the stumbling shapes into the man on her mind.

She got two for the price of one.

"You've got to be kidding me." Popping up from the top step, she bounded down to help Rick. Her father sagged against her lover, arm propped over the younger man's shoulder for support.

"You know this guy?" Rick asked, looking about as shell-shocked as Sidra felt.

"He's my dad."

She picked up her father's other arm and wrapped the dead weight around her shoulder. Together, with minimal shuffling on Jack's part, they got him upstairs, into the house, and to his bed.

"So do you live here, too?" Rick asked, now standing and watching as she wiggled Jack's shoes to loosen them.

"Downstairs apartment." One shoe fell with a thud. "I moved there when I was twelve."

"All by yourself?"

She set the other shoe down and glared at him. How dare he ask questions when he had left her to stew on her own all evening! Leaning, she yanked the wastepaper basket from the spot near Jack's desk and plunked it by the bed, in case he needed to get sick in the night. With that thought in mind, she gently rolled her dad over on his side. Nothing more for her to do, she thought, standing quickly. Too quickly. Rick's arms were there as she swayed from the head rush.

"What happened to you?"

"There was a bloke to the right of me at the pub who took slight offense to one of your father's recitations. I just happened to be the unfortunate middle man."

"I didn't mean your eye," she said through gritted teeth, although before she realized it, she was gingerly fingering the bruise blossoming along his right cheekbone. She was glad it hadn't been her father's doing. "Let's get some ice on it." Ice was one thing Jack made sure was fresh and plentiful in his otherwise empty freezer. Sidra wrapped some in a towel.

"I swear I had all good intentions. I came downtown and my hand was even on the door and—"

"Intentions?" Sidra's fuse sparked hot. "You talk of *intentions* like they're an excuse! Do you know why I ask you to set intentions before yoga?" His gaping mouth registered with her, but she didn't let him answer. "It's more than just a connection between mind and body. It's a vow that has been birthed in the very core of your heart—the place of your deepest truth."

"I was scared, okay?" he shouted. "That's my deepest bloody truth."

"And you think I'm *not*?"

Patience.

The memory of her mother's voice echoed in the long hall. Their shouts may not have been loud enough to rouse a drunk, but they had raised the dead.

What if she didn't have the time to be patient?

Patience is bitter. But its fruit is so sweet.

She wanted to move forward, to see where time might take them. To reap the fruit and savor its swollen sweetness. To love, and to be loved. A surge of emotion tumbled over her, timeless and nameless. It rendered her spent and calm, like a crying jag in her mother's arms used to, after all the tears had been shed.

Rick's arms held her now, like she was a treasured thing. She took the ice pack and gently applied it to his bruised cheek. He kissed the inside of her wrist, nuzzling against the thin skin there. She reveled in the solidness of him. He was strength and vulnerability as he murmured apologies and reassurances.

"Any news?" he asked quietly.

"I saw my doctor today. We're starting with a diagnostic mammogram."

"When?"

"Tomorrow. She's hoping it rules out anything serious, but..." Core needle, fine needle aspiration . . . Her brain had stopped processing during the biopsy discussion. "One step at a time."

Sidra wasn't quite ready to stay indoors. Especially not in her father's apartment with Rick, with this conversation hovering stale and scary above them. "Do you want to take a walk?"

It was a beautiful night. The breeze was a gentle reprieve from the heat. Sidra thanked the garbage gods that it was not collection night; no roaring trucks or sour-smelling cans on the streets. Rick kept one hand on his eye with the ice and kept the other holding hers.

"You came up Bowery? There are shorter ways to get here."

"Hey, it's not like old Jack was much help. I'm just a tourist in your town. I stuck to the streets I knew. Or at least I thought I knew. When did CBGB become a clothing boutique?"

She gently tugged him down her block. "A while ago. We've had to make our peace with it. Better that than another Starbucks or a bank."

"You think?" His expression closely resembled someone in mourning, Sidra observed. "CBs was my first music experience in the States. I was fifteen. You can imagine the impression it had on me."

It gave Sidra a funny feeling to think of Rick in her neighborhood without her. She had always been proud of and territorial about her Village. Yet she knew New York and all its landmarks belonged to everyone, day-trippers and city dwellers alike. It was all here before she arrived and would most likely be here long after she was gone. *But for now,* she thought, sliding her arm through Rick's, *relish the moment. Show him your New York.*

As they turned onto First Avenue, Rick's eyes widened. "What is that place?" They were approaching a storefront lit by hundreds of tiny chili pepper lights. "It's a bit over the top, isn't it?"

"It's two places, actually." Sidra could see the red lights reflecting in his spellbound stare. "Rival restaurants. They've been there for years." She laughed, thinking of their identical interiors, with their gaudy lights dripping down like red-hot icicles and their similar, competing Indian menus. "Keep walking," she warned, not making eye contact with either of the gentlemen standing in their respective doorways at the top of the shared staircase. "Or they will begin to fight over us."

She steered him onto the next block, tentatively watching for his reaction. She wanted to see it through his eyes. New eyes. Capturing that feeling of seeing something for the first time. When you grew up in a place, you saw it, but didn't really *see* it, day after day.

Rick's steps slowed. She gazed around as he did, eyes drawn to more twinkling lights, although not as manic or abundant as those they had just passed.

"This is Little India." She sighed. "Or what's left of it. Isn't my village pretty?"

RICK
ROCK STEADY

RICK TURNED and rested his lips gently on her forehead. "No, *you're* pretty. Your village is magical." In his head were a hundred words to describe what he saw before him, but he wanted to keep it simple.

She smiled, bumping a hip against his leg to get them walking again. "It's like carnival meets curry. There used to be thirty different restaurants on this one block. Now there are, like, nine." She pointed out a red awning on the opposite side of the street. "My grandparents owned that restaurant for years. It was the jewel of Curry Row."

"What happened?"

"Rents kept going up. Insurance after 9/11 skyrocketed. The novelty wore off." Sidra bit her lip. "And the city never was the same for them after my mother died. They're retired now, down with my great-aunt in Florida."

Rick thought of Jack's rant about women leaving via a pine box. "Oh, luv. I'm so sorry."

"She was only thirty-five. Pregnant at the time."

"How old were you?"

"I was ten." She paused by one of the merrily lit shopfronts, reaching up to finger a single bulb on the strand that had burned out before the others. "A young Indian woman dying in childbirth . . . that's something you think would only happen in Third World Calcutta or something, not here. Not in the eighties in the United States of freaking America."

Rick detected bitterness beneath all the sadness, but her eyes—all shades of tiger iron—revealed fear and guilt as well. He collected her to him, and her head found his shoulder. He pressed the towel, damp and cool from the long-gone ice, against her cheeks, dabbing at the tears.

"Aortic dissection. It's rare, and almost always fatal to mother and fetus. The doctors didn't know if it happened during that pregnancy, or . . . one before. And it went undetected."

Rick stroked her hair off her face and gently kissed her temple. "I know," he began gruffly. "The loss feels . . . unending."

He couldn't tell her about Simone's stomach cancer, not now, with her own health in question. But her eyes were searching his face, seeking out something: assurance, acquittal? Her words sunk into his thick skull and embedded their guilt-tipped talons: *She* had been the prior pregnancy; she thought she was to blame. Maybe someone had told her she was, or had implied it in a rash moment of sheer grief and utter despair.

The enormity of that notion slammed him sideways, like a wave on the Na Pali coast. His own children came to mind once again, clinging to his legs and arms like barnacles in the bubbling surf. Simone bending to peel them away from him, her laughter carried with the wind as the waves slammed the backs of her knees, almost taking her down. You want to protect your children forever, even when you cannot protect yourself. Who had been protecting Sidra?

He was aware of his own breath roaring in his ears, like in yoga class. "Stay in the present." The words were ones Sidra had shared in class, but he heard them leaving his lips in a soothing mantra as he held her close.

"But what if . . . what if I brought all of this on myself?"

"Shhh, no. Let's get you home." Rick threaded his arm behind her and led her back around the block. As they rounded the corner, he had a queer feeling of déjà vu. Compared to the deadweight burden of her father, Sidra was featherlight. Rick allowed himself to dig deeper in the comparison. Jack blotted the pain by getting blotto. Sidra masked her pain by flitting above it all, like a bird tending to her various nests: her father, her brother, her yoga studio. Him. He had thrown himself at her mercy, had thrust himself into her life as another project.

As she sagged against him, he heard Thor's words about not knowing a sure thing when he saw it and fucking up every good thing that'd come into his life. The thought of the blueprints and his involvement flashed before his eyes. *Am I the predator, destroying her nests one by one?* In the past, such thoughts would have dripped cold panic until it froze into a sharp icicle that needled at his nerves until they were frayed. But the heat of her body in his arms, the warmth of her breath against the hollow of his neck, caused all anxiety to dissipate. *She needs a rock. She needs you. To hell with everything else right now.*

"Stay the night?"

"Of course, luv."

She led him through a bottom door, tucked under the brownstone's stairs. "It's small," she explained, "but it's all mine. And Seamus's, too, when he's home." Rick took in the cozy nook of a living space. "I know, I bet it's the size of one of your walk-in closets," she mumbled. "You've probably got something modern and sprawling on a cliff overlooking a beach, right?"

Rick gave a chuckle. "You've got the beach part right. But no, it's . . ." He thought of his bungalow back home, which had been an old Buddhist mission before being converted into a house. How he and Simone had fallen in love with it upon first sight. How she had insisted it had chosen them and not the other way around. It had been compact, for the five of them.

And then there were four.

Then three. Then one.

All alone, he had felt like the walls were closing in around him.

Being with Sidra in her place, as tiny as it was, didn't feel like that at all. More like an extension of the lounge space of her yoga studio, warm and peaceful.

The first thing he noticed was a small statue of a dove with its young nestled under its wings. With a gentle steady hand, Rick reached to stroke the small smooth head of the mother dove. Its glaze had crackled over time, but the cool solidness was a comfort.

"My mother was a sculptor." There was pride in Sidra's low voice.

He turned to her and looped a thick lock of hair behind her ear with a smile. "She had amazing models to work with."

Sidra picked up the small bird and brought it to her lips, kissing it with a tenderness and grace that completely blew Rick away. "I've studied up on its symbolism," she explained. "Trying to get to know the woman who was my mother. The dove represents sexuality in Indian culture. Lust and life. But look at its wings."

Rick's hands eclipsed hers, bringing the sculpture closer to inspect it. The pattern on the feathers took on a familiar shape.

"It's a *triquetra* . . . the Celtic knot." She gazed up at him. "And the Celts say the dove coos to the softest sides of our awareness. She pays a visit after a time of suffering because she recognizes our need for sanctuary." Her voice was barely above a whisper, and her hands shook beneath his. Together, they placed the mother dove back where she belonged.

Gathering the woman before him into his arms was a

wholly new experience. He felt her hands, warm on his back, her chest expanding to fill the space left when his contracted. *Life, lust, sanctuary* . . . How could the universe grant him another glimpse at the greatest gift, then threaten to take it away?

Over her shoulder, Rick spied an open doorway leading to her bedroom. Sidra squeezed him. "Come this way."

SIDRA
FALL IN LIGHT

SHE STARED AT HER LOVER, naked in the moonlight. Together, they had slowly undressed each other, taking the time to marvel as the layers were shed and skin was exposed. Seeing, perhaps for the first time, beneath the sheen of lust and excitement. Accepting each other's offerings for what they were: a blessing, a gift. Taking their time.

Sidra ran her thumb over the hard ridge of skin in the crook of his elbow. She had never noticed the scar there before. It was strange to think that healing could harden parts of you, while it softened others. She loved the hollow of his throat, its pulse vulnerable under her kiss. And the way his fingertips ghosted against her earlobe and traced her jawline, as if treasuring something priceless.

"I don't know if I'll be able to sleep tonight." She felt the warm breath of her admission as she pressed her lips into the caress of his hand.

"I'll be keeping watch over you if you do."

She turned in his embrace, gingerly touching his regal shoulders. "Don't worry."

"Don't *you* worry, luv."

He ducked his head to her breast and gently kissed each ripe mound, where areola met skin. An overwhelming surge of tenderness came over her as she watched him. Her fingers stroked the curls at the crown of his head, as if he were the one who needed comforting and protecting.

Sometimes the lightest touch conjured the heaviest of emotions.

RICK

LIGHT OF DAY

RICK'S MOBILE was like a wasp, buzzing overhead, pestering relentlessly. He waved an arm up and finally knocked it off the shelf to the floor, waking Sidra in the process. She sighed and rolled lazily across his chest. "You're in high demand."

"Apparently so." He stroked her hair, loving the way it pooled across his belly and tickled at his ribs. Reality could wait a few moments longer.

"Rock star."

Rick smirked. He was probably public enemy number one up at the studio right about now. He could picture Sam cussing him out, Adrian pacing. Thor seething. The captain had jumped ship. But for the first time in a long time, he felt no sense of "what if" or impending doom. The King of Doom was content.

Sidra sighed.

Oh yeah, that.

"Your appointment today . . ."

"Noon. Fiona is coming with me."

"You're sure you don't want—"

"I want to stay in bed. Right here with you." He could feel her lips pouting against his sternum.

"Probably too much to ask for you to stay here until I get back, right?"

"Is that all you want of me?" he teased. "You're asking too little."

"I'm pretty low maintenance." Sidra sat up with a grin. She pulled the orange ribbon, shiny and familiar, from the nightstand and absently wound her hair up.

"Do you have an endless supply?"

She didn't answer right away, turning her back to him to pull on her tank top. Catching the satin between thumb and forefinger, he pulled gently and freed her thick mane once more. "Hey!" Sidra playfully grabbed the slippery length of ribbon back and went to work tying what curls of Rick's she could gather into a ponytail, then twisted it into a tight, knotted bun. "Cute. You look good in orange."

She rolled out of bed and padded barefoot to a high dresser, fetching something from the top drawer. Rick could see it was a flat paper wheel—a spool of the same ribbon. He watched as Sidra carefully unwound a good measure and snipped it with a pair of tiny gold scissors. Methodically, she set the supplies back into the drawer and again slowly and deliberately drew back her hair. Her fingers shook as she tightened the bow. "I don't have much of it left," she said softly, and busied herself in the drawer again.

Twisting the bedsheets around his naked torso, Rick sat up fully now, somehow aware that a great gift was about to be bestowed. It was a bittersweet gift of memory and trust swathed in delicate tissue paper that faintly smelled of spice and rain.

Sidra smoothed the creases out of two identical silk dresses after laying them gently on the bed near Rick. The golden fabric was intricately festooned with tiny multicolored jewels, and at the hems were borders of the silky orange contrast. "My mother was making us matching saris," Sidra said softly. She held up the miniature replica of the full-size. "For me and the baby."

She didn't have to go on. Rick could see the larger of the two was unfinished. But she swallowed hard and pressed forward anyhow. "I was so busy that summer, I couldn't be bothered with my mother lumbering after me, pestering me to try it on. So she set mine aside and worked on the baby's."

Sitting cross-legged on the bed in just her panties and tank top, Sidra held the tiny swath of fabric to her chest. *I want to take it all away from her,* Rick thought. *All the pain and guilt and grief. And I want to give her everything good in its place.*

He felt an odd stirring; it was out of place and inappropriate. *Everything?* his loins mocked. Sidra had seemed pretty adamant about her decision to not have children, yet watching her made him ache to change her mind. Or to at least have fun trying. Vasectomies could be reversed. *Yes, you egotistical bastard. As if she doesn't have enough on her plate already without you trying to sow your seed.*

"She never got to finish what she started," Sidra said flatly. She methodically began to refold the fabric. Rick could tell it was something she had done time and again, her fingers rubbing over the uneven beading and pulling on the hems so they lay flat.

"She would be so proud of you, you know."

She kept her eyes down, making a production of wrapping the delicate fabric in the rustling tissue once more. With a muted *plat*, a tear hit the paper and blossomed into a dark circle as fat as a quarter. Rick watched helplessly as another one fell and the paper thirstily soaked it up.

"What if I don't get to finish?" she choked out, practically keeling over off the bed. Rick was up in a flash after her, but the bedding ensnared him like a thick vine of two-hundred-thread-count cotton. He tumbled, swearing, to the floor and took the teary, gorgeous mess that was Sidra down with him.

Half laughing, half kissing him through her tears, she managed to get out, "Thanks for lightening the situation, but oof, you're heavy!"

"Sorry, my love. I am so sorry." He blotted her tear-stained cheeks with his stubbly own, murmuring against her hair. "Don't you talk like that, though . . . you hear me?" he gently scolded her, bestowing a necklace of kisses around her throat.

"Hey, Sid, I'm just gonna—Okay, whoa, didn't see THAT coming!" A whirl of perfume and leopard print hit Rick's senses: Fiona. She was in and out of the doorway so fast that they barely had time to react, except for collapsing and laughing again.

"It's okay, Fi. We are decent. Kinda." Sidra wiggled out from Rick's embrace and fashioned a flowing loincloth for him from the top sheet. "There," she said, pulling him to his feet. "It's a dhoti. Hot." She bit her lip to keep from laughing.

"Hot like Gandhi?"

She tucked a loose end around his navel so he wouldn't trip again. "Nice abs, nice butt," she commented, giving him a pat. "Must be all those stacked side planks someone's been making you do."

"My yoga instructor is a real whip-cracker."

Fiona appeared in the doorway again, her long, airbrushed fingernails drilling impatiently against the woodwork. "Like I was saying. I was gonna suggest we grab a cab so we won't be late." She cracked her gum and gave Rick a knowing once-over.

"Give me ten?" Sidra asked. "I just need a quick shower and to put on a pot of coffee for my dad." Turning to Rick, she pulled at the ribbon that was still in his hair. From the same dresser drawer where she stowed the saris came a key, which she tied to the ribbon. "You don't have to stay here all day," she said shyly. "But promise me you'll come back?"

"Absolutely."

"I'll brew the coffee for the papa bear hibernating upstairs," Fiona said. "Just get ready already, wouldja?"

Rick stood in the doorway, as proud as a prince in his pima cotton finery, smiling as he overheard Fiona whisper loudly to Sidra, "Well, I wouldn't kick *him* out of bed for eating crackers. Unless, of course, he was better on the floor?"

RICK
SHOP BOOK

Freshly showered and key in pocket, Rick contemplated his morning. He could head uptown to Adrian's apartment for a change of clothes. Or over to the studio to show his face. The band's two-month lockout to get this album recorded was almost up, yet half the tracks still needed work.

The bright sunshine stopped him in his tracks. Something about the morning was totally different on the Lower East Side than on the Upper West. Its scents and its energy, its sights and sounds. Buildings were lower and older. And despite the noise and number of mammoth construction vehicles already biting into the last small parcels of available earth around them, the neighborhood had a small- town community feel.

He'd missed a text from Thor last night and had barely glanced at his mobile since. Pulling it from his pocket now, he saw the message:

I've made an offer. Last chance to redeem yourself.

Guilt followed him like his shadow did, impossible to escape. Doggedly there, mimicking his every move. Gloria was pulling strings downtown to expedite his request. But he still needed to tell Sidra. How? And when? Furious with himself, and with his so-called colleague, he thumbed back:

I meant what I said. Don't touch that property, Thor. If you fuck with the beast, you will get the horns.

A line snaked out a door, two-deep. Heavenly scents of bagels and Scottish smoked salmon caused Rick's feet to join the crowd, shuffling inside Russ & Daughters Cafe. Talk about your mosh pits! But all the jostling, shouting, and chaos were worth the coveted spot he was awarded at the counter of the New York institution. Rick went full-on, even ordering a frothy, sugary egg cream with his meal. Which, in fact, contained neither egg nor cream, but a rich concoction of chocolate syrup, seltzer, and milk.

Isabelle pestered him via his mobile. Rather than letting her call go to voice mail so she could record her unique brand of harassment, Rick pushed the Talk button and set the phone back down on the counter. Isabelle drowned in an earful of Lower East Side Jewish delicatessen din and dropped the call after forty-three seconds. Today was all about Sidra. The last thing he needed was Isabelle giving him grief.

He had been addicted to grief for much too long now.

Back on the street, he meandered. He thought about his lover, sitting in a sterile environment somewhere, surrounded by the steely machines that would diagnose her future. He wished he were with her. They'd get through this.

Rick knew in his heart he wouldn't make it uptown today. He strode from Orchard to Rivington and didn't stop until he felt his hand on the doorknob of Revolve Records.

"HIRE ME."

Sidra's cousin looked at Rick like he had lost his bleeding mind. "*What* you?"

"You're down two men this summer. Put me to work."

"I don't think I could afford you, dude," the shop owner said slowly.

"So I'll do community service. No pay necessary."

"I'm a New York State employer." Mike's chest puffed proudly. "Everyone in my shop is on the payroll. I pay into work comp, and disability, in case anyone were to get hurt."

"I'll take minimum wage, then." *And donate it back by buying records.* "When do I start?" Mikey made a face, so Rick added, "I'm not taking the piss, mate. I need this."

I need all the help I can get.

"Don't you have an album to record?"

"Eventually."

Rick thought he saw a little of Sidra in the man's wary gaze. They were family, after all. "You got a visa? Green card?"

"I'm a permanent resident, if that's what you're worried about."

"I don't want Immigration in here, breathing down my neck."

The principal shareholder of Rotten Graves Holdings, Ltd. gave a full-bellied, throaty laugh.

"Fine. You can start with restocking. And help me with inventory. Stay away from the register." He thrust an application at Rick. "You'll need to fill this out."

Rick smiled and did what he was told.

"Good. Can you sign these, too?" Mike was holding the used Corroded Corpse albums he had in stock. The men exchanged a grin.

Mikey needed all the help he could get, too.

SIDRA
PURE ROMANCE

SIDRA LOVED the Astor Place Starbucks. Although the lines always made her wonder if they were giving coffee away, she loved tucking into a seat along the windows looking out over the entire neighborhood. The vantage point overlooked a complex myriad of intersecting streets disconcerting to anyone who relied on the city's numbered grid. But for Sidra, it was a crossroads she had traveled throughout her entire life.

You could watch people ascend from the 6 train and see the tourists take their lives in their hands as they tried to cross both Lafayette Street *and* Cooper Square during a single traffic light change. On any given day, there were buskers or skaters loitering near the Cube, a huge steel sculpture that perched on one of its eight corners. It had been there since before Sidra was born, and she could count on her hands the number of times she had been recruited to help spin it.

Now she watched with a smile, latte to her lips, as a group of four kids, incoming NYU frosh age, beckoned a lone pedestrian to cross over to the traffic island and help them. The guy tilted his head as the ringleader of the group gestured wildly with his hands while the others, two more boys and a girl, stood back and looked on shyly. He turned and contemplated the task. In his hand was a bright bouquet of flowers. Sidra watched as he handed them off to the girl with a flourish before reaching up to lean on one side of the cube. The other guys followed suit, and together the four of them began to slowly rotate the cube on its vertical axis. The girl did a little happy hop dance before snapping pictures with her phone camera. Sidra delighted in watching their triumph, while the rest of the busy intersection barely took notice.

"Bravo," she murmured moments later as she fell into Rick's embrace. "You're officially a New Yorker now."

"Is that so?" he said against her temple as kissed it.

"It's not so easy to get that thing spinning." She thought of the times she and Seamus, kids barely tall enough to touch it, plotted out their methods for moving the "Alamo" cube. And later with Charlie's band, all of them too drunk to stand, let along coordinate a mass push against eight hundred and fifty pounds.

"I was about to tell them to pull the other one; it's got bells on it." Rick laughed when Sidra eyed him queerly. "You know. I figured they were putting me on. Having a laugh at the old man. Then I realized, blimey, this thing really does move!" He suddenly remembered the bouquet in his hand and brought it gently to her chest. "For you."

"Oh, Rick. They're gorgeous." She breathed in the barely there scent of the roses, all yellow with their tips tinged in red. Their blossoms were tight but voluptuous, and she marveled at their symmetry.

"They had wildflowers that reminded me of you, and I considered a mixed bunch, but they were all different heights, and I thought, no, like in yoga, you'd appreciate everything squared off." He chuckled.

Sidra grinned. It was true; she was a broken record of "square your hips" and "stack your shoulders" during class.

Yoga demanded perfect alignment. Now, holding Rick's flowers close, she felt her legs turn to jelly and had to sit back down. "They are perfect. Thank you."

Charlie used to whip a dozen red roses out from behind his back every Valentine's Day without fail, and she had always been embarrassed and confused by her own reaction: polite appreciation, feigned to mask disappointment. Now she understood why. Flowers for no occasion was pure romance.

"Tell me," Rick urged, pulling a chair close, "how'd it go?"

The diagnostic mammogram had been the longest thirty minutes of Sidra's life, an uncomfortable haze of squeezing and pressure and question after question. *When was your last period? Have you had a previous mammogram? Are you pregnant or could you be pregnant?* Then there had been the ultrasound. Sidra shivered at the memory of the cold gel and the transducer passing around and around on her skin, searching for abnormalities. Scary, darkened masses that might seal her fate. She remembered bargaining with herself, wishing she were there for any other reason. *Really?* Her brain dared her to think the previously unthinkable. *Any other reason, even . . . ?*

Yes.

It had been shockingly easy to imagine the technician sliding the wand just a few inches lower, and hard not to fantasize what it might be like to hear a little heartbeat galloping. The thought of ever growing a life inside her was still terrifying, but at the same time . . . slightly less inconceivable—no pun intended.

Rick took her hand, and her own heart quickened its pace.

"The radiologist said the tests appeared normal, just dense tissue, thank goodness. But he'll still send the full report to my doctor." She took a deep cleansing breath and shook her head. "Then she'll decide if I need to go back for any follow-up."

She hadn't been aware of the tension Rick was holding until she saw his jaw twitch and all of his neck muscles relax. The change in his demeanor was almost imperceptible, but Sidra had made it her mission over the last month to help quell his panic attacks. She noticed.

"What?" she asked quietly, gently, but he just gave a shake of his head and a gusty exhale before smiling and kissing her cheek.

"That is great. So relieved for you. Let's celebrate. After classes, of course."

"Actually, I asked Gretchen if she could cover my classes today. I wasn't sure I'd feel up to it." She'd also texted Rick from the waiting room to meet her out, rather than back at the apartment. She had decided whether the results were good or bad, she would be too emotionally drained either way to face the walls of her apartment. And think about the tiny dresses in her drawers. Or her father sleeping off the drink upstairs.

It was the first time she'd ever "called in sick," so to speak. The camp director had been very understanding, and Gretchen had been more than willing to step in. Now Sidra felt a little giddy, like a kid playing hooky from school. It was Friday afternoon, and the whole weekend waited for her.

"Oh, Banana Louie!"

A few Starbucks patrons turned their heads at Sidra's outburst, and Rick leaned back with an amused look. "Come again?"

"Yes, let's celebrate. But first there's something I have to do."

"So this is how you spend your weekends while I'm upstate, eh?" Rick tapped the top of the iguana cage gently. Banana Louie was happily back under his bulb and munching on some kale after Sidra had taken him out for some exercise. "What's so funny?"

"Oh, my friend Reggie's latest note. He stays here during the week and takes care of Louie." She held out the scrap of paper. *Fresh okra and sweet potato in fridge. Just changed the basking bulb. Used Evie's toothbrush to scrub the shit out of cage.* "Neither of us is a fan of Charlie's girlfriend. So when we swap notes, we usually have to say something disparaging about her." She laughed.

Rick flipped over the paper and wrote: *Louie ate all the kale. I gave him a bath. Then Rick and I had sex in Evie's bed.*

"Richard Rottenberg!"

"The ladies prefer to call me Riff Rotten." He snaked his arms around her waist. "And I will gladly soil your reputation rotten, my dear."

"I am not having sex with you in that bed," she exclaimed. "Besides, you wouldn't want to touch me if I'd cleaned the cage."

"We could always shower." He cocked his head toward Charlie and Evie's tiny bathroom.

"You're serious, aren't you?" She contemplated his expression, then decided he wasn't. "You goofball."

"This bloke is Charlie, then?" Rick gestured to various framed pictures hanging on the white cinderblock walls. Charlie as leader of the band, Charlie shirtless with a low-slung guitar, Charlie barking wide-mouthed into a microphone. "Takes himself rather seriously, does he?"

"Oh, you have no idea." When she was alone, Sidra barely glanced around at her surroundings. She dutifully tended to Louie's well-being and made sure she locked the door behind her. Now, she took in the sad sagging middle of their Bohemian couch, the attempt at hipster bric-a-brac, and didn't envy Charlie and Evie's love nest one bit. "Can you do me a favor, though?"

"Anything, luv."

"Go check out their bedroom and tell me what it looks like."

Rick raised a brow. "My offer still stands, you know."

Sidra laughed. "I know." She turned back to the cage as

Rick embarked on his mission. Banana Louie arched up to her hand for petting. Sidra found it amazing that he seemed to remember her and trust her after all this time.

"Well?" she asked when Rick emerged, poker-faced and seemingly unperturbed.

"Nirvana poster on the wall. Cheap IKEA furniture. And she's got an old stuffed animal on the bed that has clearly seen better days."

Sidra snorted. "That's Charlie's."

"What were you expecting?"

Sidra shrugged at Rick's question. *A den of iniquity? Red tapestries, candles burning? Sex swing hanging from the ceiling?* "I don't know," she admitted. "I guess, just … something more?"

She had built walls of solitary confinement with her anger and her hurt to protect herself from their betrayal. Had assumed the fortress they'd built together would somehow always be larger, stronger, better than hers. But Rick's flippant description made it pedestrian, boring. Evie and Charlie were just boring, normal people.

"He's a hack, Sidra. And a fool to give up everything you had to offer."

"I know," she said quietly. She looked up at him and, with conviction, nodded and smiled. "Let's get out of here, okay?"

They left Alphabet City behind, winding up St. Mark's Place hand in hand. Rick told her about visiting St. Mark's over the decades, first as a teenager on his visits with family to the States, then as an upstart musician.

They swapped stories of "remember when" as they crossed each numbered block, recalling the days when sushi places were record shops and bars were institutions, not trendy flavor-of- the-month franchises.

"I've been wanting to do that, right on this very spot," he said, breaking his soulful kiss with a boyish smile and a nuzzle to her nose.

"Um, what?" She laughed. "Kiss me next to a garbage can, between a pizza place and a body piercing shop?"

"No, silly girl. Under the caryatids." He gestured up toward a residential building sandwiched between the businesses. Sidra gaped at the half-naked ladies making up the stone support columns that decorated each side of the doorway.

"I've walked by here hundreds of times, and I never noticed them," she marveled as he kissed her again. In some ways, he knew her village better than she did. "They're beautiful."

"Stunning." His eyes sparkled a memory. "Like you, in Mermaid pose."

As they approached Third Avenue, an aging punker was hopping down the graffiti-and sticker- covered metal stairs of an old storefront. He looked about as old as Trash and Vaudeville, the rock and roll clothing store whose gaudy red neon sign winked above his head. The shop had been inspired back in the seventies by the rock and roll meccas surrounding it: Electric Circus, the Fillmore East, and, of course, CBGB. All had faded away, but Trash and Vaudeville remained as one of the last holdouts of the old East Village.

"Riff fucking Rotten!" He landed in front of them with a thud of his steel-toed Doc Martens. "Not to disturb you with your lady friend, but if you could give me a few minutes of your time, I'd be much obliged, dude."

Sidra discreetly took in the stranger's appearance, from Mohawk to facial piercings down to his Bouncing Soles, with amusement. It was funny to hear such polite and reverent banter coming from pierced lips, heavily smeared in black.

Rick's reaction was even more interesting. She felt him raise himself even taller beside her as he met the guy's gaze, a guarded but friendly expression on his face. Sidra realized he must've spent years during his band's heyday having to gauge fans' zeal. She trusted he had a built-in meter that crossed from Normal to Crazy in these situations, and she wondered at what point the needle hovered currently. "What can I do for you?"

The guy reached his lanky arms across his chest and pulled his T-shirt up and off in a lightning-fast movement. "I've got everyone's autographs but yours, man. All of Corroded Corpse, see?" He hunched over for inspection and, sure enough, tattooed on his back were three signatures surrounding the Corroded Corpse logo inked on his spine.

"Crikey, you don't look old enough to have collected all of these," Rick marveled. He turned to Sidra and explained, "The band broke up in '88, you see."

"Sam's was the first one I got, back on the first US tour," the guy called over his shoulder. "Then I got Adam's before he went all Jesus-freak and stopped wanting to play. I traveled all the way to London to see your show at Hammersmith and thought for sure I would get all of youse guys there, but it didn't happen and then the band broke up. I found Digger in Washington Square Park, like, two years ago. Pushing his kid on the swing, but he gave me this." His finger, covered in silver skull rings, pointed at a scrawling signature that snaked across his scapulae. "I went right over to my girl on the West Side and she inked it before the marker had even dried! Digger said if he hadn't had his little one there, he would've gone with me to get a new tat, too."

Rick chuckled. "That sounds like something Dig would've said."

"And now"—the guy extracted a black Sharpie from the back pocket of his stovepipe jeans, as if he had just been lying in wait for such an opportunity—"if you could complete the tattooed tetralogy, I would be massively stoked."

"Of course," Rick said without hesitation, taking the marker from the guy.

"Do you have a phone? I could take your picture," Sidra offered.

"Yeah yeah, awesome!" He handed off his smartphone. "Thanks." Sidra snapped multiple pictures as Rick leaned over the guy and carefully added his signature to the work in progress. "I think I'm going to get, like, a ring of thorns around the whole thing," he told Rick excitedly.

"Look at me, guys. Smile!" Sidra snapped a photo of the two of them, grinning and hanging on to each other like brothers.

"Here we go, one more," Rick joked, and held the bouquet of roses he had kept in his hand the entire time up to their chins. The Mohawked man beamed like he'd won the lottery, and Sidra could hear the rings in his bottom lip hit his teeth.

"Are these your kids?" Sidra asked as she handed him his phone back. Two brown-haired beauties smiled sweetly on his wallpaper screen.

"My twin girls. They just turned fifteen." He held the display up with shaking hands. "Proud of my girls. Honor students. This one is Siren, and this one is Simone."

RICK
TESTING, TESTING, 1-2-3

RICK WAITED for the dread and bile to rise. It didn't. He braced himself for the prick of panic that primed his nerves for the attack, but it never came. He expected anxiety to flatten him right there on St. Mark's Place like a hit-and-run. He thought the world would freeze to a stop with the incantation of his late wife's name.

From the corner of his vision, he caught the slow, steady movement of the Cube he had helped push earlier. It was being rotated again.

The world still turns. Life goes on.

Fancy that.

The fan profusely thanked them; his day had been made. Both parties moved on. With his arm slung over Sidra's slim shoulders, Rick felt like his own day was brave and new. Sidra's fingers roped through the belt loop that rode low on his hip, her steps in synch with his.

Red lights were an excuse to let his lips linger on her temple, her lips, her neck. The blaze of the afternoon sun was a reason to tangle up together under the shade of Washington Square Park's trees. They talked and touched, watching people squander their hours happily near the fountain. Sidra shared memories of her mother bringing her and Seamus to the park when they were little. Rick told her about each of his boys. And about Simone.

"So, that fan?" Sidra puzzled over the new bits of information. "He named one of his daughters after . . . your wife?"

"No. He named *both* of his daughters after songs." Songs Rick had sung so often that their words no longer had meaning. They had never been his words, anyway. "Do you want to come up to the studio? I want to play something for you," he heard himself say.

DREAM DEPTH MUSIC Studios emptied out early on Fridays, save for a few engineers tweaking knobs on deadline. Adrian had already trekked up to the lake house; they'd traded a few texts and Rick had begged off joining him, Kat, and Abbey for the weekend. Thor was thankfully nowhere on site.

Sidra marveled at the live rooms and consoles, taking it all in with the wonder of a foreigner in a new land. She admitted that even with a brother who was rarely without drumsticks in his hands, she had only witnessed music performed live, never in the process of being recorded. With his permission, she ran her hand over Jim's snare, tapping it with the pads of her fingertips.

"It's got to be like . . . like childbirth, bringing something totally new into the world like that. Isn't that scary?"

Rick contemplated her comparison and she waited, watching him with those incredible eyes, both dark and bright. "Yes, in a way it's bloody terrifying," he admitted. The creating and the coaxing, making sure what you envisioned in your head translated into reality and not just a shadow of itself. "But the excitement and exhilaration trumps the fear."

He popped a pair of headphones on her ears and backed out of the room with a grin.

Behind the console, he flicked switches, adjusted levels, and pressed the talkback button. "Pay no attention to the man behind the glass," he whispered, but Sidra's broad smile told him the console mic had sent his fluid murmur to her ears crystal clear.

She tentatively tapped the double-mesh screen of the microphone in front of her. "But don't you worry, once it's out in the world . . . what everyone thinks of it? Of you?"

"I used to get caught up in it. But you've just got to trust and make peace with the fact that you put in—and put out—your very best effort."

The track he chose for her flowed not only through her headphones, but the speakers of the console in front of him as well, its beat and melody causing the indicator lights to jump and fall in time. Sidra's eyes closed and her frame rocked slightly. *To me,* Rick thought.

That's my music, moving her.

It was the piece he had composed after the first time they had made love, high over Central Park. He'd wound her ribbon through his fingers and had let her bind around his heart. He didn't have all the words yet, but they were coming.

They would be his very best effort.

"That sounds incredible. That's you? The guitar?"

He isolated his own playing, separating it from Adrian's staccato arpeggio. Glass-like chords formed his rhythms, but he had his share of solos, too. "That's all me." His signature dropped-D tuning created a thick and creamy sound, adding depth to the already complex composition.

"It's so . . . different than I imagined. Heavy, but . . . pretty."

Sidra's elegant hands cupped the cans on her ears as she swayed and grooved to the music. Rick left the console room and joined her, kissing her eyelids and long lashes, her jawline and her throat. Sealed in the live room without headphones of his own, he heard no music. The only sound Rick was treated to was the breathy sigh that escaped her perfect lips. And that alone was all he needed.

His hands roamed her body, turning her gently to fit against him. She shivered as his lips found the nape of her neck. He spanned fingers across her collarbone like he was forming perfect bar chords, while his other hand caressed her middle, pushing up under the thin linen of her shirt. She gasped as his broad thumb plucked against her navel. "Is this how we celebrate?" she asked, carefully removing the headphones.

He took them from her hands and tossed them onto a nearby stool. "I'm about to celebrate all over you, if I'm not careful."

"Is that so?" She was warm and pliable as she turned and molded her exquisite body against him: her curves to his hollows, her fingers lacing with his, and her open mouth capturing his groan.

"Hard at work, I see." Sam's baritone rumbled through the speakers on the wall. "Get a room, you two!" His intrusion in stereo surround-sound continued. "Or at least use the isolation booth."

Rick leaned over Sidra's shoulder and addressed his bandmate through the mic. "Why are you here, Summerisle?"

The bassist grinned behind the glass that separated them. "I could ask you the same thing. Still working to salvage that bridge. You and your bloody B string! Besides, nothing better to do on a Friday, now that Franny threw me out. And the twins are on holiday. I'm down to my last three Day of the Week panties."

Panties? Sidra mouthed to Rick. *As in . . .*

"Don't ask," he murmured. To Sam, he replied, "Stop airing your dirty laundry, mate." Silent laughter shook Sam, his blond locks bobbing around his massive shoulders. "Look at that great gaping gob. He's forgotten to press the talkback button."

Sidra laughed. Sam's lips were moving a mile a minute, and his meaty paws were gesticulating wildly. He hadn't a clue. Rick gave him a sarcastic thumbs up, brows raised comically. "Let's get out of here before he says something he's going to regret."

Sidra took the hand Rick offered. "Where to?" she asked.

If Sam had come back to rework his bass part in "Demons Above," then Thor couldn't be too far behind, Rick surmised. And seeing him was definitely not on Rick's agenda for celebrating. He'd ignored Thor's last text: *Found another investor. You're off the hook.*

"How about dinner at one of those competing Indian establishments on your block? You know, with the crazy lights?"

Sidra looked at him like he was crazy for suggesting it. "I'm afraid you might surpass the maximum height requirement inside." She laughed and stroked back his long unruly curls as he lifted an arm to hail a cab. "Your hair might catch fire under all those lights. But they do make a good chicken tikka!"

RICK

BEST INTENTIONS

THEY WALKED ARM IN ARM, drunk on spice and mango lassi. Sidra had been right; Rick had had to duck his head to even get to their cozy corner table. But once inside, they were treated like royalty.

The interior was like an exploded Christmas tree: Lights, balloons, ornaments, and flags dripped from the ceiling. Music and people and endless plates of naan rotated through the small space, but all Rick remembered was Sidra. And how the low-hanging lights caused the flecks of pyrite in her eyes to spark. And how her lips had tasted as exotic as the foods placed before them when he stole kisses between bites and conversations. Even in that manic atmosphere, they were able to shut out the world. It had been just the two of them, exploring each other, learning more, growing closer.

A woman pushing a jogging stroller approached. Despite the humid evening, she wore a long skirt and her arms were covered. Her pretty face was partially obscured by the thick, straight hair of what appeared to be a wig. Rick remembered . . . it was Friday, and they were within the *eruv*.

"Shabbat Shalom," he said as they passed.

The woman happily echoed his greeting, sending a bright smile their way.

Sidra squeezed Rick's arm. "You surprise me." Her whisper was an echo from the day of the blackout in the yoga studio.

He'd come to her sanctuary seeking something, and yet it felt as if he had found so much more. It went well beyond yoga, and attraction; it was the sense of belonging and well-being that had been eluding him for such a long time. Of having everything he needed and needing to look no further. He squeezed her back, wordless, happy.

"I almost forgot it was Friday," she commented. "No work today has thrown me off."

"You deserve a day off once in a while. Today, especially." He kissed her temple. "You know, in Jewish poetry and music, Friday—the Sabbath—is described as a bride. And one welcomes her and greets her. Quite mystical, really."

"That's beautiful." Sidra flashed him a smile as they turned onto her street. "You're quite the Renaissance man. Heavy metal, religious symbolism, yoga . . ." Her tone matched the warm night breeze that teased through their hair, tangling her straight tresses with his thick curls.

"Nah, just an old dog learning some new tricks, that's all."

"I know this is going to sound silly, but my dad . . ." Sidra paused at her gate. "He's been wanting to meet you."

"You don't think he—"

Sidra shook her head. "He won't remember the Whiskey Ward. Trust me. I've had Fiona monitoring his food and drink intake all afternoon. It will be like meeting an entirely different Jack."

Rick stared up the steps of the brownstone, remembering the shock and embarrassment on her face that had greeted him as he stumbled down the block with Jack draped over his shoulder. Had that really only been yesterday?

She led him inside her apartment, through the Lilliputian

kitchen, and out a back door. Three concrete steps up and they were under the stars again. Sidra noticed Rick's gaping expression and laughed.

"It's just that I . . . I never considered New Yorkers could have a backyard!" he sputtered. He thought of all those high-rise dwellers and what they were missing. Even Adrian, with his park views, couldn't walk into his private patch of green at midnight. "This is incredible!"

He took a tentative step off the small patio and onto the grass. High wooden fences cordoned off the space on either side, and the windowless brick of a building from the street behind served as the garden's back wall. Strands of tiny white lights suddenly twinkled on, dancing along the fences and through a few of the trees. It was as if the stars had decided to drop in on the party.

"Dad!" Sidra turned toward the house. A laugh emanated from an open window above them. "Here he comes."

Jack emerged moments later, carrying a hurricane lantern in one hand and a six-pack in the other. Sidra bounced over, kissing his cheek and relieving him of the beer. "Dad, this is Rick."

"Jack Sullivan." Sidra's dad thrust his free hand into Rick's open palm and pumped it warmly. "Finally, we meet."

"It's a pleasure, sir." And it was. Sidra had been right. When not clouded by drink, her father's blue eyes were sharp as they subtly gave her suitor the once-over.

"Sir, bah. Call me Jack. North London?"

"Yes, Hampstead." Rick followed father and daughter up the flagstone path to a small set of chairs and a table. Sidra lit tiki torches in a halo around them while Jack cracked the tops off three of the ales.

"It's nice to hear RP without a hit of Estuary."

"You got all that in less than ten words?" Rick accepted the bottle Jack handed him with a nod.

"Dad. Stop showing off," Sidra teased. She picked up a beer and took a healthy swallow. Rick detected a tiny smile of pride hiding behind her bottle.

"An accent can tell the history behind a person. Often, better than the person behind the accent," Jack said, kicking his feet up onto the extra chair.

Rick wondered what else his accent said about him. Embarrassed at an early age by his parents' wealth? Rebelled against their regard for higher education as soon as he had finished his posh public schooling? Self-conscious of his covenant with God whilst growing up under the shadow of the Church of England? He had traded the silver spoon in his mouth for heavy metal in his veins, learned life lessons from every city on the road, and prayed to very different gods now.

"Your mother," Jack continued, staring down the neck of his now half-empty bottle, "moved here from India at age three. Spoke no English until school began for her at five. She taught her parents English as she learned it herself. She had barely a trace of an accent by twenty." He pinched his thumb and index finger together and squinted an eye. "Like the tiniest hint of spice in a dish. But I fell in love with it. And then I fell in love with her."

The way Sidra was hanging on to her father's every word told Rick she had never heard this story before. He had a feeling Jack didn't speak of his wife often.

The three of them chatted easily as the evening grew louder around them. Crickets and katydids trilled their night songs, blending with distant sirens and the vibrating clack of subway cars. It was only when Jack lurched up to use the bathroom inside that Rick noticed the man had consumed four beers to their one, effectively killing the six-pack.

"Walk with me?" Sidra was luminous in the moonlight, her hand like a cool, smooth shell in his palm as she led him through the small garden. So small, they couldn't walk far, giving Rick the perfect excuse to press Sidra against the brick of the back wall and kiss her sweetly.

"Thank you."

"For what?" She nipped his lip and smiled up at him.

"For showing me this exists." If questioned, he didn't know if he would be able to put into words what exactly "this" was: The nature, the beauty, the stillness all humbled him. Just as life, and love, energized him.

Sidra bent and touched a rock by their feet. Light illuminated it briefly as Jack pushed open the back door, and Rick saw it wasn't a rock at all. It was a ram's head, sculpted from terracotta in fiery burnt orange. It was rough-hewn and obviously one of a kind. Grass and clover grew up around it, rooting it there and making it seem as if it had been a part of the natural landscape for a while now.

"You have your mother's fingers," he murmured as Sidra lovingly traced the ridges of one of the curved horns. Her hands were an exact fit in the grooves.

"Her name," Jack bellowed from the patio, "was Satya." He was now nursing a brown beer jug the size of a small infant that he must have retrieved from inside. "It means 'truth.' Meant," he corrected himself, swearing under his breath and taking a swig as if to punish himself. "Satya *meant* truth."

"Dad . . ." Sidra's dismay led her back to her father; Rick followed.

"I'm sorry for your loss," he said. It didn't seem adequate. "May her memory be a blessing." *And not a curse.*

Jack's face was close enough for Rick to see the broken capillaries splayed across his nose like the red lines on a subway map. "You don't know what it feels like to lose your truth!"

"Actually, Jack . . . I do."

"Dad! Stop." Sidra inserted herself between them.

"Enough." There was a brief tug-of-war with the bottle, but Jack held fast. "Why don't you go inside?"

"No, I think I'm gonna go down to ABC." Smiling Jack was back, but again, his eyes belied his smile. "For a growler fill."

"Can't you just stay home tonight?"

Rick heard the little girl lost in his lover's voice. Jack kissed his daughter on the forehead. "Just ducking out for an Easy Blonde." He winked at Rick. "That's the name of the draft, if you get my drift. You kids have fun tonight."

RICK STARED at the bars on Sidra's bedroom window once they were inside and wondered if she even realized she was a prisoner. He wanted to free her from every cage binding her in and holding her back, just as she had freed him from the rusty, unforgiving traps of his mind and body.

And those were truly his very best intentions.

SIDRA

WRITTEN IN THE STARS

Sᴏᴅʀᴀ ʟᴀʏ with her back to Rick, smiling. Her bed felt like an island. No, like a shimmering oasis. He had laid her gently down and drunk her in, savoring the entire length of her body as if he would never quite quench his thirst for her.

Now propped on one elbow, he leaned and kissed each vertebra. "Even more beautiful in the starlight."

"My mother wanted to name me for the starlight," she said softly. "*Sitara* in Hindi. Sidra is the Latin form for *starlike*."

"Perfect."

"What's my name in Hebrew?" she asked, resting her chin on her shoulder and gazing up at him.

"Well, let's see. There are no vowels, so we go by the consonants." He traced each Hebrew letter on her back with his finger as he recited them aloud. "*Samech* means 'support'; to trust and rely on." She leaned into his touch. "*Dalet*," he continued, "is 'door.'" He kissed her slightly parted lips. "*R* is *Resh* . . . 'beginning.'" She shifted her body, twining her legs through his so it was hard to tell where she began and he ended. "And lastly . . ." His voice caught as his finger made its last loop on her body. *"Hey."* He slipped his hand down her hip to her belly and pulled her close. "To behold," he breathed into her hair.

"My name means all those things?"

"To me, yes. But the word *sidra* means something else." He held her in silence.

"Well, are you going to tell me?"

"The word means 'order.'"

She contemplated that. All her life, she loved the idea of being named for the boundless beauty of the stars. Now, she considered the grounding reality of order, arrangement, and responsibility. She felt the hot spring of tears, then Rick's fingertips mingling with them on her cheeks.

"Your mother named you for the stars because she wanted you to follow your dreams. It's not your job to save your dad, Sidra. Believe me, if you ever have kids—"

"I'm never having kids." Fear had momentarily opened a small, pondering window that morning in the radiologist's office, but all Jack's talk about her mother tonight had slammed it shut. It hurt too much to go there.

"Hear me out. Children grow up and out. They have to live their own lives. Your dad wouldn't want you to give up your dreams to take care of him. Nor would Seamus. You cannot replace your mother. And you are not to blame."

The fear and toll of the last few days, and the sweet relief of its outcome, made her feel weak and weepy. She tried to take care of everyone, even absolute strangers passing through the door of her yoga studio, but the last person she considered needing care was herself.

She had been just a young, scared girl when her mother died. There was no order to that, no divine arrangement. Rick was right; she was not responsible. It had been just as senseless as Rick losing Simone. Just as random as her own scare and false alarm. She was alive. It was time to live.

"Erm, luv . . . do you realize there's a shoe nailed to your wall?"

The gentle kisses between her breasts had felt like a dream, but the vibration of Rick's voice and his breath on her skin both warmed and awakened her.

"Yes, it's my flip-flop." The gorgeous guy who had shared her bed for the second night in a row was now working his way down her body. Sunlight streamed through the windows, bronzing his strong shoulders. She captured one of his curls between her fingers as it tickled its way across her tummy and lazily twirled it. "You're only noticing it now?"

"My mind is usually elsewhere when I'm in your bedroom, luv. As is my mouth."

Sidra groaned, twisting his hair in her fist. "Talk about driving your point home," she panted as his tongue darted against her tightest, most tender spot. "Oh, my . . ." His arms gripped her thighs as he lifted her.

"I could drink from you all day, Goddess."

Those dark eyes flicked a glance at her so intense, she nearly came on the next long lap of his tongue. But he wasn't nearly through with her. He kissed her very tip, making her tremble and buck up against him.

He licked slow circles around her glossy core, stroking out each whimper and sigh as his personal prize. Heat spiraled in her belly, and her breasts ached. She ran her hands over them, marveling at their heaviness, before plunging her fingers into his hair. He groaned, pulling her against his mouth and sucking her sweetly.

"Make love to me." She had never wanted anything like she wanted him inside of her now. Her whole being begged for him. "Rick . . ."

She summoned, and he responded, climbing her gently, sliding kisses across her hips, her nipples, her throat, covering her with his lean, hard frame. "I love you, Sidra." His words and his actions were solemn, sacred. His thumbs caressed her chin and she cried out, biting at his lip as he filled her. He rode the wave of her orgasm, giving her a taste of the highest high as he whispered her name and plunged deeper. She clenched him, meeting his every thrust, never breaking eye contact. An overwhelming surge of tenderness toward this amazing man overtook her, and as they moved as one, slow and sensual, she knew.

Love was just the beginning of their journey.

She climbed with him, watching his face as she embraced the words. He was changed. From that first encounter in the elevator, all steely-eyed and desperate for an escape. And different from the man who had first stepped into her studio, wrestling demons he couldn't even name.

The bliss of his release sent shock waves through her, and they gasped in unison, laughing and kissing their way down to solid ground once again. Rick rolled onto his back, chest heaving, spent. His eyes searched above, and he broke out into a smile. "I want to wake up every morning and see that shoe."

Sidra cuddled up against his chest, fingers trailing along the soft hair at his navel. "I nailed it there as a reminder, after meeting you. That there are good guys out there in the world. And in hopes that one would come to my rescue again."

Rick's brows rose as he regarded her. "Have I been successful in my quest?"

"Why, yes, brave sir," she whispered. "You've rescued, and you've captured, my very heart."

∾

"WELCOME TO SATURDAY, New York City! *The Mookey & Dean Show* is coming at you live from South Street Seaport all day, and it's a block party weekend of your favorite classic rock."

Sidra didn't remember dozing back off, but she vaguely recalled singing emanating from the shower and Rick kissing her good-bye. "I set your alarm for ten," he'd said. "Just in case. Don't want you missing your first class."

"Hey," she'd protested. "Stay." He'd laughed at her sleepy demand and had said something about working for a few hours today.

Now that she had heard part of the album and seen where he spent most of his days, she understood. And was excited to hear the finished product. But a small, selfish part of her wanted to tie him to the bedposts with pieces of orange ribbon and never let him go.

She smiled and stretched, thinking about how yesterday had turned out to be one of the best days of her life.

"Another hour of rock coming atcha after this commercial break."

She made a halfhearted attempt to shut the clock radio off, but missed it on her first swipe. *Whatever. I should tell my students to do this in bed,* she thought as she reached both arms back over her head, stretching from fingertips to pointed toes. A full-body stretch. She elongated and engaged her torso, bringing a slight arch to her back. She stayed like that, concentrating on the rise and fall of her breath.

She had twelve kids registered for her tween-and-teen yoga at noon, but an open kids flow class before that. Some weeks it was just her and a couple regulars, but other times it was a madhouse. Mikey loved it, because the parents would usually nostalgia-shop in his store.

"So get this: Times must really be tough in the music industry. You know, with music streaming and all. Rumor has it that Riff Rotten is working retail."

Sidra sat rod-straight, wondering if she really just heard the DJ call her lover by his stage name.

"That's right, folks. The lead singer of Corroded Corpse

fame has been spotted on Rivington, working in a record shop. What's the name of that place, Mookey?"

"It's called Revolve Records."

She threw a hand over her mouth, but a delighted laugh managed to push through. "Oh my God, Rick. You're crazy," she whispered to herself, rocking out of bed. This she had to see.

"There you go, folks. Revolve Records . . . one of the last remaining vestiges of vinyl in this town. And now you can go down there and catch a glimpse of the King of Doom. Think he'll bite some heads off the rats down on Rivington?"

"It's Riff Rotten, Dean. Not Ozzy."

Sidra quickly showered, not even bothering to dry her hair. The morning sun would do the job on her walk to the studio. She found herself humming "Bohemian Rhapsody" as she toweled off, the song Rick had been singing in the shower. After a bite of toast and juice, her father occurred to her. She hadn't heard him come in.

Rick's words from last night echoed in her head. He was right. She couldn't be his keeper. Still, she hesitated as she pulled the front door closed behind her. Without Seamus here . . .

You're only one person; you're doing the best you can.

It was a mantra that had been a long time in coming, and she needed to embrace it.

"Rubbish, rubbish . . . perhaps . . ." Rick was sorting albums at the counter under the watchful eye of Mikey when she arrived. "No scratches," he observed, holding the edges of a glossy black record between his palms before gingerly flipping it over. "Twenty bucks, maybe?"

Her cousin thumbed through his dog-eared copy of *Goldmine's Price Guide to Collectible Record Albums*. "Hot damn! Right again." He glanced up at Sidra. "It's like a Jedi mind thing. He just *knows*."

Rick laughed, aiming a wink in Sidra's direction.

"I heard good help is hard to find these days," Sidra said, leaning on her tiptoes to kiss the newest employee of Revolve Records. "Better hang on to him."

"Looks like you got that covered, Sid."

She blushed at her cousin's comment and slowly untangled her arms from around Rick's neck. "When did this come about? And how?"

"Oh, you know . . . my girlfriend's got this full-time yoga gig, so I figured I needed something close by to occupy my time." He slid another record out of its sleeve and pretended to inspect it. But she could see his smile betray him.

The shop was buzzing, practically bursting at the seams with people. Fiona was taking money, hand over fist, at the register. The New Arrivals bin looked picked clean, and it wasn't even noon yet. Couples crowded around the listening stations, but many pairs of eyes were aimed at the counter. The Heavy Metal section was overflowing with customers Sidra had never seen before, jockeying for space and pulling albums out left and right.

"Plus we're getting trade-ins," Mike crowed, nodding toward the pile of vinyl Rick was making his way through. "Some guy came in with all of those in exchange for one of these." He gestured behind him, where several signed Corroded Corpse albums were displayed prominently behind the counter.

"Oh, *this* will be worth something." Rick pulled an obscure hard rock album from the pile. "This band had already gone platinum with their debut album in the late eighties. Then they discreetly put this EP out, pretending it was an indie live release from *before* they were famous, and their fans snapped it up. Meanwhile, their record label had funded it as a marketing scheme. Extremely rare. Especially in its original cellophane. At least three hundred dollars, maybe five."

Mike was busy with his nose in the book. His hoot confirmed the validity of Rick's provenance. "Dude, I could kiss you! You know," he quickly added, "if you weren't rich and famous and if my store wasn't filled with all these people and if dudes turned me on."

Sidra laughed. "Want me to take over, Fi? My class doesn't start for another half hour." Fiona's long, red nails were flying over the register keys and she was bagging purchases so fast, she was like a leopard-print blur.

"I think that was the initial rush," she called, sagging against the register to catch her breath. "*Someone* had the bright idea to call the radio station. I mean, who does that anymore?"

Mikey chuckled, bouncing his cell phone in his hand. "Oh, looks like a little birdie tweeted about it, too."

"Hey, don't exploit my boyfriend," Sidra joked, shifting out of the way to allow a few hesitant fans through to say hi and grab an autograph. It was fun to watch Rick in action as he nodded and genuinely listened to whatever they had mustered up the courage to say. Each person earned a smile from him as he handed over whatever he had signed. The jangle of the bells above the door signaled more visitors, and he looked up expectantly.

Sidra followed his gaze as it landed on the too-tan-to-be-trusted man who had met with her uncle last month. And he was arm-in-arm with the woman from the limo.

RICK

LOCKOUT

"A for effort, Riff. Really."

Rick had always disliked the sound of a slow, sarcastic clap. But now, as the sound of Thor's hands cracked and echoed in the cavernous space, he hated it—and the man—even more. He intercepted the producer at the door.

"You have no business being here." His tin-man jaw was back in full force as he choked out the words between clenched teeth.

"Oh, but I do." Thor wound his way through the bins toward the counter, Isabelle in tow. Rick felt his fists tighten as they both gave Sidra the once-over. *This isn't happening. No. Not now.*

He'd thought of a dozen different ways to come clean to Sidra over the course of last evening, but it had been too perfect to puncture. *Can't the universe give me a bloody break for one night?*

"Nice to see you again, Miss Sullivan."

"Don't talk to her. Don't so much as look at her, Thor. I'm warning you."

"At ease, Riff. I've just come to show my new *partner* the potential space."

"Isabelle, you can't be serious—"

"Oh, please." She flicked her heavily made-up eyes heavenward. "Like I'd make it my business to come slumming down here for anyone but you." She sighed and swept a hand toward the door like she was a game show hostess. "If you'd taken my calls yesterday, you would know I was merely the messenger."

"Rick?"

He heard the confusion in Sidra's voice, but couldn't pull his eyes from the door.

Wren.

Corroded Corpse's former manager strode into the shop like he already owned it. No, make that owned it, surveyed it, and planned to take a wrecking ball to it. The counter bit into Rick's back as he bumped back against it, adrenaline pumping at the memory of the smoking hole Wren Blackmoor had left in his wake the last time business brought him within ten feet of Rick. The band in ruins at his feet.

He'd stolen from them. Lied to them. But worst of all, he'd systematically ground them down, one by one, and pitted them against one another.

"Hello, old friend."

Rick hadn't heard that voice in an age. And Simone had still been walking this earth the last time he'd uttered a word to the man standing before him. He refused to alter that fact. Old history. Dead history. Nothing could change it.

"I know the front is shabby," Thor was saying, handing Wren a copy of the building's specs. "We'll do a small reception area up here, all in marble. Maybe a slate floor? Something sleek." Holding up a small USB drive, he proclaimed, "Amazing that something this small can supersede all *this.*"

He flicked a hand at all the vinyl before dropping the

thumb drive into Rick's front shirt pocket. "Turns out the beast is bigger than all of us," he murmured in Rick's ear.

"You know what would be cool?" Isabelle piped up. "You can break all this vinyl—you know, take a hammer to it—and do a mosaic on the floor, under poly or Plexiglas. White, with all the black? So hip. Maybe even do the ceiling, too."

Thor nodded. "Then we'll get rid of whatever rattrap's upstairs now and build up to house the musicians. That brilliant idea was Riff's, actually."

"Don't listen to him, Sidra."

"Ah, Riff Rotten not wanting to take credit for something?" Wren laughed, looking pointedly at him. "That's a switch, eh, mate?" The wanker dared to add a wink.

The air left the building, left Rick's lungs, and he saw spots behind his eyes.

"You must be Junior." Thor clapped a hand on the shoulder of a stunned Mike. He had been gaping like a fish from the moment Isabelle mentioned taking a hammer to his inventory. "Your dad said you'd show us the back if we were to pop by."

Turning to Wren, he added, "Its bones are perfect for a state-of-the-art recording studio. Worth the wait, trust me. And its acoustics border on orgasmic. Am I right, sister?" He chucked Sidra under the chin playfully. "Riff can vouch for that, too . . . I'm sure."

"Fi," Mikey managed. "Take the gentlemen to the back. I'll be there in a moment." His gaze slid to Rick, then to Isabelle, with cool familiarity.

"You two know each other?" he demanded, protectively ensconcing his cousin under a beefy arm. Sidra avoided everyone's gaze, choosing to stare down at Isabelle's show-stopping shoes.

Rick remembered his request to his publicist, asking where the limo had dropped Sidra that long- ago day. God, how stupid he had been! And it was all coming back to bite him in his pompous arse. "It's not what you think, I assure you. Sidra, I was trying to find—"

Sidra shook her head, as if to rid her mind of any thought of him. "To find a way to use me? To get inside here, to survey my *space*?"

"No! Tell her, Iz. Please."

"Kismet, darling." Isabelle smacked her lacquered lips to his cheek. "Sometimes it's a bitch. Nothing personal," she added smugly, casting a thinly apologetic look toward Sidra and Mike. "It's just business." She clacked away on those horrid stilettos. It was a sound that would haunt Rick, along with the wounded look in Sidra's eyes as she finally regarded him, for the rest of his days.

"Sidra. Hear me out." He made a move to touch her, but her cousin played defense, blocking the path.

"To make me think you wanted me to *help* you." Sidra's voice broke. Those tiger-iron eyes were like polished stones behind tears that she would not let fall. "To make me think you wanted *me*," she whispered.

"Luv, let me—"

Not only would Sidra not hear him out, she did the cruelest thing she could possibly do. With a push and help from Mike, she locked him out.

SIDRA
WOUNDED WARRIOR

THANK GOODNESS FOR THE CHILDREN. Sidra watched as they invaded her space, their feet slapping happily on the wooden floor and their chatter echoing up to the stained glass windows.

"You're welcome to stay," she hollered to the building's buyers, where they huddled deep in discussion on the bimah. She plunged the lights down to their dimmest. "Join the class."

The children knew exactly what to do. Low lights was their cue to grab mats and form a circle with them on the floor. Today they were twenty strong, spreading the circle generously, their energy as bright as the sun. Sidra set her mat in the middle of them and sat cross-legged, in lotus position. When she nodded, all of her young students fell dutifully into prayer, their starting pose of the day. Kneeling wide, their tiny rumps in the air and their foreheads to the mat. Sidra felt like Aditi, the Hindu sun goddess, as their little arms all stretched toward her in the center of the ring. *Aditi, mother of all,* she remembered learning as a child. *Keeper of the light.*

There was no way she was going to let Thorton Young rain on her parade. Or Thor, as his friends— like Rick—had called him. The Norse god of thunder would not storm on her day. Not when she had this circle of light around her.

Sidra smiled in satisfaction as the only three people still standing had to pick their way out, tripping over foam blocks in their haste. They twisted and stepped wide to avoid the mats and bodies in their path to the exit door.

Her mother had once sculpted Aditi in relief, glazing her in a brilliant orange sari and sitting her on a majestic purple lotus flower. It had been one of her favorite pieces.

You've got flames in your hair, my golden goddess.

The memory of Rick's words from the first time they made love slammed into her from behind, and she broke, just like her mother's sculpture. She fell into her own prayer pose to hide her tears.

"Sid?"

The door wasn't locked, but Mikey knocked anyway. Sidra didn't feel like moving from her spot under the light. An hour of Karma Kids on the stereo had forced her through the children's class, and she had powered through the next hour with her teens to Enya. Now she lay, allowing complete silence to surround her. No students, no music . . . just her and the *ner tamid*. For now.

They'd knock it down, of course.

She remembered the day Thorton Young had introduced himself, on his "exploratory visit." How he had said he'd had a vision, more than a purpose, for the space. And it hadn't been just his alone. *My investment partner . . . he's in entertainment, keeps odd hours.*

Rick knew all along, she thought, rolling onto her side. *How could I have been so blind?* She felt the twinge in her lower back, left over from that same day, when she had popped too fast out of that warrior pose.

The battle was over. She had no reserves with which to fight any of this.

Until she turned, she hadn't been aware of the tears. Now she let them roll, hot across the bridge of her nose and down into her ear.

Soft footfalls made their way toward her. Her cousin sat on the wide edge of the top step. "Fuckin' A," was all he said.

"Fuckin' A," Sidra repeated tonelessly.

He grabbed a nearby brick and twirled it between his thick, blunt fingers. Sidra wiped her nose with the back of her hand.

"Hey, we're the fighting Irish. Well, you're half Irish. But that's half the battle. We can do this. Shillelagh law." He raised the brick in his fist.

"No, Mike. We can't." There would be no protests. No lying down in front of the bulldozers that would come in the name of gentrification and progress. The building that had been in their family for three generations would morph into some sort of hipster oasis. For musicians and their entourages, women wearing thousand-dollar shoes. And showing up in limos.

Meeting Rick in the elevator that day may have been chance, but she had been a fool to believe that anything after that wasn't just some desperate fantasy she had conjured up. No rich rock icon could ever be happy slumming in her shabby neighborhood, her tiny apartment. Or in her sad little life.

"Kind of ironic that my record store is closing because of a recording studio." Mike blew out a defeated laugh. "Can't they just do that shit on GarageBand? With laptops and USBs?"

Sidra thought about how distressed Rick had been about CBGB closing down. Yet watching him behind that console yesterday, she saw how in control and focused he was. Like a metal monarch behind the glass walls of his castle. When it came to business, *his* business, he probably had no trouble acquiring kingdoms. No doubt just another part of the deal he'd made with the devil. She, Mike, and Sully just happened to be in the path along the way.

And as Charlie would say, everybody has a price.

"I'm sorry, Mike." Her whisper was almost too hoarse to decipher. "So, so sorry."

"For what? Like this is somehow *your* fault? Get outta here. My dad was looking to unload the building long before—"

"You can say it. Before I let another heartless musician trample all over me." She pulled her knees up, curling into fetal position.

"Hey. At least you didn't put him on your payroll."

Sidra forced a smile. She knew her cousin was just trying to lighten the mood. But even as they were bathed in the warm golden light from overhead, there was no denying it: Things looked pretty bleak.

"What say we round up Fi and Reggie and go get toasted?"

Sidra sat up slowly. "Reggie's got that summer share on weekends, remember? Fire Island?"

"Well, fuck it. Let's hop on the Jitney and burn that shit down." Just like her brother's hand flexed in anticipation of playing percussion, Sidra's cousin milked his fist at the thought of an ice-cold brew in hand. *Happy-go-lucky Irish party boy,* she thought, *or just another Jack in training?* Sidra wondered how far the scale had to tip to register the point of no return.

"You go." Banana Louie was waiting for food, water, and a lightbulb change. And her father, well . . . hopefully he'd remembered to eat, shower, and leave a light on for her. She would make her rounds. And then she would go home.

Mike stood to his full height. He tossed the foam brick from one hand to the other. "For what it's worth, Sid . . ."

"Yeah?"

"Sullivan and Son . . . and grandkids. We had a good run."

It was after dusk by the time Sidra rounded 5th Street and plodded up the path to her apartment. How could this possibly be the same day that she had burst from her front door into the sunshine on her way to see Rick at the record store? She didn't even feel like she was on the same planet, let alone in the same time zone. If depression dulled the senses, why did everything around her appear so different? Her block looked shabbier, traffic sounded more crass than usual, and her outside vestibule smelled foul and foreign.

A figure swayed out of the darkness, under the brownstone stairs, lurching heavy against her and knocking the key from her hand. She screamed, the weight and confusion bringing her down, and her knees scraped the pavement.

"Lost her . . ." A plaintive mumble slowed her racing heart. "Lost my truth."

"Daddy." Sidra wrapped her arms around her father's slumped shoulders. Not Jack, not Dad . . . She needed that father figure she remembered from her childhood.

But he wasn't that.

And he was no longer the distinguished NYU professor on a summer bender. He was broken.

Jack still wore the same clothes he had had on the night she and Rick visited with him in the back garden. He smelled of sweat and tears. "Let's get you inside," she said.

She brought him through her apartment door rather than trying to get him up the steep steps of the brownstone to his second floor bedroom. Once he was slumped on the couch, she figured he would pass out peacefully. But instead, he grabbed the mother dove statue from the console table.

Her heart sank.

"Dad . . . let go." Her words fell on deaf, drunk ears. She didn't worry that all hell would break loose, like when she was little, and that he'd throw it like all the others. No, his death grip on it worried her more.

Even in death, her sweet mother had such a grip on him. Sidra wondered if he would ever be free.

Jack squeezed the sculpture so hard, she thought it would pop and shatter to dust in his hands. "You're holding her too tight." The sharp edge of one wing bit into his unfeeling flesh, drawing blood. "You're hurting . . ."

Who, Sidra? Himself?

"You're hurting me!" She yelled the words, even startling herself. "And you're hurting Seamus!"

He started. Looking stunned and unsure. "But I lost . . . her."

"Yes. But you didn't lose *us*. We love you, Dad. But you need to get help. Will you agree to get help?"

There was a lucid look to those watery blue eyes, and he slowly nodded.

RICK

LOYALTY LIES

"How long has he been like that?"

"Dunno. I just got here."

"What should we do?"

"Let's wait for Digger."

Rick could hear Sam and Jim whispering. A door slammed. There was more whispering, then Adrian's low murmur. Footsteps.

"Is he breathing?"

Rick slowly rolled out of the Plow pose he had been holding, one vertebrae at a time. He kept his legs together and steady as he brought them down.

"Yes, Sam. I'm alive."

Now that his neck wasn't in a compromised position and his feet were no longer over his head, Rick could see his bandmates' concerned faces as they surrounded him. The inversion he'd held was known for calming the brain and reducing stress.

A pity he couldn't stay there indefinitely.

He arched his back and pushed into Fish pose to counterbalance, then slowly came to rest in Corpse. He let his eyes close. "I fucked up. Big-time."

Night settled over Dream Depth Music Studios as the band-mates sat and listened to his sordid tale. All of it: from the beginnings of the botched business deal with Thor to Wren showing up and everything in between. Including all the fights with Isabelle over the album, a burden he had considered his, as bandleader, to bear.

Then came the personal stuff. The highest highs of falling in love with Sidra all summer in the city were counterbalanced with the lowest lows. Lying to her. Losing her. Letting her building fall into the hands of Thor. The guy who had his hands in everything, including the future of their album.

"He's going to leak it."

All heads turned. Mason, Thor's assistant, was standing in the doorway. "I saw him duplicating multiple thumb drives from Pro Tools."

"Why should we trust you?" Sam demanded. "He's your bloody paycheck."

"I trust him." Thanks to Rick, Mason had become a fervent follower of Sidra's yoga. He was a good kid. And sharp. Rick touched his hand to his chest pocket, remembering the USB Thor had dropped in there and what he had said. About the beast being bigger than all of them.

Thorton Young was no upstart in the business. He had been bred by the machine. And fed by the machine. He was pissed that their dealings were going south. And once he found out Rick had hired Gloria—not to dig into his past, but rather into the past of the building—he'd want Rick's blood. And the best way to siphon it would be through the veins of the band itself.

"We'll go to the label and demand a new producer. It's a conflict of interest." Adrian was adamant. "We'll storm the gates and take it right to the top if we have to."

"Don't you get it?" Rick scrubbed a hand over his eyes, his cheek, his mouth. "We've been trusting the wrong gatekeepers all along!"

The look Sam and Jim exchanged, followed by a quick glance at Adrian, confirmed something Rick had been denying the entire time. All his talk about control and doing it their own way this time around—he had marched them right into the jaws of the bloody machine again. And for what? The glamour? The fortune? They had had all that. What was the point?

Corroded Corpse had rid its old shackles like a snake shedding its skin, becoming the Rotten Graves Project. But for all intents and purposes, they were still in captivity.

Rick had confused guilt for loyalty. Aligning himself with Isabelle because of her connection to Simone had been his first of many mistakes. She'd done nothing but push deadlines and force stress on him. And he had mistaken attention for validation. Signing on to a 360 deal just because one had been offered, the first of its kind to a metal band of their stature, had not been what they needed. Or what he thought he had wanted.

And his mind and his body had been trying to tell him that all along.

"So what should we do?" Sam ventured.

"We beat him to the punch," Rick said.

"Oh!" Sam's eyes widened. "In this case, I am all for a premature ejaculation of this nature."

"It can't be the rough cuts, coming from us." Adrian rubbed his goatee in thought. "The press will rip us apart."

"The fans will go bonkers, though. They've been dying to hear new material," Jim pointed out.

"Bloody well right!" Sam boomed. "We've been dusting off and hauling out the old standards live these past four years. They deserve a taste of the new."

Rick spoke up. "What if we were to record one of the tracks, live? And interlace it with the studio takes?"

The rest of the band agreed, but which track?

"Track eight."

It was the song he had been composing for Sidra. And in light of all that had happened, it couldn't wait. Not for the album's official street date, not months from now.

"Track eight? It doesn't even have a title," Sam pointed out. "Or lyrics!"

"It does now," Rick said.

RICK

CASHING IN

"You gotta lotta nerve, Riff Rotten."

Fiona cracked her gum and gave Rick her best stare-down. Her cadence was downright melodic; he had missed it. Along with everything—and everyone else—within the four walls of the Rivington Street structure.

"I'd like to speak to the owner."

"Which one? New one? Old one?"

"Come on, Fi." Rick could've sworn her expertly penciled brow twitched at the sound of her nickname. "Page Mike for me. Please."

She feigned boredom, pressing a long pink nail down on the store intercom button. "One of the *investors* is here." Fiona glared at him as if he'd brought an infestation of rats along with him.

"We're not taking in new stock," Mikey said as Rick hoisted the heavy crate full of albums onto the counter.

"Trust me. You'll want these."

Mike folded his arms across his chest. "Why? So that bitch in the heels can take a hammer to them after I'm gone? I'd rather her claw my fucking eyes out."

Rick pulled out the first album in the pile. "Recognize this?" He tapped the windowed artwork on the front of Led Zeppelin's *Physical Graffiti*, but was met with a blank stare.

"No? You should. That's the front of 96–98 St. Mark's Place. Mick Jagger sat on that stoop, too, during the video for 'Waiting on a Friend.' " Rick singled out the Rolling Stones' *Tattoo You* from the bunch. "Then he and Keith walked around the corner to St. Mark's Bar & Grill on 1st and met the rest of the band inside."

Mike stole a glance, but didn't make a move for a closer look. "So what of it?"

"*So,* it's your neighborhood." Rick pulled the Allman Brothers out next, followed by the Velvet Underground. Hendrix. The Dead. "You're too young to know about the Fillmore East or the Electric Circus. But they were the stuff of legend, the places that made me want to leave England to come here! And I did."

Out came the Ramones, Blondie, the Pogues. "I bought half these records at Sounds in the 1980s. A little shop on St. Marks. Gone. CBs, Sin-é, Coney Island High. Some of those have to ring a bell, right? But they're all gone now."

"Tell me something I don't know." Mike shifted his weight impatiently to the other foot.

Rick slapped down another album: Corroded Corpse's *Palladium Live.* "We were one of the last rock bands to play there, before it turned into a nightclub. Then it was demolished."

He leaned on the counter and leveled Revolve Record's proprietor with a steely stare. "So you're right. I *am* invested. I had forgotten the history. The significance. Until I found this place. And until I found Sidra. I'm not the enemy, Mikey."

"How much do you want for them?"

Rick shook his head. "I don't want money. I'm looking for a trade."

SIDRA

STANDING ROOM ONLY

"Just let everything dissolve . . ." Sidra advised. But it was hard to settle into the final relaxation as the floor beneath her students resonated with a steady *thump, thump, thump* from somewhere.

Perhaps it was a good thing that half her class had already vacated. One by one, their phones, set to silent, had begun lighting up like Christmas trees twenty minutes into class. The publicists made like lemmings for the door, followed by several others. Apologies were murmured, gasps could be heard as they scurried out, until only Pixie, Deuce, Benny, and a few of her old regulars remained.

"Come on," Pixie had protested. "Did Lady Gaga have a wardrobe malfunction? What kind of musical emergency could possibly impact this many people in the business?"

"Moving on," Sidra had prompted, and led the meager holdouts through their poses. It was depressing enough that she could count on her fingers the number of classes that remained before the place was shuttered for good. She'd hoped that quality would make up for the shrinking quantity, but her tranquil environment was already being infringed upon.

Over the past week, surveyors, architects, engineers, and interior decorators had paraded through, all on Thor's payroll and with no heed to business hours or class schedules. Her uncle was too busy meeting with lawyers and liquidators to even care.

Applause and a collective cheer erupted from somewhere up front.

"It sounds like the roof is caving in." Benny struggled to a seated position. "Benny wants to know what is going on!"

"Sounds more like a party no one invited us to," Deuce commented, pushing his mammoth digits together and bowing his bandana-clad head. "Namaste, Sidra."

"Thank you for allowing me to—"

"*Chhhheeeeeeck . . . check one, two.*"

"—to guide your practice," Sidra hollered over the amplification that echoed through the space. *What the hell?* The thumping had now been replaced by a low buzz. "Namaste, everyone. And remember: If you aren't coming to a class again before we close and haven't used up your punch cards, take them with you. I've made arrangements with Yogatality on Houston to honor them."

"Will you be teaching there?" one of her regulars asked. Hopeful murmurs from the others followed.

Sidra slowly shook her head. "No, Gerta. I'm afraid not."

After many hours of quiet contemplation, using the cheap flip-flop on her wall as a gazing point, Sidra had made some decisions. She'd stared at her $5.00 drugstore *drishti* until her eyes unfocused and her mind became clear.

She had somehow lost sight of her happiness, and of who she was, hoping that some knight in shining armor would come and rescue her. It hadn't begun with Rick, or even with Charlie. But being wronged by them had reinforced the notion that something was wrong with *her*. She'd forced herself to look way back, to her original knight in shining armor: her father. Jack had relegated himself useless without a mate. Worthless, Sidra had realized, like the lone shoe hanging on her wall.

Life is what we make of it, she'd decided, reaching up and wiggling the nail out of the wall with strong fingers. The flip-flop dropped to the bed, and Sidra slipped it on. *Do you render yourself obsolete, or do you work with what you've got?*

She'd fallen into Corpse pose on the bed, lifting her foot and inspecting it. She'd let the shoe dangle until it dropped off.

She wasn't going to ever wait to be rescued again.

"I've been offered a job at a renowned yoga retreat in the Berkshires," she told her students. Testing out how that sounded. She and the director of the institute had had an hour-long discussion last week, when she had dropped Jack off for their highly successful twelve-step yoga and meditation recovery program.

She wasn't going to wait for her father to drink himself into a place he couldn't come out of. It wasn't her job to rescue him, but then again, it wasn't her place to enable him, either.

Hopefully Jack would be well enough to come home before his semester started, but regardless, she was seriously considering taking the teaching job upstate come autumn. A new start, she envisioned, as the leaves shed their brilliance all around her.

The buzzing noise increased when she opened her studio door, echoing off the walls. The sound vibrated through her body like a mantra chant, leaving a ringing in her ears.

Fiona pounced on her. "I didn't want to disturb your class. But you need to come see this."

The first thing Sidra saw were bodies, five rows deep, lining the hallway. People swayed, impatient, and craned their necks to see over the heads of those in front of them. Deuce parted the crowd with his body like it was the Red Sea, allowing safe passage for the rest of Sidra's yoga students.

"Fi, this is a fire hazard!"

"I know," Fiona hollered, grabbing her by the hand and pulling her through the corridor. "Isn't it great?"

Guys from the Local 1 and 4 were in front of a makeshift stage in the corner of Mike's record shop. A half hour ago, they had been prone on mats in her studio. Now they were testing lights and stringing cable. Stagehands, still in their yoga gear, scuttled to adjust mic stands and pedalboards. Every PR person who had vacated her class either had a phone to their ear or was ushering in the news media they had alerted.

Revolve Records had hosted live in-store appearances before, but nothing like this.

"Where the hell is Mikey?" Sidra stood on her tiptoes, seeking out her cousin. The traitor. "So I can kill him dead."

"Sid, can you blame him for wanting to go out in a blaze of glory?" Fiona pointed out. "Come on. He was offered an exclusive. Who wouldn't jump at the chance?"

Exclusive, ha. Sidra had learned what happened when you trusted musicians and their exclusivity. Girls like Evie happened. And texts and calls from ones named Gloria.

More gear was loaded in, and a Plexiglas shield, like the one that had surrounded the drums in the recording studio she'd visited with Rick, was erected on stage.

This was more than just a simple in-store performance.

Vivian, from the beginners class, waved a hand madly in Sidra's direction from behind the sales counter. The vibrant senior citizen hadn't been in attendance today, and now she was sporting a Rotten Graves T-shirt.

"If it's too loud, you're too old, Benny!" she crowed, watching her classmate as he made for the door with his hands over his ears.

"Vivian, what are you doing back there?" Sidra asked.

"I've come to get autographs for my grandkids. You didn't tell me we had a genuine troubadour in our midst!"

Sidra allowed her gaze to follow the straight line of Vivian's elegant fingertip, and felt her rib cage contract as the breath left her. Rick was stepping up to the small stage, a guitar slung on his shoulder just as naturally as Sidra slung her yoga bag.

RICK
SIDRA'S SONG

"YOU ALL RIGHT, MATE?" Adrian bumped a shoulder to Rick's from the high stool next to his.

Rick stared at the word tattooed on the knuckles of his best friend's hand, where it rested easily on the body of his twelve-string guitar. *Y E S !*

Yes. I can do this.

He gripped the neck of his own guitar. The sunburst-on-black pattern of his Martin Marquis reminded him of the sun, rising to flame Sidra's hair from behind that first morning they'd made love, high over Central Park. Was she here?

I have to do this.

Rick had passed up the chance to sing to someone he loved once before, and damned if he was going to make the same mistake twice.

A sea of faces stared up at him. The empty record store he'd stumbled into while lost that long ago day was now packed to the gills. Beyond the windows, he saw the masses had spilled into the narrow street. Metalheads and music fans intermingled with the residents of the Lower East Side. Rick had fashioned a rock and roll *eruv* of sorts, arranging listening parties in every bar within the radius of Rivington, a live feed to appease the overflow of eager listeners. Private security had been hired for crowd control so he and the band could take their performance art to the next level.

Behind him, Jim began a shimmering intro that gently began to tap out a heartbeat. Sam picked it up, thrumming a bass line that strengthened the spine. Rick and Adrian cued themselves with barely a glance to each other. Even after their prolonged estrangement, their muscle memory from making music together for years was still there, along with their awareness of their effect on the crowd.

Bodies in space.

His fingers found the strings. As flesh and steel became one, he remembered his hands on Sidra, playing her body as it melted against his.

This was mind-body connection. It was no wonder he'd felt so disconnected in the sterile recording studio. His world had always existed on the stage. But now, as he prepared to share his true intentions, from the very core of his heart, he realized his world wasn't complete without her.

He embraced that deepest truth, breathing deep and allowing his mantra to come forth. And into the mic, he murmured, "This one is called 'Dove.'"

She carries the word on her lips,
>   *And I feel it in my bones.*
>   *For one kiss upon her shoulder*
>   *I'd give up every kingdom, all my thrones.*
>   *Soften up, she says,*
>   *Those wings made of steel.*
>   *But they're wrapped up in*
>   *These chains of silk*
>   *That I can't even feel.*

She carries the world on her shoulders,
But she lies with me alone,
Firing up the very core of me,
Binding skin to muscle,
Muscle to bone.
Soften up, she says,
Those wings made of steel.
But they're wrapped up in
These chains of silk
That I can't even feel.

She smiles but hides
The truth from herself,
Never daring to fly.
She holds her own wings
Closed tight,
But she's watching the sky.

I've been kicked in the teeth,
Can barely stand.
Everything's out of reach,
Can't honor thy commands.
Did I take her wings for granted?
Did I pull her to the ground?
Did I tear her feathers, one by one?
Did I bring her down?

Maybe she'll learn to fly again
And I'll learn to feel
Once we
Soften up those chains of silk
Wrapped up in
Wings of steel.

The crowd let loose its collectively held breath, and a cacophony of whistles, hollers, and claps broke the spell. Perfume and leopard print whirled into his line of vision, and he grasped for Fiona in the crowd. "Did she hear it?"

But one glance over her shoulder hollowed his heart. He spied a snatch of orange ribbon as it was swept from the black curtain of hair. Sidra let it fall to the floor on her way out the door.

SIDRA
FLIGHT OR FIGHT

Typical, Sidra fumed. *Leave it to a musician to think he can solve everything with a song.*

While her heart ached from the beauty and truth she'd heard within it, her head advised her better. She didn't need a song to tell her it was time to shake off the roots and fly.

Especially one penned by the guy who had pushed her from the nest and then pulled the welcome mat up from under her feet. His clever way of saying "tough shit, suck it up and move on."

Pushing through the throngs in front of the shop, she ducked down the alleyway and into the receiving door. Seamus's steampunk bike was parked patiently amid the boxes and broken-down bicycle parts in Sully's storage space. She carefully toed up the kickstand, swung a leg over, and took herself far from Rivington, Revolve, and Rick.

RICK
CREDIT DUE

"It's an absolute zoo out front," Sam shouted. "We'll have to wait it out."

Rick felt the vise grip of panic at his throat. He couldn't go after Sidra, and he couldn't get away from the throngs of admirers that were magnifying his anxiety tenfold. *What the hell had he been thinking?*

"'Play 'Simone'!" someone yelled from the crowd, and mob mentality took over. "Si-mone, Si- mone, Si-mone!"

"Through the back," Rick choked out.

"We can't leave after one song," Jim reasoned. "They'll tear this place down to the rafters, going against everything you're trying to do."

The crowd undulated, causing Rick to feel dizzy. He let his seat find the stool, shielding himself with his useless guitar. Jim was right. Even with private security, he couldn't just leave Mikey to deal with the aftermath. Not of the mess he himself had created.

"Si-mone, Si-mone, Si-mone!"

"I say we play it. Give the people what they want." Sam, stubborn and insensitive as he had been in their youth, back when he and Rick used to butt heads routinely, put his foot down. "Bloody hell, Riff. Get over yourself!"

"No," Adrian said.

"You wrote the poxy song!" Sam turned on Adrian now, stating the obvious. "Despite what it says on the album credits. Don't kowtow to him! He's not the bloody king."

"Damn right, I wrote it. But it wasn't my place, then . . . or now. So, no. Sam. *No.*"

Adrian reached out a hand, tattoos shifting as his biceps strained, and he helped his blood brother to his feet.

"Let's play 'Cat with the Emerald Eyes.' And then let's get the hell out of here, because I have a tuxedo fitting in two hours."

Rick gripped his friend's arm in thanks. Adrian Graves was still the strongest man he knew.

"How do you do it, mate?"

"What?"

"This! Surviving. Thriving. What's your secret?"

"Kat. The first day I met her, her kiss literally caused my life to pass before my eyes, making me realize it was a bloody great shipwreck that I hadn't been brave enough to salvage."

Adrian's eyes shone with care and concern, making Rick realize that the one secret Kat never gave up was his panic attacks. "Are you all right?"

"I . . . I haven't been. Anxiety attacks have plagued me since . . . hell, since the band originally split. I'm sorry, mate." He slung his guitar over his shoulder once again and covered the mic with his hand as his lead guitarist prepared to take over lead vocals. "I never gave you enough credit. Not for the song back then . . . or for being able to balance home life, your happiness, and music now. You deserve that credit. Full stop."

Adrian mouthed his thanks, astute and sincere. And then he launched into the song that had helped make peace with his own past.

THE BAND SEQUESTERED itself in a studio up near the lake house and got down to work. There was no time to waste.

And no time to dwell on Sidra.

Rick didn't have to. She was the name on his lips when he awoke. Her voice was in his head as he took himself through his morning yoga routine to tackle each long day in the studio. And the memory of her touch carried him through each endless night.

She had permeated his entire being.

Rick wasn't sure if his rock and roll Hail Mary attempt to reach Sidra had fallen on deaf ears. He wasn't sure exactly what he had hoped to accomplish that day. But as they carefully mixed his live vocals into the studio track, he realized he never could've captured the essence of the song in a recording studio. No, he had had to do it on her turf on the off chance she was there to hear it, in order to capture its true power and vulnerability.

It was equal parts exhilarating and terrifying. He trusted and made peace with the fact that he'd put in, as he had confided to her at the recording studio, his very best effort. And with that, he let it go and released it into the world.

"Leak it. Leak it like your life depends on it, Mason." The young engineer had not only aligned himself with the band on this matter, he had worked alongside them as a producer for the first time in his career. "I want her to hear it everywhere she turns."

"I know Thor won't be happy that we messed with his blueprint," Adrian commented later as they shared a celebratory beer over the fire pit by the lake. "But I have to say, the track is bloody brilliant."

Rick couldn't help but smile at Adrian's choice of words.

And at the thought of the phone call he had received from Gloria a few hours prior.

"I think Thor is going to be far more livid about the other blueprint I messed with," he said.

Adrian quirked a brow. "Care to share?"

"Let's see . . . how did Kat phrase it, after she first tracked you down, and then me? Ah yes. *Never underestimate the power of a good research librarian.*"

SIDRA
CLOSING TIME

"Yo, Sid!" Mike burst onto the yoga studio floor. Shoes on.

"Mike," she scolded. "Just because I don't have any students doesn't mean I haven't dedicated this time to my practice."

She had just spent the last hour loosening her body, grateful for its resilience. She had come to a peaceful state, a place she mindfully told herself to revisit several hours from now, when the closing on the building would take place.

"Yeah, yeah. I know. Sorry." He stepped aside so his father and a pretty blond woman could peer in.

Not another one, Sidra thought darkly. Rick's little publicity stunt had done nothing for the plight of the property. Thor's worker bees had continued to stream in. She had no desire to watch her uncle show around yet one more person intent on "transforming the space."

She glanced around. Except for her mat and the light above it, everything else had been removed from the room. Bricks, mats, straps . . . it hadn't taken too many boxes or trips to the storage space she'd rented.

She moved into Mountain pose, steeling her feet to the warm wood floor one last time.

"Let's go up front," Sully was saying, but he wasn't addressing the woman. He was talking to Sidra. And Mike. "I want you kids to be a part of this, too."

Sidra slowly lowered her arms, losing strength in the pose. *This is it,* she thought as she followed the procession up front. Her collective body moved, but the sum of her parts—her head, her heart, her happiness—protested greatly.

As she passed the time clock in the hall, she realized she would never hear its distinctive thump again. Nor would she have the built-in response that followed it: the elation and joy of knowing she was about to share her practice with the students at Evolve.

Everything else was gone from the space, except for the row of lockers. Something poking from the top locker caught her eye. It was the locker Rick liked to use. She stopped and pulled at the colorful, glossy triangle, but it was wedged tight. Somehow she found her fingers on the keypad and the word on her lips. D-O-V-E.

The impulsive guess paid off; the door sprang free. She pulled the magazine out. It was a rock publication, not unlike the ones Mike sold up front on a rack by the counter. Used to sell, anyway.

A punch card peeked out, flagging a page within. She could tell it was Rick's unlimited card, just by the sheer number of holes. Touching each one felt like a punch to her heart. They had spent a lot of time together, in here and on the mats. But there was no time to torture herself, thinking about it all now. She quickly tucked the magazine into her yoga bag and moved to catch up with the others.

She had avoided walking through the record shop since the day she'd stormed out. Emptying it of its contents wasn't going to erase the ghosts of rock stars past, haunting the corners with their sad songs.

Sure enough, Sidra was met with Rick's fluid voice, playing over the store's sound system. *So much for family loyalty.*

And there was her uncle's lawyer, chatting amicably with another guy in a sharp-looking suit. The legal profession truly was full of vultures, Sidra thought. Always showing up to pick at the carcasses. Death, divorce, or dissolution of property—as long as money was lining their pockets, they made nice. As casually as neighbors across a white picket fence, the two opposing sides communed over the New Release bins.

Which were still full to the brim with records.

"What . . . Why haven't you packed all this?" She turned to face her cousin before reeling back at all the vinyl, still in their bins. Was he planning on leaving it for the design team to trash, after all? "And will you please take that stupid CD off rotation?"

"That's the radio, Sid. Not a CD. They've been playing that new song nonstop over the airwaves since it got leaked online. What rock have you been living under? And my dad told me to hold off packing, like, a week ago." Mike shrugged. "If you showed your face around these parts, you would've known."

"There's been a new development," her uncle said with a sweeping gesture. The blond woman handed a business card to Mike. "A very interesting wrinkle."

Mike studied the card before slowly handing it to Sidra. "You're from the city's Landmarks Preservation Commission?"

"You're . . ." Sidra glanced from the name on the card to the woman and back to the card. "Gloria?"

The woman laughed. "Yes. And yes." Her eyes sparkled. "I may have been guilty of calling your boyfriend once or twice, Sidra. But only because he called me first. Once he put this location on my radar and pointed out its architectural, historical, and cultural heritage, I was hard-pressed not to make a case for preservation."

"Meaning?" Sidra asked.

"Meaning the new owner's ass will be trussed up in red tape

for years, trying to get permission to renovate the interior or the exterior of his new building!" Mike was as gleeful as a kid on Christmas.

"Well," Gloria explained, "even though I've expedited the process, it's not a done deal. First comes a public hearing. And then it still needs to be voted on by the commission. And then the city council gets involved. They have several months in which they can approve or deny our recommendations, and even then, the mayor could veto their decision. But this is the official notice of the formal review."

She handed Sully a manila envelope stamped with the city's insignia.

The song over the store's PA finally registered with Sidra. She recognized the heavy instrumental parts of the song from that afternoon in the recording studio, but now it was laced with the mellower live performance from the store: crisp acoustic guitars layered with the transporting power of Rick's voice.

She heard the strength and sensitivity in it, and realized "Dove" sang to the softest sides of her awareness, that it had come at her time of need; the need for sanctuary.

If he hadn't been invested in Thor's project, *had* he been invested in both her future and her freedom all along? And in the village she called home? With vivid clarity, she recalled their kiss on the street, under the stone statues. Rick claimed he was just a tourist in her town, but in some ways, he knew it better than she did.

And maybe he knew her better than she herself did.

She had been fighting against every thought of him, protecting herself from the pain that could possibly follow. But now she surrendered and settled into the notion, like letting go of her edge and going deeper into a pose.

"So . . ." Sidra was trying to wrap her head around all the

details. "Thor bought a building that he potentially cannot alter?"

Sully's lawyer spoke up. "Not exactly. He, too, was informed of the commission's intent. That's part of the designation process. And it was Mr. Young's decision, along with that of his investors and advice of counsel, to withdraw his offer and seek out a less . . . controversial space."

Sidra and Mike both turned on Sully. "When exactly did this happen?" Sidra asked. "You told us the closing was today."

Sully grinned as the younger attorney now stepped up.

"I'm here on behalf of Richard Rottenberg," the man said with a smile. "And he would like to propose a counteroffer."

RICK
FRIENDLIER SKIES

"Tell me why we're doing this again?" Rick talked around the unlit cigar that was wedged between his teeth.

"Because I am the most awesome future brother-in-law in the world," Adrian replied, chomping on the end of his own Camacho Corojo from the duty-free shop. "And you've got time to kill."

The two rockers stood in the arrivals terminal of JFK, shades on, awaiting the onslaught of passengers from flight 3029 from Portland. "And because it ain't over until the fat lady sings. Or gets back from the loo."

"Sorry, sorry, sorry!" Kat's friend Liz scuffed toward them, noticeably with child. She'd expanded exponentially since Rick had last seen her, at karaoke night. "I have to pee, like, every five minutes. It's very inconvenient for a city girl. I hate public restrooms."

"'Tis okay, luv. You haven't missed anything."

"You guys are the best. It'll really soften the blow, coming from you." Liz thrust a teddy bear in each of their hands. She'd obviously kipped into the airport gift shop in between bathroom visits.

"Gee, think he'll get the hint?" Adrian wisecracked, giving a little blue bear a shake.

Rick squeezed his furry pink charge and murmured out of earshot of the pacing mum-to-be, "Let's just hope he doesn't run screaming in the other direction."

"Ah, there's our fan club now."

Kat's brother was the quintessential music fan that never quite grew up. The successful restaurateur wore spiky bleached locks, earrings in both ears, and an ever-present Corroded Corpse T from his vast, rotating collection. In fact, Rick had never seen the guy wear the same shirt twice.

His jaw, sporting stubble after the long red-eye flight, unhinged at the sight of his two favorite musicians as his own personal welcome wagon. Clutching teddy bears and grinning from behind their shades and cigars.

"Dooley! I know you're behind this."

Liz tentatively stepped out from behind the men. "Hey, Underwood."

He stared long and hard at her changed middle. Then he dropped his carry-on backpack. "This really isn't the best timing," he said, kneeling and rummaging through it.

Liz's smile began to fade. Adrian and Rick exchanged a look, slowly removing their cigars.

Kevin continued to make a production of searching, annoyed that he couldn't find whatever he was looking for. It was very small, apparently.

"I was going to wait until after my sister's big day to give you this, but I suppose I should make an honest woman of you ASAP."

"B-b-but . . . Bite Me?" Liz stammered, at the sight of the open ring box her high school sweetheart had produced on bended knee.

"Never heard a response quite like that before." Rick leaned toward his bandmate for confirmation that his ears weren't playing tricks on him.

Adrian tilted his head and murmured, "That's the name of the restaurant he owns back in Portland."

With his free hand, Kevin whipped out his phone and thumbed to a photo of the building with a big Sold sign in front. "It took me just about as long to find the perfect owner for it as it did to find the girl of my dreams."

"I've been here all along," Liz squeaked.

Rick turned away, to both give privacy and to take a moment to breathe deep. He thought about the For Sale sign on Sidra's building and whether he'd ever have the chance to step back inside. And he thought about what lay ahead of him back home.

He felt Adrian's hand on his shoulder. "You sure about this, mate?"

"Yeah. It's for the best. I'd better get to my gate."

Rick wedged Pink Bear into the newly engaged couple's embrace and tucked his cigar into Kev's backpack. "For your rock and roll shrine in the attic."

"You're coming back for the wedding, aren't you?" Adrian asked.

Rick gave an affirmative raise of the metal horns. "I've always got your back."

"And I yours."

The two friends exchanged thumps to the back. "Here's something to occupy your hands, and your mind." With an impish grin, Adrian slid an assortment of industry rags into Rick's grip. "The latest issues, hot off the presses. I know how much you value up-to-date news."

~

"Aloha, Mr. Rotten. Can I get you anything?"

Rick pulled his gaze from the first-class window.

"Some paper if you have it. And a pen?"

He turned his attention to the trade papers in front of him. *Billboard, Pro Sound News,* and *Variety* all had similar sensational headlines:

ROTTEN GRAVES PROJECT LEAK: ACT OF
REBELLION . . . OR PUBLICITY STUNT?

A "GRAVE" MISTAKE? OR PROGRESSIVE
MARKETING?
INDUSTRY INSIDERS WEIGH IN.

THUNDERSTRUCK:
FAMED PRODUCER THOR YOUNG BACKS OUT
OF CONTROVERSIAL PROJECT, CITING
"CREATIVE DIFFERENCES"

LOVE IT OR LEAK IT!
(IF IT'S ROTTEN, YOU FIX IT FIRST)

The last headline had him chuckling and reading on. Of course the band's chief biographer would weigh in on the matter with typical panache. Actually, this one was old news . . . to him, at least.

Alexander Floyd had dropped off a copy after it went to press. And Rick had Mason deliver it to Evolve Yoga, with explicit instructions on where and how to leave it.

He only hoped Sidra would take the time to read it.

Let's be real. Heavy metal has always been the bastard son of the music industry. Written off as self- indulgent, aggressively theatrical, obnoxiously provocative, and overtly masculine, many will stand by their claim that the genre just hasn't aged well. More politely put, metal is a slowly acquired taste to some. But that doesn't mean the infamous genre is without merit.

And it certainly doesn't mean its long-standing forefathers, such as the Rotten Graves Project—the band known in a past life as Corroded Corpse—cannot roll with the punches of the modern day and still rock out.

When learning the most raw and vulnerable tracks on Demons Above, *their forthcoming album, had possibly been compromised, the band took extreme action—and matters into their own hands.*

"The creative process is such a fragile thing," frontman Riff Rotten states. "You're crafting from the deepest part of your soul. One moment you're soaring to the sky on your brilliance, and the next, you're crushed to the ground under the weight of your fears. It's completely normal to doubt oneself in the process."

Rotten is no stranger to highs and lows in general—the forty-four-year-old guitarist/vocalist has suffered from anxiety and panic attacks since 1988, but has recently discovered how to control them, through mindfulness and yoga. "The thought of those songs being unleashed before they were ready just about crippled me. But then there's the thought: Perhaps they are ready to be heard. And you've got to get over what's been holding you back, do your best and stand back and let it happen, you know?"

The band live-recorded and self-mixed the eponymous "Demons Above" and several other songs, but clearly the true title track of the album is "Dove," a transporting ode that soars above and beyond conventional label expectations, the producer's vision, and even the hopes of its creator.

Rotten, who up until five years ago barely believed in using e-mail, trusted the power of social media and the fans to be the true judges. Within minutes of leaking the first track, fans flooded the forums and blogs and Web-based streaming services. The verdict: utter gold.

But was it breach of contract? The jury's still out on whether the band violated its monumental 360 deal with the record label. But even the shrewdest spin doctors can't deny: The press has been oh so good.

"So we might not sell a ton of records," Rotten says with a laugh. A mellower, humbler version of the man emerges. "But our story will sell. We grew fans exponentially through our live shows, and they will still come. The songs are on their hard drives, but there's loyalty in their hearts. They will always support us."

This is more than just a matter of making a silk purse out of a sow's ear. It's about moving beyond the comfort zone, being true to oneself and trusting the process.

"Someone very close to me asked recently if I found it scary, bringing something totally new into the world," Riff confides. "I became a father at nineteen, whether I was ready or not. And I was raising my three kids alone by the age of thirty-one. Yes, it's terrifying. But the rewards have to trump the fear."

Like he's learned through practicing yoga: "Sometimes if this is your edge, you stay there. But if you find you can make that push and go deeper . . . you never know what lies beyond it."

Leaking one's own tracks used to be considered on par with retail suicide, with heads rolling from the upper echelon of the monarchy we all still bow to, the Modern Music Recording Industry. But as the dust settles on this latest incident, perhaps the Kings of Doom have kicked the first big crack in the castle wall.

The groundbreaking song is their first foray back to the field of hard rock ballads since their eighties mainstream mega-hit, "Simone," which was recently revealed to be the sole creation of guitarist Digger Graves, after years of speculation. How high will "Dove" fly, once it officially releases? Only time will tell.

But Riff Rotten, dare we say, is Zen about it all.

Rick tucked the magazines into the pocket of his first-class seat and leaned back. He realized he had mastered dynamic tension, on the mat and off, during this whole process. It was a matter of pushing forward and reaching for what you want and believe in, while at the same time not being afraid to pull back and let it all go.

Meeting Sidra—and falling in love with her—had taught him: Even when he thought he was standing still, he was moving on.

The flight attendant returned with his requested items and a smile.

"Mahalo." And with his thanks, Rick began to pen his ultimate—and final—love letter to Simone.

I'm heading home, my love. And I've been traveling a long time. I've crossed the globe trying to shake you, yet I've been seeking something elusive as well. I'd hoped to feel your presence, and felt guilty when I didn't. But now I know. You're not in that cemetery in Brooklyn. You're not at the hospital wing that bears your name. You're not in the childhood mementos or the synagogue I visit once a year. You're no longer in our Hanalei house, and you're not in the songs I write . . . or in the songs I choose not to sing.

You have a place in my head, and my heart. The memory of you will always live there. But I've realized for your memory to truly be a blessing, it needs to be just that. Your blessing. For me to move on, to find love, fulfillment, and happiness . . . with myself. And with someone else, someday.

Maybe I'll place this letter with the others, in the hatbox. And maybe I will plant it under the purple naupaka on the mauka side of the house, because that flower always reminds me of you. But it no longer saddens me. I love you, Simone.

RICK CROSSED one-lane bridges and looped past waterfalls, the landscape of his adopted hometown so familiar, yet so different from what he had come to know. It was like leaving one dream and reentering another. The house itself even looked larger, compared to the row upon row of tight brick and stone he'd gotten used to in New York.

The For Sale sign out front was new.

Rick gathered air into his lungs, collected from the dewy Hawaiian morning. Then he released it audibly. *Ocean breath,* he thought. *Lion's breath.*

"He's here!"

"Dad!"

Ari came barreling out the front door, and Jonah appeared from the side yard. Strong, grown men had replaced his little lion and dove as they fought over Rick's bags and pounded hugs against his back. Paul waited on the porch, as tan as the Greek coffee he no doubt drank lots of in Thessaloniki.

"There's our viral Internet sensation," he joked. "Finally, you see technology can be your friend."

"You're back," Rick said simply.

"Of course. You didn't think we'd let you do this by yourself, did you?"

He'd called them all first and gotten their blessings before hiring the Realtor. Now, father and sons worked side by side, tossing stories back and forth, from room to room, as they boxed the house's contents.

Rick stood in the doorway of the living room, the hatbox full of letters in his hands, smiling while he listened to each boy vying to one-up the others with their tales and good-naturedly trying to get him to take sides. He had raised them well, he realized, as remnants of their happy childhood packed their rental cars and kept them laughing through dinner together.

They didn't stop until the place was empty, but their hearts were full. Then they raced to the beach, sailing Frisbees high over one another's heads and tackling one another in the soft sand.

"So what now, Dad?" Jonah shook the beach out of his dark, shaggy hair. "You staying here, you going back, or what?"

He thought of the black, silky sand of East Hawaii. There was no way he'd be able to run it through his fingers without recalling Sidra's hair. Or lie on the sugar-sand beach here in the west without thinking about the warm, sweet scent of her skin.

"Can I have the turntable?" Ari asked. "Paul said you've got all of Mom's old albums."

Rick gave a wry smile. "Well. It's a long story. But I can recommend a great little record shop next time you visit me in New York."

SIDRA

LOST AND FOUND

THE TINY NATIVES were getting restless on the big yellow camp bus. Sidra hopped down the steps. "What's the holdup?"

Tasha, the camp counselor standing beside the bus, consulted her clipboard. "Abbey Lewis hasn't been counted in."

"Hmm, lemme check." Sidra climbed on board and took inventory down the aisle, making sure the little curly-haired girl hadn't slipped by unnoticed during the head count. "No sign of her," she called back down.

Tasha got on the two-way radio with the camp director before hauling herself up the steps. "He said to go ahead, to keep the bus on schedule. The kid is having a meltdown apparently. Her parents have been called to come get her."

Sidra frowned. That didn't sound like happy-go-lucky Abbey. "Where is she?"

"In the changing house. Won't come out."

"Hold on," Sidra called to the bus driver. "I'm getting off. You got this, Tasha?" Her coworker waved her off, and she made for the large log cabin that housed the girls' changing area.

Pacing in front of it was the camp director, clearly not

versed in how to handle little girls who refuse to change out of their bathing suits.

"I can sit with her, Harlen. Until her mom comes. I know her."

With a sweep of his hand, he gratefully ushered Sidra in. Immediately, the smell of her own childhood camp experience hit her memory triggers. While the digs hadn't been as luxurious, probably just the local town pool out near Uncle Sully's in Queens, the same chlorine combination with equal parts mildew and coconut sunscreen was present. She smiled as she moved through the maze of wooden benches and cubbies.

"What's the haps, girlfriend?"

Abbey sat on the end of a bench with her swim towel tented over her head. "I lost my moonrise shell." Her voice was muffled by the thick terry cloth, but her misery was clearly apparent.

"Knock, knock." Sidra tugged gently on the towel. "May I come in?"

Abbey lifted the corner. If Sidra were two feet tall, she might have been able to slip in. Still, she took it as an open invitation. Scooting next to the little girl, she ducked her head under.

"Whooo, it's hot under here. And it smells like corn chips."

"I had Fritos at lunch." Abbey sniffed. Her cheeks were flushed, and her curls a frizzy mess. She wiped her eyes with the towel before slowly sliding it off both of them.

"Tell me about your shell," Sidra encouraged in a gentle tone. "Did your dad give it to you?" She knew Abbey had lost her dad at a young age. And she knew all about treasured mementos loved ones left behind.

"No, my uncle did. I brought it for show-and-tell. It was *makana aloha*," Abbey wailed, "a gift of love. And it was here before swimming and now it's gone!"

"Oh, sweetie." Sidra put her arm around the girl as she

dissolved into another fit of tears. She wished she could slay the dragon of unhappiness that preyed on her young friend. Her more pessimistic side wanted to tell her that mean people sucked. And that some other little kid probably did take liberties, and the shell. But it was probably best to take a more neutral route.

"How about you get dressed and we check the lost and found?" Perhaps a walk in the fresh air down to the main camp building would help calm the girl down, at least until Kat arrived.

"Okay." Abbey rubbed her face with the towel, then pulled her tiny jean shorts up over her bathing suit. Pushing her feet into her sneakers, she stated matter-of-factly, "I guess if it was a gift of love, it's never truly lost."

Sidra was taken aback; that was pretty esoteric thinking for an eight-year-old.

"How true, Abbey. Because you can always find it here." She tapped her heart's center, and then her head. "And here."

"And in the stars, where my dad is," Abbey was quick to add. "Ouch!"

The girl wriggled her foot, and her little Skechers went flying. Something small and colorful cartwheeled onto the ground. "Hey! My shell!" She scooped it up and grinned. "Here, you can carry it, Miz-ess!" She pushed her foot back into her sneaker and went running in the direction of the blue and white Mini Cooper that had just rounded the camp drive.

Sidra turned the small shell over. Despite having just been kicked out of a shoe, it was perfectly intact, and its colors were like nothing she had ever seen before.

"Mom! I thought I lost the moonrise shell, but me and Miz-ess found it. You *did* tell her she could come to the wedding, right?"

"Oh, Abbey," Sidra replied as Kat's eyes grew wide and

apologetic. "Weddings are mainly for family and very, very close friends. You're sweet to think of me, though."

"I did promise Abbey she could invite a few people who are special to her," Kat supplied. Her grin was sheepish as she ran a hand through her curls. "I've been so crazed with the planning, I've been sort of MIA. I meant to mention it before the summer disappeared. Really. Please come. It's going to be very casual. Right at the beach near our house next Sunday morning. Shoes optional."

"Funny, I'm actually someone else's date that day, for a . . ." Sidra paused. The lakeside wedding upstate for the sister of Liz's estranged boyfriend sounded suspiciously like Abbey's mom's big day. "Wait a minute. Liz Dooley wouldn't happen to be on your guest list, would she?"

Kat's reaction was one of delighted surprise. "She's one of my bridesmaids, as a matter of fact. We've been friends since high school."

"That's so crazy," Sidra marveled. "I've known her for years. My brother works for her!" She shook her head. "Oh, so Kevin is *your* brother? Oh my God, this is all making sense now. What a crazy coincidence."

Kat laughed as Abbey grabbed her hand and swung it. "Small world, for sure! When Liz RSVPed with a guest, I didn't dare ask. She's been a little . . . hormonal, if you know what I mean." She pointedly dipped her head toward her daughter and raised her brows. Sidra nodded. "Although she picked up my brother from the airport yesterday, so I'm hoping they work out their drama before the big day. I'm so glad you are coming!"

"Thanks. Me too." Sidra was looking forward to getting out of the city for the weekend. With Jack away and Mike on the hook to feed Banana Louie, she had less weighing on her mind.

"Yay!" Abbey crowed. "You'll get to meet my uncle after all. Maybe he's got a shell for you. It's a gift of love," she singsonged.

"Jump in the car, you!" Kat swatted Abbey's denim-clad butt. "She's been trying to matchmake all summer," she apologized once her daughter was out of earshot. "Don't mind her. Come on, I'll give you a ride to the station." She swung her keys from her finger as they walked. "Kids get ideas; they have no idea how complicated things are."

Sidra rubbed her thumb over the ridges of the shell like they were beads on a rosary. *Kids aren't the only ones,* she thought. "No need to apologize. I roll with the punches. But I don't think your brother would have any interest in me."

"Oh, it's not *that* uncle she wants to set you up with," Kat was quick to assure her.

"And not Unkie Luke, 'cuz he has a husband," Abbey piped up from the backseat. "It's my uncle Riff. Remember? I *told* you he's not my real uncle."

"Riff?" Sidra repeated.

"He's my fiancé's best friend," Kat explained. "He may as well be family. They're in the same band." She turned the key in the ignition, and "Dove" filled the small space. "Speak of the devil," she said with a laugh. "Here's their latest hit!"

Abbey began to list the merits of her unreal uncle as Kat navigated them off camp property, but none of it registered with Sidra. It was all so . . . much.

All these connections. Like unique and separate movements in yoga, yet all woven together to create the tightest flow.

Rick was everywhere she turned. He was ingrained in her. Like a vinyasa. Body and breath. Head and heart.

He was there for the long term.

Out of all the different roads and paths, Sidra mused as Kat wound the car through Bear Mountain. *And all these people along the way . . .*

Under the guiding light of the *ner tamid,* she had read the article he'd left for her. And she had meditated over, and memorized, every line of his song while on her mat. But she had stayed at her edge, waiting. Listening to the truth behind his words. And watching the sky. Her mother's voice gently reminded her of omens and opportunities. *It's a day for a new journey, my love.*

Spending the last few months with Rick had made her the happiest in her heart. There was no need to wait for a certain holiday, or for the moon and the sun to be at their brightest. She was done with bittersweet patience.

Carpe punctum. Seize the moment.

At the station, she handed Abbey her shell through the open window. "Abbey, I'll be there. With bells on."

RICK
BOOTED

SAM SHOOK the raindrops from his mane of hair and kicked his muddy boots into the pile of river shoes by Adrian's porch door. "It's fit for neither man nor beast out there," he proclaimed. "The cabbie who dropped me just told me the storm's been upgraded to a nor'easter, and guess what they've named her? Isabelle."

The band had a good laugh over that. Leave it to their self-appointed Queen of Everything to be a pain in the ass, even on the eve of Adrian and Kat's big day.

"Speaking of friends, both foul and fair-weather," Jim said, leaning over to inspect Rick's caller ID as he deftly dealt another hand of poker, "who invited Isabelle to the bachelor party?"

"If she ends up popping out of my cake," Adrian dead-panned, "I will disown you all."

He was actually smoking that cigar from the duty-free shop at the airport. Rick waved the pungent smoke toward the screens of the lake house's enclosed porch. The best man had arrived on the last flight in and hadn't had time to plan anything elaborate for the groom's last night as a single man.

He guessed they always had Sergeant Pepperoni's Karaoke Night if they got desperate.

"Put 'er on speaker," Sam demanded.

Rick pushed the speaker button, then placed his bet. He had a pretty good hand.

"Do you realize the damage you fuck knuckles have caused by leaking that track?" Isabelle screeched.

"No idea what you're talking about." Not that his lawyers had advised him against talking about it, but it was fun to play devil's advocate with Isabelle, for once.

"The hell you don't."

"It could've been anyone," Sam added, tossing some chips into the pot.

Adrian talked like a tough guy, cigar wedged between his teeth. "It could've even been you, Isabelle."

"Not a chance. I never even heard the finished product! And don't go blaming Thor, because he only had his rough cuts. That sounded nothing like a rough cut."

"No," Rick said slowly. "Because the rough cuts with him were utter crap."

"Well, there's more than one way to polish shit into a diamond," Isabelle sputtered. "But you never, ever give it away for free!"

"Way of the world these days," Adrian said. "Any album worth its salt has the possibility of being leaked. And honestly, the day the fans *don't* want to get their hands on our music any way they can is the day I worry about."

Isabelle blew a raspberry at Adrian's comment. "Well. I just heard from my contact at the label. Do you realize how many hours of PR and dollars of advertising and artwork you squandered, with the click of the mouse?"

"Funny, I just spoke with *my* contact at the label," Rick countered. "They love the track and haven't had this much advance buzz about a comeback in years."

In fact, suddenly the band had become the most talked-about name on the roster. Thanks to the runaway single, the label had decided to put even more muscle behind the comeback album. Including moving up the street date, and adding a signed, limited-release LP format to the deal.

"Ninety-five Metascore," Jim supplied, quoting the latest review aggregator stats.

"THREE HUNDRED THOUSAND ILLEGAL DOWNLOADS!" Isabelle raged. "And you won't ever see a penny of it."

"And neither will you, from us, from here on in. Isabelle? You're fired, luv. Nothing personal. Just business. We don't like how you conduct it."

SIDRA
ADORNMENT

"SO MUCH BETTER THAN A WILD, drunken bachelorette party," Liz said with a sigh as Sidra stepped back to admire her henna artwork. The bridal party had opted to stay in the night before the big day, using Karen's spacious home as a girls-only refuge. And Sidra had offered to apply mehndi—henna art—for the excited bride and all her friends.

"I don't think you could've fit through the bar door, Big Red. Even if we'd wanted to go drinking and carousing," Marissa said. She waved her hands to speed up the drying process of her hennaed hands.

"Kiss my big fat pregnant ass, Falzone!" Liz sassed. Marissa flipped her a festooned middle finger in response. Liz held up her tank top so Sidra could put the finishing touches on the intricate pattern that swirled around her belly. "Ahh, that feels so good!"

Sidra smiled. The cooling paste was calming, and she loved the fresh smell of the natural henna, combined with just a little lemon juice, sugar, and lavender oil.

Her Old World aunties would've insisted on including certain patterns and protective images to guard against the evil eye and any malicious spirits, but Sidra focused instead on the joyous celebration as her friend entered her final phase of pregnancy. Especially now that Liz had set things to rights with Kevin.

Sidra kneeled in front of Kat again. Her bridal mehndi, even while more modernized and American than the traditional Indian, had been the most time-consuming and intricate, so she had started with her first, before the bridesmaids.

"One last detail for you." She admired the sophisticated patterns on Kat's hands and feet. "It's tradition to place the groom's initials somewhere, for him to search for on your wedding night."

"Good thing you got a bikini wax," Leanna said, clinking her wineglass to Kat's with a wicked gleam in her eye.

"Somewhere in the henna," Sidra added, chuckling. "Pretty PG-rated, I'm afraid."

Kat smiled. "What a beautiful tradition, Sidra. I love it. Thank you."

Sidra carefully stroked the letters into the simple, pretty flower and vining combination along the inside of Kat's wrist.

Liz waddled over, showing off her pretty baby bump. "Kat, do you think Luke would photograph this masterpiece?"

"Totally! So someday my niece or nephew will see what a wild one you were, with your henna tattoos."

"Speaking of tattoos, Kat," Sidra said, "I hid *your* initials somewhere on Adrian, earlier today, when he dropped Abbey off."

Kat bit back a smile, her eyes shining. "I can't imagine where you managed to find a free spot, but I will uncover it before our wedding night is through!"

All the women roared with laughter.

Adrian had been ready, willing, and able when he heard about the tradition, whipping off his black Western-style shirt with a grin. It had been a shock for Sidra to see his misericorde tattoo, which mirrored Rick's, at such close range, but a comfort, too. She loved the idea that her lover had such a close confidante, and couldn't help but wonder if Adrian knew her connection to the man he called a blood brother.

"I hear my stepdaughter-to-be is playing matchmaker tomorrow," he'd murmured as Sidra carefully added his bride's initials to the hilt of the dagger, close to his clavicle. "She's pretty good at it."

Sidra laughed. "Yes, I heard the story of how you and Kat met. I bet you never imagined meeting the love of your life in a library!"

Shrugging back into his shirt and buttoning it, he'd winked. "We rock stars often find ourselves— and love—in the darnedest places."

As he'd turned to leave, he'd added, "And a word of advice. This guy . . . he's a little hardheaded. But right here?" He'd tapped his heart with his tattooed knuckles. "He's a softie."

Alone in Karen's spare bedroom that night, as the other women slept around her, Sidra carefully, and hopefully, placed double *R*s within the heart design on the palm of her hand.

Perhaps a little old-fashioned auntie superstition couldn't hurt.

RICK

THE HEAD AND THE HEART

"I DON'T WANT to walk to the beach with the bridesmaids." Abbey pouted. "I want to go with Uncle Riff." All morning long, the flower girl had flit back and forth between the two houses on Love Street, leaving a trail of rose petals in her wake.

"Bee . . ." Adrian frowned into the mirror, adjusting his bow tie. "What'd your mum say?"

"Me mum is fine with it!" Her dead-accurate imitation of Adrian's accent caused Kat's brother, Kev, to choke on his coffee with laughter.

"It doesn't matter how metal you are," Rick reminded the groom, fastening his cufflink for him. "If an eight-year-old asks you to escort her to the beach, you go."

Adrian chuckled. "Wise words. And speaking of heavy metal . . . take good care of these, won't you?" He dropped two platinum wedding bands into his best friend's palm. The rings were thick and festooned with intricate thorns and flowers. A perfect blending for the union of rock star and librarian.

Rick dropped them into his shirt pocket and reached for Abbey's hand. "Ready to rock and roll?"

They walked in silence to where the pavement became

gravel, then dirt, and finally sand. "Shoes optional," Abbey reminded him, and kicked her sandals off. Rick followed suit, removing his stiff dress shoes and rolling up the bottoms of his trouser legs.

Abbey led the way to the small lake, detouring around the large white tent that had been erected for the reception later. "It's got a real wooden floor inside it." Her voice contained a mixture of awe and distain. "Over the sand."

"You call this sand?" Rick's tone was teasing; he loved to rile the eight-year-old until she buzzed like a little irritated bee. "Gravel, compared to Hawaii's beaches."

She snorted. "Still. Why dance on wood when we can dance on sand?"

"Very good question."

Abbey was full of them today. "Are you leaving after the wedding? Will you live in Hawaii or go back to England? Would you stay if you found someone, like Adrian found my mom?"

"Ah, Bee. I wish it were as simple as that. Even when you *do* find someone . . ." He trailed off and stared out at the murky blue. The calm after the storm. Amazing how nature was able to settle into a powerful stillness, even after all the chaos. Sidra had been right about that all along.

Abbey fidgeted, impatient with him. She pulled her small hand out of his and plunged it into her flower girl basket. "Did you give her *makana aloha*?"

"I tried."

Buying the old building, in hindsight, had been a bit over the top. But how else to show her he was invested and in it for the long haul? The test of time? Then again, her father had run a twenty-year bar tab to drink away his guilt. Had Sidra assumed he'd thrown money down in the same fashion, to assuage his own? Is that why she hadn't reached out to him?

He jammed his hands in his pockets and kicked at the sand.

He was done with guilt and grief. Sidra had taught him to learn to let it go, and he would always thank her for that.

Abbey ran ahead, dropping something out of her basket as she went.

Rick stooped to retrieve it. Not a rose petal this time. But the small familiar shell of his adopted homeland that he had given the little girl the first time he met her.

Back when he thought such a rarity was found once in a lifetime.

Twice, if you're lucky, he heard Kat insist. A memory he had carried since he had given away the shell four years ago.

And a memory, along with Simone's, that *was* a blessing. He was allowed to live, and love, again. Sidra had taught him that, too. But it was he alone who had had to instill it into his head and his heart.

Funny how far he'd had to travel just to realize the journey had been within his grasp all along.

He jogged to catch up with Abbey. "You don't want to lose this," he said, stooping to deposit the moonrise shell back into her basket.

"Silly Uncle Riff. You can't lose love!" She laughed, tugging at his waistcoat to keep him at her height. "You can find it, but you can't lose it. 'Cuz it's here." She tapped the spot above the pocket where Adrian's and Kat's rings were stowed, and then smoothed back a rogue curl as the wind blew it across his cheek. "And here." She patted his head. "And," she whispered, as if she were bestowing a great secret, "in the stars."

To his utter surprise, Abbey dipped down into a Deep Forward Fold like a skilled yogini. The little girl grabbed the shell from the basket, made a perfect Reverse Swan Dive up, and chucked it as far as she could throw it, toward the water's edge.

"Abbey!" he exclaimed. But there was no time for admonishment. Guests were spilling onto the beach for the cocktail hour Kat and Adrian had wisely decided to have before the ceremony, so friends and family could meet, mingle, and break the ice.

"Please don't be mad at me, Uncle Riff."

Rick's own ice floe, the one that had dammed in his chest since the band had reunited, melted away as he glimpsed the bride and groom, together for the first time on their wedding day.

Kat, swathed in an elegant dove-gray gown, seemed to float across the sand. At arm's length, she playfully held the hand of her partner in crime. He was all at once debonair and devilishly doting. And the happiest Rick had ever known him to be.

"Adrian on marriage" was going to be a beautiful thing.

Abbey careened away in the direction of the tent, where the rest of the bridal party was assembling to take pictures.

But just beyond that . . .

Like a vision, the woman named after starlight walked barefoot along the shoreline in a beautiful orange sari. Her hair was loose, no ribbons today, and the lake breeze blew ripples in it, like a wave.

Something by the shoreline appeared to catch her eye. Rick watched in wonder as she gracefully gathered the hem of her flowing gown and bent, slowly and deliberately, in a one-legged balance to retrieve whatever it was.

And he felt every grain of sand, hot under his heels, as he dug in and raced to join Sidra by the water.

SIDRA
MAKANA ALOHA

SIDRA STOOD FACING the lapping shore, eyes closed, and formed a perfect Tree pose. Her lower body was rooted, but her arms light. She was all at once balanced, strong, attuned. Sun and shadow caressed her face, and as the breeze picked up, she sensed she was not alone.

Strong, warm arms bound her waist from behind, and she slowly lowered her pose, bringing her prayer hands to her heart's center. Leaning into the solid familiarity of Rick.

"What did you find, Goddess?"

His question was spoken softly against her, lips brushing against the silk draped over one shoulder. Without a word, she opened her clasped hands to reveal Abbey's moonrise shell.

"Ah, the rare *makana aloha*," he remarked, his rough fingers sliding over her smooth ones to caress the delicate treasure resting on her palm. "And what's this?"

He moved the shell aside to study the mehndi adorning her hand, tracing the heart pattern. Like their relationship, it hadn't taken long for the henna stain to mature and deepen. Rick took her hand in his and pressed his mouth against the spot where his initials blended with the intricate designs. She felt his smile blossom there. "Looks like a gift for me."

"How did you spot them so fast?" she marveled.

He slowly turned her in his arms until they faced each other. "I've learned to appreciate the details . . . but not worry so much about how they fit the big picture."

"I think I read somewhere you've become rather Zen," she teased. "And speaking of the big picture . . ."

Abbey, just a pinwheel of color far down the beach, turned a perfect cartwheel in the sand, fancy dress and all.

Rick laughed. "I don't know how she did it, but I am sure she will fill me in later."

The lake seemed to want in on the joke. Sidra gave a yelp as it surged against their ankles, darkening the hem of her sari.

Rick stepped in deeper to steady her, the water weighing down the rolled edges of his dress pants.

"I don't care," he said, dismissing it with a glance. "This is the calm after the storm I've been waiting for."

"Thank you," Sidra blurted. "For my song."

"Thank *you*, for giving me courage to find the words." He wove his fingers between her beautifully adorned ones.

There was something wholly new in his kiss, something that went way beyond rescue and redemption. Sidra tried to think of the words she needed to string together to convey her gratitude for what he had done to help save her building and her business, but only one emerged, like a new mantra, buzzing with energy as he repeated it back, reminding her that they were, indeed, together in this process.

"Love . . ." she breathed, allowing it to linger in her sigh as he captured her mouth once more, waking vibrations within her.

EPILOGUE
ON WAVES AND WINGS

Seventeen thousand fans can't be wrong.

And even if they were?

Rick Rottenberg needed no validation. All he needed was the music, flowing like a straight line of energy from bandmate to bandmate across Madison Square Garden's vast stage. And love, waiting patiently for him in the wings.

Right, wrong.

Soft, strong.

It hadn't mattered, all along.

Jim rode his Paiste 14" Rude hi-hats like they were his one-way ticket out of the gates of hell. Sam was hot on his heels, bludgeoning the bass strings with exactly the kind of force needed to show the devil he meant business. And Adrian played licks off their backbeat that left scorching burn marks in his wake as he strode toward stage left. Rick watched the sea of arms undulate in the same direction as his lead guitarist. Pride and admiration swelled within him; his best mate had not only salvaged his shipwreck, he now sailed it victoriously from the heavy metal helm.

And the King of Doom? He was just getting started.

Rick raised his mic stand like a scepter and not only heard, but felt the crowd hold its collective breath, as if preparing to be pulled into the undertow.

Sidra stood side-stage with Kat, her eyes delighting and dancing, luring his gaze more than once during the evening's performance. While the gig had been sold out for months, tonight he sang for her, for memories old and new. And for himself.

He ran his fingers through the bits of orange ribbon festooning the stand. Starting with a soft growl, he allowed his voice to grow seamlessly into a strong, sustained full sound that quickly evolved into an effortless scream.

Lyrics followed, channeling through him perfectly; he delivered each one with rhythmic intensity, never losing musical momentum.

Destined to do this? Perhaps.

But no matter what, he was enjoying the journey.

Casting another glance side-stage, he was surprised to see Abbey had replaced his fan club. She stood, coltish legs splayed and kid-size noise-canceling headphones on, throwing double rock horns his and Adrian's way.

Her stepfather threw an amused smile at her and raised his brow at Rick before subtly nodding in the direction of the barricade.

It wasn't exactly a coffee klatch down there, but the girls looked out for each other in the pit. And at home, while the band was on tour. They weren't road widows. They were warrior women.

Stronger than steel, and softer than silk.

Rick swung the eight pounds of guitar that had been slung behind him back to front and center, joining Adrian's dual guitar attack as if they were battling unseen forces to the death. Never missing a note . . . until something came sailing from the crowd.

His peripheral vision registered the incoming object, but his mind was unable to reconcile exactly what it was as it struck his sternum with a muted thump. He jerked his hand, breaking a guitar string in the process, and stepped back.

Like a jousting knight, Rick had collected his share of lady favors throughout the years. Rock and roll–style tokens of appreciation: bras, panties . . . and most recently, a lone flip-flop.

But this?

"Is that . . . a diaper?" Jim's voice flowed through the rest of the band's in-ear monitors on the private mix. Their drummer sounded incredulous, but his hands and feet didn't miss a beat.

Sam stepped up to his pedal board and kicked his own mic-mute to join the band-only conversation. "If that's a nappy, I 'ope it ain't a soiled 'un!"

The band's backline tech deftly swooped in and unstrapped the guitar with the busted string, freeing Rick's body from its customary armor. Leaving him free to retrieve the bounty at his feet.

It had a date written on it. A due date.

Sidra's head was slowly shaking, but she was quick to grin. *Not me,* she channeled up toward Rick's questioning gaze. *Not right now, anyway.*

Together, they had agreed to stay in the present. But who knew what the future held?

But as Adrian's song had predicted, emerald eyes held it clear.

Kat's hand was to her mouth, eyes wide and apologetic. She had missed her mark.

Adrian was playing both rhythm and lead in the improv instrumental jam going on. He had a stubborn "the show must go on" jut to his goateed chin, but his eyes glittered in realization as Rick held up Kat's message.

"Mazel tov, Dad." Rick hadn't bothered using his own toggle

at his feet to keep his message between them. He let it be known through public decree. Anything that took away from Corpse time, Rick now knew in his heart, wasn't a threat. Not when the payoff was so much sweeter. The crowd roared their approval, too.

Fancy that.

The tide had shifted. Rick studied the sea before him. Thousands of hands were raised open in supplication, while feet were planted firmly. Dynamic tension at work.

Rick lifted his eyes to the rafters, turned his back to the crowd and, with arms wide, surrendered himself to the infinite possibility.

ACKNOWLEDGMENTS

Gratitude and yoga go hand-in-hand. They say it's all about the journey and not so much the destination, but as I reach the end of this tale, I have to give props to those along the way:

First and foremost, to the book-lovers and readers of my words: thank you for your time, your support, your reviews and your love of these characters.

Super-huge thanks to Nalini Akolekar: for your guidance and advice, and for falling in love with Sidra and Riff on the early pages.

Kristin Contino and Pat O'Dea Rosen: thank you for lending your eyes and your thoughts, chapter by chapter. I know we never reached "the end" together on this one, but you were with me in spirit when I crossed the finish line. And thank you to my very best bestie, Alysa Cohen, for reading *Deeper Than Dreams* and *Softer Than Steel* back-to-back, and texting me comments and encouragement!

Thanks to Amanda Usen—I have so much fun plotting and posing with you! You're a true friend for letting me drag you halfway across Atlanta during RWA Nationals to attend a Metal Yoga class. A big thank-you as well to Neda, the owner of Tough

Love Yoga in Atlanta, for flying the heavy metal yoga flag and showing how such music can have a place in people's practice.

And finally, I am ever grateful to my favorite yoga teacher and supportive friend, Kimberly Locke Gionis. Your words linger in my head after each class I take with you, and you helped shape Sidra and Evolve. Your knowledge, patience and energy are inspiring on and off the mat— Namaste!

ABOUT THE AUTHOR

Jessica Topper has been in love with the beauty of the written word ever since she memorized Maurice Sendak's *Chicken Soup with Rice* at the age of three.

After earning a B.A. in English Literature and her Master's Degree in Library Science, Jessica went on to work as a librarian in New York City before trading in the books for book-keeping. For seventeen years, she worked in the production office of an international touring rock band.

Jessica broke the rock romance mold with her 2013 debut novel LOUDER THAN LOVE. Her follow-up romantic comedy, DICTATORSHIP OF THE DRESS, was named one of Publishers Weekly's Best Books of 2015.

She lives in Western New York with her family - including two cats that love to walk across her keyboard.

Visit her online at jessicatopper.com

ALSO BY JESSICA TOPPER

The "Love & Steel" series:

Louder Than Love

Deeper Than Dreams

Softer Than Steel

More Than Merry

The "Much 'I Do' About Nothing" series:

Dictatorship of the Dress

Courtship of The Cake

Sign up for Jessica's newsletter for exclusive content, news, giveaways
and more!

https://tinyletter.com/jesstopper